Tell Me You're Mine

Tell Me You're Mine

ELISABETH NOREBÄCK

TRANSLATED FROM THE SWEDISH
BY ELIZABETH CLARK WESSEL

G. P. Putnam's Sons
New York

PUTNAM

G. P. PUTNAM'S SONS
Publishers Since 1838
An imprint of Penguin Random House LLC
375 Hudson Street
New York, New York 10014

First published in Sweden in 2017 as *Säg att du är min* by Bokförlaget Polaris

Published in the United States in 2018 by G. P. Putnam's Sons

ISBN: 9780735218543

Printed in the United States of America
1 3 5 7 9 10 8 6 4 2

Book design by Elke Sigal

Tell Me You're Mine

Stella

I'm lying on the floor.

Legs pulled up, arms around my knees.

Inhale. Exhale.

My heart's still pounding in my ears, the pain in my stomach has turned to nausea, but at least I've stopped shaking.

My name is Stella Widstrand now, not Johansson. I'm thirty-nine, not nineteen. And I don't get panic attacks anymore.

A gray autumn light streams in. I still hear rain pouring down outside. My office at the clinic looks the same as always. Tall windows, moss green walls. A large landscape painting and a wooden floor with a handwoven rug on it. My old, battered desk, the armchairs in the corners, just inside the door. I remember decorating this room, how carefully I chose every detail. I no longer recall why that felt so important.

I always imagined that I would find her. Not that she would track me down. Maybe she was driven by curiosity, wanting to see who I am. Maybe she's come to accuse me, so I won't ever forget.

Maybe she's here for revenge.

It's taken me so many years to rebuild my life, to get to where I am today. But even though I've left what happened in the past, still I've never forgotten. There are things you can't forget.

I'm lying on the floor.

Legs pulled up, arms around my knees.

Inhale. Exhale.

Henrik kissed me on the cheek before he left for work this morning. I ate breakfast with Milo and dropped him off at school, then headed to

Kungsholmen. Just a normal day. Fog on the windows, traffic over the Traneberg Bridge, mist hanging above the gray waters of Lake Mälaren, and no place to park when you get to the city.

Her appointment was an hour before lunch. She knocked, I opened the door, and I knew immediately. We shook hands, introduced ourselves. She called herself Isabelle Karlsson.

Does she know her real name?

I took her wet jacket. Said something about the weather and asked her to come inside. Isabelle smiled and sat down in one of the armchairs. She has dimples.

As I usually do when I meet a patient for the first time, I asked her why she sought help. Isabelle was prepared. She played her role very well and claimed she's been suffering from a sleep disorder since her father's death. She needs help dealing with grief. She said she felt lost and insecure, that she found social situations difficult.

It all felt extremely practiced.

Why?

Why didn't she just say what she wants? There's no need to hide her real reason for coming.

She's twenty-two now. Medium height, an hourglass figure with a narrow waist. Short, unpainted nails. She has no visible tattoos or piercings, not even in her ears. Her straight black hair hangs down her back. Still wet from the rain, it glistened against her pale skin, and it struck me how beautiful she is. More beautiful than I ever could have imagined.

The rest of the conversation is a haze. It's difficult now to remember what I said. Something about the dynamics of group therapy, or something about communication, or how our self-image determines how we see others.

Isabelle Karlsson seemed to listen attentively. She tossed her hair and smiled again. But she was tense. She was on guard.

At first I felt sick to my stomach, then came the dizziness and the pressure on my chest, making it difficult to breathe. I recognized the symptoms. I apologized and left the room, went into the bathroom in the hallway. My heart raced, a cold sweat ran down my back, and the throbbing behind my eyes sent flashes of light through my head. My stomach knotted up, and I dropped down on my knees in front of the toilet and tried to vomit. I couldn't. I sat on the floor, leaning against the tile, and closed my eyes.

Stop thinking about what you did.

Stop thinking about her.

Stop thinking.

Stop.

After a few minutes I went back in, told her she was welcome at group therapy next Wednesday at one o'clock. Isabelle Karlsson pulled on her jacket, lifted her hair from her neck, and tossed it. I wanted to stretch out my hand and touch it, but I stopped myself.

She noticed.

She saw my doubt, my desire to make contact.

Maybe that was exactly what she'd hoped to accomplish? To make me feel unsure?

She slung her bag over her shoulder, I opened the door for her, and she left.

I've dreamed of this day. Fantasized about how it would happen. How it would feel, what I would say. It wasn't supposed to be like this. And it hurts more than I ever could have believed.

I'm lying on the floor.

Legs pulled up, arms around my knees.

Inhale. Exhale.

She's come back.

She's alive.

Isabelle

"Isabelle!"

I hear Johanna's voice and turn around. I'm back in the M-building at the far end of campus. The lunch hour is almost over, the room is full of students, and every table and chair is occupied. It's always packed here at lunchtime. I spin around, but don't see Johanna until she stands up and waves.

"Come over here," she calls out.

I have no desire to do so. I've spent the last hour on pins and needles. It felt like I might explode from holding all those feelings inside.

Grief. Rage. Hate. And the struggle to hide all of it. To smile and act nice. Be someone I'm not.

I'd much rather eat my sandwich alone before the next lecture starts. Think through what happened at the therapist's office. *But I always have a hard time saying no.* I pull my bag up on my shoulder, then start winding my way through all those people, all those backpacks on the floor, all those green tables and red chairs, until I arrive.

Johanna's the closest thing I have, have ever had, to a friend. And she has been ever since that first horrific period at KTH, the Royal Institute of Technology, when she took me under her wing and let me move in with her. Why, I don't know. We're not at all alike. She's done so much, traveled all over the world. She has purple hair, pierced ears and nose, also a tattoo on her lower back and another on her forearm. It's of a unicorn spraying fire. She's cool, confident, knows what she wants.

Susie and Maryam, who are sitting next to her, are also very nice. But I can relax with Johanna, actually be myself.

"Where'd you go?" Maryam says. "I didn't see you at the mathematics lecture."

"I wasn't there," I say.

"Did something happen?" Susie puts a hand over her heart. "You never miss anything."

"I had to take care of something." I pull out the chair next to her, hang my jacket over the backrest, and sit down. It still surprises me when people even see that I'm here. When somebody notices me. Maybe even misses me. I'm so used to being invisible.

I open my bag and take out a sandwich I bought at 7-Eleven. It's seen better days, so I throw it back in again.

"Is it still raining?" Johanna says.

"Same as this morning," I answer.

"Ugh, Mondays." Susie sighs while flipping through a textbook on mechanics. "Do you understand any of this?"

"I wrote down a bunch of stuff about momentum last time," Johanna says, "but I can't make sense of it."

They laugh. I laugh, too. But part of me feels like I'm in a glass cage looking out. I feel like two different people. One is the person people see. But the other one, only I see. She's the real me, and the difference between the two is profound. Inside me is a ravine of darkness.

And a tendency to be melodramatic.

"Isabelle, you understand it, right?" Maryam asks, turning toward me. "The panic is setting in, we need to start prepping for our exams soon."

"I promise, if you read the book you'll get it," I say.

"Just say it. If we spent our time studying instead of partying, we'd understand it, too." Susie nudges me and grins.

"Admit she's right." Johanna's napkin hits me in the head. "Admit it, Isabelle."

"Do you think I'm boring?" I say. "You think I'm a stick-in-the-mud, a nerd who doesn't know how to have a good time? You'd all be lost without me, you slackers."

I throw the napkin back at Johanna and burst out laughing when two more hit my head straightaway. I throw them at Susie and Maryam, too, and soon there's a full-on napkin war at our table. We laugh and scream and everyone in the lunchroom stands up and starts shouting and—

My phone rings.

I do this way too often. Disappear into a fictional dream world. Play ridiculous little movies in my head. Scenes in which I'm as spontaneous and natural as everyone else.

I fish the phone out, look at the screen.

"Who is it?" Maryam asks. "Aren't you going to answer?"

I send the call to voicemail and put the phone back.

"Nothing important."

After the lecture I head home by myself. Johanna is going to her boyfriend's place. I wish I could have gone straight home after my appointment with Stella, considering how exhausting it was to meet her, but I didn't want to miss anything important at school.

Now I'm on the subway. Alone, one of many strangers. When I moved here I hated that, but now I don't mind. And after a year in Stockholm I can find my way around pretty well. In the beginning, I was terrified of getting lost. I mixed up Hässelby and Hagsätra, triple-checked how to get wherever I needed to go. In spite of that, I traveled around quite a bit, visited most of the shopping centers that were within reach of Stockholm public transportation.

I've taken the commuter trains to their final stations, tried out all the subway lines, and taken most of the buses in the city center. I've walked around on the islands of Södermalm and Kungsholmen, through the neighborhoods of Vasastan and Norrmalm, and spent a lot of time in the city center.

I look at my fellow commuters and pretend I know everything about them. That old lady with orange hair and ruby red glasses, she works out at Friskis&Svettis twice a week, wears colorful leggings from the eighties, and stares saucily at men in the gym.

The couple holding hands and kissing each other: he's a medical student and she's a middle school teacher. They're on their way home to their studio apartment near Brommaplan. They'll cook something together and watch a movie and fall asleep next to each other on the sofa. Then she'll go to bed, and he'll take out his computer and watch Internet porn.

The tall, skinny guy in the suit, coughing until he's bent over double. He's dying of lung cancer. No one knows how long he has left. How long do any of us have left? Life could end at any moment. *It could be over today.*

I miss Dad. Four months have gone by since that day in May. Four long, empty months. Afterward, I found out that he'd been feeling sick for several weeks. Of course, he didn't go to the doctor. I didn't know a thing. Dad was hardly ever sick. Why would he bother me unnecessarily?

To say I feel guilty doesn't begin to cover it. I went home too rarely. The last time I saw him was at Easter. I didn't even stay the whole weekend.

Was it selfish of me to move? Dad wanted me to take this chance. He encouraged me to stay in the city, hang out with my new friends on the weekends, and to break free.

Only after he was gone did I learn the truth. And I will never forgive her for what she did. With all my heart I wish she was dead. I hate her.

Hate her.

Hate her.

Hate her.

Stella

I wake up in our house on Alviksvägen in Bromma. I've been sleeping on the bed under a blanket. It feels like I've been lying here for days.

I asked Renate to cancel the rest of my patients and blamed it on a migraine. Hailed a taxi in the rain on St. Eriksgatan. I don't remember anything after that. I must have paid the driver when we arrived, left and gone inside. Took off my shoes and my coat, and climbed the stairs up to my bedroom. I don't remember any of it.

My eyes ache, I have a pounding headache, and for a moment I wonder if I imagined everything. If I dreamed that a woman named Isabelle Karlsson came to my office.

I wish it was so.

Avoiding pain is a basic human instinct, trying to escape rather than face what hurts.

And I do wish I could escape.

At the sound of Henrik's Range Rover rolling down the driveway, I get up from bed and walk over to the window. It's still raining. Our neighbor is standing at the fence in a raincoat with his little yapping dog. Milo jumps out of the car and runs toward the house. Henrik greets our neighbor and follows after. The front door opens; I hear him shout hello. I close my eyes a few seconds, take a deep breath, and go down.

Milo slips past me, asks what we're having for dinner. When I say I don't know, he goes to the living room and throws himself onto one of the sofas. Henrik picks my coat up off the hall floor, hangs it, and says he tried to reach me.

I tell him my phone must be in my purse. He turns his face toward the floor. It's lying next to my shoes. He picks it up, hands it over to me.

"We wondered if we should pick up food," he says. "You didn't make dinner." It's more of a statement than a question.

"I haven't had time."

"Did something happen?"

"Why do you think that?"

"Your car?"

My Audi is still parked on Kungsholmen, not in the driveway.

"I took a taxi."

Henrik examines me closely. I give him a quick kiss, avoiding his gaze, and head into the kitchen. He follows me.

"Milo needs to eat," he says, opening the fridge. "He has to leave soon."

I forgot about Milo's basketball practice. I never do that. I sit down at the kitchen table, check my phone. Two missed calls and one text message. Henrik takes a plastic container out of the freezer, shouts to Milo that food is on its way.

"How was your day?" he asks after a while.

"Good."

"Everything okay?"

"Yes," I answer.

"Are you sure?"

"I'm sure."

Henrik stirs the pasta and warms up the Bolognese. While telling me something about plans to visit his parents in the country next weekend and Milo's basketball game on Saturday. Also, his day at work. He sets the table: plates, cutlery, and glasses, fills a pitcher with water. Tells me more about work.

It's just like any other Monday, meeting at home after a long day, chatting in the kitchen. My husband is the same, my son, too. Our beautiful home is unchanged. And yet it all feels so foreign. As if I've been transformed into someone else. As if I'm a stranger in my own life.

Henrik calls out to Milo to tell him the food is ready. No reaction from the living room. He tells him to come now, but Milo dawdles. I walk to the living room, go over to the sofa. I take off his headphones and pull the iPad out of his hands. I snap at him that he's in a hurry. Milo is surprised at first, then annoyed. He strides past me and sits down at the kitchen table.

Henrik puts his hand on my arm when Milo's not looking. I know exactly what he wants to say. *Take it easy. What's the matter with you?*

I should tell him what happened. Should talk to him. It's not like me to keep secrets. I am, after all, a psychologist and a certified psychotherapist. I verbalize my emotions, I discuss things, figure out where the problem might lie. Especially when it comes to something that could transform our lives. Plus Henrik is my best friend. We're always open with each other, we talk about everything. He knows me better than anyone else, which is what makes it so hard to hide something from him. I've never wanted to, either. Until now.

I can't choke down any dinner. Henrik and Milo talk to each other; I don't know about what. I hear them, but also don't. My thoughts constantly return to her.

Isabelle Karlsson.

I wonder why she's using that name. I wonder how much she knows.

Milo is telling us about some super-sweet bike he wants. He takes out his phone to show us. I apologize, get up from the table, and leave the kitchen. I go to the laundry room and try to compose myself.

A panic attack. Only one, in twelve years. I'm losing control and can't do anything about it. Panicked terror and paralyzing anxiety are taking over my body, invading my thoughts and feelings. Like boarding a runaway train, then being forced to ride it all the way to its final destination. And I never wanted to go there again. I'd do anything to avoid going there again. The thought of exposing my family to this terrifies me.

If I'd known what this meeting would entail, would I have gone through with it? If I'd known who she was, would I have been brave enough to meet her?

If it's really her.

I can see myself asking her. Looking into her eyes, formulating the question, watching my words reach her consciousness, starting some chain reaction.

No, that's not me.

Truth? Lie?

Yes, that's me.

Truth? Lie?

I don't trust Isabelle Karlsson. How could I? How could I trust her, when I have no idea what she wants? I have to find out more. I have to know.

Henrik is standing behind me; he puts his hands on my arms.

"What is it?" he says. "Talk to me, Stella."

"I'm tired."

"It's not just that," he says. "I can tell something happened."

He won't give up. I turn around.

"I had a shitty day," I say. "I got a migraine, canceled everything, and went home." I imply that it has to do with Lina, a patient I've had problems with recently. I can tell he understands. Knew he'd interpret it that way.

Henrik touches my cheek and holds me. He asks if I have been contacted by the Health and Social Care Inspectorate. I haven't. Not yet.

He tells me the last few months have been stressful, but it will all work out in the end. He'll take Milo to practice tonight, I can stay home.

I stand at the kitchen window watching them leave.

Go up to the attic. Look in the bag.

The handbag in the attic. I haven't touched it since we moved here, but after twelve years I still know exactly where it is. I don't intend to look inside it. If I do, I'll lose my mind again.

Twenty-one years ago my life was destroyed, but I rebuilt it. I can't forget that. I chose to live. I couldn't do anything else. The only alternative was death, and that was something I couldn't do.

I focused on my education, on my goals. Five years later I met Henrik and fell in love.

I buried her. That doesn't mean I forgot.

Look in the handbag, in the attic.

My panic attack today was a singular event. It won't happen again. And I don't need to go to the attic. What I need is sleep.

By the time I reach the bedroom I feel too tired to shower, too tired to wash off my makeup. Don't even have the energy to brush my teeth. I take off the wristwatch Henrik gave me and put it in my bureau. My pants and shirt I throw on the chair next to the door. I take off my bra and crawl under the blanket.

The rain's still beating against the windows when I wake up in the middle of the night. I must have slept deeply, I didn't even hear Henrik and Milo come home. The room is pitch-black thanks to our thick curtains. I usually prefer that, but tonight the darkness is suffocating.

Go up to the attic. Look in the handbag.

Henrik's arm is draped over my waist; he grunts when I lift it off. I climb out of bed and pull on my robe. I sneak out of the bedroom and close the door. I pull a chair down the hall and place it under the hatch that leads to the attic. I climb up, grab the handle, and pull it down. Hold my breath when it creaks. I pull down the ladder, climb up, and turn on the lights.

The handbag is in the corner. I move a few boxes before I'm able to see it. A blue and wine-red paisley pattern, given to me by my mother years ago. I pick it up, then sink down to the floor and unzip it.

The spider has soft, limp legs of purple and yellow and a big silly smile. I pull the cord under its belly, but nothing happens. It used to play a few bars of "Itsy Bitsy Spider." We found it hysterically funny.

A white blanket with gray stars. A small blue dress with lace around the neck and sleeves, the only garment I saved. I bury my nose in it, but it smells only of mothballs.

Photographs. In one stand three happy teenagers. Daniel; his sister, Maria; and me.

I've almost always had long hair. It's thick and dark brown and naturally wavy. When this picture was taken it hung to the middle of my back. I'm wearing a yellow dress with a wide black elastic belt around my waist. Daniel's arm is draped around my shoulders, he seems cocky and self-assured. His black hair is as disheveled as ever, and he wears a pair of worn jeans and a flannel shirt with the sleeves cut off.

I wonder where he is right now. Wonder if he's happy. If he ever thinks of me.

I look closely at Maria. Her waist-length straight hair is as black as Daniel's. The resemblance to Isabelle Karlsson is uncanny. They could be sisters. Twins.

But it's a coincidence. It has to be.

More photos. A seventeen-year-old holding a small baby. She's barely more than a child herself. Both she and the baby are laughing. They have dimples.

My eyes sting, and I rub them with the sleeve of my robe. At the bottom of the bag is a red hardback book. I pick it up.

DECEMBER 29, 1992

Heeeeeelp! Shit, shit, shit. I'm pregnant. How could this happen? Or, I know how. But still. So that's why I'm so tired all the time. So that's why I've been so insanely moody and weepy.

Or like today. Me, Daniel, and Pernilla went to Farsta Center to try on some clothes. I found a pair of super-cute jeans, but couldn't button them even though they were my size. I really tried, but I couldn't get them closed.

I totally overreacted, I know. I cried in the fitting room. Daniel didn't get it at all and was insensitive, like he can be. "You on your period? Try on a bigger size, what's the big deal?" I got so angry I cried even harder. Pernilla chewed him out for me. We skipped shopping and got coffee instead.

How am I gonna tell Mom? She's gonna hit the roof. Helena will think it's awful. And Daniel, what's he gonna say? He's going to be a father. That's not what we planned.

My emotions are out of control. My whole life is spinning.

I can't believe we were so stupid. So irresponsible. All my plans, what am I gonna do now?

It feels like I'm going crazy. I go from laughing to crying every other second. I'm overjoyed. I'm terrified. A human being. Just like that?! Is it possible to already love this little creature inside me?

I want this baby. With him. I hope he wants it, too, because I can't do anything else.

So, hello and welcome, whoever you are. The rest will have to wait.

Isabelle

It's mid-morning rush hour at Östra Station. Susie is a few steps below me on the escalator. I just turned around and noticed her looking at me. That means I'll have to converse with her the rest of the way. Try to seem carefree, normal.

Normal. I don't even know what the word means.

To be like everyone else?

Will I ever truly learn how to do that? So nobody sees what a weirdo I am? How evil I am?

Evil. I can't call it anything else. I don't do mean things. But sometimes I'm afraid I will. The hatred inside me, the ever-increasing rage. That's what makes me evil. I don't know what to do about it. And I suspect it will end badly. These thoughts I have, these feelings swirling inside me will surely lead to something terrible.

Am I being melodramatic again?

I step off the escalator and wait for Susie.

"Heeey, Isabelle!" she bursts out and comes over to me. She always speaks in exclamation marks. "So crazy that it's not raining! It's been such crappy weather for days! Where's Johanna!"

"She's grabbing something to eat, I think."

"Grabbing something to eat." She laughs and mimics the melody of my country bumpkin accent. That happens more rarely now, and I don't feel as embarrassed as I did in the beginning.

"Where's the lecture?"

"Q1 hall," I answer.

"Did you do the homework?"

"Yes," I say. "And you?" I toss my hair. *A habit I'm trying to break.*

Susie grimaces. "You're so smart. I hope I don't get called on today."

She chatters the rest of the way, about how thankful she is it's Friday, tells me everything that's happening this weekend, how some people are going out on Saturday and do I want to come along, and then about how her dog threw up yesterday, and did I know her friend is a veterinarian, and, boy, do they see some gross stuff, ha ha. She reminds me that half of September has gone by, time is moving so fast, and it's going to rain again soon.

I listen, hmmm sometimes. When we get to the hall, she heads off to the bathroom. I open the door and enter. The lecture won't start for another eleven minutes. I look around before heading down the stairs. I choose a spot near the end of the third row.

I always sit close to the front. *And always get there early.* Sit with my notebook and pencils in front of me, ready to take copious notes. Every number and letter. I use different colors to mark things, underline them, and draw connections as a memory aid. There is something slightly neurotic about it. I know that. I've read about it. I have a thing about numbers. Even if I know I'm going to remember them, or will never need them again, I always write them down.

See you at three twenty-six. *03:26.*

Take bus five-fifteen or sixty-seven from Odenplan. *515, 67.*

Height sixty-four inches, weight one hundred and twenty-three pounds. *64, 123.*

A lot of people think I'm too serious. Every student I know here at KTH takes their studies seriously, but they party, too. A lot. On Fridays there's cheap beer at the student union, then there are the dinner parties where everyone wears coveralls over their nice clothes and ends up getting wasted, there are also the beer-drinking contests and the pub crawls organized by the various classes, and when exams are over there's always a huge blowout to celebrate. Not to mention all the house parties.

Johanna and Susie always try to get me to go to them, but I've only done so a few times. The freshman party last spring was the only big party I've been to.

It's not that I don't *want* to join. I want to be one of the gang, and I wish it were easier for me. Easier to forget who I am.

Still, moving here is the best thing I've ever done. The number of friends I have on Facebook has increased drastically. I have more followers on Instagram. And I have Snapchat. *I love it!* I document my daily life. I take selfies. My digital reality is awesome, crazy, insane. When you look at my pictures you see a life filled with unforgettable moments where I'm surrounded by all these amazing friends who love me. Every like, every comment makes me happy. I know it's superficial, but I don't care. There's nothing wrong with being superficial. And until last summer I was social in real life, too, not just online.

Then Dad died.

There's a movement at the corner of my eye, and I look up. A guy I don't recognize. He's good-looking. He asks if he can pass by me, and I feel myself blushing. I stand up, and he smiles at me before squeezing into the row. Throws a long glance at my short dress and my knee-high boots.

One thing I've gotten used to this year is guys looking at me. *At home I was invisible.* My hair was the only feature I was satisfied with, even proud of. But my body? Sometimes they check me out, like now. It's weird. But at the same time, I like it. No one looks beneath the surface, no one looks behind the mask. No one sees how fake, nasty, ruined, and twisted I am. No one is allowed inside.

Johanna and Susie gave me a makeover. It started when I borrowed a shirt from Johanna, which fit really well. Then they made me try on one of her shortest dresses. It was definitely too short. But according to them, that was the point. My legs were made for showing off.

They dragged me to H&M, Monki, Gina Tricot, all over the place. I discovered the secondhand stores here are way better than in Borlänge. Now I have a whole new wardrobe. Clothes in sizes and styles I've never bought before.

I've gotten used to being noticed. Realized it's not that bad. Quite the opposite. It's easier to hide that way. You can choose who you are in other people's eyes.

My newly won freedom. My new strength.

I just wish I could forget the real me completely.

And that's where Stella Widstrand comes in.

My thoughts are interrupted when the lecture begins. I listen closely and take notes until the break. Then I stand up and let the people in my row file past me into the aisle. I'm considering if I should leave the hall or stay, when I hear his name.

Fredrik.

I look around the hall. He's sitting a few rows above me. He looks up, meets my eyes, and nods briefly. *I know I'm staring.* He rises and turns around, looking for Medhi. He shouts out something to him that I don't quite catch.

Fredrik is slender and slightly taller than me. He has a thick mop of blond hair that he often tosses to the side or runs his hands through. He laughs a lot. I can imagine the seven-year-old version of him in his school picture. Pretty much like now, but with a tooth missing in the front.

He usually wears jeans or chinos low on his hips and T-shirts. He's a skater and coaxed me onto his long board once. He ran along beside me, holding my hand and laughing so hard. When I asked why, he told me I squeal like a girl. He's cute, cool, handsome. And he's a good dancer. I know from experience, at the freshman party.

He can never, ever know what I'm really like.

There's a gorgeous, rail-thin brunette sitting next to him. She stands up, pulls on his hand, and he looks at her. Laughs at whatever she's telling him as they climb up the stairs toward the exit. He's obviously tired of me. Maybe he suspects something. Maybe he knows.

Maybe everybody knows there's something wrong with me.

I sit down again. Wish my life was different. Wish I fit in, that I was like everyone else. That there was no shadow inside me. Nothing to hide. But my life is not like anybody else's.

And it's *her* fault.

I want revenge.

I want her to suffer, like I've suffered.

I want her to cease to exist.

I want her to die.

Stella

Thunk, thunk, thunk. The sound of basketballs bouncing against the floor and walls. Now and then a ball actually hits the backboard with an echoing racket. The noise level is deafening.

I'm headed down the bleacher stairs at the Vasalund Hall in Solna. A firm grip on my paper cup of scalding-hot coffee. I sit down and nod to some familiar faces, then take out my phone to avoid conversation. I spent the week going to work, listening to my patients, buying groceries, cooking dinner, doing laundry. Pretending that everything is the same as always. But I haven't been able to think about anything but Isabelle Karlsson. I think about her all the time. It didn't matter to me that Henrik was working late every night or that Milo hung out with his friends too much.

Marcus sent a text message:

Does dinner Wednesday work for you? My brother defers to you.

I've always liked Henrik's little brother, but I have no desire to socialize with anyone right now. Still, I reply that we're looking forward to finally meeting his new love interest. And seeing him and the kids, of course.

Another basketball mom I recognize asks if she can sit down. I scoot over on the bench and look out at the players. Milo is dribbling on the other side of the court. I wave but he doesn't see me. I take my diary out of my purse, balance it on my knees. In my teens I kept a diary almost daily, and this ended up being the last one.

There's obviously page after page about Daniel, but also about what I wanted to do with my life. A teenager's thoughts, plans, and dreams. I wanted to be a tailor. Or a ceramist. Maybe work in fashion or interior design. I wanted to do it all. I wanted to be a Renaissance woman, working in some creative field, traveling around the world, spending a month here or there.

Daniel didn't share my dreams. He had no interest in traveling or studying or learning new languages. He wanted to stay in Kungsängen, the suburb of Stockholm where we grew up, and eventually open an auto repair garage. He was content with his cars, some street racing, and a few beers with his buddies on the weekends. We were very different. But I was in love, and we were happy.

In the fall of 1992 Daniel and I spent all of our time together. We drove around in his red Impala, having fun, with no clue what was in store for us. We both wanted to keep the baby. We even talked about having more.

I wrote about the pregnancy, about my anticipation and my fear. About the looks people gave us. We were teenagers expecting a child and not everyone thought it was as wonderful as we did.

The birth, the first time I held her to my breast. Daniel with tears in his eyes and Alice in my arms.

The first time we met the little person who would turn our lives upside down. Her scent. I could smell her forever. Her sweet little mouth. Her dimples.

I thought I'd feel more when I read about all of this. That every word would grab me, give me joy and laughter, or sorrow and tears. Honestly, I don't remember much of what I've written. It's like a story told to me by an acquaintance.

As long as I refuse to think about that day a year later. As long as I keep the door closed to that room. I don't know if I have it in me to face the pain, if I could handle hearing the accusations. I just don't think I can go back, let guilt drag me down again.

Why weren't you there?

I flinch when someone scores a basket, and the man behind me roars.

Milo takes the rebound and dribbles across the court.

When he was younger I went to every practice, every game. Both basketball and tennis. Even though I don't need to anymore, I still go to many of them. He's thirteen. And I am hopelessly overprotective. He's my only child.

I wonder when I stopped thinking of him as my second.

Both of them got their smiles from me. Milo has my curly hair and Alice, my eyes. Otherwise they both favor their fathers.

Alice. Daniel.

Milo. Henrik.

Different lives.

Are they colliding now?

What will that do to me? To my family?

It must be a coincidence. It has to be my imagination. I've spent enough time hoping and believing. I can't handle more anxiety and useless suspense. Nothing will change what happened. I'll never get back the time I lost.

As we leave Vasalund Hall, I throw the diary into a trashcan.

JULY 29, 1993

I'm a mother now!

Alice Maud Johansson is one week old today.

There was no way I could have imagined what it feels like, I know that now. My life has changed completely.

Who knew I was capable of feeling instant love for a person. She is the most perfect thing you could possibly imagine. Little, tiny chubby fingers and toes. Tons of hair sticking out in every direction. She was born with her own fur hat, Daniel says. Just like him. Thick, black hair.

The world's cutest little mouth. I think she even has dimples. Especially one on the left side, like me. Her right ear looks like Daniel's and Maria's. Elf ears. It's genetic.

She looks more like her dad, but she has my eyes. She's a mix of the two of us. I have never been so happy in my life.

She's also so helpless, completely dependent on me.

It's a lot of responsibility.

It hasn't been that long since I waddled home lugging bags of groceries—which Daniel chewed me out for afterward. Apparently, I wasn't supposed to lift anything heavier than a carton of milk or a loaf of bread. Then he put his ear on my belly and listened. He sang Elvis songs to it, "Teddy Bear" and "Love Me Tender." Then he fell silent and stared at me with wide eyes, whispered that he could feel her moving. Then he ran his hands over my stomach, searching for our baby, trying to feel her feet. That was just a week ago. It could have been a century ago.

I was in labor through a whole night. It hurt like crazy, and I thought she'd never come out. It was awful, but also the most awesome thing I've ever experienced. When they finally put her on my breast, all pink and wrinkled, her big eyes stared straight into mine, and it was the most beautiful moment of my life.

Daniel didn't like seeing me in so much pain. I squeezed his hand so hard he thought he might faint, too, he told me later.

And he did actually faint! At the precise moment Alice was born. He fell like a tree and hit his head against a chair. He doesn't want me to mention it, but he got five stitches near his hairline. My love. My brave hero.

The first time he held her, he cried. I feel more in love with him than ever.

Mom and Helena were here today. Even though Mom thinks we're too young, she could barely bring herself to let go of little Alice. Helena was kind of stiff, both to me and Daniel. She still can't relax around him. And she didn't want to hold my daughter. It made me sad.

We're becoming so different as time goes by.

I brood more and maybe I'm a bit on the introverted side. But how do you get anywhere if you don't reflect and think? My sister likes to get things done; she doesn't like to think so much. She carries on no matter how she feels. I got pregnant accidentally, and I don't really know what to do with my future; she spends her time focusing on minor details.

Do I wish I were different? How could I? Who would I be then?

Life is unpredictable. Anything can happen.

No matter how much I brood or how much Helena plans, neither of us knows what to expect. Isn't that what makes life interesting? I know I'm being silly now. A teenager trying to sound deep or whatever.

I need to sleep. Daniel and Alice are lying next to me, sleeping like logs. My family.

Stella

Today is Wednesday. Time's been moving unbelievably slowly.

I finish my morning coffee, put the cup in the dishwasher, and close the diary lying open on the kitchen table. It was stupid to throw it away. As if doing so would change anything. When we got out to the car in the parking lot, I told Milo to wait for me. I ran back to Vasalund Hall and fished the diary out of the trash. Dried it off and put it back in my purse.

Eventually, reading it brought the past back to life. Just like I had thought it would. The guilt, the anxiety. Knowing what I did, what I can never undo. But I have no choice, I have to go on. Meanwhile I keep trying to pretend like nothing happened. Henrik can't know. Not yet.

I've locked the front door and am headed toward the car when our neighbor shouts my name and waves. Johan Lindberg somehow manages to always be outside when we leave or enter our home. He was recently fired from his position as a financial adviser at a big investment firm, let go immediately when it was discovered he'd been sending dick pics to his female coworkers. But of course, they gave him a golden parachute. When a man at that level crosses the line, his landing is a soft one. Johan Lindberg will never have to work again. We call him the investor. He's always around home, boasting about his new life as a day trader. He's annoying, but harmless, and sometimes almost pleasant to talk to. But I don't feel like it today, so I wave back and drive off.

I pass by the reception desk and say hello to Renate. She asks me how I'm feeling, thinks I look pale. I don't mention my sleepless nights or loss of appetite. Instead, I smile and blame my genes, I always look pale. She laughs. I laugh, too, for good measure, and continue down the hallway toward my office. I hang up my coat and change my shoes. Sit down at my desk, take out my calendar and MacBook Air. I look through the calendar, taking note of today's sessions. Two in the morning, then group therapy after lunch, and one session after that.

It's been nine days since I met her. The woman who calls herself Isabelle Karlsson. Nine meaningless days. Nine days of suffocating nothingness. I've been drinking more than I should. Self-medicating of course, what else?

I don't like the red wine Henrik persists in bringing home. I don't even like wine. It tastes bad, gives me headaches, and makes me feel ill every time I drink more than two glasses. But for the last few nights I've gulped it down just to be able to sleep. And even that has barely helped. Still, it's better than sleeping pills. When I use those, my brain ceases to function the next day. Then again, in the long run I know alcohol is not truly an option. The risk of relapse increases the more I drink.

The uncertainty is excruciating. Not knowing, never being able to silence the swarm of thoughts and questions buzzing around inside me. And I waver constantly between certainty and doubt. So sure my instincts are correct, and then just as sure that I'm wrong. My mood is terrible; I have no patience.

Isabelle Karlsson. Today she'll participate in group therapy for the first time. I don't remember the last time I felt this nervous about a therapy session. Or scared. Maybe my self-esteem as a psychotherapist isn't what it used to be. But no. I know that what happened to Lina Niemi wasn't my fault. I'm good at what I do.

Still, I should have detected the problem sooner. I tried for a long time, but I couldn't help her. In the end, she became dependent on me, wanted me to always be available to her.

Lina Niemi's staged suicide attempt occurred following my decision to refer her to someone else. Last May she took a handful of antidepressants and washed them down with alcohol. Her mother found her. She spent one night in the hospital for stomach pains, that was all.

Her life was never in danger. But according to Lina herself, she'd almost died. She claimed everything was my fault: I wasn't responsive enough in our conversations, I didn't care about her problems, I didn't heed her cries for help. She said I was unprofessional, fostered her destructive dependence on me.

Lina's parents listened only to their daughter. Which I suppose is understandable. But afterward Lina's mother started blogging about me. I'm manipulative, my methods are dubious, I get off on being needed. I'm never mentioned by name, but there aren't many psychotherapists with the initials SW who practice on Kungsholmen.

Still, I was surprised when they reported me to the Health and Social Care Inspectorate. I took it hard. Did I make a mistake in my treatment of Lina? I've analyzed it so many times, and every time I come to the same conclusion.

No, I did not.

However, I am far from sure that my colleagues share that opinion. Of course, they want to cover their backs. Several times they've asked me if there were really no signs of self-harm. Every time I have assured them I did everything I could for Lina Niemi. They've also wondered if maybe I need a break, even suggested I take a leave of absence. I made it clear to them that I don't think I need that.

I submitted Lina's patient journal for review and gave my version to the Health and Social Care inspectors. I'm still waiting for a decision.

Right now, I can't afford more complaints.

I need to be professional around Isabelle. The problem is I have no clue what her intentions are. And it frightens me.

There's a knock at the door. It's nine o'clock. My first patient has arrived.

In a few minutes, it will be one o'clock. My fear has increased. I can't handle another panic attack. I try to calm myself down. I try not to let my emotions get the better of me. I try to think rationally, to talk some sense into myself.

It's just a figment of your imagination, Stella.

There has to be some rational explanation. It's a coincidence.

It's a misunderstanding.

It can't be her.

Inhale. Exhale.

It doesn't help.

Nothing helps.

Anxiety gnaws at my stomach, and my field of vision narrows to a single blurry point of light.

I rush out into the hall and down to the bathroom. I fall on my knees in front of the toilet and throw up. Then I stand up, holding on to the edge of the sink, and close my eyes. Wait for the dizziness to subside.

I rinse my mouth, wipe my forehead and the rest of my face with a paper towel. I study my expression in the mirror. Attempt a smile. I leave the bathroom and go to the lounge.

Nine red armchairs circle a round rug. Someone, probably Renate, has prepped the room, and the air is fresh. I sit down in my usual chair and force myself to relax, breathe.

Sonja comes in next and sinks down in the chair closest to mine. When the session is over, she'll be the first to leave. She has social anxiety disorder and has been in this group the longest. Still, she never speaks. I greet her; she answers with a motion of her hand.

My armchair is placed with its back to one window. To the left of me is another wall with high windows, to the right is the door. I look at the clock above it and glance at my wristwatch. I'm always careful to come just before the session begins and finish exactly ninety minutes later.

Two minutes left.

Still no Isabelle Karlsson.

Clara is already in place, afraid as she is of arriving late.

She sits on my left. Her expectations for herself are incredibly high. Despite a good job as a project leader in a successful media company, she constantly doubts her own abilities.

Magnus is here, too. He sits in the chair opposite me with his eyes glued to his old shoes. He looks up, brushes his hair out of his eyes, then looks down again. Chronically depressed.

Isabelle opens the door.

Her black, shiny hair is pulled up in a ponytail. She is wearing light blue jeans, a black top, and a dark brown leather jacket. She gently closes the door behind her and slides down into the armchair next to Sonja.

I realize I've been holding my breath and release it.

Her face is impossible to interpret. I resist the impulse to stare at her. To my great relief, the strong emotions of the last meeting do not return. She isn't as similar to Maria, Daniel's sister, as I thought the first time. At least that's what I tell myself.

Our eyes meet. I realize this isn't a coincidence.

Isabelle is here for a reason.

She must have tracked me down to see who I am, not just for therapy. I have to find out what she's really searching for. I have to find out what she wants and why she's so secretive. Before I dare to confront her. Everything would be so much easier if she'd just be honest with me. I have no idea why she's not.

I am about to start when Arvid pulls open the door and rushes in. He throws himself into the chair next to Magnus. I give him a long look and hope he understands how much I disapprove of his habitual lateness. He ignores me. Takes out a box of mints and puts one in his mouth.

I begin: Welcome. As I told you last week, we have a new group member starting today. Her name is Isabelle.

Short silence. Everybody looks at Isabelle. She smiles, pretending to be shy. She does it well. Where did she learn to lie so convincingly?

Magnus: I don't think Anna should have left. She was just starting to get somewhere.

Clara: She had to stop in order to keep progressing, she said. This is more about you and how much you dislike change.

Magnus: Maybe. But still.

Silence.

Clara: How's your week been, Arvid? You had a family reunion to go to, right?

Arvid: Ugh. I thought I was gonna go insane. Being with my family for a couple days, what a fucking nightmare. My sister was weird. As usual. Dad drank, Mom was a nervous wreck. Then we pretended to be a "happy family" for the relatives. Good God. Total fucking fakes.

The door opens, Pierre comes in.

Pierre: Sorry. Stuck in traffic.

I give another long look. Doubt he even notices it. Pierre pulls out the armchair next to Isabelle. She seems embarrassed.

Me again: Welcome, Pierre. Nice of you to make it. As I told the others, Isabelle is joining the group starting today.

Pierre: Hi, Isabelle. Hope you contribute more than some of the others in here.

He looks meaningfully at Sonja. Isabelle lowers her gaze to the rug. Is she annoyed?

Pierre: Therapy is pointless if you never open your mouth. So why are you here?

Isabelle: My dad died.

Her voice catches. She clears her throat, looks at me, looks down again. She seems genuinely sad. Have I misjudged her? Or is she acting again?

Isabelle: It went so fast. I wasn't able to make it home in time. We never had the chance to say good-bye. I didn't even know he was sick.

Arvid: Home? Where do you come from, is that a Dalarna County accent?

Isabelle: Yes, I'm from Borlänge.

She blushes. If she's just acting she's really good at it.

Isabelle: I moved here a year ago August to study.

Me: Were you born in Dalarna?

The rest of the group reacts to my direct question. But I can't control myself.

Isabelle: I was born in Denmark. But I've lived in Borlänge most of my life.

Magnus: Do you like Stockholm?

Isabelle: It's thanks to Dad I'm even here.

She laughs, seems embarrassed. I smile encouragingly. I don't know what to think. Is she really that similar to Maria? Maybe I'm wrong.

Me: It sounds like you were very close to your father?

Isabelle looks at me. Defiant and scornful. Aggressive. She knows. There is no doubt about it anymore. She knows. But can she see that I know? Can she see that I know who she is? And if so, does she realize I've seen through her carefully constructed façade?

Isabelle: He was everything to me. That's why it came as a shock when I found out he wasn't my real father.

Now we're getting there. Here it comes. In just a moment everyone will know her real reason for being here.

Arvid: Did you think he was your biological father?

Isabelle: Yes. But he adopted me when he and my mother met. I don't know who my real dad is.

Adopted?

Did she tell me that at our first meeting? I don't remember. Who is the woman she calls her mother? *Is* it her mother? Her biological mother?

The conversation continues, but I find it impossible to concentrate on what anyone is saying. Is time standing still? Or is it going faster than usual?

"Stella? Thank you for today?"

I snap out of it, meet Pierre's derisive look and glance up at the clock on the wall: 2:33. My wristwatch shows the exact same time. Unsure if I can trust my voice, I nod and stand up.

I'm aware of how strange I've been acting. I let us run overtime, I haven't paid attention for the most part, and I asked Isabelle a direct question, for no apparent reason. Usually I only speak when the conversation stalls, sometimes to help someone progress in their reasoning. But never like this. Not in this clumsy way.

Sonja is first out of the door; the others follow. I usually leave the room immediately, too. But today I remain standing, unable to move. I can tell my breath stinks. My armpits are sweaty, and I hope it's not visible.

I can't tear my eyes away from Isabelle.

She drapes the strap of her bag over her shoulder. As she turns, her ponytail dances to the side.

Her right ear is pointed and slightly longer than the other.

There are only two other people in the world with an ear like that.

Her right ear looks exactly like Daniel's and Maria's.

That insight is a punch in the stomach. My nausea returns.

I hear Daniel's voice. As clear as if he were in the room. *Yes, I have an elf ear, are you gonna make fun of me for it? You know it just means I'm gonna bring magic into your life, Stella.*

"Isabelle?" I say.

"Yes?" she answers.

I want to tell her I've been waiting for this day for over twenty years. I want to go over to her and take her in my arms and never let her go.

"Thank you for today," I whisper. That's all I can manage.

Isabelle smiles. The dimple in her cheek deepens. She leaves.

She's gone.

I sink into the armchair, close my eyes, and clench my trembling hands.

I buried you. We stood at your headstone in the cemetery. We wept and said good-bye.

Still, I never stopped looking for you. I searched for you in every crowd, in every face, on every bus, and in every street. Year after year.

Hoping. Wishing. Waiting. One day you would come back.

But then I stopped. Stopped hoping, stopped wishing. I had to move on. Either that or I had to follow you, to disappear. I moved on. For my own sake, for my son's. Was that wrong?

I don't understand why you pretend we're strangers. Do you want to see what kind of person I am?

Want to see if I feel regret? If I'm plagued by guilt? Do you hate me as much as I hated myself?

Do you want to punish me? Make me feel pain?

I already do.

The pain of you never leaves me. It's as much a part of me as you are. It never lets me forget. What is it you want to know, what do you want me to say?

I can only say sorry.

Forgive me, Alice.

Kerstin

I put the phone on the table and stare at it. Wait for it to ring. Isabelle rarely answers when I call these days. And she never calls me back, either. It's not fair to be treated like this. After all these years, after everything I've done for her. I did the best I could. You can't do more than your best. I'm only human.

I stand up and walk over to the coffeemaker on the counter. I reach for a mug in the cabinet, but there are none left. I look at the sink. Ever since the dishwasher broke, it's always full.

Hans would have fixed it immediately. Hans Karlsson could fix anything. But he's gone now, and I'm alone.

It smells. Dirty plates, glasses, coffee mugs, and cutlery. Piled up in a jumble. I should do the dishes. I don't have the energy. It's so depressing to cook and eat by yourself. Easier to just make a little sandwich, drink a cup of coffee. Who cares if the dishes are dirty? It's only me here.

I roll up my sleeves and rinse out a mug. I pour myself some coffee, put in two sugars, and as I'm reaching for a third I hear him reproach me. *Think about what you're putting into yourself, Kerstin.* He always scolded me for that last cube of sugar.

How can he be gone? Of course, he was twelve years older than me, but fifty-nine isn't old. And he took good care of himself, didn't smoke, only one cup of coffee a day, drank in moderation, and watched his weight. It didn't matter. He died of a stroke.

I defiantly put a third cube of sugar into my coffee and take the mug with me to the library. That's what he called the small room just inside the kitchen. I take a sip, stare at shelves filled with books. His books, of every sort. I myself rarely read. Don't get the point of it. Spending your time dreaming of some other world, hearing words in your mind that aren't your own. No, thank you. I'd rather watch TV. Some sweet, funny movie, a series maybe. A bit of romance, but preferably no sex scenes. Though they're hard to avoid these days. You can hardly put on the boob tube without having nakedness inflicted upon you.

But aren't the walls in here a bit drab? Yes, I do believe they are. When we decorated this room, I thought that brown was a beautiful, soothing color. Maybe it's time for an update?

I'm trying to trick myself, it's obvious. Because, of course, that will never happen, I know that. I'm the only one who has to stare at these walls now; it's not worth the trouble.

Since he passed away, and Isabelle left, the house has been far too lonely and quiet. The clock on the wall ticks. *Tick tock, tick tock, tick tock.* But somehow time is standing still, not moving an inch. I can't stand the sound of it anymore.

I walk out the front door, follow the gravel path around the house to the back. The air is fresh, the sun shining. But the garden is in the shadows. The trees around it have grown high and barely let any light through. It's like living in the middle of a forest.

I look up at the house, a classic country red with white trim. It was perfect for our family, a bathroom and bedrooms for each of us upstairs, a living room, library, and kitchen on the ground floor. But it looked different before. Now the paint on the window frames is flaking off, and the gutters are hanging aslant. The red needs repainting, too.

As if that weren't enough, a pipe is leaking in the bathroom upstairs and a stain is starting to spread in the kitchen ceiling.

How will I be able to handle it all? How will I afford it?

I sit on the back steps with my mug, staring at my uncut lawn. I've only managed to mow it once. It was the yard that first drew me when we moved here almost twenty years ago. Isabelle helped me do the planting every spring. But as she got older she thought it was boring. Lately, I've quit doing that, too. Everything is overgrown now.

I should put the garden furniture into the shed. Our nice outdoor furniture, the plastic was once completely white. Now it's gray.

"Hello, Kerstin, it's been so long since I've seen you out here." My neighbor is standing not far away.

"Hello, Gunilla," I say.

She pulls off her gardening gloves and wipes her forehead with her sleeve. Gunilla is in her mid-fifties. She dyes her hair a copper brown in an obvious attempt to hide the gray. But her body is fit, and she's energetic and sporty.

She prides herself on doing the Swedish Classic every year, skiing the Engelbrektsloppet, swimming in the Vansbrosimningen, running the Lidingöloppet, and biking the Vätternrundan.

Both she and her husband, Nils, are outdoorsy types. They have no children and spend their time on sports and running. Maybe they're fulfilling some sort of need, I don't know. They store their equipment in an immaculate garage that sits next to their cozy house and perfect garden. They have no idea what it means to raise a child. To care about somebody more than yourself, to constantly have your needs take a backseat to someone else's. It's hard not to find them annoying. And they hate having me as a neighbor.

"Perfect day for some gardening, don't you think?" she says.

"Maybe," I say.

Gunilla tilts her head to one side. In her eyes I see both sympathy and contempt.

It makes me wonder how others perceive me. I look down at the shapeless, washed-out sweater I usually wear. I push my hand through my hair, which surely has its fair share of gray. Not so strange considering how life has treated me. My wrinkles have multiplied and deepened. I am hollow-eyed, and the skin beneath my chin sags. And I've put on weight lately. I feel far older than Gunilla. I *look* far older than Gunilla.

"You know, Nils is heading to the recycling center in Fågelmyra later today," she says. "He has room for more if you want help carting away anything?"

That short hesitancy says everything. The pile of trash Hans and I cleared out of the shop is what she's referring to. We abandoned the project and left everything in front of the house when he started feeling sick. It's an eyesore for all our perfect neighbors. But it can stay where it is. I have the right to do what I want. I don't owe anyone anything.

"No thanks," I say.

Gunilla seems taken aback. She stretches, getting ready to go. "I was just trying to be kind."

I sigh, so she'll understand that I feel embarrassed and am aware how unpleasant I must have sounded.

"I'm sorry," I say. "Thank you for the offer, Gunilla."

I make an effort to smile, but it feels more like I'm just stretching my face. She sits down on the stairs below.

"You know, Kerstin, we'd be happy to help you. This place must feel pretty empty now that Hans is gone. And with Isabelle in Stockholm, too. We've been worried about you." She puts her hand on my knee but pulls it away when I stiffen. "We care about you."

"Thank you, it's nice of you to say so," I answer.

"You always used to be out in the garden."

"I just haven't felt up to it."

"I understand that. I really do."

"Oh, you do?"

"What do you mean?"

"First, my daughter moves out. Then I lose my husband. I'm completely alone now. How do you know how that feels? How could you possibly understand?"

"The only thing I'm trying to say is that we are here for you. We don't want to disturb you, but isolating yourself doesn't seem like a good thing, either."

"I'm grieving. There's a difference, Gunilla."

She looks down at her brightly colored running shoes and sighs. Neither of us speaks for a long time.

"Just tell me if we can do anything," Gunilla says, then stands up and goes back to her own yard.

I wish I was better at small talk. But I'd rather sit with my own thoughts. Things were easier with Hans. Now, after he's gone, I realize he made me a better person. We were happy, in our way. We had a fine family. And Isabelle wasn't as angry as she is now.

She's changed. I don't know why. She doesn't tell me anything anymore. She's just unresponsive and cold. Something has happened, but I don't know what. It's more than just mourning her father. Every day I wonder what she's doing, what she's thinking. I wish she would tell me stuff, share things with me. Like when she was little, and she was my doll. My darling little girl. We used to get along so well, talked about everything, made each other laugh, and we comforted each other when we felt sad.

Suddenly I am on the verge of tears. This is not the life I dreamed of. It wasn't supposed to turn out like this. I dump the rest of the coffee out next to the stairs and stand up. I open the patio door and walk back into the dark, silent house.

Isabelle

I'm standing on the platform at Fridhemsplan subway station, waiting for the green line train. Line 19 toward Hässelby is arriving in three minutes.

I'm thinking about Stella. I think about her a lot, can't help it. She's beautiful, looks so young. I wonder how old she really is? But I see glimpses of a hardness in her. She probably doesn't realize it herself. I wonder what she's trying to hide. Or to protect herself from. Is she afraid? Maybe.

She should be. You never know what might happen.

Never.

I stifle a yawn and sit down on a bench. I'm tired. Barely have the energy for anger anymore.

Stella's nails were painted a different color today. *Cerise red.* Not one hair out of place. Tasteful makeup, discreet lipstick, lovely earrings that looked expensive. Her black pants fit perfectly, her gray top made from some fancy material. She seems so put together. *She must be rich.* She's married, too; a wide gold band sits on her left ring finger. *With diamonds on it.*

Everything is easy for Stella Widstrand.

She sits with her back straight, but relaxed. She seems so confident. How did she become like that? Maybe she's good at maintaining a mask. What does she look like when she takes it off? Is she as ugly and evil as me? I wish I knew more about her than I do.

Right before I walked into group therapy, I was sure I wouldn't be able to handle it. I wanted to blurt everything out. Tell them all of it. But I couldn't. Everyone was staring at me. The words got stuck; I couldn't pull them out. They're too heavy.

And Stella stared at me. Does she know? Does she understand?

I had the opportunity to reveal everything when Pierre asked me what I was doing there.

They were waiting for my reply. But I couldn't get any of it out.

Not a single word of what I intended to say. I felt Stella's inquiring eyes. I'm sure she was staring straight through me.

If any of them knew what I know, if any of them knew who I am. How is it possible to walk among all these people and not a single one of them can see?

The train enters the station. I board and sit down across from an old lady. She holds her purse tightly, but smiles when she meets my eyes. *She doesn't see it, either.* I smile back, lean against the window and close my eyes, feel the coolness of the glass against my forehead.

Everyone is afraid. Everyone. But we smile and pretend, we lie with our faces so that the real us doesn't shine through.

But I've made up my mind. Next time I'm going to tell you. I'm going to tell you everything.

The whole truth.

Stella

Damn, they're here already.

I'm in the kitchen, listening to the sounds in the hall. The stamping of shoes against the hall carpet, the rustle of jackets and the clink of hangers. The shrill voices of little girls, backslaps, men's laughter, a high and penetrating woman's voice that demands attention and immediate response.

Henrik reminded me this morning of the dinner, and I pretended to be looking forward to it. Unfortunately, it was too late to cancel. I called a catering company, and they arrived with their fancy autumn menu. The staff set up in the dining room, placed the food onto serving dishes and plates, and then put those into a food warmer.

How am I going to make it through this?

After group therapy today, everything else seems insignificant.

I take a deep gulp of wine, thankful Henrik managed to make it home before they arrived.

Glue on a smile and go out into the hall to greet our guests.

"There she is." Marcus lights up and gives me a big hug.

"Stella," Jelena chirps and gives me a kiss on each cheek. "We meet at last. I've heard so many amazing things about you."

Marcus's new girlfriend is a model. According to her. But she does indeed look like one. She's a devoted blogger on beauty, health, and mindfulness. She flashes her unnaturally white teeth constantly in a wide smile. Her body lacks even an ounce of excess fat and her long, shapely legs are golden-brown. She's enjoying showing them off in a short little black dress. She can't be more than twenty-five, and she's insufferably perfect and obvious as only a woman of that age can be.

Ebba and Sophia, Marcus's daughters, are nine and five years old. They're loud and squabble without interruption. To my great relief, Milo comes out of his room and offers to let them play video games. I have to remember to reward him abundantly for that. Henrik takes Marcus and Jelena into the living room and handles the conversation.

I follow in their wake without really feeling present. Instead I'm thinking of Isabelle Karlsson.

Of Alice.

Seeing the dimple in your cheek. Your ear. Your careful smile that reveals none of your thoughts. I've thought about you more than you could ever know. You've been an ache inside me since the day you disappeared.

Where have you been?

Why don't you want to tell me?

The same questions arrive over and over again. Impossible to silence.

But I do try, by drinking more wine.

Jelena declares she wants a tour of our house.

I escape to the kitchen with the excuse that I have to deal with the food.

I empty my glass, refill it again as Jelena arrives to share her enthusiasm with me.

She's completely in looooove with our huge gray sofas, with our rug and the copper urns and the giant cacti in them. She adooooores the black-and-white photographs on the wall near the patio, the huge landscape, the rugs, such adooorable rugs, and those small sculptures in the bookshelf, she loves it all! Our home could totally be in an interior design magazine, it's just crazy how nice our house is.

Henrik comes into the kitchen and saves me. Says I've always had a feel for design. Or maybe she's the one he's saving; probably he can see how she gets on my nerves.

Again I empty my glass. Needing to go farther into the fog. Needing some escape from the sharp, prickly reality pressing all around me.

I'm almost totally absent during dinner.

Voices rise and blend with each other, chairs scrape, cutlery clicks against plates, there's chewing and slurping; the sounds assail me, stick in my ears. Henrik is telling them about his company. How well it's going, how they're expanding, their sales increasing, new exciting challenges lie ahead. And us? We've been together for sixteen years, married for, how long has it been, honey? Jamón Serrano, parmesan, curry-roasted scampi. Well, that's been. Oh my goodness, how was it now. Soon fourteen years and Milo is thirteen, and we've been in this house for twelve years, and it must be five years since we redid the kitchen, right? Honey? Sun-dried tomatoes and oven-grilled vegetables in garlic vinaigrette. And when we got there we went straight to the hotel and. Yes, this weekend we'll see you at the Widstrand country house outside Nyköping; it will be so lovely. No, it's been so long since Henrik went moose hunting. Feta and halloumi and asparagus and then it's. In Abu Dhabi when we.

All these words seem to be coming from another room, another house, where people sit around another table conversing in a language I'm no longer fluent in. Henrik puts his hand on my thigh and squeezes. *Come on. Wake up.*

No, we have no plans to move; we love it here, right, honey? Another meaningful squeeze. I nod and smile like an idiot, like I've never done anything in my life besides nodding and smiling.

"And you're a psychotherapist?" Jelena bursts out and leans toward me.

I straighten up in my chair. "That's right," I slur.

"How can you listen to other people all day?" she says. "All their little worries and problems? I'd go crazy. Must be super depressing."

So much for mindfulness.

I hand my glass to Henrik for a refill. He sends me a worried look that I pretend not to notice. He pours just a little. "Psychotherapy isn't about dwelling on problems for their own sake," I say and can hear that I sound like a robot. "The purpose is to detect patterns or behaviors that can be changed. To learn how to handle our fears. Exchange old habits for new ones. Develop as a person." My default response, a simple guide to therapy for idiots.

"How did you decide to go into that line of work?"

"I met someone who inspired me."

"It's super impressive," Jelena says. "I mean that you're able to help all those people." She glances affectionately at Marcus and caresses his neck with her fingertips. "According to Marcus, you're always happy," she continues. "And you seem so balanced."

Balanced? I want to stand up, throw all the dishes on the floor, and scream at all of them to go to hell.

Henrik puts his arm behind my back. "Stella is amazing. She's strong, single-minded, accomplishes whatever she puts her mind to," he says. "That's why I fell in love with her."

"Has she always been so calm?" Jelena says.

Marcus laughs. "Stella has a temper, I swear. But she's settled down over the years. Or what do you say, Henke?"

Yes, Henke, what do you say? Has Stella calmed down?

He grins at me. "Only on the surface."

Idiot. I love you, Henrik, but tonight you're an idiot.

After dinner, Marcus takes Jelena to inspect the second floor. She's already seen all the rooms downstairs. I hide in the kitchen again. I make coffee, set the table with the fine Rörstrand porcelain service we got from Henrik's grandmother. Though I have a good mind to throw all of it against the wall.

"You haven't said much tonight." Henrik comes in and leans against the kitchen counter.

"Did I need to?" I take a drink out of my wineglass. Again.

"Sweetie." He puts it away. "Now you're being unfair. And you're drinking more than you usually do."

Jelena's heels *click clack* above us.

I point to the ceiling and hiss, "She's absolutely hysterical, the clearest example of borderline I've ever seen. Besides the obvious, what does Marcus see in that high-strung bimbo?"

"If anyone is being high-strung, it's you," Henrik answers and looks at me. "You seem like you want to throttle her; it's not like you."

He takes my hand and draws me close, kisses my hair. I let him hold me for a moment before wriggling loose and telling him I have to go to the bathroom.

I enter, sit down on the toilet lid, and put my head in my hands. I'm an awful person. And I feel very sorry for myself.

· · ·

It's quiet in the house now. The catering company picked up the food warmer, trays, plates, and bowls, cleared the table and did the dishes.

The guests are gone, Milo is asleep. Henrik is behind me in bed, caressing my body. It's been a long time since we indulged in more than a good night kiss. I try to enjoy his touch, but can't relax even after all the wine I drank. I'm too angry. Too sad.

After a while he pulls back. He gives me a kiss on my shoulder, mumbles good night, and turns around.

When I'm sure he's asleep, I leave the bed. I go fetch my handbag from the hall. I creep onto the sofa and open the diary.

AUGUST 5, 1994

Pernilla came by today. It was fun to converse in something other than baby talk for a while, a nice break from my usual days. I'm so thankful for her; all my other friends have disappeared.

But we're tough, my little fur ball and me. Most of the time she's happy and content. (Everyone asks if she's a "good" baby, like she's a dog or something. "Yes, she's so good, she doesn't bite at all," or "Well, she's never mean on purpose.")

But lately she's been fussier than usual. And she's a light sleeper. As soon as I lay her down, she wakes up and protests. If I'm lying next to her and try to stand up, she starts to scream.

Could she be teething? That's what we've been saying for weeks. It's become a joke between the two of us, as soon as she's unhappy. "It's the teeth." But we haven't seen a glimpse of any new ones yet. Gas? Hungry, too full, tired, too warm, too cold?

Maybe it's just a phase. Not a fun one.

Anyway, Daniel turned twenty, and his parents gave him the most thoughtful present. A mini-vacation for the three of us. Yippee! We're leaving next weekend. Headed to Strandgården, a place on the Blue Coast in Småland.

Doesn't that sound delicious? Strandgården. The Beach Garden.

Maybe we'll sleep better there than we do at home, who knows. Hope so, because we're pretty exhausted. Daniel has worked his butt off all summer, morning to night. We've hardly seen each other, and when we do we can barely stand each other. We need this.

Need to get away somewhere together. Cruise around in the car singing silly songs. We'll be staying in our own little cabin, sunbathing and swimming.

I can't wait!

Stella

I get dressed and make coffee early Saturday morning. I should eat something, but that will have to wait. I gulp down the last of my coffee; it's hot and tastes a bit like dishwashing soap. I rinse my mouth with water, spit it out in the sink.

Then I go out to the Audi. I start the car and twist around to look out the back window while I reverse. I pass the gateposts and am just about to turn the wheel when there's a knock on the passenger-side window. I brake and look around.

Johan Lindberg grins at me. His little dog is behind him, trembling. I roll down the window, expecting a brief account of how he just killed it on the stock market, or maybe too much information about his "open" relationship with Therese.

"Are we in a hurry?" he says.

"Sorry, Johan. I didn't see you."

"I hid behind the hedge, Stella. Not your fault."

I start to roll up the window again. Johan puts his hand on it. He leans forward and winks.

"And you just get hotter every time I see you."

I look at the time. Give him a smile that can only be interpreted one way.

"And what have you done with Henrik? Does he know the little missus is headed out on a solo adventure?"

"Please don't tell Henrik. Don't betray me." I continue backing up. Johan Lindberg refuses to let go of the window. He looks at me with a shocked expression on his face.

"Are you joking, Stella? Wow, that's cool. Like I say, that's how you keep a relationship strong. A little excitement. You go, girl!"

I turn out onto the street and drive away. In the rearview mirror, I see our neighbor standing with his tiny dog in the middle of the street. For some inconceivable reason, he's holding his fist high in the air. Solidarity with the struggle? I laugh to myself. If Henrik were here, we'd laugh together.

I've only been driving for an hour when my phone rings. I jump a bit behind the wheel; the ring is so shrill and sudden. I turn in to a rest stop and answer.

"Did I wake you?" Henrik says.

"No, no," I reply. "Are you having a good time?"

The wind blows in my ear; it sounds like he's outdoors.

"Milo is still asleep. I went running. Now I'm having coffee in the garden. What are you doing?"

"Nothing," I lie.

"I miss you," he says. "But it's good you're getting some rest."

"I miss you, too," I answer.

They're at the Widstrands' country home, a manor house with horses, hunting grounds, and a private beach on the sea. I was supposed to be there, too. Instead, I'm on my way somewhere else.

We talk about the house and the boat for a while, about what they are going to do today. He says his parents send their love. I tell him to send mine to them and give Milo a big hug. We finish our conversation, and I drive out onto the road again.

The Widstrands belong to a different social class than me. I grew up in the working-class suburb of Kungsängen, in considerably simpler circumstances than Henrik. I was raised by a single mother, just Mom, me, and Helena, my seven-years-older sister. Henrik comes from the expensive Stockholm suburb of Lidingö, went to good schools, sailed, played tennis and golf. His ex was a law student named Louise Von-Something-or-Other. She had a trust fund and a huge apartment in the traditionally aristocratic neighborhood of Östermalm.

Mom and Helena didn't think it would last between us. But Henrik's parents welcomed me. His mother, Margareta, was delighted that their son had found a sensible person to share his life with. They've become as much my family as his.

I'm nearing Nyköping. Their country house isn't far from here. Yesterday, Henrik made one last attempt to convince me to go with them.

He tempted me with peaceful evenings by the fireplace, crisp autumn walks, sexy nights, and sleeping late. I said I felt off, that I was tired and antisocial. I needed some alone time, needed to rest.

Usually, I'd feel guilty. Not now.

I drive past the exit.

Two hours later I turn off toward Storvik and Strandgården. Last time I came here, Daniel drove. I didn't even have a driver's license yet. I remember him swearing through the last few miles. The gravel road was dusty, the potholes deep, and the turns tight. He was worried about the shocks in his car, worried what the gravel would do to the paint, and he claimed he was afraid of colliding with some nutty country bumpkin.

Now the gravel road is broad and paved. Storvik used to be mostly forests and fields, now there are rows of newly built houses. House after house, as if they were delivered straight from a catalog. Rolled out the perfect lawns, the red tricycles, the obligatory trampoline, and the stone sundial. There's not a tree on any of the plots. Some of them are still construction sites.

After that the asphalt ends, and the old gravel road takes over. There are no new houses or ongoing construction projects there.

I step on the brakes.

A large red deer is standing in front of me. It stares at me with dark, gleaming eyes. Its huge horns are like a tree. I open the car door, climb out, and hold out my hand. Why, I don't know, perhaps as a greeting. The deer turns away from me. It takes a leap and heads out over a field on the other side of the road. I watch it until it reaches the edge of the woods and disappears into the trees. Then I get back in the car and drive on.

It's nearly lunchtime when I turn onto the forest lane. After more than four hours, I'm at my destination.

Strandgården. The sign still hangs above the driveway. It looks just as I remember it, just weathered by wind and rain. The forest road consists of two deep grooves with grass growing high in the middle. On either side stand dense bushes, and tree branches arch over the road. I drive slowly through an orange tunnel of leaves and arrive at the parking lot.

An old camper with no doors and broken windows has been abandoned here. A few rusty bikes lean against the pines. The field is covered with leaves, needles, and pinecones.

I climb out of the car and stretch my stiff body. I follow the gravel path toward the main building. Behind the low house, the lawn spreads down toward the sea like a wild meadow. The mini–golf course to the left is covered in grass and brushwood. The verandah along the house is missing some boards here and there, and the bushes below have taken over. The windows are shuttered. This seaside resort seems to have been abandoned a long time ago.

I walk around the main building, follow the gravel road to the right toward the six cabins. They stand a bit off from the main area, between tall trees near the water's edge. Number one is the farthest away.

We're staying in a private cabin right by the beach. Number one. I'm sitting on the porch, Alice is sleeping in her stroller between the trees. Sleeping in the country air does her good, I think. Leafy elms and birches provide cool shade.

There are more cabins at the edge of the beach. All of them are occupied and the camp down the road is full. There are a bunch of Germans and Dutch people here, and a lot of families with kids and retirees with RVs.

Our cabin is secluded, calm, and cozy. Just Daniel, Alice, and me. We live in our own little bubble. These days have been wonderful, couldn't be better. But tomorrow, our mini-vacation will be over and we'll head home again, so it's important to make the most of today.

The cottages are also in need of restoration. Almost all the paint has flaked off the sunny side, and on the other side, the roof is in bad shape. I walk up the verandah to the cabin we stayed in and peek through the windows. The table and three chairs by the window are gone, as are the brown-and-orange sofa and the double bed that took up most of the bedroom. Nothing remains.

I don't feel anything special. No anxiety, no thunderous emotions. I'm at Strandgården. Where it happened. It doesn't feel like I thought it would.

I turn around and go down to the beach.

The wind from the Baltic Sea. The smell of salt and seaweed. I breathe in, let the fresh autumn air fill me. I crouch down and touch the water. It's ice cold. Even though it's only September, the summer feels long gone. I stand up again, look out over the blue sea.

That night when Alice woke up and we went outside. We sat right here looking at the full moon. Just the three of us.

It feels strangely peaceful to be here.

The silence is broken by a muffled bark.

"Buster!" An old woman in a large, shapeless coat dashes after her dog with surprising speed.

The dog sprints out into the water, then sees me and joyfully bounds in my direction. It stops in front of me and shakes its wet fur. It's an enormous dog. Drool flies in every direction as he tosses his big, wide head.

"Don't worry, he's not dangerous," the old woman shouts, wrapping the coat around her as she approaches. The whole scene is so comical I can't help laughing.

The dog is red-brown, short-haired, strong, and almost as big as its owner. I smile at her and pat the dog.

"Unfortunately, he's got no manners," the woman says as she leashes him.

"He's cute," I say.

"Do you hear that, Buster, you miserable cur?" Her tone is kind, and the dog responds with a deep bark.

"What's the breed?"

"An English mastiff. The best lapdog you could ever imagine." The woman squints at me. "And what brings you here? It's not often we see someone at Strandgården."

I look around. "I was here on vacation once. A long time ago. I was driving by and I wondered if it looked like I remember it."

"I'm afraid not, not anymore." The woman holds her arms out to her surroundings. Then she laughs and pushes her hand in my direction. "But what am I thinking. My name is Elle-Marja. We live on the other side of the hill. I've lived there for more than forty years, Buster for the last eight."

"Stella," I say, and we shake hands. "It used to be so idyllic here. Flowers everywhere. Plants of every color, flower boxes and flower beds, shrubbery and trees trimmed to perfection."

"When were you here?"

"Ninety-four. August."

"It's a shame how this place has been abandoned. Back in the day Strandgården was well cared for. And popular. Always buzzing with guests in the summer."

"Why doesn't anyone take care of it?" I wonder. "The land must be worth a fortune."

"There have been developers who've been snooping around over the years. Everyone wants to get their hands on it. But here it stands, year after year."

"How could that be?"

"Well, let's see, you were here in ninety-four, you say?"

I join Elle-Marja and walk down the beach, listening to her. The sun is high, the sea glittering. Buster is on the loose again, running ahead of us, and rooting around in the driftwood and debris on the beach.

"Memory has a tendency to fail you in your later years, you'll learn as much," says Elle-Marja. "But some things you never forget. A little girl drowned here that summer. The family were guests. Those poor parents had to go home without their daughter. It was tragic. Lundin took it hard. He owned Strandgården and ran it pretty much on his own. It was his life's work. He died soon after that. Very sudden. His daughter owns it now. But she doesn't do anything with it. Haven't seen her since then."

We continue down the beach, past the main building, past the remnants of the mini–golf course. Elle-Marja snorts before continuing: "She moved here for a bit that year and then she disappeared again. She had a baby, and I guess this place was too much to take care of on her own."

We arrive at the end of the sandy beach. In the distance a few seagulls circle in the air and caw. Buster lumbers away to inspect them.

"Are we already here?" I say. "I remember this beach as endless."

"Memory plays tricks on you," Elle-Marja says. "It'll get worse. You live as long as me, and you'll see."

We continue down the path, through the tall grass that grows beside the rocky beach. I'm reminded we used to call it the Path of Problems.

"I remember this," I say. "There were stations along this path where you could meditate."

We stop in front of a ring made of large stones. In the middle of it lies a pile of smaller, fist-sized stones. Beside the ring, a sign sits leaning on its peg. Elle-Marja bends over, puts her hands on her back, and peers closely.

"If you have good enough eyes, you probably can read what it says. I don't see one iota. Can't remember, either." She taps her forehead and chuckles.

"The Ring of Troubles," I say.

I enter the ring. I pick up a rock and rub it. I think about what worries me, about the troubles I have. I release them by throwing the stone away from the ring. I do it with the utmost seriousness and feel my troubles ease. When I turn around, I see Daniel grinning at me.

"Maybe I should throw you out of the ring, Stella. You've only meant trouble since the day I met you."

With a howl, I chased him along the path. We laughed and hugged, kissed in the grass. Unaware that our lives would be destroyed in a moment.

I stand in the ring. I pick up a rock and rub it. Throw it as far as I can. I feel no relief. Just bottomless agony. I fall down on my knees. I sob and scream until Daniel comes and carries me away from there.

I snap out of it when I feel Elle-Marja's hand in mine. She squeezes it, takes me by the arm, and we move on.

After a bit the path continues up a steep hill. Just below us lies a gravel road. That's where we separate. Elle-Marja and Buster are going to head home on the road because it's quicker.

"Buster becomes difficult otherwise," she says. "He's prone to low blood sugar, you know."

"I know how it is," I say. "My husband is the same."

Elle-Marja laughs, and we hug each other. I head up toward the hilltop. I reach a high cliff and see some trees to the left. Another building stands there, partly hidden behind the trees.

I continue in a different direction, toward a rocky cliff that faces the sea. I never came up here last time; we couldn't take the stroller this far. From here you can see out across the Baltic Sea for miles. The cliff ends in a sharp drop. I walk closer and look over the edge. Far below the waves crash over large rocks.

A small stone deer stands in the bush beneath me. Always just about to flee, but frozen here forever. I sit down next to it and gaze out over the sea.

On my way back, I stop at the Ring of Troubles. I go inside and pick up a stone. I rub it in my hand. Then I throw it away, into the trees.

Isabelle

"Isn't it beautiful?" Johanna stretches out like a cat on the blanket next to me.

I close my eyes to the sunlight. "Wonderful."

"That's what I said, Dracula."

It's Saturday, and we're at a class picnic in the Tantolunden park. I'm glad Johanna convinced me to come along. *Stop obsessing, forget about all that for a while.* I've decided to resume what minimal social life I had before Dad died.

I open my eyes when she tells me Axel's arrived. She waves to her boyfriend, stands up and walks over to him. They hug and kiss.

My life could be like a movie. A feel-good movie about college life, giggling and girls' nights out. If only I could relax; if only I could just go for it. If only there were more romance. Johanna, Susie, and Maryam share all the details of what they've done, what they've seen and heard. And it makes me realize how hopelessly inexperienced I am. I've made out with a few people. But never gone farther than that. *It's time to do something about it.* I came close at the freshman party. I drank more wine that night than I'd drunk in my whole life leading up to then. I wore a tight black dress. *I was talked into it.* Although I was tugging at it all night, until the wine made me forget. But I didn't miss a single glance I got because of it. And I do confess, the more wine I had, the more interesting those glances got.

Every time I think about that night, my whole body tingles. *Now is no exception.* Fredrik dragged me onto the dance floor. His hands on my waist. His hands on my hips. His hands on my buttocks. I pressed closer to him, could feel him getting hard. He took my hand, drew me away to an empty corridor. Nibbled on my throat, my ear, on the pointy one, which I have a bit of a complex about sometimes. He tickled my body as we kissed. *If Mom only knew.*

His fingers were on their way inside my dress when one of his friends shouted for him. He asked me to wait and left. My mistake was that I started thinking. Just the thought of Mom destroyed everything, so I went home.

I sit up on the blanket and see that more from our class are here now. Some are playing softball; some are just hanging out. One guy's strumming a guitar.

Fredrik is here, too. He's sitting a few feet away with a beer in his hand. When he leaves the group he's talking to, I screw up my courage and wave.

"Hey."

He looks at me and smiles.

"Ciao, Bella."

"How're you?" I say.

"Good, and yourself?"

He flings himself down beside me and opens a new beer.

"I didn't think you'd be here," he says. "Want some?"

I take a drink and try not to grimace. I hand back the bottle. Fredrik takes it and lies down. After a while, I lie down as well.

"Did you have a good summer?" *I can hear that I sound like Mom, dry and polite.*

"I worked a lot for my dad," he says. "Short trip to Berlin, then Saint-Tropez. You?"

"I worked the whole summer," I answer. *Such an interesting girl. Really.*

"Back in Dalarna?"

"No, at a grocery store in Vällingby."

"I didn't see you at any of the barbecues."

I shrug my shoulders. "Couldn't come."

"Too bad."

He offers me the bottle again. I don't really want any, but it feels so right to lie here together like this. Sharing a bottle of beer and pretending I mean something to him.

"Do you miss Borlänge?"

I think about his question.

"No," I say. "Or, sometimes. Both yes and no. Mostly in the summer, I guess. Stockholm is lovely, too, but it's cozier at home."

"Are you crazy? What could beat the midnight sun in the archipelago? All those outdoor bars and restaurants? Sitting in Kungsträdgården eating ice cream, having a beer in the park, taking a stroll on Djurgården . . ."

"A stroll?" I tease. "Are you retired?"

He pokes me in the side. I laugh.

"Don't forget having to squeeze into the subway with a bunch of sweaty passengers," I remind him. "Usually with your nose pushed into someone's armpit. Yuck. Blech."

"Ha ha, funny. What's so great about Borlänge then? Hillbilly cars? Folk costumes and screechy fiddles?"

"You don't get it."

"Explain it to me then."

"The calm. The silence. The blue mountains. Magical summer nights on the meadow next to Grandma's house."

"Blue mountains and magical summer nights. Sounds poetic."

"Imagine biking to the lake and feeling the wind in your hair. Wandering out into the woods and not running across another soul for hours. Hearing nothing but birdsong."

"Imagine getting lost, getting eaten alive by mosquitoes, and ending up hundreds of miles from civilization."

"Don't be silly. When you're tired of the woods you can go to Leksand, or Noret along with all the corny tourists. Get a burger at Mitti. There's swimming at the sandy beach next to Leksand's Summerland—do you know how cold it is in Lake Siljan? Ice cold."

"Sounds like a blast."

Now I poke him in the side.

"Have you ever been to Tällberg? It's gorgeous. Dad always drove through really slow so we could look at all the houses. And the road is narrow and curvy. Sometimes we drove down to Hjortnäs Bridge. Every time we went up to Vidablick, we ate ice cream and looked out over Lake Siljan. The view is incredible. We'd end our trip by walking out on the long pier in Rättvik. When I was little, it seemed like it never ended. We'd race back to the shore."

I fall silent.

"What are you thinking about?" Fredrik wonders.

"My dad."

"I heard. I'm really sorry. Or is that the right thing to say?"

"Thank you."

"You should have said something."

"Said what?"

"You should have told me what happened. You just disappeared. Said no to everything and nobody heard from you."

"I know."

He looks into my eyes. I want to stay here forever. With him. He asks me how I feel now, and I hadn't planned on saying anything, but I confess that I've started going to therapy. He doesn't seem to think that's so strange. *I don't tell him everything, of course.*

We lie in silence for a moment. Then I start telling him about how I went with Johanna and left a sample at the blood bus last spring. It feels good to give blood; not enough people do. Recently I received my first summons to donate.

I keep talking. I want to get the mood we just had back again, want to make him stay for as long as possible.

I say I'll probably faint and fall over and split open my whole arm with the needle and my blood will spray all over the room and the nurse will start slipping around on it. Fredrik laughs out loud. He takes his phone from his pocket and scoots in close to me. He holds it above us and takes a picture. I protest and say I wasn't ready. He takes one more.

"Better?" He hands the phone to me for my approval.

"Okay, a little better."

"Come on, we look super hot, right?"

He gets a text, reads it, and sits up.

"In one of my weaker moments I promised to drive my sister to Ikea," he says. "Gotta go. Unfortunately. But I'll see you."

I sit there smiling like an idiot. That is, until I realize there can never be anything between us. When he finds out who I am, I'll disgust him. He'll fear me.

I fear myself.

I'm afraid of what's inside of me.

Stella

After more than eight hours behind the wheel, I'm home again. I fall asleep in a hot bath and wake up in cold water. I climb out and dry off. Thinking about Henrik.

I still don't know how to tell him. Tell him Alice is alive, and I've met her. Tell him I didn't stay home to rest, but went to Strandgården instead. That it's for real this time.

His T-shirt is draped over the chair in the bedroom. I pull it on and lie on our bed. I open the diary.

The summer I was pregnant, 1993, the year it reached eighty degrees at the end of April—which ended up being the warmest day of the year. Otherwise the summer was long and cold and rainy. The next year, we had a heat wave, and Alice crawled around everywhere in just her diaper.

The apartment in Jordbro. We were able to get the lease because the landlord was a friend of Daniel's father. The scent of honeysuckle outside the kitchen window, the dirty gray-striped wallpaper in the bedroom, full of holes. In the end, I papered over it with newspapers.

Daniel, my first real love. He was a year ahead of me in high school, and he ran around with all sorts of girls in his souped-up car. I showed him I was interested, but I didn't chase him. Somehow I still managed to catch his attention. I lost my virginity in the backseat of that car.

Daniel was wild and restless, intense about anything he was interested in. He annoyed my big sister to no end. She thought he was a bad influence; he didn't fit into Helena's ordered worldview. We stayed out late, street racing, partying. We had a lot of sex in the backseat of his car.

Helena was always the reliable one of the two of us. I'm a dreamer, always have been. Spontaneous and impulsive, did whatever I wanted. My sister was responsible, did what she was supposed to. She grew up too early because our dad died.

When Mom ended up alone with us, she struggled to make ends meet. At night she mended clothes for extra money, sometimes she worked double shifts at her day job as a cleaner. I was only five, and Helena had to stay home and take care of me.

My sister and I grew apart as we got older. The fact that I got pregnant at seventeen didn't help matters.

Daniel was overjoyed when he found out he was going to be a father. He did what his parents wanted him to do, finished high school, got his diploma. Then we moved in together. He got a job in a garage. We lived on minimum wage and stubbornness. Just the two of us and Alice.

I loved being home with our baby. Looking into her eyes while I nursed her, watching her mouth search for my breast, the happy sigh when she found it. I loved her scent, loved listening to the little sounds she made, her complete trust and the tenderness she evoked inside me.

Alice's first year. I read entries about how she learned to sit, how she started turning from stomach to back, the teeth that eventually came in. Her first birthday. When I baked her first cake, a balloon popped, and she started crying until Daniel made her laugh again.

Pernilla's visit just before we went on our highly anticipated vacation.

I stop reading and put the diary on the nightstand. Not sure I can continue. I get up from bed and dry my hair. Pull on a pair of leggings and a sweatshirt. Pick up the diary again. Sit down on the edge of the bed. It comes back to me.

The beach, infinite, white. The sea, calm. Flowers of every color, everywhere. Oppressive heat. Trees swaying. Cabin number one.

Her red stroller, turned over in the sand.

Alice, where are you?

AUGUST 15, 1994

What did you do? Where were you?

Why weren't you there? Why didn't you hear anything?

Why didn't you notice she was gone?

The same questions, over and over again.

I wasn't away long. I wasn't, was I? I was close by.

They think I hurt her. My own child, my baby daughter.

They think I injured her. That I killed her. I see it on them, in their faces, in the looks they give each other. I hear it in their voices.

I did something unforgivable. The worst sin a mother can commit. I didn't take care of my child. I left her alone. I wasn't there to protect her.

She was sleeping in her red stroller there among the trees. I went on a short walk just down the beach. Sat there for a while, just thinking. A few minutes.

They ask why I didn't notice anything. They say it's time for me to tell the truth. Tell it all, it will all come out in the end.

But I have told them, I have explained. Again and again and again.

She couldn't have overturned that stroller by herself. And I would have heard if she woke up. I wasn't away for long. I was close by. Someone must have taken her. But who takes someone else's child? It's impossible. People don't steal children. She has to be here somewhere. Maybe someone is taking care of her. Because I didn't. Her young, selfish, immature mother who went off by herself for a while.

She'll come back. She has to. She'll come back soon. She didn't overturn that stroller on her own, didn't crawl away, didn't drown in the sea. She did not, it's impossible.

Alice, where are you? Are you sad? Is someone else holding you now?

We've been searching everywhere. No trace, nothing. But she's here, I know it. Come back to me. Listen when I call for you. Come back. You have to come back.

You are my everything. You are my flesh and blood! Without you I don't want to live. You are in my blood.

Stella

Mom mutters to herself while rooting around in the kitchen drawer. "Stella, where did you hide that can opener?" she says, pulling out another drawer. The way she says it you'd think she'd already scoured the whole house.

"In the second drawer," I respond, forcing myself to be calm.

"No, it's not here. It's nowhere to be found."

"It's there." I wonder why I invited her here. So I wouldn't be alone? So I'd spend my time being irritated with her instead of thinking about Alice?

"That's it, right there." Mom picks up the mail from the kitchen counter. "Is it okay if I put this on the microwave?"

"Sure."

"It looks like the local newspaper and . . ."

"It's fine; put it there."

"Shouldn't we make enough food for Henrik and Milo?"

It's the third time she's asked.

"Margareta will see to it that they're fed before they leave," I say. "Or they'll pick up something on their way."

"Are you sure? We can always freeze the leftovers. You'll have food for tomorrow," she says.

"Mom. This will be enough."

She throws up her hands in surrender. "Just trying to be helpful. Sorry for intruding."

Mom has a tendency to take over. She starts baking and cooking, asks if she can help with the laundry and the vacuuming. It's convenient for a while. But it also gets on my nerves.

"Have you heard from Helena?" I ask.

"She called this week. She and Charles and the children might come home for Christmas. I hope so."

"Do you think she's happy? In Oxford, with him?" That was stupid. Here we go again. Why do I keep doing that? Am I trying to start an argument? Mom wrinkles her forehead before she answers. "Yes, I think so. Don't you?"

"She's still there, I guess," I say.

Not long after I had Milo, my sister met Charles while visiting London. He's an English professor with an affinity for brown corduroy and long-winded monologues.

For thirteen years she's lived in Oxford with him, and they now have three well-groomed sons.

"When was the last time you talked?" Mom says as she stirs the pot.

"Just before summer, I think."

"How did this happen? Why don't you two keep in touch with each other anymore?"

"We're just different; we always have been."

I hand Mom a wineglass. She sits down at the table and takes a sip.

"You gave me more trouble than Helena," she says. "You always wanted to know *why*. She was content to accept things as they are."

"She's always been afraid of conflict."

"We all have different ways of handling things. You of all people should know that."

"She didn't even talk about Alice once, after what happened. Never asked how I was doing. She pretended like nothing had changed. Would only discuss practical things—what do we eat, who should do what. She still does that. I hate it."

"What's the matter with you? You sound so angry and grumpy."

"You two always want things to stay the same. You ignore anything difficult. What happened to me affected all of us, but nobody will acknowledge it."

Mom puts down the wineglass. "Have you ever thought about what part you might have played?" she asks. "You pulled away from us. You wouldn't let us talk about it. You didn't want to. There were long periods of time when we barely saw you." She stretches out her hand toward mine. I pull away.

"I brought you home from a party," she says. "Pernilla called. You'd drunk too much, probably taken something else. You had an anxiety attack. Scared the wits out of everyone who was there."

I don't say anything. Stare down at the floor. I don't want to hear this.

"I should have done something about it earlier. You're right that I kept my eyes closed for too long, and I'm sorry for that. Then you started therapy. You felt better. Life goes on, you said. And it did. For all of us. So don't be so hard on Helena."

My mother's words make me feel ashamed.

She continues. "You talked about this with Henrik when you met him. He wasn't afraid, he was able to bear your grief. I know things have sometimes been tense between us. But I'm always here. I hope you know that."

Now I take her hand. "I'm sorry, Mom. I know I've been unfair to you. And Helena, too."

"Why are you thinking about Alice? Isn't it better to let it be? You have Henrik and Milo now, a good life. Let it go, Stella."

I get up and give Mom a hug. She's right, I should let it be.

"Have you been to her grave recently?" she wonders. "Sorry, I know you'd rather call it her memorial stone."

I shake my head. After we've eaten and Mom leaves for home, I sit in the kitchen thinking over our conversation.

I have only vague memories of the time between Alice's disappearance and ward five. Mom had me committed in the spring of 1995. I was put into a secure psychiatric ward. I didn't eat, lost weight. I was deeply depressed.

Eventually I came in contact with Birgitta, a psychotherapist. I got help, allowed myself to look toward the future, decided to live. Later, I studied psychology with the goal of becoming a psychotherapist. I'm good at what I do.

I used to be.

Not anymore. Right now I can't help anyone. I can't even help myself.

I stand up, wipe down the kitchen counter, and pick up the local newspaper Mom put on top of the microwave. An envelope falls down onto the floor. I pick it up. It's handwritten and addressed to me, Stella Widstrand, formerly Johansson. No postage, no address. Someone put it directly into the mailbox.

I open it. There's a piece of paper folded inside the envelope. It has a cross drawn at the top. The text beneath is written neatly in black ink.

> Stella Widstrand,
> born November 12, 1975,
> has suddenly and unexpectedly left us.
> She will not be missed.
> No one mourns her.

Isabelle

The cold seeps straight through my clothes. Even with a thick scarf wrapped around half my face, I feel naked. I hunch my shoulders against the rain and dash down Valhallavägen. The storm rumbles above Stockholm for the third day in a row. We only had one lecture and many stayed home today. *Like Johanna.* If it weren't for group therapy I would have, too. Or at least *considered* it. But I don't want to miss my appointment with Stella. Too much is at stake.

Forty-eight minutes until group therapy begins. I've been looking forward to it all week.

What if she's not there?

I walk across the street toward the bus stop. The bus arrives, I hop on, and the air on board feels heavy, damp from soaked clothes and dripping umbrellas. The windows are foggy; the lights outside glow as if in mist.

Ever since I found Stella I think about her. Maybe too much. Last time she looked at me very thoroughly. As if she already knows who I am. As if she understands why I was there. But she doesn't. She can't know anything about me or my life. She has no clue.

The bus stops outside the Västermalms Mall. I push my way through the doors and hurry toward the clinic. I open the front door and walk in. I ride up to the fourth floor. Greet the receptionist, pay, and head toward the lounge.

I sit down in one of the armchairs, put my phone on silent. Stella comes in at exactly one o'clock and closes the door behind her. I examine her. Beautifully dressed in a knee-length dress today, her hair pinned up in an elegant, thick knot.

Everyone seems like they're in a bad mood today. Clara is nervous about a presentation she has to give to corporate management tomorrow. Pierre snaps that she's always worrying and whining, but then everything always goes well for her. She snaps something back.

I glance at Stella again. *It's difficult to read her.* So far, she hasn't spoken. She just sits there.

She's listening. Studying us one by one. After a while, I feel Stella's gaze on me.

I meet it and smile. She does not smile back.

Stella

I regret recommending group therapy to Isabelle Karlsson. Given the social difficulties she reported having, this kind of therapy seemed appropriate. But that was before I knew.

Others have talked today, but not Isabelle. So far, she hasn't said anything. Not a word.

The group has been silent for a while. I have to make her say something. Have to find out why she's here.

I take the floor: How has your week been, Isabelle?

Isabelle: It's been okay. We started a new group project, and I like my group. Which is nice. And I became a blood donor.

She smiles again. The dimple on her left cheek appears.

Isabelle: Yesterday was the first time I donated blood. I'm a little afraid of needles. Like my mom, she's ridiculous about them. But it went better than I thought.

She's silent for a moment. Who is this woman she calls "Mom"?

Isabelle: By the way, she wants me to come home this weekend, but I really don't want to.

Magnus: Why?

Isabelle: We're not really getting along right now. She was the one who told me Hans wasn't my real dad.

Arvid: How did it come about?

Isabelle: I was crying. I told Mom I missed him. Told her it doesn't get any easier, like everyone claims. I said I would never get over it. She couldn't take that. She got angry and told me that I should be thankful I still have her.

She takes a deep breath and looks around. Is her story true? Is what she says real?

Isabelle: Dad and I were close. I know she wishes I was close to her, too, that things were as natural between us. But they're just not.

Her voice quivers; she's close to tears. It's genuine. No one can be that convincing without real feelings. What does it mean? Am I wrong? Did I imagine everything? Is this not Alice, but just Isabelle?

Isabelle: So she said, he's not your real father anyway.

Clara: What a terrible way to say that. Awful.

Pierre: So freaking mean.

Arvid: Just sick. How do you feel about it?

Isabelle: I don't know. She's sad, too. I don't want to be unfair to her. It's been hard for her as well. She hasn't had an easy life. She's done her best to be a good mother.

Is it a coincidence that Isabelle is sitting here? Imagine if she actually doesn't know anything. It can't be that simple. She must be hiding something. But what?

Clara: Of course, she's grieving, but still.

Arvid: It's still not okay. You don't tell someone something like that so callously.

Isabelle: It would make more sense if Mom had been the one who adopted me.

Me: What do you mean by that?

Several of the participants stare at me and exchange looks with one another. I don't care. I need to know.

Me: What's her name, your mother's?

Isabelle: Kerstin.

Me: Do you and Kerstin have a close relationship?

Isabelle: There's close and then there's close. How should I say this? I could talk to Dad about everything. Me and Mom, we might as well be from different planets.

Arvid: What mother doesn't come from another planet?

Relieved laughter from the group. I try to smile.

Arvid: My own mother insists on visiting me in the morning. I never learn to say no.

Clara: You have to set boundaries.

The conversation changes focus and the participants continue the discussion among themselves. I want to hear more about Isabelle, but can't interrupt without arousing suspicion. I think Isabelle wants to talk about Kerstin, the woman she calls Mom.

It would make more sense if Mom had been the one who adopted me.

What does that mean?

Does she know Kerstin isn't her biological mother? Does she want *me* to know she knows? Who is this Kerstin? And what does she know?

It's impossible to concentrate. I have no idea what the group is talking about anymore. There is too much moving through my mind.

Alice, everything that happened when she disappeared and the aftermath.

What happened later, twelve years ago, when my life fell apart again.

The visit to Strandgården.

Lina Niemi's report.

My own death notice.

Who would put something like that in someone's mailbox?

Is it a warning?

A threat?

Henrik was upset. Mostly because I didn't think it was necessary to report it to the police. Unfortunately, it's not uncommon for a therapist to receive threats. But this is the first time I've received a threatening letter. Whoever is behind it was at our house. He put it into our mailbox himself. But the idea that someone intends to physically harm me seems improbable. Nobody hates me enough to go that far. As far as I know.

And what could the police do? The letter is handwritten, there's no signature, no return address.

Henrik assumed it was from Lina or her parents, the only client in my years as a psychotherapist who's been openly hostile.

Maybe he's right. It could be Lina's parents, one or both, who wrote it.

It could be Lina herself. Or it could be completely unrelated. Another patient of mine. It could be someone sitting in this group.

It could be Isabelle Karlsson.

I've been lost in my own thoughts for far too long, so I straighten up in my chair.

Pierre is going on about social media. He can't understand why people spend their time on Facebook or Instagram—why would forty-eight likes give your life meaning, and why do people seek confirmation for a photoshopped picture of an imagined reality. He wonders if Isabelle ever posted a picture of her "father," with air quotes, if she wrote: *I will never forget you*? People do crap like that all the time. *I think about you every day.* Like, your mother or your cat has been dead seventeen years. It's bullshit. People forget. There's no way you could go seventeen years and still think about someone every day, *miss* someone, he says. You grieve, you move on.

"What is grief?" I say. "What is it to miss someone? When someone is taken from you, they take a piece of you with them. A piece that can never be replaced by anything else. The grief, the loss is there forever. And it hurts. It bleeds and aches. It becomes a scab, and it itches, and then it falls off. And it bleeds again. One day it becomes a scar. The wound heals, but the scar remains."

Everyone is staring at me. The silence is oppressive.

"After a few years, sadness and loss have changed you," I continue. "They've become a part of your interior. They help to form the rest of your life. No day passes without that grief being there. You never forget. It's part of you, of who you are."

Without looking at any of the participants in the group, I stand up and leave the room.

SEPTEMBER 2, 1994

Twenty days. The longest days of my life.

A living nightmare.

Don't give up yet. You have to take care of yourself. You have to believe; you have to hope. That's what everyone said in the beginning. They meant well; they were trying to be supportive, to comfort me. Their words are empty.

Now they tell me she's gone. Alice has drowned; she no longer exists. She's dead.

I refuse to believe it.

But my hope is gone.

It took only a second. The blink of an eye.

My little girl has disappeared forever. How can I live with that?

They are afraid of my grief. Mom, Helena, Maria. As if I might be contagious.

Daniel is silent. He won't look me in the eye. I hate the distance between us. I wish he would scream at me, blame me as I blame myself. I know he does, but he won't say it.

We have lost Alice. And in our grief we lost each other, too.

Stella

People are crouched under their umbrellas, hurrying down St. Eriksgatan. I step into Thelins Bakery, buy a coffee, and sit in a corner near the front. I left the building without telling Renate, without canceling my next appointment. I've never done that before. And this is the first time I left a therapy session early.

I put my head in my hands, stare down, and see myself reflected as a dark shadow in the black coffee. I straighten up and observe the other customers, who are either reading or in conversation with each other. We are in different worlds. We have nothing in common. My hand shakes as I lift my cup.

I must be more affected by the death notice than I realized. Somebody hates me. Someone wishes me dead. Who? And why?

Once again I go through every problem, every question. I try to sort it all out, think through it logically, but I'm too upset.

Four mothers enter and sit down at the table next to mine. They park their strollers and start to strip layers of clothes off crying and screaming babies. Over and over again they tell their children to be quiet, stop climbing on tables and chairs. They laugh, they discuss the houses they want to buy and winter vacations they want to take.

It feels like an invasion. I get up from the table without drinking my coffee and leave. I go to the left, take the stairs down to the subway, and regret that I had Henrik drive me here this morning. Wet commuters squeeze in around me on the train headed toward Alvik. The air is stuffy, smells damp and sweaty. Everybody wants to be home already, or at their destinations. Everyone wants to be anywhere but here.

The back of my neck burns, as if someone behind me is staring.

I turn around, study the other passengers. Nobody is paying any attention to me.

I switch to the bus at Alvik. The rain flows down the windows. The streetlights shine along the wet streets. The outside world is blurry and diffuse. The sky is dark and indifferent. I get off and walk homeward in the rain.

Again, I have the unpleasant sensation of being watched. I stop and turn around but see no one. I speed up my pace.

I hang my coat in the hall, lean my purse against the bureau. The house is empty. Milo should be home soon, Henrik will come shortly after, if he's not working late. I should cook dinner. Can't. Won't.

Why didn't I let Mom make enough food for the whole week? I should call Henrik, tell him to buy something on his way home. I never know when to expect him nowadays.

I go into the living room and stand by the window. I lean my forehead against the cold glass and close my eyes.

A glass of wine. A hot bath. Then sleep. That's what I need. The symptoms are clear, and if I don't take them seriously, this will end in disaster.

I open my eyes.

A man is standing in the street. He's wearing a dark, shapeless raincoat with the hood obscuring his face. His arms hang rigidly at his sides.

I gasp for breath and take a step back. The man watching me doesn't move. I turn around, grab the phone from the living room table to call the police. When I look back, nobody's there.

The wind whips the trees; the rain pummels the windows.

I stand with the phone in my hands, ready to call. I look out over the garden, across the street.

The man in the raincoat is gone.

Kerstin

I've probably spent half an hour organizing the shelves in the nursing home's storage room. Messes make me crazy. If everyone just pitched in to keep things tidy, just did a little bit, then I wouldn't end up having to do this.

But I like routines. I've always found them important. Going to work, doing the same tasks every day, it makes me feel calm. It gives me a sense of purpose.

Anna-Lena sticks her head in. "Kerstin, do you have a second?"

"When I'm done in here," I answer.

What does she want now? I look at the time and notice she came in forty minutes early today. She often does that. And it doesn't matter if anyone notices. Efficient, responsible Anna-Lena. She's only thirty-five, but she thinks she's better than the rest of us. However, I've never seen her cleaning up the storeroom. It will never happen. She's far too important to concern herself with such things.

I arrange the cleaning sprays on the shelf in neat lines. I'm in no hurry. I lock up the storage room and walk leisurely through the corridor. I don't intend to stress.

"You needed something?" I say when I get to her office.

"Sit down." Anna-Lena gestures to the chair on the opposite side of the desk. She finishes what she's working on before turning to me. "I've been told things aren't going so well lately."

"I think things have been exceptionally calm. Who said otherwise?"

"It doesn't matter who." A searching look, a regretful smile. "You've been impatient and hard on the residents."

"So this is about me? I'm the problem?" Anna-Lena refuses to meet my eye and fiddles with a few papers. "I'm sorry to hear that," I continue. "What exactly does this *person* claim to have seen?"

"Well, she didn't say anything specific, but—"

"Then it's hard to talk about it," I interrupt. "Right? If *she* didn't see me doing anything wrong."

"Well, she has that perception. And Greta has complained."

"Greta?" I laugh to show what I think of her. "What *doesn't* she complain about? That woman thinks everyone is wrong. She's never satisfied. You would know that if you ever worked the floor."

Anna-Lena sighs. As if I've said something unusually stupid.

Drama at work exhausts me. Especially battles of this kind. The others gang up on me, complain that I switch my shifts, that I don't work all my hours, that I go home early. They'll invent anything to make me feel terrible. But there's no reason for any of it.

I'm not the most social and chatty person on the staff, I know it. That must be why. Yet I've been here longer than any of them. Me and Ritva, sixteen years soon. They wouldn't know what to do without me. New shooting stars like Anna-Lena rarely last long. To cope with this job, you need more than just the desire to play boss. It's not like it looks on paper. Theory is one thing, practice is another. Some people are totally out of touch with reality, that much is clear.

"Yes, well, I just wanted to check in with you," Anna-Lena says and makes a snooty face.

"There's nothing wrong with how I do my job."

"Please, Kerstin, why do you always get so defensive? We need to talk about this. You have received a complaint. Again. I know things have been difficult lately, because of your husband and such. But we can't let it affect your work."

She doesn't understand. She doesn't understand anything. She doesn't understand shit.

Without a word I stand up and leave the room. Anna-Lena follows me into the corridor and calls after me. I pretend not to hear.

To say I like it here would be an exaggeration. There's always some foolishness, differing opinions on routines and how tasks should be performed. Easy things end up getting complicated, and it creates twice as much work.

I somehow always end up getting the short end of the stick. And these young people who get paid by the hour. Shouldn't a work ethic be a basic requirement? They ignore the old folks and do the absolute minimum. They're always causing trouble, trading shifts, calling in sick at the last second, always on Friday nights or Monday mornings. I sub for them, pitch in when I can. But I'm the one who gets shit for it. The world is a thankless place.

Working somewhere else sounds appealing. But I'll be fifty soon. I'm too old, nobody wants me anymore, the job market is closed. I'll stick to my routines here at Hällsjö Home, no matter how unpleasant my colleagues are or how incompetent the management is.

I enter the staff room.

"Soon I'll be home at last," Ritva says in her thick Finnish-Swedish accent.

"Yes," I answer. "At last."

"Me and the old man are going to Ikea. You been there yet?"

"No. I don't need any more furniture than I already have."

"The old man is happy they've opened a store here in Borlänge," Ritva says and laughs. "He won't have to drive to Gävle all the time."

"Hello," Cecilia says, bouncing into the kitchen.

I turn away. I can't stand her. What is she, twenty-three? Twenty-four? Some little nursing student who thinks she's in possession of infinite knowledge. I'm glad she doesn't work with us every day. She likes to tell you how to improve everything. Know-it-all kids, is there anything more annoying? Brats who take that tone once they land their first real job.

Right behind her comes Hattie, around forty, a woman from Iran, I think. She rarely talks, but she's pleasant and modest, humble in some way. Not pushy and self-important like some people around here.

"Do you want coffee, Kerstin?" Ritva holds out a cup to me. I sink down in the nearest chair and put in three sugar cubes. I deserve them today.

Ritva pours one for Hattie, who takes it and smiles gratefully.

"None for me, thank you," Cecilia says, though no one asked her. "I don't see how you all can drink so much coffee every day." She makes a great fuss of fixing herself a cup of herbal tea. "This job really fucks with you. How can you stand it year after year?"

"Lucky you won't have to then," Ritva says and sits down next to me. "You've always been in nursing, right, Kerstin?"

"More or less," I answer. "But you do get worn down."

"There's too much to do," Cecilia says, throwing her feet up on the chair next to her. "Too little time."

"You have to take it easy," Hattie says. I smile encouragingly at her. She's getting better and better at Swedish. Imagine if everyone were so ambitious and goal-oriented.

"Someone has to do the job," Ritva says and frowns. She's gruff and doesn't fawn over anyone. She does what has to be done and goes home. No bullshit. Just like me.

"How's Isabelle? Does she still like Stockholm?" Ritva asks.

"Seems like it." I don't want to tell her how worried I am about my daughter. In just a few minutes I'll report to the evening staff, change my clothes, and go home. Home to silence. Still, I carry on. "But it would be for the best if she moved home again."

"Why?" Ritva says. "Best for who?"

I'm startled by this blunt question. But Ritva is just like that, I know. I swallow my annoyance.

"I think it would be best for *her*. It's been hard for her since Hans passed. She's started therapy."

"You make it sound like that's a bad thing," Cecilia says.

"I didn't say that."

"If she's having a hard time, sounds like it might be good for her to have someone to talk to?"

"Maybe," I answer. "But she can talk to me. I don't know if I believe in sharing private matters with strangers."

My spoon rattles around in my coffee cup. My face turns hot as they stare at me. I shouldn't have said anything.

"I know my daughter," I continue. "She's very vulnerable right now."

"You don't have to worry," Ritva says. "Isabelle is a good girl."

"I think it's useful to talk to an outside person sometimes," Cecilia says. "Everybody should go to therapy now and then, I'm certain of that."

Of course you think so. And if you think so, I guess it's automatically right?

You are half my age, but of course you know best. You have no idea how much I miss my girl, or how worried I am.

"Of course I support her," I say after a while. "If that's what she wants, I'll do what I can to help."

I've been abandoned. What do they know about that? Do they lie in bed at night worrying about their own flesh and blood? Do they know how it feels to watch their only child become a stranger? Isabelle is slipping farther away from me with each day. They don't understand, they can't imagine what it's like. It's meaningless to even try to explain. I drink the rest of my coffee and leave to report to the next shift.

My old Nissan starts on the first try, thank goodness. Before I leave the parking lot, I clear the fog off the window with my sleeve. I drive down Hemgatan and turn onto Faluvägen. Some driver behind me honks his horn and blinks his headlights. A young guy passes me and gives me the middle finger. Yes, yes, I should have stopped at the intersection. It's all too much right now. My head is swimming with thoughts and speculations. I'm not really myself.

I turn into the driveway. Just sit in the car thinking. It was nice to leave work, but I don't want to enter that emptiness. If only Isabelle would move home. Then we'd have each other. Like before. Everything would be just like before.

To my great surprise, she called me yesterday and told me about her therapy. Until now the subject had been completely taboo. She refused to tell me anything. She'd been quite rude and said it didn't concern me. Now she was all excitement. She's getting so much out of it, tons and tons. But when I asked *what* she wouldn't tell me. Apparently everyone in the group is on her side, can you believe it, Mom?

No, I don't. I don't understand any of it.

In my world you solve things on your own; that's how it works. I want Isabelle to talk to *me,* not total strangers in group therapy. Who knows who they are, what kind of baggage they have, what kind of advice they're giving? I want the two of us to figure everything out; I want us to have the chance to talk through things properly. But I'll have to let her try this first.

I'll wait and see. In time, everything will work out for us, I'll make sure of it.

My purse is in the backseat, and I have to wrench my body around to grab hold of it. I'm so stiff. On my way to the house, I stop and stretch. I forgot the mail. I turn around and go back.

I bought the mailbox next to the gate at an auction just after we moved here. It looks like a miniature house, painted yellow with gingerbread trim and a fence and tiny, fine details. I just had to have it.

Later Isabelle biked into it, it fell over, and its tiny fence was destroyed. She must have been around seven then? It made me so sad and a little upset. Isabelle got sad, too. Hans fixed it as well as he could and put it up again. It's still nice, even if it's not like before.

I talked it through with Isabelle, showed her how you can be upset and disappointed, and it's no big deal. You can be friends again later. I bandaged her skinned knees and taught her that life goes on. I taught her we stick together no matter what happens.

The front door of the neighboring house opens. Gunilla comes out and stands on the top of the stairs. I have absolutely no desire to expose myself to her well-meaning babble. I go up the path without looking to the side. She calls my name, but I don't care. I fumble with my keys, unlock the door, open it, and go inside. I close the door behind me and lock it. Then I sink down onto the hall floor.

Sweat runs down my back, my heart is racing, and I feel dizzy. I don't know what's wrong. It must be the stress. All those disappointments. All those worries and anxieties. The grief after Hans.

I'm grieving for him. I feel both sorrow and relief. Freedom. Are you allowed to feel like that?

Life is strange. Can you ever master it?

I stay there for a while. Then I pick up the phone and call Isabelle.

She misses me, too, I know it.

Stella

Milo and Hampus, Pernilla's son, are sitting in the backseat with their heads close together, staring at their phones.

"Can you believe you boys have known each other your whole lives." I see them exchange glances in the rearview mirror. "You're both so cute."

"Mom," Milo exclaims.

Hampus laughs. "You're just as embarrassing as my mom," he says.

"Embarrassing, how could that be?" I say, and park outside Konradsbergs Hall, which sits opposite the Dagens Nyheter Tower. "I'll leave your bag with Pernilla, Milo."

"Thanks, Mom."

They're already out the door by the time I shout out a good-bye. Milo raises his hand in answer as he saunters away. It strikes me again how similar he is to Henrik. Tall and lanky and with the same boyish charm.

I watch them walk away with their gym bags and basketballs. As they enter the glass doors, I start the car and head toward Pernilla's apartment near Kungsholms Strand.

Pernilla and I grew up on the same block, went to the same school from first to ninth grade. She's like a sister, closer to me than Helena. She had Hampus the same year Milo was born, and the boys hang out a lot outside of basketball, too.

She was one of the few who stayed in my life after I had Alice. Other friends disappeared. They went to high school, partied, lived their lives. And after Alice vanished, Pernilla was the only one I kept in touch with. Or rather, she was the only one who kept in touch with me.

No one else saw how bad it got for me. Not Mom and definitely not Helena. Only Pernilla.

I was manic. Did everything I could to suppress the guilt, to forget my grief. I just kept going. I drank. I escaped into a haze of partying, drinking, doing drugs. I slept with unfamiliar boys and strange men. Afterward, I remembered none of them, not their names or what they looked like. From the outside it looked like I was reliving my lost teen years. But in reality it was something else. I was headed toward a complete mental breakdown.

I'm looking forward to an evening with Pernilla. Talking to her, telling her about everything that's going on. I find a parking spot on Igeldammsgatan and walk down toward Kungholms Strand, where she lives.

"Do you want a glass of wine, or are you driving?" Pernilla says when I sit down on the sofa.

"Uncork it. I'll pick up the car tomorrow," I say. "I'm so glad that Milo can stay the night."

"It's fun for us."

I stare through the big windows, looking out over the canal and Karlberg Palace. Pernilla puts on some music, pours a glass of wine for me. I flip through the magazines on the coffee table. *"Health & Fitness, iForm, Feel Good, Fitness Magazine,"* I read aloud. "You're taking this new hobby of yours very seriously."

"Don't make fun of me," Pernilla says. She settles down on the sofa next to me. "It's not a hobby. It's a lifestyle."

"Does that lifestyle include wine on a Thursday night?"

"I believe in balance." Pernilla raises her glass as in a toast. "It's never too late, Stella. You're slim, but even you could exercise a bit. Fit over forty—check out the hashtag on Instagram."

"I don't have Instagram," I say.

"You're a dinosaur," she replies. "And you'll end up all wrinkled and flabby if you don't start moving. Come with me sometime and pound the shit out of your body in the gym—it's wonderful."

"I exercise. I play tennis sometimes."

She snorts. "I can offer you a gaggle of ripped personal trainers to ogle. You're not gonna find that at the tennis court."

I laugh. Pernilla never changes. I'm glad I came here.

"It's been way too long since we did this," I say, tucking my feet beneath me.

"Got soused on a weekday?"

"Is that the plan?"

"I'm flexible," Pernilla says and hands me a tray of cheese and crackers.

"I saw Mom this weekend."

"How was that?"

"It was good."

I take a cracker and taste it. Pernilla's cell beeps; she picks it up, reads something, and puts it away.

I gather my courage and ask, "Do you have any contact with Maria nowadays?"

"Maria Sundkvist?"

"Or Daniel? Have you heard anything from him?"

I try to make it sound like an innocent question.

"Not so much in recent years. We're friends on Facebook. Maria lives in Arvidsjaur, Daniel in Bro." She glances sideways at me. "Why? Why do you ask?"

I shrug my shoulders. "Saw someone who looked like Maria."

Pernilla seems content with that. She stares at her cellphone again, laughs at what she sees.

"I've been thinking a lot about Alice lately," I say.

Pernilla wrinkles her forehead and finally looks up. "So that's why you ask. Why have you been thinking about her?"

"Why?" I say. "What kind of question is that?"

"Sorry, Stella, I didn't mean it like that." She creeps closer to me on the sofa and puts an arm around me.

"When I saw Milo and Hampus today I wondered about her. How she would have looked, what she would have been like right now."

"Don't think like that, sweetie. Dwelling on that leads nowhere."

"What if she's alive?"

Pernilla grabs my hand and looks into my eyes. "You can't do this. Do you remember last time, how bad you felt? Let it go, Stella. You have Henrik and Milo. Alice is gone."

"How do you know that? What if I know she's alive and that—"

"Stella, stop. I was at her funeral." Pernilla impatiently shakes her head.

Her cell beeps again, and she can't stop herself from looking at it. "Maybe it's the stress? Work's been pretty rough lately, hasn't it?"

I think about the death notice. About the menacing-looking man in the raincoat standing on the street watching me through the window. I want to talk to her about it. But Pernilla isn't listening.

"Okay, let's forget it," I say, grabbing the wine.

"Is everything good between you and Henrik?"

"It's nothing like that."

"You need a hot weekend just the two of you," Pernilla says and winks. "Send Milo here. Get away and have some fun together."

There's no point. I thought I'd be able to talk to her, thought she would understand.

"Who are you so eager to chat with?" I nod to the phone.

Pernilla smiles. "My personal trainer. I'm happy you were so kind to him when you met."

It's that easy to change the topic of conversation. Apparently, we're just going to shoot the shit for the rest of the evening. I regret coming here.

"Yes, he was nice," I say. "Henrik liked him."

"Did he really?" Pernilla seems relieved. "Hampus likes him, too. I know he's a little young, but he's sweet. And funny. He makes me feel special."

Pernilla goes off on a long monologue. *Sebastian is so nice, so wonderful, more mature than anybody she's ever dated, he's charming, attentive, kind, and he's good in bed, handsome, in great shape, young and strong and so hot, and she's never felt this way about anybody before.*

I let her prattle on. Drink my wine. Feel miserable.

I've tried talking to Mom, tried talking to Pernilla. Neither has shown the least bit of understanding. Both think I should forget the past and focus on the future.

I think about Daniel. I miss him, long for him even. I want to see him; I want to hear what he has to say. But I'm not sure he'd want to listen to me. Not after last time.

Pernilla gives me a long hug when I'm about to go and says she'd gladly meet again soon. If I want to talk. I don't tell her that's why I came tonight. She's completely absorbed by this new relationship.

She wants to call a taxi but I explain I'd rather walk to the subway, get some fresh air. We hug again, and I leave.

It's cold outside; I wrap my coat more tightly around me as I walk up Igeldammsgatan. The time is almost half past nine, but the street is deserted. There's not much life on Fleminggatan, either. I'm rarely afraid, still I speed up. Wish I'd skipped the wine so I could have taken my car.

I turn right on St. Eriksgatan, descend down the stairs to the subway. I take out my subway card, continue through the turnstile toward the escalator. Steps echo loudly in this desolate hall. Is someone following me again? Or is it my imagination? On my way from Pernilla's I had that odd feeling. As if someone was watching me. Surveilling me. Following me.

I walk even faster.

The man outside our window. Standing in the rain staring at me. I see his shapeless raincoat in front of me. The hood pulled forward over his face.

I stop and turn around. No one is there. The escalator is too slow. I run down it with my eyes on the steps. When I get to the bottom, I stop and look around again. I continue forward and crash into someone who grabs my arms. I scream and take a step backward.

"Look out there, lady." A close-cropped, beefy security guard. The smile he gives me is friendly.

"Excuse me," I say. "Didn't see you there."

He wishes me a nice evening and continues upward.

I'm on edge during the whole subway ride. In Alvik, the bus takes forever to come. I consider ordering a taxi after all, or calling Henrik and asking him to pick me up, but that feels silly. I don't want to give in to fear. In the end, the bus arrives, and I get on.

It's dark when I get off at my stop. The streetlights are broken, and I start running. I look behind me, but nobody is there. I run up the driveway to the front of the house. Breathless and shaking, I struggle to find the key in my purse, and it takes me a few attempts to get it into the lock. I get the door open, hear a sound behind me, and swing around. The wind has pushed the branch of a tree into the gate. It's fallen down and lies there between the gateposts. I tear open the door and throw myself inside. Close and lock it.

It's dark inside. Henrik still isn't home. I send a text message to him, asking how long he'll be at work. Receive no response. I want to talk to him about Alice. I want to talk to him about the man in the raincoat.

I sink down to the floor in the hall. My heart is pounding, blood rushing, I have difficulty breathing, and my field of vision has shrunk to a fuzzy circle of light.

I lie on my side and pull up my legs. Arms around my knees.

Inhale. Exhale.

The attack has ebbed out.

I get up from the floor and go into the living room. I draw the curtains. Go to Milo's room and grab a golf club. I turn on the TV, flip to some ridiculous sitcom, and raise the volume. I lie on the couch with the phone in one hand and the golf club in the other.

Isabelle

It's Friday, and we're sitting at the café outside the KTH library. Johanna, Susie, Maryam, and I are working on a mechanics assignment. I've started staying behind after lectures again so we can study. Sometimes when we're done we have a coffee or even go into town together. I find it easier to do every time I join them. It feels good to be part of a group, no longer just an outsider.

I got through primary and secondary school by focusing on my studies. Never made any close friends. I wanted to get out of Borlänge the whole time. I longed to start over, to become the person I wanted to be.

A school counselor encouraged me to study at the university because my grades were so good. Dad thought I should go for it; he understood me and my need for independence. Mom didn't understand at all. She still doesn't. I'm not sure why. She moved around when she was young, but when it comes to me, she worries about everything. She wants to know every detail of my life, wants to protect me from everything. She has a long-held suspicion that the world is terrible, that people are dangerous. You can't trust anyone. It's awful.

And it's poisoned me.

If Dad had died before I moved, I never would have done it. I know that. I would have ended up on the hamster wheel, working at a grocery store or at the nursing home like Mom. No friends, no life. Just like Mom.

My life has been so different from the lives of other people my age. It's like I'm from another planet. My very own lonely planet.

When they talk about music, I'm lost. Mom doesn't like "that pop music." It gives her a headache. They've taken vacations in France, Thailand, Greece, the US. We visited my father's relatives in Norrland.

Fashion? What a joke. Most of my clothes came from secondhand stores in Borlänge. *Old, sad, shapeless.* I've been taught it's unnecessary to buy things new, it's too expensive. And the worst part is that sometimes I feel the same way as my mother. Just as judgmental, just as petty, inexperienced, and jealous. I never want to be like her. Never.

I'm glad I got away. Yet there are times I miss Dalarna. Mostly, I miss spending time with Grandma.

My grandma Aina is just what a grandmother should be. White-haired and round and kind. She still lives in a house next to the railroad in Kyna. It's country red with white trim and a front door painted bright blue.

The garden is bigger than ours, more open and inviting. The flower beds are well cared for and full of pink and white peonies, so many kinds of roses, and quite a few lilies. Of course, most of them would be done blooming now. There's a knotty apple tree in the middle of the garden; its branches bend under the weight of apples at this time of year. At the far end of the garden sits a playhouse. A trampoline used to stand next to it. I would jump there for hours, waving at the trains passing by.

As a kid, I spent a lot of time at Grandma's house. She'd pick me up after school, and I'd stay with her a few weeks every summer. We baked and played games; we did crafts and spent time out in the garden; we picked apples and raspberries and made jam; we found tons of blueberries in the woods. I would go over to the farmhouse next door and play with the kids that lived there. They had cats, chickens, and a horse. I used to go to the stable and loved to pet the horse's silky throat, feel the warm puff of his breath. And every day we went down to the lake and swam.

When I think of Grandma, it hurts. Without her, I don't know how I would have made it. I don't want to lose touch with her. But we haven't talked for a while, and it makes me feel guilty.

"Your expressions are fascinating, Isabelle," says Susie, interrupting my thoughts. "Amused, thoughtful, terrified, sad. What's on your mind?"

"All sorts of things."

"Did you really never visit Stockholm before moving here?"

"Never. We mostly went up to Norrland. I've been to Gothenburg and Malmö a few times. Stockholm stresses Mom out."

"Surely you went to the Gröna Lund amusement park with your school, though? Every kid goes there."

"I broke my arm and ended up in the hospital that day."

I remember how I begged and pleaded to be allowed to go and still Mom refused. It was too dangerous; it was too unsafe. How could a few adults handle such a large group of children? She would never forgive them if something happened to me. But my teacher talked to her, and she eventually gave in. Unfortunately, I hurt myself the day before I was supposed to go.

"How's it going at therapy?" Maryam asks.

"*In* therapy," Johanna corrects her.

"Are there any freaks who, like, drool or twitch?" Susie wonders.

It annoys me. I regret telling them where I go every Wednesday after lunch.

"They're just regular people," says Johanna, who always defends me. "Maybe you should try it, Susie. You seem to need it."

"Yes, *I'm* gonna need therapy after this horrible class." Maryam bangs her head on the table. "Mechanics. Who invented it and why do we need to learn it?"

Everyone laughs at her and I feel better again. Next summer I'm going to go to Gröna Lund, damn it. I'm going to do all the things I haven't done yet. I'll live my own life.

Dad would have wanted it that way.

And I'm going to talk to Stella. I'll say everything I didn't dare to say last time. I want to get rid of this hate inside me.

Stella

My head aches: what's left of my hangover. It's not yet ten-thirty, but it feels like I've been at work for much longer than that. I'm sitting at my desk with my laptop open, and I should be working on my patient notes. I can't seem to formulate a rational sentence. I can only think about finding out more about Isabelle.

I open her journal, read the notes I've taken so far. Read her referral.

The referral.

I pick up my phone and call the GP clinic in Vällingby. I leave a message for Dr. Siv Rosén asking her to call me back concerning an urgent matter. While I wait for her call, I wander around the room. I stand by the window and look down onto the street below. I rearrange the things on my desktop. When the phone rings, I pick up before the first ring falls silent.

"Hi, Stella, what's on your mind?" Siv Rosén wonders.

"You sent a patient to me recently," I say. "Isabelle Karlsson."

"Yes, that's right."

"Why did you send her to me particularly?"

Siv Rosén is silent for a moment before asking: "Is there a problem?"

"Not at all, I'm just wondering if you know anything more about her."

"Any more? What I know is in the referral—did you receive it?"

"Did you have her as a patient for very long?"

"I've only met her once."

"Do you know anything about her family?"

"What I know is what I've written." Siv Rosén sounds annoyed. "Her father passed away in May, she's depressed, has some social difficulties. You're a good, well-respected therapist. And—well, maybe this will sound strange, but something in how she carried herself . . . something told me you'd be a good fit for her. You'd be just the kind of person she needs to talk to. So I sent her to you."

"So she didn't mention my name? Didn't ask for me specifically?"

"Certainly not. You sound upset—what exactly is the problem?"

"Nothing."

"Are you sure?"

"Nothing at all," I answer. "Just wanted to check with you. Thank you for your time."

I hang up. Cradle my head in my hands.

Isabelle didn't seek me out. She doesn't know who I am.

JULY 22, 1996

I'm searching for her. She's still in the cabin. I hear her crying. Hear her voice when she calls out.

I dive into the water. Swim down, farther and farther. I search everywhere, but she's not there. Only darkness.

If I give up, stay here in the deep, will I find you then?

Today you turn three. It's been two years since you disappeared. Yesterday we buried you at Skogskyrkogården.

A "farewell service." Your name on a stone, beneath a white dove. But you're not there.

Everyone wants closure. Everyone wants to move on. Everyone but me.

Stella

The sun is shining when I get down to St. Eriksgatan. I buy some spring rolls at Mae Thai. Carry them in a take-out bag and head toward Kronobergs Park. From the playground, I hear the shrieks of toddlers wearing the yellow and pink reflective vests of their various preschools. One young woman from a doggie daycare is walking nine dogs. The smallest is a Chihuahua, the largest a Great Dane. It seems quite comical. And also difficult.

I lose my breath from climbing up the steep hill to the top of the park and remember what Pernilla said about the body's decline in middle age.

I'm still annoyed with her. She of all people should understand. But she's completely obsessed by her sexy boy toy.

The benches at the top are empty; I sit down on one of them. It's a bit too chilly to be sitting outside, but the autumn wind and the clear blue sky feel so good.

Mourning a child is a lonely business. The longing and the loss are impossible to share with anyone else. And now? What happens to that grief now that I know Alice is alive? I don't know why, but there's a kind of sadness in her return, too. I should be overjoyed, should be screaming with happiness. But all I feel is the weight of what we lost. Those years. Those stolen years.

My child, she knows nothing about us or our history. She's unaware of any of it.

I wonder how Alice ended up in Dalarna. She disappeared from her stroller in Strandgården, but then? How did she get to Borlänge? And when? Does she feel as I do, that there's a bond between us? What does

Kerstin know, and how did she end up with custody of my daughter? Is she a victim, too, just like me?

Who stole my child? *Is* Isabelle really my child?

I could be wrong. The constant questions are driving me mad, I know that. Their obsessive quality is a sign that something is not right. The panic attacks could also be the beginning of a more serious mental breakdown. Just like when Milo was little. Maybe I've lost the ability to see myself objectively.

A woman approaches and sits down on the bench next to mine. "Excuse me," she says, "I hope I'm not disturbing you."

"No, no," I answer but still feel annoyed. I take out one of my spring rolls and bite into it. I've lost my appetite, and I put it back in the bag again. When I'm about to leave, the woman apologizes again.

"I don't want to intrude," she says, "but are you okay?"

I turn, about to give her a sharp reply. She smiles at me, and I realize I'm overreacting. The woman is obviously just lonely and wants to chat. There's no reason for me to be dismissive.

"I'm miserable," I respond and try to laugh. "I hope that changes soon."

I expect her to say something encouraging, like "It'll be fine soon enough." Or react with embarrassment, apologize, and leave. Instead she sits quietly, looking at me. She doesn't ask me to keep it together, doesn't try to be cheerful. Just a meeting between two people. It feels surprisingly liberating.

"My life is chaotic right now," I say, and my voice breaks. "Everyone is afraid and wants me to act like nothing has happened. How can I do that?" Tears stream down my face. I feel like an idiot. I don't want to break down in front of a complete stranger.

The woman stands up from the bench, walks over, and sits next to me. She gives me a clumsy pat on the back.

"Oh, dearie, what's happened?" she asks.

Pernilla's voice was impatient; Mom's was concerned. Henrik would be afraid and angry. This woman shows compassion.

"My daughter disappeared when she was a year old," I tell her. "They said she drowned, but I knew she was still alive. And now I've met her again. It's so much harder than I thought it would be. Worse than anything I've ever been through, except when she disappeared."

"I understand," the woman says. "I can really understand why."

"Why did it take so many years, why did it take so long for her to come back?"

I must seem incoherent and confused. But the woman just keeps patting my back.

I stop crying. "My mom and my best friend are worried about me. They think I'm making it up."

"Why?" she says, and takes out a pack of napkins and hands one to me. "They must realize you're serious."

I pull out a napkin and wipe my eyes and nose.

"I've been wrong before," I answer. "I thought I saw her once. I was wrong. I became severely depressed. I was hospitalized, put on sick leave. They're afraid it may happen again."

"But what about your husband?" She nods to my wedding ring. "What does he say?"

"I haven't told him," I say. "I don't know if I can handle that right now. Having him wonder if I'm sick, if I need to be committed again."

The woman watches me attentively and answers only *hmmm*.

"I don't know what to do," I say. "I've never felt so lost."

"What do you *want* to do?"

"I want to get to know her. But what would that mean? For me? For my family? And for her?"

The woman looks out over the park. "Yes, who knows," she says.

"I'm sorry," I say. "I probably don't seem so with it. Stella is my name." I hold out my hand.

"Eva," she says, taking it between her own. "Life is short. We only live once, remember that. What's your daughter's name?"

"Alice."

"A good name."

"I never thought it would be so difficult. That it would hurt so much."

"Think about what would hurt more. Leaving things as they are and learning to live with it. Or doing what you need to do to find the truth, and letting everyone else think what they want about you."

I don't know how long we sit next to each other in shared silence. After a while Eva stands and wishes me good luck. I watch her walk down the hill and out of the park. It's ridiculous, but I hope we meet again. People who truly listen and show compassion are rare.

When I get back to my office, life feels a bit easier again. I'm not superstitious. But the meeting in the park feels like a good sign.

Isabelle

I left home a while ago. Stopped by the Åhléns department store and walked through H&M in Vällingby shopping center. Now I'm on the platform waiting for the subway. I'm early, but I don't want to get there late like the first time.

I just started therapy, but it's already raised so many questions and memories. They've always been there, I think, but only now do I dare to think about what they mean. It's totally new for me. I'm also not used to saying what I feel and owning it. Like last time when they wondered how I reacted to my mother's way of telling me about Dad. I have never been so angry with her. The hate I felt was so intense it scared me. *I will never forgive her for the way she told me.* Can you hate your own mother? It is terrible to feel like that. I wanted to talk about that last time, but I didn't dare. I wanted to talk about it the very first time I met Stella, but couldn't. It's like carrying a wild animal inside of you. What would happen if I let it go? Would it consume me? Or is it already consuming me from within?

I'm starting to risk sharing a few things. It's so unfamiliar that no one questions whether I have the right to feel or say as I do. No one gets hurt or sad or angry. Nobody takes what I think or feel personally. *On the contrary, they seem to be on my side.*

My phone rings. I pick it up and see it's Mom. She wants to know everything about therapy. Interrogates me about every detail. I never should have called last week and told her how good I think it is. That was a mistake. I put the phone in my pocket again without answering.

As soon as I told her I was going into therapy, I regretted it. I knew there would be questions. I knew she'd try to interfere. Knew she'd start snooping. She means well, of course. She always wants to be useful. She always wants to understand, but she never does. She suffocates me. I'm not ready to talk about it yet. Not with her. Sometimes I wonder if I'll ever be. She's like a leech, a parasite sucking the life out of me.

It's ringing again, and I take out my phone. Watch it until it stops. I get off at Fridhemsplan and climb onto the escalator.

She calls again. I answer.

"Hi, Mom."

"Hello, my dear girl. Are you on your way to therapy?"

"You know I am," I say. During my upbringing I learned to suppress any negative feelings. Now it's as if I've lost the ability to pretend. My voice betrays my annoyance.

"You don't have to be so angry. I'm just asking."

I control myself. Take a deep breath. "How are things at home, Mom?"

"Quiet. They always are nowadays."

Here comes the guilt trip. Dad is dead. Mom is alone. I'm a bad daughter.

"Maybe you should try to meet someone," I say. "Have you been to Grandma's lately?"

"Your grandmother is busy," Mom says. "Sewing circles or whatever it is she does now."

"Do you know anyone else you could visit? You haven't always lived in Dalarna."

Silence. A silence that means I've wandered into forbidden territory. I know it well, still I go on.

"Where did we live when I was little? You've never told me about that. Just that we were somewhere in Denmark before you moved to Borlänge and met Dad."

"Hans, you mean?"

I'm not allowed to say *Dad*. She wants to take that away from me, too.

"Who was my *real* father then?" I say. "Are you ever going to tell me about him?"

It's been a long time since I dared to push this far.

Mom clears her throat.

"How exactly does this group therapy work?" she says. She sounds friendly and somewhat interested. But I know she just wants to snoop.

Beneath the surface she's angry. And I don't want to answer. It's private. Still, I feel obliged to smooth things over. Try to calm her down.

"We go there, sit in a circle. Then you can talk about anything. And the therapist—"

"Stella?"

"Stella is good. She asks questions that make me think. Reflect. I'm able to work on things."

"What kinds of questions? About us? About me?" Mom's voice is cold. "Should a therapist really be asking you questions like that? You're young, you're grieving. What does she know about our lives? Her questions could do more harm than good. Don't you see that?"

"They're not those kinds of questions. You don't understand."

But I remember Stella's blunt questions. How everyone fidgeted in the face of her intensity. She makes me feel unsure sometimes. I don't know why, but it feels like she's more interested in me than any of the others.

"What are you telling them? What do you need to process?"

Angry, mocking, patronizing. Mom is just like she's always been. She roots around in my mind and demands total transparency.

"That's my business, Mom," I say. "I have to go now."

"Well then, I'm sorry."

And now that hurt tone of voice. She's misunderstood, but she means well.

"Not all therapists are good, you know," she says. "They can have a lot of influence. They believe they're the bearers of the truth; they want to tell other people how to live. For someone vulnerable and sensitive like you, it can end badly."

"Stella never claimed to know everything," I say.

Mom sighs. "Sweetie, I'm just worried about you. You're coming home soon, right? It's awful to have to talk on the phone like this."

"I don't know," I say. "School is really intense right before exams."

"But I thought you had a free week before your exams?"

"Yes, but I have to study really hard during it."

"Isabelle, come home instead. You need it."

"No, Mom, *you* need it. I need to be left alone."

I hang up and turn off the phone.

. . .

Arvid: You seem to be in a bad mood, Isabelle?

Me: I screamed at Mom. I can't believe I did that.

Clara: You seem to be taking it pretty hard. Is it so terrible?

Me: I feel terrible. I haven't done that since I was little.

I hear Pierre snort.

Pierre: What do you think is going to happen?

I look down at the rug.

Me: I don't know. I'm not supposed to act like this. She gets hurt. Everything is worse now that Dad is gone.

Stella: Last week, you said it would make more sense if she'd adopted you. What did you mean by that?

I twist my hair between my fingers. A nervous tic of mine. It was hard to have a conflict with Mom, and it's even harder to talk about it afterward.

Me: I don't know if I can explain. She's not like other mothers. She wants us to be best friends. At the same time, she always insists I show her respect, because she's my mother. She wants me to confide in her, but tries to pull it out of me before I'm ready to tell her. She wants to know everything. Every detail. My most inconsequential thought. Then she uses it against me. I can't explain. It's sick. Nothing is easy with her. Everything with her is one long battle.

Stella: You've lived with her your whole life?

Me: Yes, but I remember very little from my childhood. And I've never felt comfortable in her house. It's been such a huge relief to move away from home. Scary, too.

Stella: Go on.

Me: The more she wants to be close with me, the more demanding she becomes. She gets disappointed and sad. She gets angry, and I've learned how to keep her in a good mood. I've learned to be who she wants me to be. To think what she wants me to think. Every time I try to take my own path, I feel guilty. I've even hated her, sworn I'd never forgive her. I've wished she were dead. Some days, that's all I think about. How much I hate her. I almost feel like killing her. It's sick, I know. There's something wrong with me.

Tears run down my face; I'm sobbing now. I feel both relief and embarrassment, crying like this in front of the others. I wonder if I've said too much. Maybe I exaggerated. Because I'm angry. No matter what I do it's wrong.

Stella: But has she been kind to you? Comforted you when you were sad? Has she ever hit you?

Now she seems so intense again. Several of the others seem nervous. Is something wrong?

Me: Hit me? She would never do that. And comforting me is what she does best.

Maybe I've gone too far. Maybe I've said too much.

Me: We've had our good times, too. And she hasn't had an easy life. When I was little, she was often left alone with me. Dad had to travel far away for work, and I was sick a lot. She had a lot on her plate.

I have to clear my throat. It feels like something's stuck there.

Me: And she almost died when I was born. She's Rh-negative, and I'm Rh-positive. Our blood mixed, and she ended up with blood poisoning. So she means it when she says she'd give her life for me.

Clara: That's not how blood poisoning works. And if the blood were to mix, it's the infant that gets sick, not the mother.

Me: Are you sure?

Clara: Yes.

Me: Weird. She must have told me that story a hundred times. I must have misunderstood something.

The room falls silent. I feel stupid. It feels like I'm the only one talking today. And Stella.

Me: I've often wondered if she was jealous of Dad for some reason. Maybe it's because we had an easier relationship. Better than what she and I have ever had.

Stella leans forward, gripping her knees.

She asks: Has it always been like that?

Has it always been like that? I suppose so. We've had our good times, too, we definitely have. But basically it's always been like that. I don't know why, though, I really tried. I've tried to be a good daughter, haven't I?

Stella: Alice?

Pierre: Who's Alice?

Stella

A distant, fluctuating noise streams in from the street. I pull the curtains and sit down at my desk. The muscles in my back and neck have cramped up, and it doesn't help to massage them. It's like kneading a rock. The pain behind my eyes is so intense I feel nauseous. I search my purse for the painkillers Mom gave me. I swallow one and close my eyes.

The blankness in her eyes when I said her name.

Alice. Her real name.

It means nothing to her. She doesn't know who I am. I could be anyone to her. I'm a stranger.

She hasn't been searching for me. She hasn't tracked me down. She hasn't thought about me. She hasn't been waiting or longing for me. She doesn't miss me. She doesn't know I felt her grow inside me. That she's my daughter, and I carried her for nine months. That I spent a never-ending night enduring the worst pain of my life for her. She doesn't know I fed her at my breast, gazed into her eyes, that she slept in my arms.

I don't exist to my own child. What was it Eva said in Kronobergs Park? I can let this be.

I can go on like before. Maybe I shouldn't meet Isabelle again. Maybe I should let her go.

Never.

It's impossible.

How could I possibly live like I did before when I know Alice is alive? There is nothing that can tear me away from her again.

I have to continue. I need to find out what happened to her, need to get to know her. It will turn our lives upside down, it already has, but I'm prepared for anything.

Whatever I choose to do, there will be serious consequences. That's inevitable.

Can Isabelle handle the truth? She's already found out that her dad was not her biological father. And now neither is her so-called mother. I'm going to cause even more problems for her. Her entire life will be destroyed.

I missed her childhood. Missed watching her grow up. And I'm far from sure that she's had it easy.

Alice deserves to find out the truth. Both of us deserve it.

What does Kerstin know? What's her explanation for raising my daughter?

My phone vibrates on my desk. I don't recognize the number. I answer. One of Henrik's assistants informs me that Henrik will be picking up Milo from tennis today, so I don't need to. I thank her and hang up.

Milo. How will he take it? How am I going to tell him his sister is alive?

There's a knock at the door. Renate sticks her head in: "Stella, your patient is waiting."

"My patient?"

"Are you okay?"

I smile. "Just fine, thank you."

"Kent is in the waiting room. He says his appointment was supposed to start a quarter of an hour ago."

I totally forgot about him.

I tidy my hair, grab my coat and my purse, and go to the reception area. I stretch out my hand and greet Kent with a quick handshake, then tell him I have to cancel our appointment today. Didn't he get my message? How unfortunate that it didn't reach him. I ask him to book a new time with Renate.

I should be ashamed of my lie. But all I feel when I leave the office is relief.

Stella

I park on Engelbrektsgatan. I take the path through Humlegården park that leads to the National Library. The ground is covered with red and yellow leaves. High above me, the treetops look like they're on fire. The building itself is quite beautiful, and two rows of large windows cover the main building. I walk up the front stairs, enter a small marble hall with pillars and two large statues. I turn to the right, deposit my coat in a locker next to the café, turn the sound off on my phone and put it in my purse.

I go back to the front desk, say hello to the young man sitting there as I pass through a turnstile. I go down five flights of stairs covered by a glassed-in extension. The microfiche room is located at the very bottom.

A slim, slightly bent woman in her sixties is sitting behind a high desk. Her glasses hover at the tip of her nose, about to fall off. She pushes them up as I approach her, but they slide down again.

I ask for help finding articles from Småland that appeared between August and October in 1994. She accompanies me to the other side of the room, toward large shelves of Swedish newspapers in microfiche. She bends her head back, peering through her glasses, and finds the shelf we need to access. When she finds it, she cranks a large knob on the side, moving it laterally. An aisle opens up between the shelves.

We go in, and she takes out a box from a Småland newspaper marked *Autumn 1994*. She shows me how to mount the film in a reader and scroll between pages.

I thank her for her help and get started.

There aren't many articles about the disappearance. They occur more frequently those first few weeks, and all basically contain the same information.

A one-year-old girl disappeared from Strandgården around noon on the 13th of August.

The stroller was found overturned near the beach.

A Stockholm family were on holiday over the weekend.

The teen mother left the child unaccompanied.

The father was seen in Oskarshamn around the time of the disappearance.

The teen mother was interviewed by the police.

The teen mother has been cleared of suspicion.

The police have no leads; the public is asked to report any possible tips.

One theory was that an animal might have overturned the stroller. Maybe someone saw a child by herself and took care of her. Or the child rolled it over herself and crawled away. Speculation, all of it more or less likely. Every theory except that Alice was taken. No one thought that sounded believable when I said it. Not even Daniel. Who would take our child? It was too far-fetched, the police said. I hadn't witnessed anyone showing any excessive interest. They investigated whether or not any of the guests had a criminal record, but no one did. A search was organized, but led to nothing.

Since no animal tracks were found, and no one came forward with information on where she might be, it was assumed that the child had crawled into the water and drowned. There's a steep drop-off, and the area is known for its strong currents. The police searched the water despite little likelihood of finding such a small body. A tragic accident. The parents interrogated. No suspicion of a crime.

After a few weeks, the articles dwindled to a final short notice. *Child still missing. No tips have led to discovery of the one-year-old. She is assumed drowned, her body removed from the scene by the current.*

The police investigation has been discontinued. The girl has been declared dead.

I think about what would have happened today. My possible guilt, my negligence, all of it would have been dissected and debated online. Just the fact that we had a child at such a young age would have been considered irresponsible. Unflattering images of me would have appeared all over the Internet. The tabloids would have dug into our private lives, reported on our breakup a few months later. Everyone would have wallowed in our tragedy.

I keep moving forward. Find nothing. Still nothing. Until a headline catches my attention.

Strandgården has closed for business immediately, no new management will be taking over.

This was what Elle-Marja told me about. Roger Lundin, manager and owner of Strandgården, passed away suddenly due to complications from diabetes. Elle-Marja said Strandgården shut down permanently in August of that year.

I go to the shelves and search for another local newspaper. Load the film and start to scroll. The same articles again. A missing one-year-old. A young mother questioned, but never formally under suspicion. The girl assumed drowned. Case closed.

I see a familiar face. The police officer responsible for the investigation. Sven Nilsson was his name. I remember him as compassionate and understanding. The scent of the steaming coffee cup he gave me, the blanket he wrapped around my shoulders. His younger colleague was more insensitive. I find his name farther down in the article. Per Gunnarsson. He thought I was guilty. He was sure I'd killed my own child and tried to cover it up by reporting her missing. He was the first one who interrogated me at the police station.

We have a witness who puts your boyfriend, Daniel, in Oskarshamn at the time in question. What were you doing?

Why did you leave your baby alone?

Why were you not there?

How long were you away?

If you were so close by, why didn't you hear anything?

Where exactly were you?

You're so young. Do you like being a mom? It must get pretty tough sometimes. Hearing the kid scream all the time. Sometimes you wish you could escape.

Have you suffered from postpartum depression?

Was there an accident you don't want to tell us about?

You can talk to us. We'll understand if something happened.

The truth always comes out in the end. It'll go better for you if you're the one who tells us what really happened.

What did you do to your child?

Hard eyes full of suspicion. I was not formally a suspect. But I *was* suspected. Sven Nilsson interrupted the interrogation and explained that they had no reason to keep me there. He'd talked to a woman who backed up my version of events. She'd seen me rock Alice to sleep in the stroller under the trees. Soon after, she'd seen me walk down to the beach.

I take out my laptop. Search for Oskarshamn's police station. Sven Nilsson must have retired a long time ago. I have no idea how police work is archived, but old investigations have to be kept somewhere. It's worth a chance.

I walk out through the front entrance and stretch my back. I call the police, am connected to the police station in Oskarshamn. I'm thinking about what to say and I'm just about to hang up when a woman answers.

My words rush out. August 1994, Strandgården, on a visit from Stockholm over the weekend, an abducted girl, she was only one year old, the police, an old investigation, closed, of course, Sven Nilsson, Per Gunnarsson—

"Per Gunnarsson? He's gone home."

Silence on the line.

"Hello?" I say and wonder if she hung up.

"Wait, you're in luck, he's still here. You can speak to him. Please hold."

"Hello. Per Gunnarsson." His voice is raspier than I remember. But I recognize it.

"My name is Stella Widstrand. Johansson is my maiden name. You were at Strandgården in August 1994. When my daughter disappeared. She disappeared from her stroller."

"Ninety-four? What the hell is this?" Impatient and irritable. He was back then, too.

"At Strandgården. In Storvik, north of Oskarshamn. You came there with Sven Nilsson and then—"

"Now, just calm down for a minute. Speak slower. And a bit louder, too, please."

I clench my teeth, then start over. "You and Sven Nilsson. You were the officers who investigated the disappearance of my daughter. She was only one year old. You interrogated me and my daughter's father at the police station."

"Okay, I think I remember that," Per Gunnarsson mutters. "What's this all about?"

"I'd like to take a look at the investigation. What you did, who you talked with, those sorts of things."

A tired sigh. "Honey. It's been, what, more than twenty years? That case has been closed a long time. Don't you think we have more important things to do than root around in old files?"

"Is there anyone else I can talk to?"

Another sigh. "Do you think this is some kind of Make-A-Wish program? We're swamped as it is. We can't take on stuff like this, too."

I don't respond.

Per Gunnarsson coughs.

"Sven Nilsson. He's been retired for many years. Last I heard he'd moved to Norrköping. I know he saved some material. He often talked about some tip we never followed up on. Don't have a clue what he meant by that; he was a curious fella. We turned over every stone, as you probably remember. There were no tips we forgot about. It was a hopeless case if you ask me. But get ahold of him, that's all I can tell you. Now I have other things I need to do."

He hangs up.

I see on the screen that I have nine missed calls and ten text messages. Angry and annoyed text messages from both Henrik and Milo wondering if I'm alive. It makes *me* annoyed.

I text Henrik that I'm on my way home. Then I turn off my phone.

The evening is coming on. The air is cool and fresh, and I don't hurry as I walk through Humlegården park.

Stella

Henrik and Milo are sitting on the sofa eating popcorn. They're watching a rerun of *Top Gear* and roaring with laughter at some RVs crashing into each other.

Henrik notices that I've entered the living room and throws me a quick glance. I can see that he's angry with me. Why? Because I'm not available every second of every day?

"Hello, my loves," I say.

"Hi, Mom," Milo says. "Where have you been?"

"Yes, indeed, where have you been?" Henrik says.

"Did you miss me?"

"I waited for you for forever after practice," Milo says.

"What?" I say.

"Yeah, you never showed up, so I went home by myself."

"Did you ride the subway by yourself?"

"I had my subway card with me."

"Why didn't you pick him up?" I say to Henrik.

I sound angry but actually I'm terrified. I think of all the things that could have happened. He could have been hurt, gotten lost, been robbed or kidnapped. Why didn't Henrik pick him up?

He raises his eyebrows, and we stare at each other over Milo's head.

"Why didn't *you* pick him up?" he replies.

"Because you told me you were."

"Where did you get that idea from? You always pick him up after tennis."

"I know," I say. "But you called and said you were going to do it."

"When did I call?"

"This afternoon. Around two-thirty or so."

"I had a meeting at that time."

"It wasn't you. It was some assistant who gave me the message. Otherwise, of course I would have been there."

"Which assistant? Erica? Why would she call you?"

"I don't know her name. But she probably called because you asked her to?"

"I didn't ask anyone to give you that message. But it all turned out fine. Right, buddy?" He squeezes Milo's shoulder.

"Sorry, honey," I say, stroking his hair. "It was a misunderstanding. I didn't mean for you to have to go home by yourself."

"Please, he can handle it," Henrik says. "We talked about it before you got here. He's ready to start riding the subway on his own now."

I want to protest. I don't want him going anywhere by himself. Never. Henrik reads my reaction immediately.

"He's been riding around with his friends quite a lot lately. There's never been any problem, Stella."

I go out to the kitchen. Pour myself a glass of wine. I feel like smoking for the first time in many years. Henrik follows me.

"Where have you been?" he says. "I imagined all sorts of crazy scenarios when I couldn't get ahold of you."

He strokes my arm. I pull away.

"I was at the library."

"Why are you angry?" he asks.

"You're the one who's angry."

"Not at all. But you always let me know what you're up to. It's not like you to be so hard to reach."

He touches me again. I take my glass and go to the other side of the kitchen.

"You didn't have to accuse me as soon as I came in the door," I say.

"And you don't have to sound so pissed off. You really haven't been yourself lately. Could it be that you're projecting some of your state of mind onto me?"

"Are you trying to play psychologist now, Henrik? Please don't."

He crosses his arms.

"If I said I was going to pick up Milo, wouldn't I have done that?" he says. "I've never asked any employee of mine to call you."

"Someone called me. Or do you think I dreamed it up?"

He doesn't answer that. Instead he says, "Milo can ride the subway on his own now, Stella. He's thirteen years old. You don't need to drop him off and pick him up everywhere."

"I do that gladly," I answer.

"It wasn't an accusation."

I don't meet his eyes.

He sighs audibly and leaves the kitchen.

I see a movement from the corner of my eye and recoil from the window. Someone walked by on the street. I lean forward warily and peer out. A plastic bag is whirling across the street. I prop my hands on the sink and exhale. Am I losing my mind? A few weeks ago I wouldn't have reacted so strongly to Milo riding home on his own. Wouldn't have gotten half so scared and jittery. But lately I've been reminded what just one moment of negligence can result in.

When I left Alice alone, the consequences were devastating. I lost her forever.

And Milo, I left him alone as well. It turned out fine. Nothing happened. But afterward I swore never to be negligent again. When he was younger, I avoided places, wherever crowds gathered. I'd rather his friends sleep over at our house. Hampus and Pernilla and his grandparents are the only exceptions. I take him to all of his practices and games. Drive or walk with him to all of his friends' houses, even if they live close by. I'm overprotective.

Henrik has tried to balance that out as much as possible. He took Milo to Gröna Lund; I could never bring myself to join them. He hasn't made a big deal out of it, either. I've gotten better at managing my fears over the years, gradually eased up on my need for control. Until now.

Milo has to be allowed to stand on his own two feet. I know that. But he's only thirteen. I'm not quite ready to let go. Maybe I never will be.

I heat up the food that was on the stove, but I don't have any appetite. I poke at it and throw most of it away. I stand at the sink.

I can't go on like this. I have to talk to Henrik. He has the right to know at some point that I've found Alice. I want him to understand that it's real this time. He's going to understand. He'll help me.

I pour two glasses of wine and go to the living room. It's dark outside; the wind rocks the trees. Rain is coming. I light the candles on the coffee table and go over to the window. I'm about to pick up one of the candles when I see him. He's standing in the street behind our house. He's staring at me.

It's impossible to make out the face under that hood. The same shapeless coat as last time. The same tense posture. The same menacing figure.

I throw open the door to the patio.

I scream: "What do you want? Get lost, leave me alone. *LEAVE!*"

I try to run out to the backyard, but trip on the threshold. I grab hold of the curtains; the rod gives way and tumbles down. I fall headfirst out the door.

"What's wrong, Mom?" Milo says as he comes running in. Henrik is right behind him. They find me lying on the patio.

"Someone was watching our house," I say, pointing. "Look. There. With a hood covering their face. He's been here before. Same coat, same hood."

Henrik goes out and stares down the street; Milo follows him. They look in both directions before returning. Henrik squats down next to me; he rubs my shoulder.

"Come in now, honey. There's nobody there."

I look at him. "There was someone there just now."

Henrik looks away.

"Don't you believe me?" I say.

He takes my hand in both of his, and Milo helps me up without a word.

"Henrik? Don't you believe me?"

"There's no one there now anyway," he says and smiles.

I recognize that smile. He uses it when he thinks I'm wrong. When he wishes I weren't so emotional, so hysterical.

I look out the window. Henrik and Milo do, too. Someone is walking down the street. Someone in a raincoat with a hood pulled up. I grab hold of Henrik's arm.

"That's him," I whisper.

"Oh, come on now, don't you recognize Johan?" Henrik points. "He's out with his dog like usual."

And he's right. It's the investor. Out with his tiny dog again. The color of his raincoat is lighter, I see that now. Johan Lindberg sees us standing by the window staring at him. He grins and waves. Henrik smiles and waves back.

Then Henrik looks at me. He's not smiling anymore.

JUNE 22, 2003

I've found her. I've found Alice.

Two weeks ago, when we were at Skansen. Milo and I were standing in line to buy ice cream.

And there she was.

I recognized her. She looked just as she would have looked if I'd never lost her. One breath later and she disappeared into the crowd again.

Not again. It can't happen again.

I left Milo in his stroller and ran after her. Pushing people aside who were in my way, screaming at them to move. Shouting her name.

She was gone. Vanished again.

Then I remembered Milo. I ran back to him.

He was crying and alone. He could have been taken from me, too.

Never again. I let my child out of my sight. Never never never. I shouldn't even have gone to Skansen with him. There are way too many people. And it's easier to disappear in crowds.

Never again.

Daniel helped me. He came as fast as he could. I cried and he called the police.

All those questions. Where did you see her? When? What did she look like? What was she wearing?

I tell them. In line to buy ice cream, around three o'clock. Thick, dark hair, a dimple, and an elf ear. She has on a blue dress and is about this height. Like Milo. She was with a man.

They look at me strangely. Their eyes are blank, hard. Their voices cold as they tell me it wasn't Alice. She's not one year old anymore. She must be bigger than Milo, they say. You saw someone else; Alice would be almost ten years old.

But they don't know. They don't understand anything. They can't feel her inside like I do. They try to comfort me and be kind, but they whisper to Daniel behind my back that I'm sick, that I'm having a nervous breakdown. They're lying.

This is no breakdown. I saw my child. I saw her. I saw Alice.

I'm cold. Ice cold. I'm so cold I'm shaking even though I have a blanket around me. My back and head are burning. My hands tremble. It must be the medicine they gave me. I want to go home. I don't want to be here.

Henrik brought me here. Left me here.

I fell asleep in a bed in a cold white room. Alone.

I woke up. Drowsy. Empty. They said I had a visitor. They helped me out of bed. Took me to a visitor's room.

Daniel sat there. He didn't want to hug me. He was worried. He was angry. He said he never wanted to be part of this again. I screamed at him: Do you think I want to? Do I want to be without my little girl? Do you think I want to miss her so much, wonder about her all the time, never find any answers?

He said, That's why we buried her.

So we can move on.

And then I saw Henrik. He was in the corner. His face pale.

He looked at me as if he didn't know who I was.

Daniel said, You could have lost your son, too.

He was sorry for what happened. He wished me a good life.

And then he left.

Henrik went, too. I didn't know if he'd ever come back. I didn't even know if I'd ever get to go home again.

And after he left, I screamed at him, too.

I screamed and screamed and screamed, and I didn't stop until they made me sleep.

Isabelle

I'm alone in my apartment. Johanna is staying at Axel's tonight.

I'm in bed, staring out the window. The sky is blue, the sun shining. I find it exhausting. I have no desire to go out.

I should study. There are always things to study, and I usually find that fun. Not now. I don't want to. I don't have the energy. My room is homey, as Grandma would say. Only the bed, the sheets, and the ceiling lamp were purchased new. Everything else is secondhand. A large abstract painting in shades of blue, a gray shag carpet, the table lamps. Both the teak desk and the nightstand. The desk chair is a beat-up old kitchen chair. Plus my various knickknacks. A simple blue valance hangs at the top of the window. Johanna helped me and Dad lug it all up from his trailer.

I pull down the blinds and pick up my new MacBook Air.

I bought it with money I earned working this past summer. I check Facebook. Close it. Power down my computer. Check Instagram and Snapchat on my phone. Then I throw off my blanket and go out to the kitchen. I put on the kettle, take out a mug and a tea bag.

The apartment is bright. Large windows in every room, white walls. I got the bedroom, and Johanna made the living room hers; its glass doors are covered with batik drapes in purple and green. In the kitchen we've hung an old poster with illustrations of spices on it that we bought together. The chairs around the white kitchen table are mismatched, and the rug on the floor was woven by my grandma.

I sit down at the window with my tea. Thinking about the call I got from my mother, and what I said about her at group therapy. I feel guilty. I hate myself for how I behaved.

I was unfair. What I did was wrong. Talking badly about my mother like that, talking about her when she wasn't there. The others didn't get a fair picture. I was angry and disappointed and sad. I exaggerated.

Mom often says I'm sensitive. Impressionable. *Maybe I am.* At the moment, I feel totally confused. I'm still furious, still feel anger and hatred. My rage at my mother has taken on a life of its own, I can't control it. At the same time, I feel suffocated by guilt for feeling that way.

I'm still in shock because Dad is dead. Because he wasn't my real father. Right now, I question everything about Mom. Are my feelings valid? Am I allowed to feel like this? I do wonder how many of my memories reflect what really happened.

I'll ask Stella what she thinks about all this. I know I can discuss that sort of thing with her. When she asked how it was for me when I was little, she truly seemed to care. She was genuinely worried about me, I noticed that. It felt like she wanted to fix it somehow.

But how can I give her a true picture without being misunderstood? When I do say what I think, it usually doesn't go well. When will I learn? How do I make other people understand?

Clara wondered why it feels so dangerous to quarrel with Mom. I don't know. I just know I hate having any conflicts with her and do everything I can to avoid them. I don't want to make Mom sad. Dad was the same. *My dad, who wasn't my dad.*

Mom says I think too much. Ask too many questions. Maybe she's right. All this brooding isn't making me any wiser. But I can't stop thinking. Or feeling.

I don't know why I am who I am or why I've always felt like an outsider. Different. Weird. Odd. Something must be wrong with me. With my emotions.

I don't want to cry. But I do anyway. And I despise myself even more for it.

Stella

I'm curled up in an armchair in my office. I've kicked my shoes onto the rug and tucked my feet under me. I had to force myself to come here today, and I'm just sitting around waiting for time to pass. I haven't done one minute of work. I've stopped doing my job. The whole morning was spent thinking through all that's happened.

I received a call that no one made. I saw threatening men wearing hoods drawn low.

Was there someone in the street behind the house?

Yes, there was. I don't hallucinate. It's happened twice. Someone is watching my home. Someone is watching me. Someone is following me. The death notice makes it even scarier. I struggle to understand. Struggle to think it through. Try to figure who could be behind this. But if I go on like this, I'll lose myself. End up sick again.

This has to stop.

I'm going to tell Henrik. I'm going to tell him everything. Today. I would rather have some concrete evidence before saying anything. But it can't wait any longer. And I have to move Isabelle to another group so she can continue her therapy. I should have sent her to another therapist immediately, after the first meeting. What I'm doing now is unprofessional. Unethical.

And dangerous.

My phone vibrates. It's Henrik. I pick up, and he asks when I'm done today. He wants us to have dinner at Trattorian near Norr Mälarstrand. Just the two of us. Milo has basketball practice. I tell him that sounds lovely.

Is that how I feel? Yes. No. Not really. Maybe yes and no.

I used to like going out to eat with my husband. And I want that to be the case now, too. But it's not. The thought of talking about Alice over a dinner out feels wrong. Just as wrong as waiting any longer to tell him.

A few hours later I park the Audi on a cross street from Norr Mälarstrand. I head down toward the water and the Mälar Pavilion and see Henrik waiting there. Stubble on his face, hair ruffled, sunglasses on. He takes them off and looks at me.

"What?" he says.

"You're handsome." I hesitate before I rise up on my tiptoes and give him a kiss. He returns it.

"Just you and me," he says. "It's been a long time."

We walk hand in hand down the promenade. Watching other people and making jokes at their expense. Amateur photographers with two-foot lenses and old ladies struggling with their little yapping dogs. Parents with strollers who absolutely have to walk abreast of each other, joggers in tights ruthlessly darting between pedestrians, middle-aged ladies with walking poles in their hands.

We need this. We should take that weekend Pernilla talked about. It's been forever since my husband and I made time for each other.

We get to the dock and enter Trattorian. Henrik booked us a table at the window. While we're ordering and waiting for our food, he tells me his parents are going to France over the weekend. He says Marcus and Jelena have been to this restaurant recently. He comments on the decor and the menu, making small talk.

"It's going to be sunny this weekend," he says.

"Nice," I say.

"I thought I'd take Milo out to the golf course for one final round for the season. Does he have a basketball game on Saturday?"

"No clue. Perhaps. Probably."

I wonder why we're really here. As our food arrives, I take a drink of my wine. Try to relax. I look out over the Riddarfjärden bay. I'm sitting in a nice restaurant with the man I'm married to.

"Is it good?" Henrik asks and takes a bite from my plate.

"Quite good," I answer.

"How's work these days?"

I spin my wineglass. "It's fine. And yours?"

"There's a lot on my plate right now, as you know, but it'll get better soon," he says. Silence. We behave like two bad copies of ourselves. "Have you heard anything lately from the Health and Social Care Inspectorate?"

Here it comes. He invited me here for a serious conversation. He thinks my behavior has something to do with the inspection. I poke at my food. I wish he'd waited.

"No, not yet," I answer, letting go of my fork and pulling my cardigan up onto my shoulders.

"No need to be defensive," he says. "Since you don't talk to me anymore, I have to ask. But it was stupid for me to bring it up now. Forget it."

Forget it? A cloud will hang over the table for the rest of the dinner if I don't say anything.

"Why does this feel so tense?" I wonder.

"You're the tense one," he replies. "You've been both tense and annoyed for a while."

"I know I may have been preoccupied and absentminded," I say.

"Absentminded? You've been completely absent. You don't respond when Milo or I talk to you. You forget things, you have outbursts. And yesterday? What was that about?"

"It's been a strange few weeks, I know," I say. "But this has nothing to do with Lina. I've seen that man twice. I've received a disguised death threat. But that's not all. There's something I have to tell you."

Henrik shakes his head. "We'll talk about it later, okay? Do you want some coffee?"

I don't. I want to leave. Before I can answer, he gestures to the waiter. I look out over the dock outside while Henrik asks for two coffees, no dessert, please. The sun is reflecting on the water. It's a beautiful evening. And the distance between Henrik and me is only growing.

There is no turning back. I have to tell him. When we're alone again, I look him in the eye.

"Henrik," I say, putting a hand on his arm. He stares at me, waiting for me to continue. "I've found Alice."

Henrik puts down his napkin, but continues looking at me.

I continue. "This time I'm right. I know I'm right."

I notice that I'm too loud. The couple closest to us has fallen silent, and they're looking our way.

Henrik glances to the side. Then out over the water.

"I didn't intend to say anything," he says. "Not here. I wanted to talk about it later."

"Say what?" I ask.

"I had a visitor at work today."

Henrik's gaze is steady. My stomach aches. I have no idea what to expect, but I can see in his face it's something serious.

He says, "A woman visited me at the office this morning. She's worried about her daughter."

"Her daughter?"

"She's in therapy with you."

"What do you mean?"

"The girl has changed since she met you. You seem, and I'm just quoting"—Henrik holds up his fingers—"'inappropriately interested in her.'"

"Are you serious?" I raise my voice, and the couple looks at us again. I continue more quietly. "Who is this concerning?"

He doesn't answer my question. Instead he says, "This woman feels you're turning the girl against her. Asking leading questions about her upbringing."

"Isabelle," I whisper.

Henrik leans forward, tapping his finger on the table. "Please tell me you don't think this girl Isabelle is Alice."

"The woman who visited you, what was her name?" I ask.

"Kerstin Karlsson. She begged me to talk to you. Her daughter doesn't want to listen; she's obviously captivated by you. According to her mother."

"Why did she contact you?" I ask. "She could have talked to me directly."

He shrugs. "Does it matter? She was worried," he says.

"Guess why," I say. "Guess why, Henrik. She's trying to bury this. She's trying to hide what she's done."

Henrik looks questioningly at me. "So Kerstin Karlsson kidnapped your daughter? Then manipulated me so you wouldn't find out the truth? Doesn't make sense. You are completely wrong."

"How do you know that? How do you *know*?"

"Because it's not believable. Because no one can just steal someone else's child in this country. Records are kept on everything. You can't just show up with a child without someone noticing. And I've been to Alice's grave. She's dead, Stella. What you went through must have been harder than anyone can imagine. But Alice is gone. It's horrible, unbearable. But you have to live with it."

"I've never thought she was dead, you know that very well. But you think I've gone crazy? That's what you mean? That in my insane state I've made this up?" I slam the glass on the table too hard. The couple next to us has started whispering.

"Settle down, Stella. Settle down."

"You trust someone you've never met more than me. You totally dismiss everything I have to say."

"Don't try to put all this on me. You *have* been acting strange lately. And the woman I talked to was genuinely worried about her child. She was desperate. She didn't know who to turn to."

"And you just buy what she has to say straightaway?" My voice wavers. The anger I feel is about to boil over. "You think I'm brainwashing a patient because I'm delusional? You have no confidence in me whatsoever?"

Henrik leans over the table. "You yourself told me you think you've found Alice. Again. What the hell am I supposed to think, Stella?" He stretches out for my hand. I pull it away. Cross my arms and look past him.

"This time is different. This time I know I'm right."

"It's been more than twenty years," he says.

"Isabelle *is* Alice! Should I ignore that?"

Henrik leans backward. He folds his napkin and unfolds it again.

"Stop playing with that fucking napkin," I hiss.

He throws it down.

"You want me to believe that you've found your missing daughter," he says. "A girl you haven't seen since she was a year old. You see her in one of your patients. Whose mother is worried about how her therapy is progressing. This is serious, Stella. Say you understand that. Say at least that you understand how it sounds."

"I'm not making this up," I say. "This is not in my imagination." But I hear how shrill and pleading my voice is. I don't sound the least bit believable. Not even to myself. More diners are looking at us.

"You can't continue to be her therapist," Henrik says. "Not if you think she's your daughter."

"I already know that."

"Why haven't you talked to me? You know how this turned out last time. How you felt. I don't want you to have to go through that again."

"You mean that this is a 'relapse'?"

"I worry about you."

"You think I'm sick. I need to be committed."

Henrik runs his hands over his face. "We should go now."

He looks around for the waiter. It feels like he's stuck a knife in my back. He's sitting opposite me. But he's light-years away. We have never been so far apart.

"And you wonder why I didn't say anything?" I say. "Because I knew it would turn out like this."

I stand so quickly that the chair falls backward. Stumble between the tables as I run through the restaurant. Hear a thud, followed by the sound of breaking glass. The waiter I crashed into has dropped his tray. Everyone in the room is staring at me. I run toward the exit, rip open the front door, and rush back toward the car.

I drive across the Traneberg Bridge. I continue on toward Ulvsunda Road. I pass the airport and Bromma Blocks mall, pass by the Solvalla racetrack, and turn off toward Rissne. I'm thinking about Alice the whole time. I feel her inside me, an inextinguishable flame.

I drive through the suburbs of Bromsten, Spånga, and Solhem, and arrive at Hässelby. I turn left on Lövstavägen, heading home. But when I get to Vällingby, I turn off.

I stop in a parking lot and get out of the car. The sun is about to go down; the air is cool. I wrap my shawl around my neck and stuff my hands into my pockets.

She lives in one of the high-rise apartment buildings next to the mall. Maybe I was on my way here the whole time.

I see lights turn on and off, the blue glow of TV screens. The shadows of people move behind curtains, walking through rooms and looking through the windows. One of them could be Alice. Perhaps she's standing there right now, looking down at me. Perhaps she feels like I do, that something binds us together. Something that can never be destroyed. A connection. Maybe she's thinking about it, about me, right now.

Stella

The next morning Henrik and Milo have eaten breakfast and gone by the time I go down to the kitchen. Henrik left a plate out for me, but the coffee is cold and the juice in my glass is lukewarm. I pour them both out, throw away the sandwich, and brew new coffee.

I'm wearing makeup, my Malene Birger pants, the black ones that are slightly looser at the top and taper down the leg. A green blouse from Filippa K.

I look out the window. Everything is gray, the street, the trees, the houses, the sky. I look at the time. Half past eight. It's Friday, I have no patients today and don't need to go in to the clinic.

Henrik and I didn't speak to each other after I got home last night. When I arrived he was watching a movie with Milo. I took a bath and went to bed. I pretended to be asleep when he got into bed next to me. I could tell he lay there awake, studying me. We are living in different worlds now. All communication has broken down.

But it's not weird he would fear that I'm having a breakdown again. I have been acting strangely, as he says. I have been tense and irritated. But this is *not* like last time. This is real.

And if I had been able to tell him about Alice before Kerstin Karlsson scared him, maybe it would have turned out different. Maybe. Or it might not have mattered; he still might not have trusted me.

I take my coffee and head toward my office. I turn on my computer and log into Facebook. I've been planning to delete my account for a long time. I don't get anything out of it. It just wastes my time and energy. My "friends" are comprised of Henrik and Pernilla, plus some family members and relatives, or people I've met through work or Milo, old classmates. Or acquaintances who get in touch when our friendship is confirmed, and that's all. It's mostly for Helena's sake that I keep my account. She's on Facebook all the time and usually uses it to contact me and Mom.

I write *Kerstin Karlsson* in the search field. The number of hits is depressing. Some I can rule out immediately. They're too young, live in the wrong part of the country or abroad. I inspect three profiles of women a bit older than me. But I have no clue what she looks like at all. Or if she's even on Facebook. It's useless.

I search for Isabelle Karlsson, but there are too many with that name as well. Instead I google Isabelle Karlsson, KTH.

An article about a project she and a few others have been working on comes up. I click on it. In the group picture she's standing at the front, her arms crossed, with her hair down and her dimple prominently displayed.

She is beautiful. Radiant. I take a screenshot of the image and save it to the cloud.

Additional searches yield nothing more. I continue with Kerstin Karlsson, Borlänge.

Not nearly as many hits as on Facebook. But which of them is the Kerstin I'm looking for?

A thought occurs to me, and I search for Hans Karlsson death.

Hans Gunnar Karlsson passed away from a stroke at age fifty-nine. He's survived by his wife, Kerstin, and their daughter, Isabelle.

The notice is on the *Dala-Demokraten* website. I search for Hans Gunnar Karlsson, Borlänge.

An address in Barkargärdet. The same address as Isabelle Karlsson, twenty-two years old.

And Kerstin Karlsson, forty-seven years old.

Kerstin

Putting towels and sheets in the storage room is not my responsibility. But I do it anyway. As usual. Otherwise the laundry cart will just stand there in the corridor. People don't want to take responsibility for anything; they'd rather shirk their duties and have somebody else clean up after them.

I can feel it in my knees as I bend forward and grab the sheet at the bottom. It wouldn't hurt me to lose a few pounds. But you can't do everything at once. I have too much to think about right now. The leak in the bathroom, the car acting up again, all those bills piling up. I really need to go to the dentist. And how is a normal person supposed to afford all that? The salary of an assistant nurse isn't enough. Especially now that I'm on my own. All Hans left me were debts. The funeral took the last of our savings.

I hear a howl coming from one of the rooms; it sounds like an injured animal. I know it's Hedvig. She's on so many tranquilizers that it's a wonder she can stand at all. If she doesn't get her meds on time, she has panic attacks.

I leave the laundry and go to her room.

"Have you been hiding in the storage room again, Kerstin?" Ritva says when she sees me. "Why didn't you respond to the alarm?" She shakes her head and goes into the kitchen.

Why don't you answer it yourself? I think and head toward Hedvig's room. A young employee is standing in the doorway, obviously unsure. I pat her arm and tell her I'll take care of this.

"How are things in here, Hedvig?"

"Help me," she cries. "Heeeelp!"

"I'm here now, take a deep breath." I unlock the medicine cabinet. Very likely, someone forgot to give her the dose she should have gotten two hours ago. So typical. Now I have to write a report as well. I rip open the bag of pills, pour them into a red plastic cup, and hand them to Hedvig. She swallows them all at once and then throws herself onto the bed with loud cries and whimpers.

I sit down next to her, pat her hand, and whisper to her that everything will be fine. Then I put a blanket over her and tuck in her cold feet. I hush and hum in a quiet voice. After a while she settles down.

"Do you want some coffee, Hedvig? Maybe a cookie?"

"Don't leave me. Don't go away."

"I'm not going anywhere. I promise."

Hedvig is eighty-five and rarely has any visitors. She lies in bed, day after day, week after week, year after year. She munches on her tranquilizers, has her outbursts, gets a little extra attention. I feel for her. Ending your days this way is shameful. It's a shame for our welfare society. Our so-called welfare society. It doesn't exist anymore.

I stay there, stroking her bony arms, thinking about life. It rarely turns out the way you imagine. Even a conversation with my daughter goes off the rails. I don't understand why that happens every time we talk. I've gone over it many times, wondering what I'm doing wrong.

Hi, Mom.

Hi, honey. Are you on your way to therapy?

Already she's closed herself off from me. Maybe I should have hung up immediately and called back later, but I wanted so badly to hear her voice, remind her that I'm here and that I love her. Deep inside she must know that, even if she sounds angry. Deep inside she knows she needs me. She's not strong enough to break away. She's not ready.

How are things at home?

Quiet. It's always quiet when you're not here.

A halfhearted joke. I should have figured Isabelle would misinterpret it. She does most things these days.

Maybe you should try to meet someone. Have you been to Grandma's lately?

The fact that my daughter thinks she needs to worry about my relationships annoys me.

Your grandmother is busy. Sewing circles or whatever it is she does now.

It'll be all right, don't worry.

But don't you know anyone else you could visit? You haven't always lived in Dalarna.

What is this? Where did these comments come from? And with that tone? It's not like Isabelle. Not at all. And before I can gather my thoughts it continues.

Where did we live when I was little? You've never told me about that. Just that we were somewhere in Denmark before you moved to Borlänge and met Dad.

Maybe I handled it all wrong. But Isabelle's tone didn't make it easy. So accusatory and angry and disagreeable. Impertinent. Ungrateful. I wasn't prepared for my own reaction.

Hans, you mean?

It just tumbled out of me. I guess I wanted to put little miss in her place. It hurts when Isabelle attacks me. Of course I want to talk about it. That's obvious. But like this? On the phone?

This should have made us closer, being just the two of us. But things seem to be getting worse. If she only knew how sad it makes me. She still doesn't know what I've been through. Doesn't it matter that I'm her mother? That I carried her, gave birth to her over the slowest, most painful and awful forty-six hours of my life? That I nearly died in the process? Doesn't it matter how I held her and rocked her in the rocking chair those first few months? That I patched up her wounds and sat with her at night when she was ill. That I brought her here to Dalarna to make a safe home for her, found a father for her, the best one imaginable.

Hans meant everything to Isabelle. And Aina, Isabelle's grandmother, has a very special place in her heart. But me, I'm basically worthless. No one understands how it feels. How much it hurts. Despised and rejected, even though I built my life around her. Children can be so unbelievably cruel.

Hedvig moves anxiously, and I readjust her blanket. Poor woman, what a fate. Is this how I'll end up? Caring for my daughter only seems to push her away.

The shame I feel for the way I told Isabelle about Hans strikes me more often than I'd like. I understand she's hurt and sad, I truly do. But she's changed lately, more than she knows. She's almost always angry or annoyed. It's more than just being disappointed with me. She's totally different than she used to be.

What we need is to meet. Ideally, I'd like to take Isabelle home again, have some time to fuss over her. We need to belong to each other again. If we're together and have the chance to really talk, we'll find our way back to each other. Everything will be all right.

That's why I took care of things.

It might seem impulsive, but I thought it through carefully before I went to Stockholm. It's a long drive to do in just one day, but it was worth it. I had to do something. I can't just passively stand by while my daughter is led astray.

I chose to talk to her husband first. Henrik Widstrand. Surely he'll be able to influence her. I didn't want to storm into her clinic and confront her unnecessarily. For Isabelle's sake, I'll give her a chance. She has to understand that my daughter is vulnerable and at a very sensitive stage.

Henrik Widstrand was pleasant. He took time, showed me in, and offered me coffee. He listened, I wasn't interrupted, he let me finish what I had to say. And not once did he look at his expensive watch or show any impatience. Obviously, he was loyal to his wife. Said she maintains her patients' confidentiality, he doesn't know anything about them. He was sure she's good at her job. But he took me seriously, I could see that. I worried him. I hope I don't cause any problems between them. I wouldn't want that. But what else could I do? What alternative did I have? All I want is to protect my child. That's most important. Keeping my daughter safe.

Henrik Widstrand thanked me, took my hand and looked into my eyes. He was quite tall, handsome, in good shape. He could have been snobby, but he was warm and friendly. She should be happy to have such a good husband. I feel much better after talking to him. I actually think everything will turn out okay.

I hum and sing, stroking Hedvig's hand until she falls asleep. Then I sit with her until it's time to go home for the day.

Stella

The sky is overcast as I pass by Avesta and drive over the Dal River. I don't remember the last time I visited Dalarna.

Just before I reach Borlänge, the landscape opens up. Wide meadows and fields. The tree-covered mountains in the distance are blue. I've forgotten how beautiful this part of Sweden is, even on a gray day like today.

I turn right and drive across the Dal River again. I drive past the steelworks. Lead-colored smoke disappears into a cloudy sky.

Barkargärdet lies northwest of Borlänge, and it takes me a while to find the right address on Faluvägen. Leafy trees and firs grow high and thick. The area is dark, murky, and I wonder if the sun ever reaches here.

Most of the houses in Barkargärdet are well cared for, with neat gardens. But some houses are more like shacks: decaying and abandoned, overgrown gardens, garbage and old cars on their lawns. Hans and Kerstin Karlsson's house is one of these. I park on the shoulder, but stay in the car. I contemplate the house my daughter grew up in.

The paint is peeling and needs to be redone. It was probably a nice house once upon a time, but it gives the impression of neglect now. A pile of trash sits next to the driveway and an old dishwasher stands below the kitchen window. The garden is overgrown, the grass high, and the flower beds untended for a long time. The mailbox looks like something from a fairy tale, light yellow with intricate details. It doesn't fit its surroundings.

I want to find out who Kerstin is. What she does, what kind of background she has, how much she knows. I want to know why she tracked down Henrik, instead of talking to me directly. I want to know why she took the time to look up his business, the address of his office, then wriggled time to see him between all the meetings he has. The more I think about it, the stranger it seems.

The driveway is empty and the windows dark; no one seems to be home. A car approaches. I hunch down, it passes by, and I exhale. My armpits are sweaty. My heart is pounding. I feel ridiculous. But if it's Kerstin, she absolutely cannot see me.

I swing out onto the road and follow Faluvägen until I get to an exit. But instead of heading onto the E16, back toward Borlänge, I turn around.

I drive by the house again. Stop, turn off the engine, and leave the car. I have to try to get in. Maybe there's an unlocked door or a cellar window I can force open.

The door to the neighboring house opens when I'm almost at the gate. A woman and a man come out, wearing matching exercise clothes. They go down the stairs, and the man looks in my direction. He seems suspicious, as if he thinks I'm here to break in. On their gate hangs a sign: *Neighborhood Watch.* A red triangle with a broken crowbar in the middle, and beneath it the police logo.

I turn around and walk back quickly.

"Hello? Can we help you with something?" the man calls after me. I jog toward the car, jump into it, and drive away from there.

In the rearview mirror, I see him still watching me go.

I park farther away and wait. Then I turn and drive back toward Kerstin's house again. The neighbors are still outside; they've taken out some gardening tools. They're keeping an eye on the area; there's no way to get to the house without them noticing.

I came all the way here. I've looked at the house; I know where Alice lived. Where Kerstin Karlsson lived with my child. It's so frustrating not to be able to do more. At the same time, I'm relieved. I can't make any mistakes now. If it came out that I was snooping around like this, my career would be over for good.

I look at the house one last time. Alice grew up here. I can't take it in. It's unimaginable. Did she stand at those windows looking out? Did she run around that garden and play? Was she loved or was she mistreated? I don't know anything about the life of my lost daughter.

Isabelle

"What do you think of this?" Johanna holds up a short, sequined dress. "You'd look so hot in it."

I shrug my shoulders. "It's okay."

"Cheer up, Isabelle!" She hangs the dress up again and puts an arm around my shoulders. "Shopping is the best medicine for depression."

"Is it? Mom says you end up more depressed once your money is gone."

"She's wrong. You'll see."

I'm not at all as sure that this is helping. "Can't we go home instead?"

"If you lie in that bed for one more minute, you'll go crazy for real. Believe me." Johanna takes me under the arm and pulls me along to the next clothing rack.

She came home after the lecture, pulled up my blinds, and asked me what I was doing. At first she thought I was sick. Then she realized what was wrong. She crawled into my bed and gave me a big hug. Said she thought life was shitty, too. Then she ordered me up and into the shower. Now the two of us and about a thousand other people are at H&M on Drottninggatan in the middle of the city.

Johanna holds up a tiny silver crop top that's both silky and gorgeous. I reluctantly agree to try it on. That, the dress, and a pair of slim, black super-stretchy pants. Johanna takes the lead and heads to the changing rooms, commandeers the largest one. She sits down on the bench inside and gestures for me to get going. I take off my sweater and jeans. Try on the clothes and twirl around obediently.

I end up buying both the shirt and the pants. And maybe I do feel a tiny bit better. But probably it's more that someone cares about me than that I went shopping.

Johanna doesn't ask me until we're sitting at Joe & the Juice at Åhléns. Everyone here is so cool. The music is way too loud. She buys a juice for each of us and then sits down close to me.

"I bought you a Sex Me Up juice, I thought you might need it."

I taste it. "Thank you. It's good."

"It's been a while since you were this depressed. Is it your dad?"

"It's my whole sad life."

"Oh, Isabelle, you're so dramatic. What is it now?"

"My childhood was just so weird."

Johanna puts her arm around me. "Because you're adopted and didn't know about it?"

"Not just that. Like, we never met other people. Only Grandma. We lived like in a bubble, very isolated. And Mom always wanted me to be her little doll, who she could command and rearrange."

I take a drink, my brain whirring.

"My parents never did the things other parents do. They were so different from everyone else. I was ashamed of them. Mostly of Mom. She was strange in some way. Neither of them went to the parent-teacher conferences, they found excuses whenever our class and the other parents planned to do something together, and I was never allowed to go on class trips. I could help Dad in the garage and bake with Mom. But it's just all so weird."

"All parents are crazy. Sick in the head in some way. All of them, I promise."

"Not like my mom. She watched me all the time. As soon as a boy was interested in me she'd find out. Then she'd call his parents, threaten to report him to the police, and all sorts of things. My mom is crazy, everyone knew it. And eventually everyone avoided me because of her."

"You have me now." Johanna leans against my shoulder. "And Fredde, too? You've been texting a lot lately, right?"

"Yes."

"Do you like him?"

"A little."

"Just a little?"

"Stop it, Johanna."

"Okay."

Silence.

"Do you think he likes me?" I say after a while.

Johanna rolls her eyes. "He's so into you, you could make him do anything."

"Even though I'm weird?"

"You know what? You are not as weird as you think. It's in your head."

"Stella said something similar in group therapy once. But still. I feel like I have terrible things inside me."

"Do you think you're the only one? I feel so fucking furious sometimes. At my parents, at my life, everything. It's not wrong, the question is just what you do about it."

"Maybe. I don't know."

"But I do know. And now I want to hear what you're going to do about Fredde."

We continue to talk about boys, or men, how best to flirt via text and Snapchat, I get tips on what to say and what not to say. She makes me blush, we laugh, giggle. After a while, Johanna stands up to go buy a sandwich as well. Talking about guys and sex takes a lot of energy. I say it's my turn to buy, but she waves me away. Going out with Johanna is the best thing I could have done, even though I didn't feel like it at all. When she's gone, my phone rings. I don't recognize the number; for once, it's not Mom.

Stella

I'm on my way back to Stockholm, driving faster than I should. I feel disappointed. Angry. It was stupid to go to Borlänge. I should have stayed home and slept instead. It was completely useless. I don't know any more now than I did driving up. On the contrary, I've found even more questions that need answers. Answers that don't exist.

I pull off at a gas station in Enköping, fill up, and buy a cup of coffee. I sit down at a picnic table at the edge of the parking lot. My shoulders are tense, the skin around my eyes tight. I take a few deep breaths, fill up my lungs, and then stretch my body.

I take out my phone, make a call.

"Hello, this is Isabelle."

"Hi, Isabelle, this is Stella Widstrand."

Silence.

"Hello?" I say.

"Oh, hi!"

"Hello, I'm sorry to bother you on a Friday afternoon."

"No problem at all."

Loud music is thumping in the background. Maybe she's at some student party.

"Can you talk," I ask, "or are you still at school?"

"I'm free today. I'm out with a friend."

"Nice," I say. "Do you like studying?"

A short pause before answering.

"Yes, I do. It's a lot of work, but it's fun."

This is how easy it could be. I could just call up my daughter, ask her how she is, how her day has been. Who is she? What are her dreams? What does she want to be? I want to know everything about her.

"I'll keep it short. I have a suggestion," I hear myself saying. "Group therapy is only once a week. There's not a lot of individual time for each of you. I have an opening on Monday. You can have your own hour to talk. At eleven?"

"Okay." Isabelle sounds doubtful. "That might be good."

"Only if you want to," I say. "If you think you'd get something out of it. In the future we could meet with your mother as well. It could help the two of you form a closer bond."

"Maybe later," she says. "Can I think about it?"

"Of course. It's just an offer. You do whatever feels right."

"But Monday sounds good. Eleven o'clock?"

"I'll see you then."

I finish the call and sit down in the car. I grab my purse and pull out my calendar, write *Isabelle, Monday at eleven*. What I'm doing is unethical. But Alice is my child. I'm prepared to do what I have to to get her back.

I flip through this past week. See that I should have sent a number of e-mails, made some calls, updated some records by today. It's afternoon, and I haven't done a thing. I'm not planning on doing anything now, either.

I see a note from Wednesday, from my conversation with Per Gunnarsson. *Sven Nilsson, Norrköping.*

I haven't called him yet. The misunderstanding about picking up Milo, the argument with Henrik, the scene at the restaurant yesterday. I totally forgot to contact him.

I google and find a phone number and an address. I call, wait impatiently while the phone rings.

"Yes, hello?" A young woman's voice.

I introduce myself, say I'm calling for Sven Nilsson. I hear the woman mumble. It sounds like she's passing the phone.

"Sven Nilsson." His voice is hoarse; I don't recognize it.

"Hi, my name is Stella Widstrand," I say. "We met in the summer of 1994. My name was Stella Johansson back then."

"Yes?"

"My daughter, Alice, disappeared at Strandgården in August of that year. She was only one year old. You were the detective who investigated her disappearance."

Silence.

Sven Nilsson is old. Does he remember?

"Yes, I remember," he says. "May I ask why you're calling now?"

"I'm convinced Alice is alive. Maybe that sounds a little crazy. But I just know. I know she's alive."

"I always believed your daughter was still alive," Sven Nilsson says. "Unfortunately, I could never prove it. I'm sorry for that. It was the worst case I had in all my years on the force."

My eyes fill with tears. I wipe them away with my shirtsleeve and clear my throat.

"Do you have anything left from the investigation that I could look at?" I ask.

"Absolutely, absolutely," he says. "I have every scrap of paper here. All of it. In fact, I know there was a tip we overlooked. Can you come here and we'll go through it together? Let me see, maybe on Tuesday? Tuesday morning? Does that work?"

I laugh out loud. Tuesday feels like an eternity from now, but finally I'll get the evidence I need to prove I'm right.

I turn the music up loud and drive home.

Stella

Henrik baked bread this morning, and the kitchen smells delicious. It's Saturday, and we eat breakfast together. Henrik and I haven't talked yet, but for Milo's sake we pretend nothing is wrong. I eat a slice of bread, even though I'm not hungry, and praise how good it tastes. Then I ask Milo about today's basketball game. That's all it takes to get him started, and Henrik and I are able to continue avoiding each other.

I'm not going to the game. Henrik seems relieved I'm staying home. I say I need to rest. I'm just going to lie on the sofa and take it easy. I stand at the door waving as they leave and remember I said exactly the same thing two weeks ago. Of course, I haven't told my husband about my trip to Strandgården. Nor about the trip to Kerstin's house in Dalarna. Or about the phone calls with Isabelle and Sven Nilsson. Being the unreliable and secretive person I am.

He surely senses as much. I can't blame him for finding it hard to believe me. But I don't feel guilty.

Someone who's never lost a child can't understand. If I told him everything, what I feel, what I'm up to, Henrik would try to stop me. He'd work against me. I don't have time for his doubts or his distrust. All of his good intentions are just an expression of his fears. Henrik is afraid I'll make trouble. The only thing he wants to protect is himself. That's human. We're all like that. And that's why I haven't said anything about who I'm going to meet today.

I exit the E18 freeway. According to the GPS, it's not much farther. I couldn't help checking his profile on Facebook yesterday. Though I could only see his profile picture, places he's been, and what music he likes. The rest was private, for friends only.

At first, I didn't plan on going here. But in the end I felt I had to. I just want to see him. See how things are going for him.

There is nobody else I can talk to. No one else understands.

He's her father.

And he has the right to know that Alice is alive. That I've met her and know where she is.

Daniel lives in a charming white house in Bro, twenty miles outside Stockholm. There's a large yard with thick, well-trimmed hedges. A garage sits next to the property; inside it a man is bent over an open car hood. A sign that reads *Sundkvist's Garage* hangs on the wall. I check how I look in the rearview mirror. Readjust my white blouse. I have painted my nails wine red. I fixed my hair this morning, and it curls on my shoulders. I smile at my own image in the mirror. It smiles back, but she seems nervous and insecure.

I park outside the garage door. Daniel shades his eyes with his hand and peers at me. I take a deep breath and get out of the car.

"Stella?" Daniel smiles and comes closer. "I thought that was you," he says.

He wipes his hands on a cloth. Then he sweeps me up in his arms, squeezes me tight, and spins me around. Just like he used to. I hide my face in his neck, breathe in his scent. I've forgotten the effect he has on me. I wasn't at all prepared for the desire his touch awakens in me. Or am I? Haven't I longed to feel this again?

"What are you up to?" he says and puts me down. "All the way out here in Bro?"

"Just passing by?"

"Sure." He smiles, but I get the feeling he's on his guard. We examine each other. Daniel looks the same, but not quite. He's no longer wiry and thin. He probably works out, his shoulders are strong, his chest and arms muscular. His hair is longer than I've seen it before, and he's got it up in a man bun. It's still coal black, but starting to gray at the temples. There are more tattoos on his arms than twelve years ago. His jeans are worn and sit low on his hips. He's wearing a red flannel shirt and a black tank top underneath. He looks dangerous. Sexy.

"Your very own garage." I gesture to the sign. "You did it in the end."

He looks up at it. "It feels good," he says, turning his eyes to me. "And you? Still a shrink?"

I go over to the car he's working on.

"What a beauty," I say, running my hand along the side.

"Yep, isn't she nice?"

Daniel walks behind me and happens to graze my ass. He stands beside me. Close. He smells like engine oil and aftershave. I hear him breathing.

"I remember that red, shiny thing you drove us around in," I say, looking up at him.

"Shiny thing?" He pretends to be disappointed. "That was a 1974 Chevy Impala."

"I have some very good memories from that car."

Daniel smiles. He remembers, too. And he doesn't mind thinking about what we did in that backseat. I can see it on him. I feel it in the pit of my stomach. He walks farther into the garage. "You want a beer or something?" he calls over his shoulder.

"Some mineral water if you have any."

"Still haven't learned how to drink beer?" He returns and throws a seltzer to me. I catch it and laugh.

"No, I'm a hopeless case."

He asks about Gudrun, my mother. He heard Henrik and I bought an apartment for her a few years ago. He tells me he misses her meatballs, I have to tell her hello from him. I ask about his mother, Maud. She retired at the beginning of the summer, now she spends her days smoking cigarettes under the kitchen fan.

None of what we say matters. It's just small talk. What I feel in every part of me right now. I can see it in Daniel's gaze, how it glides over my body, he feels the same. And it's ridiculously flattering to know he still desires me.

"What a man cave you have here," I say, looking around. "Fridge with beer, jukebox. The whole package."

"Pretty sweet, right?" he replies.

I sit down on the sofa next to the fridge.

"I can't guarantee your fancy clothes will leave here in the same condition if you sit down there." He points at the couch with his beer.

"Come sit here," I say, patting the cushion next to me invitingly. He comes over and sits down. He puts an arm behind me and I scoot closer. I can't help but wonder what our life would have been like if we'd never left each other. Would we have lived this far out of town? Would we have had more children?

I'm devastated by everything that's happened to us. Everything we lost. I miss him. I miss the warmth we had between us. Miss the heat. And I want to experience it again.

"Isn't it tragic when a person who meant everything to you, who was a huge part of your life, is no longer in it?" I say. "Don't you think?"

Daniel squeezes my shoulder. "You always spent more time pondering that sort of thing than me." He's quiet for a while. "Do you still keep a diary?" he says.

"Not anymore."

"Are you happy?" Daniel looks into my eyes.

I look away. "We have a good life," I say, signaling that I'd rather not talk about it.

"Henrik's a construction engineer, or something like that?"

"Something like that."

"You've done well for yourself," he says. "Drive an Audi. Expensive and classy. Where's that girl who was too scared to learn to drive?"

"Same girl." I didn't come here to talk about my life these days. I don't want to hear any more about it. I just want to be in the here and now with Daniel.

"He seems good for you," he says. "You and I were too hotheaded."

"Maybe."

"And your son, Milo? He must be getting big now."

"Thirteen."

"Time flies." Daniel takes a gulp of his beer.

"Alice would have been twenty-two," I say.

Daniel looks at me. He takes away his arm and straightens up. He considers what to say for a long time. I'd forgotten how he used to do that. His tactics for avoiding talking used to drive me mad. They still annoy me.

"Do you think about her, too?" I ask.

Daniel twists the can in his hands. "Sometimes," he answers after a while. "Now and then. On her birthday. Life goes on." He falls silent again.

"I've been thinking a lot about her. About us." I put my hand on his thigh. "We had it good, Daniel."

"I remember the fights," he says. "How we got on each other's nerves in that tiny apartment in Jordbro. It wasn't always so romantic." He takes the elastic band off and pushes his fingers through his hair. I take my hand off his thigh.

"If Alice hadn't disappeared . . ."

"Then we would have lived happily ever after?" He shakes his head slowly and looks at me. "Do you believe that? We were so young, Stella. And you got knocked up so quick. I think you remember it differently than I do."

He dismisses our life together. So easily. Throws it all away as if it isn't worth anything. I get up and go to the door of the garage. Look out onto the street. Maybe it was a mistake to come here. I turn around and look at him.

"So what, my memories are just fantasies?"

"You wear rose-colored glasses, you always have." Daniel leaves the couch, walks over to the car, and bends over it again. He picks up a wrench and continues working. I recognize this behavior as well. He's uncertain, confused. Am I having an effect him? Is he afraid of what might happen? Yes, he is. Terrified. I awaken something in him. It's as strong now as it was then. And it terrifies him.

"I remember that you loved us," I say. "You were happy with Alice, overjoyed. Is my memory wrong? Were we just a hindrance to you? To all those plans you had? Say it, I can take it." I go over to him. I feel like an emotionally unstable character in a soap opera.

He turns around and grabs my arms. Bends over and studies me closely. "Why are you thinking about this right now? Why did you come here? It's not to talk about old memories, that much I know."

I look down at the floor before daring to meet his gaze. Then I tell him I found Alice. Or Alice found me, but she doesn't know that yet. I tell him everything. I hear myself rambling, wish I was more calm and collected. But I spill it all. From beginning to end.

When I'm done, I notice that Daniel's expression seems faraway. He stands with his legs wide apart and his back straight, his hands pushed deep in his pockets.

"Does she have thick, black hair? An elf ear?" He moves his hand to his own.

"Yes, she does. That's what made me sure." I hold his face between my hands. Our eyes meet. Everything stands still.

"And she looks like Maria?" he says. "Just like when she was a baby?" Daniel's voice is soft and understanding. Finally. I knew he would believe me.

"She is a copy of Maria. You have to see her."

I put my hands around his neck, lean against him. It was so long ago. But it feels like we've never been apart. Time has not broken the bond between us.

"And you met her, talked to her?" he says. "You're sure?"

"Daniel, she's our daughter." I want to cry with relief because he understands. With sadness for all the years that have passed. With joy to be with him, to feel the closeness between us.

"Our daughter is dead." Daniel breaks free from me. "We buried her. Don't you remember that?" He might as well have punched me in the stomach. "Damn it, Stella. How much of this am I supposed to take? How many times will we have to go through this?"

"It is her. I know it's her. I feel it with every fiber of my being." I turn away and take a deep breath before looking at him again. "I talked to Sven Nilsson. Do you remember him? The police officer? There was a tip that was never followed up. I'm meeting with him on Tuesday." I grab Daniel's hands, forcing him to look up. "I thought you might want to come with me. We'll go there together. We'll get answers. This time we'll know what—"

"Stella, listen," Daniel interrupts. "Alice is gone. You have to let go. We have both moved on. That's all we need to know."

The lump in my throat grows and the tears start to flow. I'm crying loudly now.

"Daniel, you have to help me," I sniff. "Please, don't desert me. You're all I have left." He puts his hand on my cheek and I throw myself into his arms.

"I'm as sad as you are," he says quietly. "I am."

"I miss her. And I miss you." I sob and hear that my words are incomprehensible. He hushes me and speaks quietly into my hair. He strokes my back.

It feels lovely. It feels good. And I want him. Now.

It's wrong.

I know it's wrong.

But it feels so right to be here in his arms. And the lust I felt before has returned. I caress his cheek, run my fingers through his hair, touch the scar on his forehead. I pull his face down and kiss him. Daniel pushes me off and straightens up.

"*That* is not gonna help anything. You have a nice family, don't forget that. Your husband loves you. I could see it when I met him twelve years ago. He cares about you. And he takes a lot better care of you than I ever could have."

I look down to the floor. Can't stand how he's looking at me. I'm ashamed, ashamed, ashamed.

"I don't intend to go with you," he says. "I don't want to do this again. I can't. It's not right for either of us. Go home to your son, Stella. Go home to your husband. He's probably worried about you."

"Daddy, Daddy." A girl's voice. Instinctively I back up as a small child comes in and throws herself into Daniel's arms. "We saw kittens and goats and sheep and those cafs!"

"Calves?" Daniel laughs. The girl is probably around four and has thick, dark hair. Another girl comes in, maybe eight, I would guess, with equally beautiful hair. He asks the girls where their mom is. She went inside with the food, they say in unison. He throws the little one onto his hip and puts his arm around the big one, herding them toward the door. The girls tell him Mom said it's time to go inside. Be with his favorite girls.

Did Alice look like that at their ages? Would he have looked at her in the same way, been as wonderful?

Yes, I know he would have. The pain cuts so deep, it's hard to breathe.

I see a younger Daniel sitting on the floor and cuddling our little girl. He's sleeping on the sofa with his hair in all directions and our baby on his chest. A protective hand on her little back. *We were his favorite girls.*

Will I be paralyzed forever? Will I stand here frozen until someone is merciful enough to carry me away?

I'm an idiot.

An unbalanced wreck.

Did I imagine he's been waiting for me all these years, waiting to relive that short time we had together? He has new daughters to care about. A new love.

A new life.

"Stella, Stella." Daniel is standing in the doorway. He looks at me and both girls give me curious looks. "Take care of yourself." He takes his daughters and heads to the house.

A woman is standing on the front porch, looking in my direction. She's beautiful.

I climb into my car and drive away.

Stella

I drive away like a lunatic. Pull off on the side of the road. Put my head against the steering wheel and cry. Guilt and shame circle around inside me, self-loathing hammers in its eternal message of how worthless I am. Guilt that I've been so dishonest with Henrik. Shame for the feelings that welled inside me and how I chose to handle them. Did I try to kiss Daniel? How far was I willing to go? I don't want to think about it. I still feel that longing. What we had was so strong and passionate. And when I saw Daniel today everything came back. I *allowed* it to come back. I wanted to believe it was still there. I was seeking comfort, a way to disappear into oblivion. Afraid of hurting. This is what happens when I try to flee from the pain. Right now, I lack any impulse control.

Daniel and I. What we had no longer exists. And I grieve for us. Alice was with us one moment, gone the next, as if she never existed. No one could explain what happened. Our family ceased to exist.

The days after our baby disappeared collapsed into one painful, drawn-out state of hopelessness and anxiety. Going home to the apartment in Jordbro, seeing her toys scattered in each room, seeing her high chair in the kitchen, her crib in the bedroom. I gathered her tiny clothes and put them in the laundry, her stuffed animals.

I was incapable of sharing my grief with anyone. I was paralyzed. I disappeared into our sofa and put Alice's blanket over me. In order to keep her close, smell her scent.

Daniel tried everything: he pleaded and begged and prayed, finally he screamed at me. He got no response; I was catatonic. In the end he pulled away. Gave in to his own grief. I don't think he accused me, but I'm not entirely sure. Maybe he was angry with my negligence, my carelessness, my inattention? Maybe not. He never said anything. Not once did he ask how I could have left Alice alone. But still. It must have been there. I chose not to see it; that would have been too much to bear.

Sixteen weeks passed. No sign of life from our daughter. No trace, no news from the police. Sixteen weeks passed without many signs of life from me, either. Daniel packed up his belongings and moved out. He heaved his bag over his shoulder, looked at me a long time before turning around.

I stayed on the sofa and let him go.

Milo's shoes aren't in the hall when I get home. No sign of Henrik, either, but his jacket is hung up and his car is parked outside. He must be home. My heart pounds as I walk up the stairs. I'm so pissed off I'm shaking. He let me down; he must have talked to Daniel behind my back. Warned him I was having a relapse. That I was becoming manic. *He's worried about you.* Who else has he contacted? Did he call everyone to tell them how unbalanced and sick I am?

In the bedroom his exercise clothes are hanging over the laundry basket. He's been out running. I can hear the shower from inside the bathroom. The door is open slightly, and I go in. I see Henrik behind the frosted glass door.

I pull it open. He turns around and sees me.

"Where have you been?" he says and turns off the water. He grabs a towel and wraps it around his hips. I take one step forward and slap him across the face. He stares at me as if he can't believe what just happened.

"What are you doing?" he says, rubbing his hand on his face. I shove him, pound my fists on his chest.

"How could you?" I scream. "How the hell could you do that to me?"

Henrik grabs my arms, preventing my blows. So I start to kick. He takes a tougher grip on me and turns me around. Holds me tight.

"Let me go." I fight to get free. "Let me go, I said."

"What the hell? What's going on with you?" Henrik keeps hold of me with a firm grip.

When he drops me, I bite his hand and spin around. He swears and inspects the mark left by my teeth. I raise my hand to slap him again. He catches my wrist, pushes me back against the wall, and holds it over my head.

A drop of water runs down his bare chest. He bends over me. My free hand draws his head down toward me. I kiss him. Bite his lip.

"What are you up to?" he whispers into my ear.

I don't answer. He lets go of me, takes a step backward.

Buttons fly as I rip off my blouse. Henrik stares at me in silence. I grab his hips, press against him. We kiss each other, a long deep kiss. I reach in under the towel, grab him, and fondle his erection.

He lifts me up and puts me down on the counter next to the sink. I pull the towel away, see how hard and stiff he is. I wrap my legs around his waist and he pulls me against him.

He kisses my throat, my neck, grabs my hair hard. Pushes his tongue into my mouth. He unclasps my bra, throws it on the floor, and licks my breasts. His tongue circles around my nipples and I press my lips against his ear, whispering, *Take me*.

He carries me to the bedroom. Throws me down on the bed and takes off my pants and my underwear. I try to sit up, but he pushes me on my back. He kneels and kisses the inside of my thighs, and I grab his hair and press myself against his face.

His tongue slides around, tantalizingly slow. I twist, begging for more. He licks and nibbles. I'm close to coming when he stops and leans over me, says that's enough. I pull him down on the bed, we roll around and fall over the side, down onto the floor.

I straddle him, rubbing my wet pussy against his cock. His hands are on my breasts, on my ass. I kiss his shoulders and his neck and his flat stomach. He moans when I take him in my mouth. He's big and hard and I'm sucking, licking; it gives me pleasure to see his pleasure, to hear him moan, feel his body tense, feel him getting close. He asks me to stop, says he wants to fuck me.

I sweep my hair over his chest. He grabs hold of it and pulls me to the side. We roll around. He holds my wrists over my head with one hand and strokes my clit with his other hand. He slips into me, fills me completely. Our bodies thump against each other, against the floor. I scream as I come. Scream loudly and feel a sob arrive at the same moment.

He's still lying on me, and I wrap my legs around him. His heart hammers against mine.

"Hello, love," he says after a while. He rolls off me and turns to me. "Where have you been?"

I don't respond. I want to stay in this moment. Forget everything else. Crawl in closer to him, let him hold me, his body against mine. I want to have him again. I bend over him, kiss his lips. Take him in my hand, feel him hardening again.

Henrik's phone rings. He sighs, mumbles that he has to see who it is. He moves up onto the bed and answers. I creep up into bed and close my eyes. Henrik slaps my butt, and I look up. *Don't fall asleep,* he mouths to me. But I'm too tired. No energy left. My brain is done after a long and terrible day. My body feels heavy and relaxed. I pull the blanket over me, Henrik pinches my thigh. *Don't fall asleep.*

When Henrik hangs up, he sits beside me for a long time. I don't need to open my eyes to know that he's watching me. I pretend to sleep and hear him get dressed. Before he leaves he kisses me on the forehead. He exits the bedroom and goes down the stairs.

Stella

When I wake up, Henrik is lying behind me. I turn around. He opens his eyes.

"I didn't mean to wake you," I say. "What time is it? Is it late?"

"I wasn't sleeping," he says.

"It's been a long time." I run my finger across his chest and lean over him, kiss his lips. Try to turn him on again. He caresses my cheek and looks into my eyes.

I push up against him. "Do you want more?"

"I want to talk," he says.

"Are you sure?"

I nibble at his throat.

"What happened earlier? Sooner or later we have to talk about it."

I get up from bed. Pull on a T-shirt and put my hair up in a knot.

"If I remember correctly we were horny. We had sex on the floor and—"

"Stella, please stop," Henrik interrupts. He sits up and leans back on the headboard. "You were furious with me when you came home. You hit me. Why?"

My anger returns with full force.

"Well, what do you think? Are you so stupid that you don't know why? Or are you pretending?"

"I have no idea what you're talking about. How could I? I'm the last one to know. Just like last time."

"Stop," I say. "Don't throw that shit in my face."

I grab the laundry basket, throw off his exercise clothes, and start folding towels.

"I'm sorry," Henrik says. "That was uncalled for."

I throw the towels on the floor. Stand at the window staring out.

"Honey, what did I do?" He sounds sincere. And the question is justified. I ponder how to answer. I'd prefer not to reveal what I did yesterday, that I was with Daniel.

What was it Daniel said that made me so angry with Henrik? Made me feel sure Henrik had talked to him. Broken my trust. Now, what was it again? The uncomfortable feeling that I might have misinterpreted what Daniel said steals over me.

Our daughter is dead.

There is nothing we can learn.

Alice is gone.

We have to move on.

You have a good man; he cares about you. He's worried about you.

Or was it? He *might* be worried about you? Isn't he worried about you? He's *surely* worried about you?

When Henrik is feeling guilty he can't hide it. He's essentially honest and usually takes responsibility for what he does. I do, too, usually. That's the kind of relationship we have.

Had. It's not Henrik who's being dishonest, it's me. And my guilty conscience is making me project onto everyone but myself.

Henrik rises and pulls on his gray sweatpants.

"Okay, I'll guess," he says. "You're mad at me because I don't think Alice is alive? Because I don't believe that you've found her?"

"I hate feeling like you think I'm crazy. That I'm imagining things. That you talk about me to Mom, to Pernilla, behind my back."

"First of all, I haven't talked to Pernilla. Nor your mother. I don't know where you got that idea, but it's not true."

I start to say something, but he holds up his hand like a traffic cop.

"Secondly, please don't tell me what I think, what *you* think I'm telling people. You're the therapist here, right? If you want to know what I'm thinking, ask."

He's right. And I realize he hasn't called Daniel.

Henrik continues. "Also, have you ever heard me say you're nuts or crazy? Have you?"

"No," I admit. "You've never said it."

"Then for fuck's sake, stop putting words in my mouth."

"Sorry," I whisper.

"Just because I don't jump for joy immediately doesn't mean I think you're crazy. You tell me nothing, avoid me, and then throw yourself at me. Can you see I might wonder what's going on?"

"I just wish you trusted me," I say.

"And I wish you talked to me. It's much easier for me to trust you if you tell me what's going on." He settles down on the edge of the bed again. "You're the smartest woman I know. You're usually so rational, so logical. But lately I hear nothing but angry outbursts and baseless assumptions. It's not like you."

"How do you think you'd react? How do you think you'd feel? If you met Milo twenty-one years after losing him?"

"You've met a girl who looks like Alice's aunt. That's all. Isabelle *has* a biological mother. Who happens to be very worried. Still, you're sure it's Alice. You see conspiracies everywhere. You think everyone is against you. You think that the doctors, the school Isabelle went to, all of them are lying? Do you seriously believe that someone could take a child and then pretend it's their own without arousing suspicion?"

"I've warned you, Henrik. Many times. There's something wrong with me."

"You've warned me? What are you talking about now?"

"From the beginning."

Henrik throws up his arms in defeat. "I give up. I'm not following you anymore."

"Goddamn it, Henrik. You make it sound like I—"

He stops me, points to the door.

"Milo?" he says.

"Dad?" Milo's voice sounds tiny.

"Come in, buddy."

The door opens, and Milo peeks in. He looks at Henrik, looks at me. The fear in his eyes hurts me.

"Why aren't you asleep?" I say softly, to make it clear I'm not angry.

"I was just looking for a phone charger."

"You can take the one there in the wall," Henrik says. "Next to the bureau."

"Come here, honey," I say. Milo drags his feet in my direction. I hug him.

"Do you feel better now, Mom?"

"Feel better?" I wonder and stroke his hair.

"Dad said you had a headache."

I glance at Henrik, but he's looking at Milo.

"Yes, I'm fine now," I answer. "How was the game?"

He shrugs. "Fine."

"Go back to bed now," Henrik says, putting one arm around Milo. They head down the stairs, and I can hear Henrik speaking calmly to our son. I pick up the towels I threw on the floor and put them back in the laundry basket.

Stella

It's still dark. I crawl in next to Henrik, lay my head against his shoulder. He opens his arms, pulls the blanket over the two of us.

I slept badly the whole night. I couldn't stop thinking about what Henrik and I said to each other. And what we didn't say. It worries me that Henrik is worried. I'm afraid he's angry with me, afraid my past will destroy the life we've built together. I whisper that I want to stop fighting. I tell him about the diary. Tell him I reread all the entries I wrote when I was pregnant with Alice, when she was a baby. And the day she disappeared and afterward.

The morning light filters in across the bedroom rug. The world has stopped. We are beyond time and space, in our own strange parallel world. It resembles the one we lived in four weeks ago, but it's not the same. My voice sounds distant, and it feels like I'm telling a story. Henrik is quiet, listens.

I want him to understand how painful it is to look back. How it's been like reliving it. All those memories, all that self-loathing. Grief and agony. But I don't mention the panic attacks, nor do I tell him about my visits to Kerstin's house or to Daniel.

Henrik says I should have said something earlier. Surely I know he understands? That he cares about me?

I say I was afraid. Terrified.

He doesn't want me to be sick again.

I know that.

He asks me to promise never to see Isabelle again.

He caresses my cheek. Wipes away the tears I can't stop. And then we make love slowly, gently. I lie on my side, and he enters me from behind. I close my eyes in his embrace and take pleasure from this familiar ritual. His hard body behind me, his gentle movements becoming more and more intense. When I come, he whispers that he loves me. He plunges deep into me. I tell him I love how he fucks me. He groans as he comes, his hands grip onto my hips tightly.

We fall asleep in each other's arms.

Later, we're strolling through the aisles of Coop Forum. It's an ordinary Sunday afternoon. I ask Henrik if he wants apple juice or orange juice. I forget the bread, head back. We fill up our shopping cart. We line up at the checkout counter, holding each other's hand. I pay, Henrik packs up the grocery bags. It's normal, boring, wonderfully domestic. I can finally stop thinking; it feels easier to push down the guilt that gnaws at me. We head out to the Range Rover, load it together. Henrik returns the shopping cart; I start the car. We drive home.

There's a dog in our driveway. Johan Lindberg's little pooch. It has on its leash and collar, but our neighbor is nowhere to be seen. I stop the car; Henrik throws me an amused smile. This is not the first time this has happened, and I doubt it will be the last. He steps out of the car and walks slowly toward the tiny dog. It backs up and barks its shrill, persistent little bark. After another attempt, Henrik turns to me. He laughs and shrugs. I get out of the car and scan the street for the dog's master.

Johan Lindberg is headed our way, jogging and puffing in neon yellow workout clothes, which sit a little too tight on his round body. He reaches us, puts his hands on his knees. His nose running, he clears his throat loudly and lobs a spitball on the street.

"Therese wants me to lose some weight." He groans. "She says I'm too fat to fuck."

I nod at his hydration belt and smile. "You plan on running a marathon?"

"Marathon? Isn't a few miles enough? I'm not ready to sacrifice my life for a little sex."

Henrik says *uh-huh* sympathetically. He squeezes me around the waist. I don't dare look at him, or we won't be able to hold back our laughter. We tell our neighbor good luck, I drive the car into the driveway and we carry in the groceries.

Henrik unpacks the bags, and I put the food into the pantry, fridge, and freezer. Milo hangs out by the kitchen table, laughing at us while we make fun of the investor and his dog. When Henrik's phone rings, I ask him not to answer.

"Why?" he asks, of course.

"Because," I answer. I don't want us to be disturbed. And something always does these days. Someone always wants his attention. Right now I want my husband for myself.

"It could be important," he continues.

"It's Sunday," I complain. "Surely it can wait?"

"I don't recognize the number."

"Live dangerously, Dad," Milo says.

I try to take the phone. Henrik laughs, pretends to wrestle with me for a few seconds before he answers. I turn around and continue putting away the groceries.

"This is Henrik. Oh, hello, it's been a long time." Almost immediately he seems on guard. I glance at him over my shoulder. Milo says he's going to call a friend and heads up to his room.

"Yes, thank you, we're fine. How are you?"

Henrik is using his proper, polite voice. It can't be someone he knows well. He moves a bit farther away from me. Flips through the mail. Listens before saying, "She's changed her number." He throws me a look. I wonder what this is about.

"Do you want to talk to her? She's right here."

I silently mouth, *Who is it?* Henrik ignores me, listening to the person on the other end. He's quiet, goes out to the living room. Then he comes back, the phone still to his ear. I knew it. He never should have picked up. This isn't good.

Henrik leans toward the kitchen counter and laughs, but it's not his usual, jolly, warm laugh.

"Thank you for calling, I appreciate it." His eyes are impossible to read. "I'll tell her you said so."

I wipe off the kitchen counter. Rubbing away imaginary spots.

He hangs up.

I wait.

He says nothing.

"Who was it?" I say at last. Trying to sound casual.

"It was Daniel," he says. "He wondered if you made it home all right yesterday."

Regret is a waste of time and energy. It's not something I usually feel. Instead, we're supposed to learn from our mistakes, try to do better in the future. That's the advice I give my patients. I'm not capable of following it.

I'm more filled with regret than ever. I regret driving out to see Daniel. Regret everything. I should have told Henrik. I should have been open and honest. I never thought Daniel would call.

Henrik leans over the bar counter, looking toward Milo's room. Probably checking to make sure he's out of earshot.

"Daniel was worried about you," he says. "You were upset when you left him yesterday." He looks at me like he doesn't know me. "And he told me you can call him if you want."

I know what Henrik thinks. See it in his hard look. And he can tell I'm feeling guilty about what flamed up inside me when I met Daniel. But it's not a good idea to try to explain. Whatever I say now will just make me seem even guiltier.

"It's not what you think," I say simply.

"You say you're going to stay home and rest, but you're gone when we come home. Then you suddenly show up, royally pissed off. You tear off your clothes, and we have sex."

"I know what you're thinking. But you're wrong."

"What do I think? What are you imagining I'm thinking? You seem to find it easier to tell me what I'm thinking than to tell me what you're doing."

"I don't know what to say."

"No, I've noticed that," he says. "Why were you so angry with me when you came back? You can start there."

"You're all so afraid I'm going to have a breakdown. You think if I just realize I'm wrong, drop Alice, I'll feel better. But you're the ones who will feel better."

"The ones! Do you mean me and Daniel? Pernilla, Gudrun? Who are you talking about?"

I shrug my shoulders. "You're closest at hand. You took those hits for everyone. Unfortunately."

"I can take your shit if it makes you feel better. But you don't have to slap me the next time you want to fuck."

He immediately regrets what he said. I see that. Even though I know I should just take a deep breath, I get angry again.

"And why are you so angry? I wanted to meet the father of my daughter, is that so weird?"

"You can meet him whenever the hell you want to. But why hide it? You could have told me. Do you know how embarrassing it was for me to have your ex call asking me if you're okay?"

Henrik shakes his head and walks away.

I've always been a dreamer. Felt things intensely. Just because I'm a psychotherapist doesn't mean that's changed. But I like to believe I've matured. A little. But maybe I'm wrong about that, too.

Life is easier at thirty-nine than at nineteen. I feel more secure. More sure of myself. Care less what others think of me. I've learned not to follow through on every impulse, to think before I act. I try to analyze the consequences of my choices. And then take responsibility for my actions.

Now it's as if all of that has disappeared.

If Daniel hadn't stopped me, would I have slept with him in that garage? Probably, though I don't want to believe it. Because it's Henrik I want. He's the one I love, the one I want to share my life with. The last thing I want is to lose what we have together.

I track him down in our garage, taking his golf clubs out of the car. He ignores me. I beg for forgiveness. Again. I should have told him I visited Daniel. I feel ashamed, stupid. I say it aloud and hear my voice shake. He stares at me in silence. Then he pulls out a stool for me.

"Sit down," he says. "Let's start over. What happened?"

"Daniel doesn't believe me, either. He doesn't want to know. He reacted like you. Like Pernilla. If you never heard Alice's name again you'd all feel better. It doesn't matter how *I* feel." I don't care that I sound bitter and accusatory.

"You know that's not true," Henrik says. He lays his hand on mine.

"I'm just so disappointed," I say. "In myself, in you, in everyone. I'm sick and tired of begging for forgiveness. Tired of no one believing me."

"Okay, let's say it *is* Alice. What do you do?"

Henrik waits for a moment. Lets the question sink in.

"And if it's *not* her. *If* you're wrong. What does that mean for her? For you?"

He wants answers I don't have yet. And the questions he's asking are very close to what I myself am most afraid of.

"It's too late to think like that now," I say. "Should I give up just because everyone else is afraid?"

"That's not what I'm saying," Henrik answers. "But think about what you're doing. That's all I'm asking. Think about what kind of consequences it might entail. This is the second time I've had a visit or a call about you in a pretty short period of time. Take it easy. Use your logic, you're an intelligent woman. Don't forget that."

"I don't know what I'm gonna do, Henrik."

"Maybe you shouldn't do anything right now," he says. "And please, talk to me about it. Promise me that."

I don't say anything, just nod.

I want to promise him anything he wants. I want to promise that everything is going to work out. But I'm not sure I believe that myself.

Isabelle

Someone pushes me to the side. I turn and apologize. I wind my way back between the tables at the café outside the KTH library. I put my jacket on a chair and sit down opposite Johanna.

"Did it go okay?" she asks.

"Yes, it did."

Nevertheless, I glance at my phone again. Actually, I want to call back, say I will come after all. It's not like me to back out at the last second. Especially when I don't know why. Especially when I lie about my reasons. I don't do that. Lying always makes me feel awful.

I'm not saying I've never lied. But I always follow through with my commitments. Once I make a promise. Even when I don't want to. I'm terrified of disappointing people. *Making them angry.* That's my biggest fear. But I'm working on it. Maybe it's a positive sign that I've risked making someone angry?

"Are you sure you don't want to go?" Johanna asks. She probably notices my hesitation. "We can do this later."

"Nah, it wasn't that important," I say. "It's gonna feel good to get this assignment done."

"Okay. It was kinda weird how she called you on Friday anyway."

Johanna pointed that out when we were still sitting at Joe & the Juice. She's probably right. Still, I feel guilty about not meeting Stella. Part of me wants to. Have her to myself for an hour to just talk, get her help making sense of my thoughts. Another part of me doesn't want to at all.

I like Stella. I appreciate her blunt questions. She forces me to think, to reflect. To figure out what I *truly* think, not just what I *should* think. She radiates calm and kindness. She feels safe, seems like a warm and reliable person.

But at the last group therapy her questions were very intense. She also demanded answers, inhaled every word I said. It felt off. She didn't seem like herself.

And last week I saw her in Vällingby. *I thought.* She was standing below our apartment building staring straight ahead, as if she was thinking about something sad.

Maybe she was just headed to the mall for some shopping, maybe she lives nearby. Maybe it was just someone who looked like her.

Either way, I have a lot of homework today, *that's* no lie. *Maybe we can meet an extra time next week instead.*

"Is there room?" I'm pulled out of my thoughts and look up. Fredrik is smiling down at us, Victor and Mehdi right behind him.

"Are you working on mechanics?" he continues.

"Yes, we are," Johanna replies. "Join us."

I'm glad I don't have to go anywhere.

We sit here often. At Stories café outside the library. It's more comfortable than the group workrooms or classrooms.

The café is full of students. It's noisy, but that doesn't bother me at all. Most of the tables look like ours, strewn with open textbooks, notebooks, calculators, pencil cases, napkins, old coffee mugs, and soda bottles. It's wonderful. I love everything about college life. *Even the stress of exams.*

"Do you want some coffee, Fredrik?" Mehdi asks. "Victor's buying."

"Yes, please," Fredrik replies.

Johanna bounces up. "I need some coffee. Want some?" she asks me. I shake my head.

"So, Einstein, have you come up with any good solutions to question three?" Fredrik says after they leave. He gives my hair a gentle tug.

"Well, what do you think about page fifty-three?" I answer. The book is in front of him, so I bend over him to flip through it. He makes no effort to move. I feel his gaze on my neck, making it hard to concentrate. I can't find the right page. He helps me and his hand grazes mine. I glance at him over my shoulder, laugh nervously, and toss my hair. He looks into my eyes.

"They're almost green," he says.

"What?" *Do I sound as breathless as I feel?*

"Your eyes. They're nice."

"Thanks." My cheeks are burning. Embarrassing. Embarrassing. *Embarrassing.* I hate blushing.

"And your hair is so beautiful. Is that black your real color?"

He loops it around his finger.

"Witch black, as my mother always says."

"Maybe you've bewitched me."

I'm the one who feels like I'm under a spell. When Johanna thuds down onto her chair, the spell is broken. I self-consciously back up again. Fredrik takes his coffee from Mehdi and smiles at me. I smile back.

When I'm with him, life feels easier. He makes me forget. Forget that Dad is dead, that Mom is so demanding, that it's really difficult sometimes to be social.

Fredrik's hands circle around his coffee cup. He says it's cold in here. *He's right, I'm freezing, too.* His hands are quite large. Big hands that feel so good when they're touching my back, cupping my butt, caressing my thighs. I'm staring at them. His fingers are long. I blush again. Turn even redder when I look up and meet his eyes. I suspect he knows exactly what I was thinking. He chews on his pen, sweeps his hair to the side.

He is absolutely perfect.

Mom would despise him.

We discuss things passionately, we laugh and spend at least as much time talking about other things as we do mechanics.

"Are you from Falun?" Mehdi asks.

"Borlänge," I answer.

"Maybe we've bumped into each other there," Fredrik says. "But just didn't know each other yet."

"Where would we have done that?"

"At the Peace & Love festival. I was there in 2011."

I laugh. *Do I sound hysterical?*

"Surely you were there?" he asks.

"No, I was not."

"Why not? You lived there. It's not exactly a big city."

"We could hear all of it from home."

"That's not the same thing," Victor says.

"I'm not really a festival person," I say.

"Oh, come on," Fredrik says.

"It's true," Johanna says.

Fredrik looks at me curiously.

"We should do an experiment," he says.

"Am I gonna like this?" I wonder.

"Come with us to Way Out West next summer. Maybe you're a festival person and you just don't know it."

"Yes, do it," Johanna bursts out. "I'm going, too."

"Have you all considered the possibility that I might get lost?" I say. "You'll end up spending your time searching for me instead of seeing any bands."

They roar with laughter at me. "I guess we'll just have to make sure you stay close." Fredrik balances on the back legs of his chair and won't stop looking at me.

"I won't know a single song. Or any of the artists."

"That's a long ways off now," Victor says.

"I could freak out," I say.

"Freak out?" Johanna raises her eyebrows and grins at me. "That would be interesting."

"This is a conspiracy," I complain and have never felt happier in my whole life. *Except for that night, when I made out with Fredrik and felt his hands on my body.* I wonder if he's thought about it as much as me. I believe he has. *I hope so.* I want him to think about me. In that way. Like I think about him. And I want to do more than just kiss next time. Much more.

"Do you think we've got you beat yet?" Medhi says. "Fredrik never gives up once he gets something into his head."

"And where are we going to stay?" I say.

"I have an uncle in Gothenburg," Victor says.

"We can all crash there."

"We've crashed at Victor's uncle's the last few years," Fredrik says. "He's used to it. But sleeping arrangements will be tight."

Again, that smile.

"That's fine," I say.

One person who would definitely not think that was fine is my mother. She would be furious. If she even knew I was considering sleeping in close quarters with a young, handsome guy, she'd have one of her outbursts. *They've only got one thing on their minds, Isabelle, remember that.* Is it terrible for me to say that's exactly what I'm hoping? I'm already wondering how to get away without her finding out. I definitely can't tell her where I'm going, then she'd give me hell. I haven't forgotten how she reacted when I planned to slip away to Sälen with Jocke. *The boy who kissed me in the car outside our house.* Somehow she found out and threatened to report him for rape. Jocke stayed away after that.

But I have the right to break free sometimes, don't I? I am twenty-two years old, after all. I'm a virgin. *In more ways than one.* It can't be wrong to do what I want. For once.

Long before the lunch rush begins, we think we have most of the assignment figured out.

"I'm hungry. Shouldn't we just get some food here before this place gets overrun?" Johanna looks over toward the counter. There are already a few people in line. Within half an hour, the line will snake all the way around the entrance hall.

"Good idea. No need to go out in that crappy weather. Are you staying?" I say to the guys.

"Me and Mehdi have to go," Victor says. "Our group is having a lunch meeting." He grimaces as he looks outside, and sees rain pouring down. We wave as they go.

"I brought some food," Fredrik says, "but I don't want to go out there."

Yes!

"Get in line, Johanna," I say, "I'll take care of the table."

I stand up. I raise my arms over my head and stretch. I notice Fredrik watching me. His gaze slides slowly over my body. *Over my breasts.* I pretend I don't notice and stretch a little more. I run my hands through my hair. The shirt I'm wearing is tight and low cut. As I stretch, the shirt rides up to reveal a bit of my stomach. I'm glad I chose to wear it with my light blue stretch jeans. I think I look pretty good. And judging by the way Fredrik's staring, he does, too.

I put my pencil and eraser in my pencil case. Gather up the used napkins, coffee mugs, and papers we were making our calculations on. I bend over the table. Accidentally brush against him and lean over to reach some scraps on the other side. I can feel him put his hand around my waist, on my hips. Steadying me. I linger for a moment. *Longer than I need to.*

"Everything all right?" he murmurs.

"Uh-huh." I look into his eyes again. Put my hand on his shoulder. I want to stay like that, but it feels silly. I go over to a garbage can and throw away the trash.

When I go back to the table I look out through the big windows. Rain is streaming down outside. It's almost cozy. Calming. Feels like no evil could reach me in here. A childish feeling, I know. But I am childish.

A movement outside makes me take a step back and look again. Is that Stella? A woman in a gray coat and a colorful scarf, holding a red umbrella. I've seen her before, below our window. Long, dark brown hair.

It's her.

It's Stella.

Why?

There's no reason for her to be here.

Does she know I lied? Does she know I'm not sick?

Mom could be right. There could be something wrong with Stella's questions. But Mom is always worried about me. She always assumes the worst.

I stand there, hiding behind a pillar. I see Stella walk along the windows outside. She stops occasionally and tries to see inside.

"Bella?" I hear Fredrik's voice. "Are you coming?" He approaches me and puts a hand on my arm. He reads me like an open book, sees what I feel with a glance. I wonder if he sees all of it. My anger, my hatred for my mother. What if he likes me anyway?

"What is it?" he asks.

"Nothing," I say. "I just thought I saw someone I knew."

He stands behind me and stares out. Stella is hard to see.

Nevertheless, I get the impression that she has a purpose, that she's searching for something. Searching for someone.

Searching for me.

Goosebumps rise on my arms, and I wrap them around me. I feel Fredrik hug my upper arms.

"Who is it?" he asks.

I see her pause, as if stopping to think for a moment. Then head down the stairs and disappear toward Valhallavägen.

"No, I was wrong," I say. "Come, let's go buy something to eat." I take Fredrik's hand as we go back. I squeeze it tight.

Stella

This is wrong. My behavior is abominable. I walk along the windows outside the entrance to the library at KTH. I try to see inside. It is impossible in this downpour.

I'm glad no one sees me. Glad nobody knows what I'm doing. Is this how a stalker feels? I suppose. The shame grinds away at my stomach. My inability to let it be, to restrain myself. The kick I get from crossing my own line makes it even harder to stop.

What madness it was to come here. Ridiculous. How many students are there? Thousands. Even though Isabelle told me she often sits at the café near the library, the odds are that she's not there. She could be anywhere on campus, which is as big as Old Town. She could be at home. She could be out of town.

But this isn't crazy because of how unlikely it is for me to find her. I shouldn't be here at all. I should not be trying to contact her outside therapy. I've never done such a thing in all my years as a therapist. What would I say if I met her? How would I explain what I'm doing here? I'm grateful she didn't see me sneaking around.

Finally, the bus arrives and I hurry on. I sit at the back and ride toward Fridhemsplan. I lean my head against the cool window and close my eyes. Thinking about my irrational decisions. Thinking about Isabelle.

About Alice.

When I got her message canceling our appointment, I felt both disappointed and impatient. How am I ever going to get any answers? I can't wait any longer.

The bus stops at Fridhemsplan. I hurry off and open my umbrella. My lunch hour is almost over, but it wouldn't have been faster to take the car.

I'm not that hungry, but I should eat. I have time to make it into a café for a change.

I hunch over in the wind, stare down at the sidewalk as someone approaches. I move to the right without looking up. Still, I receive a hard knock in the side. I'm about to tell them off when I notice the woman looks familiar.

"Stella," she says. "It's me, Eva. We met here in the park a while ago."

"Oh, hello again," I say, hiding my irritation.

"Terrible weather, isn't it?" Eva grabs my arm and pulls me under an overhang. "What a nice umbrella you have."

"Thank you, I like it. Definitely makes me visible to traffic." I shake and fold it. I nod to the Coffeehouse by George next to the pharmacy. "I was headed in. Would you like to join me?"

Eva answers yes and follows me. We buy coffee and Danish pastries and sit down by the window. We make small talk about the weather, and I ask if she lives nearby. She tells me she's visiting some acquaintances and only in town for a short period.

"I have to apologize for last time," I say. "I probably didn't seem altogether sane." I laugh awkwardly.

Eva puts her hand over mine.

"Life isn't easy," she says. She sounds sincere and compassionate. "What happened to your daughter, well, I can't even imagine. I don't even understand how you were able to go on. Did you have any more children?"

"A few years later. A son. With my current husband."

"I'm so glad to hear that. You have somebody to take care of."

"I do. But I've never been able to forget. Never stopped wondering. And I always imagined I'd have a big family. It didn't work out that way."

I don't know what made me tell her that. I've reconciled myself to it. Yet here I am thinking about it again. What once seemed obvious no longer does.

"What stopped you?" Eva asks and takes a sip of her coffee. I taste my latte and ponder.

"I was very happy when I got pregnant again," I answer. "But terrified, too. What if I suffered a postpartum psychosis? What if I couldn't hold on to this new life? What if I'm actually just unsuitable to be a mother? I might be a terrible mother?"

Henrik was twenty-nine and I was soon twenty-six when the pregnancy test showed a plus sign. I, or I guess we, had been sloppy. Once again I was irresponsible. For a short time I was a mess, but then I realized it was a gift. Milo was a much-longed-for baby.

"It's normal to wonder," Eva says.

"Maybe," I say. "You're probably right."

"So how did it turn out?"

"He's the best thing that ever happened to me," I answer. "He is my everything. I love him. It's wonderful to be his mother. But I've been overprotective. I'm always worrying too much."

"Why is that?"

"It's my fault my daughter disappeared." I say it quietly. I don't want anyone but Eva to hear me. "I was careless. I left her alone for a few minutes. I swore never to make the same mistake with Milo. In playgrounds, in stores, I never let him out of sight. He's rarely allowed to go anywhere on his own. He, of course, thinks I'm such a huge drag."

Eva laughs. "My daughter is the same. All mothers go through that as their children grow up."

"We talked about trying to have more children," I say. "But I reached the point where I realized I didn't dare."

I sit quietly for a moment. "My biggest fear is that something will happen to Milo."

"That's not strange at all," Eva says. "But what about your daughter? You said you think you've found her? That's incredible."

"I know I've found my daughter. I *know* it's her. And this time I refuse to let her go." I look into Eva's eyes. "I refuse to let her disappear again."

It's liberating to say it out loud.

I feel like Eva understands; this stranger is actually the support I need right now. It's an incredible relief to be able to talk to someone without being met with distrusting, doubtful eyes. Not having to weigh every word. Not being told that I'm not like myself, or that I'm making things up. Finally, I feel like someone believes me.

She even seems to have tears in her eyes. “I feel for you, Stella. I really do. You haven’t had it easy. But what are you going to do now?”

“I don’t know,” I say. And I don’t know why I tell her, but I do. “I’ve been following her. I have to know what she’s doing. I have to see what her life is like. It’s wrong, I know, and I feel ashamed for it. But it doesn’t matter. Everyone thinks I’m crazy anyway.”

Eva says, “I know what you’re going through. I lost a child, too. She passed away a very long time ago. No one should have to endure it. So I understand you. Never give up.” She looks at the clock, stands up, and looks at me intensely. “Do you hear me?” she says. “Don’t give up.”

I look after her as she leaves the café. Eva has lost her child; she knows what it’s like. She understands me, doesn’t judge me or think I’m acting irrationally.

I realize neither of us ate a bite. The Danishes are still on their plates.

Stella

The next morning Milo and I are sitting at the kitchen table. After breakfast I'll drop him off at school, then head on to Norrköping. This is going to be a good day; I can feel it. And I need it. We all need it.

I know I'll find out something at Sven Nilsson's. Something concrete, something tangible. Something that was overlooked, and it will prove I'm not living in a fantasy world.

I look at Henrik, standing at the kitchen counter. Yesterday I told him Sven Nilsson promised to show me the files from the investigation into Alice's disappearance. I didn't want to lie to him again. I want to prove to him that he can trust me.

Henrik was far from sure the visit was a wise move for me. I haven't been at my most stable lately. He didn't say that, but I know he was thinking it. But then he changed his mind. Said he hopes it helps me find some closure.

"I'll be late this afternoon," he says, drinking the last of his coffee. He pats Milo on the shoulder, and I follow him to the door. Watch as he performs his usual ritual. He ties his shoes, pats his pockets, and makes sure his phone and wallet are in place. He puts on his jacket and readjusts his tie. Picks up his briefcase and grabs his keys from the bureau in the hall.

"You look tired," he says. "Are you sure you need to go?"

"Yes, I am," I answer.

"Can't it wait for another day?"

"I want to get it over with. And he could only meet me today."

"Maybe I should come along."

I readjust his shirt collar. "Why? You said you have meetings all day. Important meetings, too, apparently."

His suit fits like a glove, his tie is beautifully knotted, he has on new shoes. He's newly shaven and handsome and successful-looking.

His phone rings, and he picks it up. He apologizes, turns halfway and answers. He smiles and laughs.

"I'm on my way. Yes, I am. I'll see you in ten minutes."

He puts his phone in his pocket and looks at me.

"Sure you can handle it?"

"I'll be fine."

"I'll be late today."

"You already said that."

He walks toward the door but stops there.

"By the way, I won't be able to take any calls the whole day. Text me if you need anything, and I'll get back to you as soon as I can, okay?"

In other words: *Keep an eye on your phone. Make sure you're back by the time Milo gets home. Please don't forget.*

"And if there's an emergency—"

"There won't be," I interrupt him.

"And eat before you leave," he continues. "I noticed you only drank some coffee."

He disappears through the door.

"Do you want any more, Milo?" I ask when I get back to the kitchen.

"Nah." He finishes his sandwich before he says, "Are you and Dad getting a divorce?"

"Why do you say that?"

"You never used to fight," he says. "Now you do all the time, even though you think I can't hear you."

"I don't agree with that. Not all the time."

"Both you and Dad seem angry. And sometimes you look sad."

"We're not getting a divorce," I say. "We're just discussing some stuff right now. And we don't always see things the same way. It's not the end of the world. I love your dad, and he loves me. Okay?"

Milo doesn't look convinced.

"Are you done?" I ask.

He nods.

"Then let's get going."

I drop Milo off at school. Wave to him and then get back on the road. I've canceled all my appointments today. They're going to start to talk at the clinic. Maybe they already are. I can't keep on like this, neither at work nor at home. That's why this meeting with Sven Nilsson is so important. After all this, I deserve a little good news. It's awful that Milo is worrying about a divorce. That's the last thing I want. I'm happy with Henrik, and he feels the same way about me. I'm sure of it. Despite everything.

It's overcast in Norrköping. I grab the bag of cinnamon buns I bought, open the car door, and hurry across the parking lot through the rain toward a row house. I ring the doorbell. After a while, a tall, skinny man opens the door. He's aged, but I recognize him. Twenty years ago his hair was thinning, now there are only a few white tufts left behind his ears. His pants hang loosely on his thin body, his shirt is only half tucked in.

"Sven Nilsson?" I say.

"That's me," he answers.

"Hello, I'm Stella Widstrand."

He looks at me uncomprehendingly. Am I at the right place? It's him, I'm sure. Has he forgotten about my visit? I try again.

"Stella Johansson?" I say. "We talked last week. You told me I could visit today; it's concerning the investigation into my daughter's disappearance."

No reaction.

"It's about Alice?"

He jerks as if I've woken him from a trance.

"Yes, please come in. What are you standing there for? Come in, come in."

I follow him into the kitchen. It's neat and tidy, smells like freshly brewed coffee and something else. The faint smell of an elderly person and their urine.

"I brought buns," I say, holding up the bag.

"How lovely. Come in. Sit, sit." He's taking down some coffee cups when a short, dark-haired woman enters the kitchen. She looks at me.

"Sven?" she says with a slight foreign accent. She takes him by the elbow and speaks more loudly. "Sven, are you having coffee with someone?"

He looks at her, smiles distractedly.

"Are you having coffee? C-o-f-f-e-e?"

"Coffee?" Sven Nilsson says. "Yes, coffee, that's right."

She takes the coffee cups from him and puts them on the counter. Sven takes the buns to the kitchen table and sits down next to me. The woman serves us coffee and leaves the room. I wonder who she is.

"Well, so you've driven all the way here from . . ."

"Stockholm."

"Yes, Stockholm, that's right. Goes pretty quick on the E4. When there's no traffic."

"Yes, it was no problem at all."

We continue to chat about the road, about my drive from Stockholm, about how rainy the autumn has been. Aren't they all rainy? But that means there'll be plenty of wild mushrooms to pick. The pride of our Swedish forests. And berries, there's sure to be a good crop this year. And how was the road? You drove in from Stockholm? Have you been out to the woods yet, found any mushrooms there, the pride of our forests?

He repeats himself a number of times. Seems like he wants to drag out our visit. Maybe he's lonely and just wants to talk awhile. I want to cut to the chase, but hide my impatience. We spend a little more time talking about the sights of Stockholm and the traffic. In the end, I can't wait any longer.

"Sven?"

"Yes?"

"You said there was a tip? I'd really like to know what it was."

He looks at me as if he has no idea what I'm saying, and it gives me the sudden urge to express my frustrations physically. I want to slap the old man until he wakes up. I take a deep breath instead.

"Strandgården, 1994," I say. "A tip that you didn't follow up? You said you had information. You saved all the files."

"The investigation, yes." Sven Nilsson lights up. "The files, absolutely. Come with me."

He stands up and stumbles a few steps to the side before he gets going. He leads me down a corridor, into an office. Inside there are stacks and stacks of boxes. The desk is covered with paper and an ancient computer with an enormous screen.

"Now, let's see. Johansson, Strandgården, 1994." His voice sounds sharper, more alert. "What you're looking for should be in one of these three boxes." He points to them. They are at the far back, close to the closet.

"Unfortunately, this old man isn't as spry as he used to be; I need to sit down for a bit. Make sure to look in the red binder. And don't hesitate to ask for help."

I squeeze his fragile, veined hand.

"Thank you, Sven." It makes him happy.

After he leaves the room, I move box after box to reach the three he pointed to. The boxes are heavy, and I'm sweaty and out of breath by the time I get to the ones I want.

I squat down and open the first box. It's full. I take away the top layer of newspapers to reveal more of the same below.

Newspapers, lots of newspapers.

Local newspapers from 2010, some from 2012, and some saved since 2002. I flip through them, trying to make sense of it. The pages are full of red marks. Seemingly random circled headlines, sometimes just a single word, arrows drawn between different articles. It's impossible to discern the pattern. If there even is one.

Does this have something to do with the investigation surrounding my daughter? I lift out the newspapers and sort them on the floor. I have to ask Sven Nilsson about it.

At the very bottom I find two overflowing binders. I open the red one. Old bills from 2006. I scroll through each page, but find only junk. This must be the wrong box.

I look at the top again, *Strandgården, Johansson, 1994*. Odd. I open the next box, same thing. Newspapers, bills, bank statements, and old tissue paper. Same thing in the third box. I don't understand. I look at the clock. Two hours have slipped by.

I stand up, intending to go ask Sven Nilsson where the boxes I'm looking for might be, but a woman is standing in the doorway. She's tall and slim and her face resembles Sven's. She seems angry.

"Who are you, and what are you doing here?" she says.

"Oh, hello," I manage to get out. "Sven invited me to—"

"When did you talk to my dad?"

"I called on Friday and—"

"Did you talk on the phone?" She looks up at the ceiling and sighs. "I told them that he shouldn't be talking on the phone with anyone other than the family." She looks around at the mess in the room. "What are you doing here? Why are you rooting around in this junk?"

I feel like I've been caught trying to steal something.

"Your father was in charge of an investigation many years ago that involved my daughter. He invited me here to take a look at his files. But there must be some kind of mistake." I point to the newspapers behind me. "I was just going to ask him about it."

The woman stretches out her hand.

"Excuse me, I should probably introduce myself. My name is Petra Nilsson. Let's go have a talk in the kitchen."

I follow her. As we pass by the living room, I see Sven Nilsson sitting in an armchair. He's sleeping with his mouth half open.

What's going on?

"Please have a seat." Petra Nilsson points to the same kitchen chair and I take a seat there again. Waiting. She pours more coffee for us and sits opposite me. "I suppose Dad promised you you could take a look at an old investigation?"

I nod, don't trust my voice.

"Unfortunately, he suffers from Alzheimer's. He has his good days, but most of the time he's just not there. Maybe that sounds harsh, but sadly it's true."

I'm not sure if I groan audibly, but Petra Nilsson looks worriedly at me.

"We put him into a facility for a while, but he got so depressed. Lost his appetite, wouldn't eat. He does much better here at home, but he needs twenty-four-hour care. We can't be here all the time. And you know how it is with home-help service."

I feel punctured. I just want to get up and leave. Or collapse on the floor and cry.

"There are no files left," Petra Nilsson continues. "We threw all that out a long time ago. As you can see, he's filled those boxes up with trash instead. We let him, because it seems to calm him. I'm sorry you came here unnecessarily."

I put my head in my hands and press my fingers hard against my eyes. A headache drums behind my forehead. If Daniel were here, his reaction would have destroyed me. Or if Henrik had come with me. I would have been incapacitated.

"He sounded so lucid on the phone," I say. My hands are shaking. I clench them tightly a few times.

"As I said, he has better days. I'm sorry." Petra Nilsson makes a resigned gesture in the direction of her father.

"Please, let me talk to him. He said there was a tip they never followed up." I can't let it go. Can't give up without being totally sure.

"It's not a good idea."

"Just a few minutes."

"He shouldn't be upset. It's not good."

"My life depends on this," I say.

Silence hangs heavy between us.

I feel Petra Nilsson's hesitation, her dislike. She looks like she'd rather throw me out. I prepare myself to keep arguing.

"Of course," she says.

"Thank you," I say. "You have no idea what this means."

"But I warn you, he'll say what you want to hear. It could be just about anything. You'll see."

We go into the living room. Sven Nilsson is awake and sitting up again.

"Dad." She gently touches his arm. "What's your theory about Olof Palme's murder? They say he was assassinated, but that's not the whole truth, is it?" Sven Nilsson lights up and bangs his fist on the armrest.

"Prime Minister Palme? It never should have been a murder investigation in the first place." He waves his forefinger in the air and looks at me. "Prime Minister Olof Palme faked his own death. Assumed a new name. He's probably living in Rio by now. With his mistress. But nobody knows exactly where he resides. Those idiots couldn't even manage a little simple police work. Hi, honey, who are you?" He peers at me. Sven Nilsson has never seen me before. I'm a complete stranger.

Petra Nilsson studies my reaction. Almost triumphant, but regretful, too. *There, you see, I was right.*

I go forward and crouch down next to her confused father.

"My name is Stella; we met many years ago. You led an investigation into the disappearance of my daughter. Alice." I take his hand and stroke it gently. Willing him to remember. To help me. To have just one moment of clarity.

"Alice, Alice, Alice," he exclaims. "And you I remember."

My hope returns. Sven Nilsson leans toward me. He gestures for me to lean closer. I ignore the smell of urine and bend forward.

Sven Nilsson whispers, "Alice Babs, Alice Timander, Alice in Wonderland, who disappeared, but came back, got small, got big. Rabbit rabbit, he's late, he's late."

He continues babbling, louder and louder, and my hopes sink like stones. I stand up, apologize to his daughter for disturbing him. She follows me out into the hall and yells for the home-help assistant to check on her father.

"Yes, he loves digging into 'old cases,'" Petra says, making air quotes. "I'm really sorry, I wish he could help you."

We go to the door. Sven is talking in the background. I stop and listen.

"Tiny little girl who disappeared, never to be found. Stones, stones, find calm, find peace. There was something, there was. The man who knew was drunk as a skunk, he just wanted to talk, oh blah blah blah."

The woman inside hushes him.

I pull my sweater around me, and as I'm turning to go he cries out.

"Stella. Stella Johansson. He wanted to tell me everything. But he died suddenly. Suddenly he died. Before he could say more." I look at Petra Nilsson. She rolls her eyes, opens the front door, and ushers me out.

Kerstin

I'll be in Stockholm soon. At Isabelle's. Thank God. I detest taking the train. Hate it. You never know who you're going to end up next to. It never fails, it's always someone who loves to talk, who has a lot of opinions, who chews too loud or spreads out onto your seat. And why is the train so packed on this normal Wednesday? What an awful trip. But the car is undependable, and it would be even worse to end up stranded on the side of the road. I had to leave it at the garage. Just hope I won't end up swindled out of the last of my savings.

Does that boy on the seat opposite me have to be so freaking loud? Parents nowadays. They're turning their children into little monsters. Letting them lash out, scream, disturb people, behave like animals. Good manners are a thing of the past. There's no respect or even basic courtesy.

I throw another angry look at his mother. She doesn't notice. She doesn't care. The boy kicks at my purse, but she pretends not to notice. In the end, I take matters into my own hands. I grab his legs and tell him to cut it out. The boy starts to cry, and the mother gets upset. She looks at me like this is my fault. Adults aren't *allowed* to take part in society today, it seems. Just let everyone run amok.

I take my bag and leave my seat. I find a free spot in the next car. Not too long left now.

I haven't told Isabelle I'm coming. She'd try to stop me. I wanted to leave yesterday, but I had to work. I have no idea if she's at home or not. Worst-case scenario, I'll have to wait in the mall until she gets home. I asked for a spare key to her apartment, but haven't received it yet. We'll take care of that now.

If she'll let me, I'd like to look over her schedule. Get some insight into her days. I'm not sure she can manage on her own. She needs all the help she can get from her old mom.

The train rolls into the Stockholm Central Station. I wait until everyone leaves the car before standing up. That horrible boy and his equally dreadful mother are walking down the platform. Our eyes meet, and she gives me an angry look. I disembark, cross the platform, enter the station. There are always so many people here. A voice over the speaker is announcing train delays, a carpet of human laughter, human language, human shrieks. The smells strike me from every direction—coffee, pizza, freshly baked cinnamon buns, perfume, sweat.

I ride the escalator down, headed for the subway. On this lower level it's even worse. An inferno. People pour down the passageway in a single torrential stream. Everyone is in a hurry, everybody is in a rush, everyone is running. Hurry hurry hurry. It stresses me out to no end.

At first I head in the wrong direction, toward the commuter trains. It's a project just to get turned around and make my way back. I'm soaked with sweat by the time I make it to the subway entrance. I search through my purse for my train card. I'm a little afraid of these subway turnstiles. Large glass gates that open and close the very moment you pass through them. But I manage. Take another escalator. Wait for the green line that goes to Vällingby.

I hop on the train and find a free seat. I'll call Isabelle when I get there. Not a minute before. Then we'll see how my daughter lives her life when she thinks I'm far away.

Stella

Wednesday morning creeps up. I meet my patients, they sit in my office and talk, telling me about all of their problems and difficulties.

I don't listen.

I'm not present.

I don't care.

I'm an unfit therapist.

While my patients talk, I fantasize about quitting. Moving to another country. Changing my name. Starting over from scratch.

Yesterday was disastrous. The setback at Sven Nilsson's is impossible for me to handle. I thought I would get some answers. Find out what exactly they did to locate my daughter. I thought he'd have some sort of clue I could follow up. Something that proved I was right. All those files thrown away? Is that even legal? Probably not. What an insult. To just throw everything away. To throw away every document about Alice. About a life.

About my child's life.

Maybe there never were any documents. Maybe Sven Nilsson just said what I wanted to hear, as his daughter claimed.

Was there a tip? There must have been. The possibility that it was all just an old man's delusion is too much to take. Sorrow washes over me like the tide over a deserted beach. It makes me sad that I'm even capable of such a cheap metaphor. I feel ashamed of how I indulge in self-pity.

Henrik got home late yesterday. He asked how it went and I told him what happened. There was nothing there. It's been too long, the person who gave the tip is dead by now. It wasn't the whole truth. I couldn't bring myself to tell him Sven Nilsson has Alzheimer's. I'll save that miserable detail for myself.

Henrik said he was sorry and wondered how I felt.

I said it wasn't too much of a surprise. What can you expect after twenty-one years?

Henrik helped me pull down the steps to the attic. I put the diaries back in the paisley handbag in the far corner, behind the boxes.

Henrik was considerate toward me all evening. He made me coffee, he lit candles, massaged my back, and put a blanket over me when I was on the sofa. My previous mistakes were forgiven and forgotten. One of the things I love most about him is that he never holds a grudge.

Besides, I think he was relieved there were no more straws for me to grasp at. And happy I didn't seem to take it too hard. Because *he* always knew that I wouldn't find any new information after such a long time. I am deeply grateful that he didn't come with me to visit Sven Nilsson.

I know he wants me to find some closure. More than anyone else. Because he loves me. Because he wants the best for me, wants me to feel good.

It's just that he doesn't believe she could still be alive.

Henrik is considerate, he cares about me. But he is terrified of my reaction if, or *when,* I realize I'm wrong. As he said, what will it do to me?

We both know.

It's almost noon. Lunch soon. Then group therapy.

Finally, I'll see Alice.

Isabelle

I've come down with a terrible cold. My head feels like it's stuffed with wet cotton, I'm hoarse and have a fever. Not a high one, but enough to stay home. *I don't want to.* But Mom has taught me that you don't go out when you're sick. You have to put on warm socks, lie down, and rest.

So here I am. I compelled Johanna to take notes for me at the lectures I'm missing. She's not as thorough as I am, but at least she's better than Susie.

The doorbell rings. I look at the time. Twenty past twelve. I wonder who it could be. I roll out of bed and glance in the mirror. I look a little pale. *No makeup on.* I push my hands through my hair and go into the hall. When I open the door, I'm glad I'm wearing my jean leggings and not my old pajama pants. I do regret my huge red hoodie and lack of makeup.

Fredrik is leaning against the wall outside my front door with a big smile.

"How did you get in the front door without the code?" *Couldn't I come up with something better to say than that?*

"Somebody went out, and I went in." He walks past me into the hall and pulls off his jacket. "I heard you were bedridden. I've come here to wait on you hand and foot." He hands me two cartons of Ben & Jerry's.

"Ice cream?" I say.

"My mother always told me ice cream is the best medicine. Didn't yours?" he says.

"She's more into disinfectant," I say. "And tea."

"Strawberry Cheesecake is my favorite. But girls are suckers for chocolate, so I brought some Chocolate Fudge Brownie, too."

He takes off his shoes. His chinos sit low on his hips and tight around his legs. He's got on a floral-patterned T-shirt in pink and blue. I can feel the goofy smile on my face. He looks up at me and smiles back. I put the ice cream on the hallway table and take a step closer to him. I don't know how it happens, but suddenly we're standing with our arms wrapped around each other.

"Hey," I whisper.

"Hey," he answers and draws me even closer. I stand on my tiptoes, lay my face against his neck.

"I may infect you," I say.

"I'll take the risk," he replies and caresses my cheek. "You're so damn cute when you smile. Those dimples."

"You think so?"

"All of you is cute."

This is the best day of my life.

I go into the kitchen with the ice cream and grab two spoons, while Fredrik looks around the apartment. I put the ice cream and spoons on the desk in my room, grab some clothes out of a drawer, and shout that I'm going to the bathroom. I pull off the hoodie, spray on some perfume, and change into a lacy black bra. Then I put on the new shirt I bought on Friday with Johanna. My leggings look good; I keep those. Before I go out I put on some mascara and look at myself in the mirror. I turn around and study my backside, squeeze my breasts and rearrange them.

When I get back to the room, Fredrik is sitting on my bed. He's leaning against the wall eating ice cream. He sucks on his spoon slowly and looks me over. *The change of clothes was a good move.*

"Are you gonna share?" I say and sit down next to him. He holds out the spoon, and I have a taste. "Didn't you go to the lecture today?"

"I left early," he says. "I missed you too much."

"Are you going back after lunch?"

He gives me a long look. "You need somebody to take care of you."

Yes, yes, yes, I need a lot of care.

We eat the ice cream, he feeds me, we discuss which kind is better and why. *He was right, I like the chocolate best.* He puts the ice-cold spoon against my bare stomach and laughs out loud when I howl. I slide down so

I'm almost lying down, and he does the same. I'm enjoying the tension between us, and his gaze, and how he teases me.

He asks if I want to watch a movie, and I tell him to choose one. He starts my computer, and I put the ice cream in the freezer. Do a little happy dance while I'm in the kitchen.

"I think I'm getting sick, too," he says when I get back into the room.

"Oh no, is that my fault?"

"Probably. As punishment, I'll expect you to take care of me."

He grins at me, and I throw a pillow at him. He grabs my hand, drags me into bed, and tickles me. I gaze into his eyes, hoping he'll kiss me. But he just looks at me. For a long time. Then he pulls away. He puts the computer on the tray next to him in the bed. I find a comfortable position while he starts the movie. He asks if I can see, and I say I can.

A romantic comedy. I wasn't expecting that. We lie next to each other in silence. I can only think of how close he is. I want to touch him everywhere. Feel his body against mine.

At one point in the story the characters do exactly what we're doing, sit down and watch a movie. I wonder what Fredrik is thinking. I scoot closer and lay my head on his arm.

The movie goes on; the main characters have sex.

I snuggle closer to Fredrik and put my leg over his legs, bend my knee and rub my foot up and down his shin. He mumbles and puts his hand on my leg, keeping it still.

"You don't seem particularly sick," I whisper. I draw my knees upward, higher and higher, feeling what I sensed when I looked down just now. *A hard bump under his pants.* He moves and looks at me.

"So you think I'm cute?" I tease.

"You make me crazy," says Fredrik quietly. "Every second next to you without touching you is torture."

"Do it then." I lick my lips, watch his eyes narrow.

"Aren't you sick?"

"Not *that* sick," I answer and climb halfway onto him.

I tuck my hair behind my ear. Feel his hands slide around my waist. I slowly run my tongue over his lips, testing. Then I kiss him. And he kisses me.

We make out. His tongue in my mouth, mine in his. Passionately, then slowly, then impatiently again. His hands are in my hair, on my body, around my butt. I draw back; my cheeks are on fire. He is so sexy lying there looking at me. Happy, pleased with himself. I want him. I want.

I lie on his arm, braid my hand with his, and sigh. *Happily.* He laughs. I pick up my phone, take a bunch of selfies of us. Some where we lie side by side, one where he bites my ear and I laugh, one where we kiss each other, and then a few where we make silly faces.

"Do I get extra credit for showing up with ice cream?" he mumbles with his lips against my hair while I look through the pictures.

"Of course. Hashtag 'world's best boyfriend.' Maybe." I hold my breath waiting for his response.

"Too bad my girlfriend ate all the ice cream on her own."

"No, I didn't!"

He laughs when I pinch him and brushes my hair aside before kissing me.

We make out again. Our tongues, our lips, we enjoy ourselves for a long time. Knowing more is coming makes me almost explode with horniness. Happiness.

And my heart pounds harder. Blood pulses into my genitals. I put my hand over his stomach, put it on his hard-on. I feel it getting even bigger. I rub it with my fingers, squeeze it. He swallows, breathes my name.

My phone rings. I look up, and Fredrik grimaces. I giggle and kiss him. Ignore the phone when it rings again. Whisper that it's not important. He pulls me on top of him. His hands on my rump. I press myself against him, rub against him, and enjoy feeling how hard he is. I whisper in his ear that I want him.

He puts his legs around me and rolls me over. Laughs when we hit the tray. He sits up, closes the computer and lifts the entire tray onto the floor. I look at his body as he sits astride me. He grins, pulls off his T-shirt, and lies down on top of me again. Kisses me more passionately now, caresses my breasts. His thigh is between mine; we rub against each other.

It starts ringing again.

I look up and swear out loud. I rarely do that, and it sounds a little stupid when I do. Fredrik tries to pull me back into bed. I turn off the sound on my phone before landing in his arms again.

"Where were we?" he murmurs and caresses my breasts beneath my shirt.

I unbutton his pants, put my hand into his underwear and feel it. It's hard, but also quite smooth. My fingers just fit around him, he's warm and nice, and I wonder how he tastes. I want to lick him, but don't dare. I touch him, rub up and down. Fredrik breathes faster, I feel him growing even more. How big is he?

He pulls off my shirt. I straddle him. My breasts show through my bra, and I drag my hands over them, can see him staring at my stiff nipples. He pulls down the waistband of my pants and puts his hand against me, strokes. I move a little so he'll have better access, feel his fingers under my panties. I moan out loud, wiggle my hips to get out of my pants. Fredrik tries to help and when one of us knocks the phone onto the floor we hear it vibrating.

"Who the hell is calling all the time?" His voice hoarse and impatient.

"I'll turn it off." I lean over the bedside and see a lot of missed calls and the first lines of a text on the screen.

All the heat in my body is extinguished. I sit on Fredrik, the phone in my hand, and enter the code. He sits up halfway. I can feel him kissing my neck, his fingers are on my nipples.

"Fuck," I whisper as I read the messages.

"What is it?" Fredrik says. He kisses me on the shoulder, pulls down the straps of my bra. I close my eyes hard and let him continue for a moment. I'm close to weeping from frustration. And disappointment.

"Fredrik, you have to go," I say, pushing him away. "You have to go now."

Stella

She never showed up. And these are the most meaningless ninety minutes of my life. A total waste.

What is the conversation about today? No idea.

Is she avoiding me? Why?

After group therapy, I have a session with Ulf.

"I know I shouldn't, but I couldn't help it. It just happened."

Ulf keeps talking. I hear him, but I'm not listening in the way I should. I wonder how many times I've heard the same thing from him over the last two years.

"Couldn't or didn't want to?" I ask.

Ulf seems shocked. He can hear from my tone that I am annoyed. Once again he's been out too late, drunk too much, and come home wasted. Once again, he started a terrible fight with his wife. And everything is his mother's fault, because she wasn't there for him when he was little. Boohoo, boohoo, poor little Ulf, such a poor misunderstood sad little boy.

He's a pig. An immature self-absorbed male pig.

What he needs most is a kick in the ass. Or a punch to the jaw. I've suggested he try another form of therapy or even get a hobby. Maybe try AA. He doesn't take the hint. And then he goes on and on, week after week. I can't stand to listen to this anymore. And for the first time ever I regret my choice of career.

I throw away the notebook I've had on my knee. "Ulf, what the hell are you doing here?" I hiss. "Really? What is the point of this?"

"What do you mean?"

"Why do you keep coming here? What do you get out of it? You're wasting my time."

He gapes at me, as if he has no idea what I mean. I tell him that he's been stuck in the same rut since I first met him. He's rolling around in the same shit and making the same pathetic mistakes again and again. He uses the same transparent excuses every time. His contempt for himself is focused on his poor mother every week. I tell him if he doesn't grow up and take responsibility for his own life, he'll always be stuck with the same problems.

"What the hell do you know about it?" he says.

I stand up, march over to the door, and throw it open. I scream: "Do not come back. I never want to see you here again."

Ulf hurries out, his face red. John, a colleague of mine, is standing in the corridor; Renate is behind the reception desk. Both stare, whisper between themselves. I slam the door shut.

Soon someone knocks.

"Come in," I say.

Renate opens the door. She looks at me grimly.

"Stella. I've always liked you. But it might be time to take a break."

I know she's thinking about Lina. They're all thinking about Lina. They believe that there are, in fact, grounds for the allegations. That the investigation is warranted. Especially now, after I've thrown out Ulf. Everyone sees it on me. Everyone knows.

I have a serious problem.

Alone in my office. Shrunk down into my chair, behind my desk. I turn off the computer, pick up the phone. I call her. Repeatedly. No answer. Again and again. Then I give up. I lean back and close my eyes. My phone dings, and I scramble for it. It's a text from Henrik.

> What! You're kidding me?! Jennie, you are amazing! Just pick the restaurant. I bet it's going to cost me.

I don't understand. I read it several times. Why is my husband writing to someone named Jennie? I don't know who Jennie is. And why is he taking her to a restaurant? What does it mean?

Henrik has been busy with his phone quite a bit lately. More than usual. He says it's work. Comes home late. Often. He gets texts and answers calls weekdays, weekends, daytime, and late at night. Was Jennie the one who called yesterday morning? Who he was picking up?

Yes, I'm on my way, I can hear him saying, remembering the morning. *Yes, I am. I'll see you in ten minutes.*

Jealousy twists around inside me.

Are you and Dad getting a divorce?

My stomach aches. I write an answer. Erase it. Start over. Delete that, too. Have to think a long time before I can write something that's not hysterical.

Sorry, I'm not Jennie. Would gladly take you up on the dinner offer though? ;)

My phone lies there dark, silent. The wait feels like an eternity. He should call me. I wonder what he'll say. How his voice will sound. It takes a while before I get his text.

Wrong person. :) I'll be home after 7.

I stand up and walk around the room. No explanation, no apology. He's pretending as if nothing happened, as if I don't know now that he's got something going on with that Jennie. I grab hold of the large ceramic vase in the corner, the one I got from Henrik when the clinic first opened. I lift it over my head and throw it onto the floor.

It shatters loudly.

But I was hoping it would be even louder. Hoping the sound would drown out my anger, overcome it. But it's not even close.

Screaming at patients and throwing vases: it's not enough. Nothing helps the powerlessness and fear I feel.

Kerstin

I'm sitting on a bench below her house, calling. Isabelle doesn't answer. I call four times without reaching her. In the end, I send a text message. After a while, I get a text back. She says she didn't hear the phone, she was resting. She'll come down and open the door. Just has to get dressed. She was home anyway. But what is she up to?

The door opens, and I stand up. A young blond guy comes out. His pants look like they might fall off any moment. His hands are pushed deep into his pockets, and he doesn't give me more than a quick glance. Today's youth don't even possess common courtesy. It's enough to drive you mad.

She comes soon after that. My big, wonderful daughter. I hug her hard and take a close look at her. She seems tired. And what is she wearing? I've already noticed some changes. Since I've surprised her, I see how she's really dressing these days. The top and the jeans hug her every curve shamelessly. The young, firm breasts, the narrow waist, the buttocks and crotch. And her top is too short. It slides up when she moves, shows her stomach. It's indecent. She looks like a whore. She might as well walk around naked.

It's that Johanna's fault. She's a bad influence. All of this is that little minx's fault. With her dyed hair and her nose ring, a person like that shouldn't be allowed anywhere near my Isabelle.

I inspect her closely. Her eyes are glazed. Has she been drinking? Did she start doing drugs?

"You'd best be careful dressing like that," I warn her. "Boys only have one thing on their minds. You should know that by now."

I see her tense up. Apparently that was the wrong thing to say.

"Are you getting enough to eat?" I ask instead. "Have you lost weight?"

"Yes, Mom, I am. And no, Mom, I haven't." She holds the door open for me.

We ride the elevator up in silence. Isabelle seems to be in a really bad mood. She unlocks the door and walks into the apartment. I look around. It's quite nice, lots of light. I've only been here a few times, but wish I could visit more often. I wish I had been here to help her move in. Hang up her curtains and pictures, help her make it a little homey. The sort of thing a mother is supposed to do. But lately Isabelle needs to prove this newfound independence of hers. To me it looks more like a revolt. I'm trying not to show how much it upsets me. But it's hard. I'm quite upset. It hurts me terribly when she distances herself from me.

Isabelle puts on some coffee, and I go to the bathroom. After I relieve myself, I rummage through her medicine cabinet. I don't find any drugs or contraceptives. Then I look into her room. The blanket has been thrown carelessly across the bed as if it were made in a hurry. It makes me very apprehensive.

Is she sleeping with someone? With many people? My very own daughter, has she started with that sort of thing? The boy I saw come out of the front door, who was he? Was he visiting Isabelle? Was he in her bed? Does she offer herself to just anyone? Screw them like a hooker, twisting beneath them while they pant and moan and take what they want from her? The thought of Isabelle in that situation upsets me. Disgusts me beyond all limits. Doesn't she understand how sad I am? But she is still weak. She still needs her mother. I have to straighten her out.

I turn and go to the kitchen. I can't let her see on my face that I know what she's up to. I sit down at the dining table and watch her putter about.

"That confounded train, all that sitting made me swell up, you see?" I pull off my sock and demonstrate by poking my swollen foot. My finger leaves a clear impression.

"Wouldn't you have been sitting at home anyway?" Isabelle says without even looking in my direction.

These constant taunts. This total lack of respect. Who has she become? Why couldn't she stay my sweet little girl forever? My daughter, who once thought I had all the answers, who thought I was irreplaceable, who I comforted and patched up. Now I'm just an embarrassment. Tiresome. Stupid. Annoying.

I swallow my vexation. "How are your studies going?"

"They're fine. I've passed all my tests so far." She sounds pleased.

"I'm proud of you," I say. "Dad would have been so proud, too."

I raised her, I remind myself. This change is only temporary. Everything will be fine.

Isabelle pours us some coffee and sets out a carrot cake.

"This tastes very good," I say.

"I made it yesterday."

"You've always loved baking. You got that from me. Do you remember how we used to bake together?"

"Why are you here, Mom?"

Only now do I realize that Isabelle is hoarse.

"Do you have a cold?" I put my hand on her forehead. It's a bit hot. Is she pregnant?

"I'll be better soon," she says.

"Maybe you should lie down? Rest a little. I'll make tea."

"But, Mom, I barely have a fever."

"Have you been home all day?" I wonder.

"Yes, I have. And I followed all your rules. To the letter. I stayed in, put on warm socks." She raises her foot and waves her toes. "I've been drinking warm things, I've washed my hands eight extra times, and I've changed all the sheets." Now she smiles at me for the first time. My sweet daughter smiles and I feel all warm inside. It's as if the clouds part and the sun finally comes out.

"That's my girl," I say, smiling back. "Good you didn't go anywhere. Not even to therapy?"

Her face clouds over again. Why does she have to be so sensitive? But we have to get through this. That's what motherhood is all about, right? To bring things up even when it's tiresome. To educate, guide, and protect.

"I just told you I was home all day."

"You know, I don't want you going there again."

Isabelle pushes her chair backward. Making an awful sound as it scratches against the floor. She stands, goes over to the sink, and turns her back to me. I know she's angry, but she'll see reason in the end. She just needs to listen to me. She just needs to come to her senses and be reasonable. I only want the best for her, nothing else.

She will understand. She has to.

Isabelle

Panic is rising inside me. I'm so angry that I'm afraid of myself.

Why does she always do this? Show up, intrude, poke around inside my privacy? Why can't she ever let me have any peace?

I focus. I don't want to let my anger take over. *It's difficult, because I'm furious.* If I don't get a handle on myself, swallow this rage, everything will just get worse.

Or is it like Stella said? That it will get worse if I don't set any boundaries? If I constantly avoid showing my mother that she can't control me.

This is my life. These are my choices. I have to be honest and say it like it is. I turn around and look at her.

"That's not your decision," I say calmly. I don't usually stand up to her. I almost never disagree. But I can't live like this anymore. A good relationship has to be able to withstand some conflict. Mom looks shocked by my statement. She's insulted. Offended. I can see it on her. Her face collapses; her mouth hangs open. She looks like I've slapped her. And I can already see she's preparing one of her speeches about how sad I make her and how ungrateful I am after everything she's done for me. How she's raised me and guided me my whole life.

But there has to come a day when I do as I please. If she's raised me and guided me as well as she claims, there's no reason for her to worry.

Mom slams her cup down and looks at me harshly. "I don't like that tone you're using with me."

"I'm an adult now," I say. "I make my own decisions. And this is something I want to do. For my sake and nobody else's."

I'm proud of myself. My reaction proves that therapy is helping me. I dare to say what I think, despite the risk of a conflict. That's a huge step for me.

Mom is not impressed. She looks at me as she did when I was little. *When I gave her headaches. When she walked away because I disappointed her.*

She puckers her lips. "There are things you don't know," she says, ignoring me. She rearranges the crumbs on the table. "Come and sit down."

I hear that unyielding tone in her voice. Even though I don't want to hear what she has to say, I sit down anyway. I know it will be tiresome. And I wish she wasn't here. I wish Fredrik had stayed with me. We would have been lying in bed right now. Naked. We would have made love to each other. It's not ugly or dirty like Mom says.

I think about it all the time, feel it in my whole body. Fredrik and I will make love. We'll make love for hours. We'll make love all night and then we'll continue making love all day long.

And making love is what we would be doing right now.

If Mom hadn't showed up.

I never should have read that text, should have been brave enough to make her wait, not dropped everything just to please her. *Hindsight is twenty-twenty.*

Mom interrupts my thoughts. "Your therapist. Stella. She has a problem."

"How do you know that? How do you know anything about her?"

"I'm worried about you. I can tell that you've changed."

"Could it be because I found out I was living a lie? My whole life?"

Mom recoils. She clenches, struggling not to lose control.

"What do you mean by that?" She whispers the words. Tears form in her eyes. I feel like I'm five years old. I want to placate her. Want to make amends. Want to be forgiven and make everything okay again.

"Hans wasn't my father, right?" I continue. "Not my real father. It hasn't been easy to find that out."

Mom sinks down in her chair, puts her head in her hands. Time for drama.

"I know. Honey, please forgive me. I understand that. I do. And I really hoped I wouldn't have to tell you this."

And Mom continues. She tells me that my therapist is in hot water. And as usual she uses that particular tone of voice, a mixture of anger, mockery, and pleasure. Sometimes I wonder if there's something wrong with my mother. Something seriously wrong.

"A former patient tried to kill herself. She was a little younger than you, and of course the parents were just crushed. They'd seen the warning signs, but still they trusted she was getting help. That's what can happen when a young girl puts her life into someone else's hands. A stranger's hands."

"How do you know this?"

"I've been worried about you for a long time now."

"Yes, you said that." That's no surprise. *She always is.* She's told me how worried she is every time we've talked recently.

"I've been researching her on the Internet. Found this information. I even talked to the parents. They seem like such nice, genuine people. And I refuse to stand by and watch while this happens to you. Do you understand?" Mom takes my hands in hers and cocks her head to the side.

"I'm not suicidal, I promise," I say, trying to laugh. Mom looks stern. Her hands squeeze mine so hard it hurts. I pull away from her grip.

"I trust Stella, Mom. It *could* be that those events weren't her fault. We don't know anything for sure about what really happened."

"Isabelle, now you listen to me. That woman is crazy. She is not normal. She is sick." Mom looks at me seriously before continuing.

"She lost a child many years ago. A little girl. She was very young then. And it's not clear what happened. She was a suspect, but they never found any evidence. She ended up committed. In a psychiatric ward. An insane asylum. How someone like that becomes a therapist is beyond me. She could be a murderer. She could have killed her own child."

I interrupt, but Mom makes a gesture for me to be quiet.

"I think she's convinced herself that you're that girl," she says. "It's tragic and sad, I can agree with that. But you should know one thing, that woman is dangerous. Stella Widstrand is sick and dangerous."

I think of Stella's monologue about grief and shudder.

Mom leans over the table. "You told me she's been asking about your upbringing. And about me. Right? Maybe she even asked you if I'm your real mother?"

My unease grows. She has done that. She has been a little too curious about my background.

Mom says, "As a therapist, she has a lot of influence on people. And she uses it. Because she herself doesn't feel good. She makes you question everything, even what you know is true. What if she's been following you? What if she's watching you?"

I saw Stella standing downstairs, outside the apartment. I saw her at KTH.

Mom is right.

What I've taken for dedication must be something else. Some kind of sick obsession.

At the same time, she made me feel safe. And I liked her from first glance. But do I dare trust my judgment? I can't make sense of it. It doesn't add up.

Mom comes around the table and puts her arm around me.

"I want you to be careful. I don't want to lose my little girl, surely you understand that?"

I look up at Mom. She's difficult, even awful sometimes. But she's my mother. And she does care about me. She'd do anything to protect me.

"I know, Mom," I say. "I promise to be careful."

Stella

Wednesday evening, I'm sitting on the sofa watching Henrik. He's leaning against the kitchen bar talking to Sebastian, Pernilla's new guy. He laughs and gestures. After sixteen years, his ways are so familiar. And yet tonight I see him with new eyes. I'm waiting for him to slip up, to reveal something. I should ask him straight-out, but I'm too cowardly. It's not like me. But if he denies it, I'll feel even more crazy and paranoid than I already do. And if he confesses, I'll be destroyed.

Sebastian and Pernilla picked up Milo after tennis. I ordered a pizza, opened a bottle of wine. When Henrik came home he greeted them and went upstairs to change. I followed him with the wineglass in my hand.

I asked him how his day was. He said it was good. He took off his dress shirt and pulled on a T-shirt. I stood there while he put on his old, washed-out jeans, buttoned them up. Placed his phone in his front pocket.

I thought he'd say something about the text message. Tell me about Jennie. Give me an explanation. Something, anything at all. He said nothing. Just wondered what we were celebrating, with a glance at my wineglass.

Love, I guess, I said.

Before we would have laughed. Now he pasted on his formal smile and asked if we were going to head down before the pizza got cold.

He seems relaxed standing there in the kitchen. Satisfied and happy and relaxed. Who the hell is Jennie? Does he laugh like that with her? What does she look like? Is she younger, hotter? How long has it been going on? How many times have they slept together?

Pernilla throws a pillow at me and I snap out of it. She's reclining at the other end of the sofa, observing me. She pokes my leg with her foot.

"What are you thinking about?" she says.

"I just had a long day, that's all," I answer and take a deep gulp of my wine. Pernilla grabs hold of my hand, pulls up my shirtsleeve. I have light bruises around my wrist.

"What did you do?"

Though I don't want to, my eyes turn toward Henrik again. He's laughing loudly at something Sebastian is saying. He turns to me, stares straight into my eyes. His face is serious. He looks away, turns his back.

"Did he rough you up?" Pernilla asks.

I feel hot inside just thinking about Saturday night. How Henrik kissed me, held my wrists, and took me on the floor.

"Love marks?" Pernilla chuckles. "I can see it on you, you might as well tell me."

"There's nothing to tell," I say and smile. "Nothing happened on the bedroom rug. Nothing at all."

Pernilla laughs. She doesn't see that my smile isn't real. Has no idea that there's another woman in Henrik's life, and I know about it. He looks at us again.

"Having fun?" He settles down on the armrest behind me.

"Have you started doing yoga, Henrik?" Pernilla says.

He laughs. "Yoga?"

"I've heard it can be amazing." Pernilla looks innocently at him. "Soft bedroom rugs are good for exercise."

"Pernilla!" I protest and glance at Henrik over my shoulder. He looks at me, then at her. He seems unwilling to discuss the topic. Why? Does he only think about Jennie now? Does she satisfy him more than I do?

"Maybe I'll have to try sometime," he says and takes my wineglass away. I take it back and refill it. I'm entitled to relax after everything that's happened. I'm entitled to feel good, even if only for a little while. And I'm happy, right? I converse. I'm pleasant and balanced. Good old, safe Stella. She's so fucking wise and understanding. Always so harmonious.

· · ·

Later I lean toward Henrik, stroke my hand over his thighs, and whisper in his ear that I want him. I promise I can make it better for him than anyone else.

He wrinkles his forehead, asks if I really need any more to drink. He looks at Pernilla. She makes a grimace toward him. *That's enough.* I pretend not to notice the glances between them, but what's the matter with them? What is wrong with everyone?

Henrik pushes my hand away and takes the wine bottle out to the kitchen. Pernilla says it's getting late. I empty my glass in one gulp.

I hear Milo and Hampus discussing a basketball tournament in Estonia.

"Mom," Milo says, "can I go on my own?"

"Your own?" I say.

"You always come with me," he continues. "You know how many chaperones there are. Please."

"I don't think that's a good idea," I say.

It takes a second. Less than a second. Fear paralyzes me like a nerve agent, makes me difficult, stubborn, and angry.

"Oh, Mom, don't get mad. It'll be all right, you know it will."

Pernilla says, "Hampus is going, so maybe—"

"You're not going abroad on your own," I interrupt. "You're only thirteen years old." I take a drink from Pernilla's wineglass. She looks at me, looks toward the kitchen. Then she stretches for her glass, but I keep it out of reach.

"It's just Estonia," Milo says.

"We'll talk about it later."

"Mom."

"Milo. We'll talk about this later, I said. Stop the whining, goddamnit."

Henrik enters the living room. He looks inquiringly at me, then at Milo.

"Dad, I want to go to a basketball tournament on my own, but Mom just gets angry."

Henrik puts a hand on Milo's shoulder. "It'll work out," he says.

"Over my dead body," I say, splashing wine on the sofa. "Never." I try to wipe the wine away with my hand, but I just spread it out even more.

Henrik wants to take the glass. I jerk it away and spill more wine.

"What are you doing?" I say and hear myself slurring.

Pernilla strokes my arm but I push her hand away. Again she and Henrik look at each other.

"Stella, calm down," Henrik says. "You don't have to scream. We'll talk about this some other time. Okay?"

"I'm not screaming. I'm not screaming. And there is nothing to talk about."

"You don't understand anything, Mom," Milo howls. "Nobody else's fucking mother goes along. You're always there. I hate it."

He rushes out of the living room.

I scream after him: "Those other fucking moms don't know you should never leave your child alone!"

I'm sitting on the sofa. Alone.

Milo has locked himself in his room.

Sebastian, Pernilla, and Hampus went home. I heard Pernilla's whispered question to Henrik, asking if there was anything she could do. He said thank you, whispered something back, I couldn't hear what. Then he knocked on Milo's door, was let in, and closed the door.

I'm sitting alone. I can feel myself sinking.

I can't control the fear.

I can't control myself.

I can't control anything.

I am sick.

Stella

My eyelids are glued together. I have to force them open with my fingers. I slept in my shirt, and it smells like sweat and alcohol. My mouth feels dry, and it reeks.

I'm lying on the bed in the guest room. Sometime during the night, Henrik must have come in and put a blanket over me. In any case, I have no memory of doing it myself. I don't even remember going upstairs and lying down. My head starts pounding when I sit up. I review how much I have to be ashamed of, and I feel sorry for myself for a while. Then I go to our bedroom.

The bed is empty. I look at the watch still on my wrist. It's not much past seven. I pull off my shirt and underwear. Take a long, hot shower. Then I brush my teeth, floss, and gargle.

Afterward I hardly feel like a new person, just not quite as bad off. I put on makeup, but I still look sallow. I put my hair up in a high bun. Put on the earrings Henrik gave me as a wedding gift. Feel an onslaught of nostalgia and magical thinking.

I open the closet. Choose a straight, knee-length dress with slits up both sides. Navy blue. Three-quarter sleeves. I look at myself in the mirror. Look away.

Henrik is sitting at the kitchen table reading the newspaper. He's dressed and ready. Black dress pants, a blue-gray wool sweater. He stands up, says good morning and asks how I slept.

I don't respond. I try to press out an apologetic smile. Henrik doesn't react. He folds up the newspaper and goes out into the hall.

We are on either side of an abyss.

He shouts to Milo to come down. I watch them through the window, how they talk to each other. Henrik laughs and pats Milo on his shoulder. They jump into Henrik's Range Rover and drive away.

I find some water-soluble painkillers in the cabinet above the sink; I put two into a glass of water. I sit down at the kitchen table, watch the tablets dissolve with a hiss, and swallow it all.

Fog on the windows, traffic crawling over the Traneberg Bridge, fog hanging over the gray waters of Lake Mälaren. It looks just like the day that all of this started.

I stop at St. Eriksgatan outside the front door to the clinic. I sit in the car and watch the traffic. People passing by on the sidewalk. I stare out the window.

A hard knock on the windshield startles me.

A traffic cop.

He says there's no parking here and gestures toward a sign down the street. I start the car and speed away.

I sit with a latte in the window of a Wayne's Coffee looking out over the square at Hötorget. Watching all those fruit and flower stalls and their customers.

Then I drive around the city for a while, wander into stores, look at shoes and clothes but tire of it.

Drive around on the southern side of the city.

Drive to Skogskyrkogården, the Woodland Cemetery. Park. Stay in the car for a long time before climbing out.

I walk to Alice's grave. I squat down and look at the stone with the white dove and text below.

Alice Maud Johansson, Forever in Our Hearts

I don't even remember the last time I was here. Maybe I should have brought flowers, but then it strikes me how stupid that thought is.

Alice isn't here.

My daughter has never been here.

Henrik and I are eating dinner at the kitchen table. I picked up some baked potatoes with Swedish shrimp salad from Erssons Deli on my way home so I wouldn't have to cook.

"Can you hand me the butter?" Henrik says.

"Of course."

"Did you have time to wash my jeans?"

"Yes," I answer, "they're hanging in the laundry room."

"The shirts, too?"

"In the closet."

"Thank you."

"You're welcome."

It feels silly that I even bothered to light the candles. The mood between us is far from romantic. He gets a text message. He apologizes and picks up his phone. He writes back, puts it down again. We eat in silence. I don't have the energy to care if it's Jennie or someone else. At the moment, I'm thinking mostly about my son. Milo is at a friend's house doing homework. I wish he were home. I want to talk to him about what happened. I want to ask his forgiveness.

"How are you?" Henrik asks.

"I'm tired," I admit and put down my silverware. The food is tasteless.

"Did you go to work?"

"Yes."

"Was that wise?"

The question annoys me. Doesn't he think I'm capable of working? Does he think I'm unfit?

He can see what I'm thinking. "Just wondering," he says. "Did you have any contact with Isabelle?"

"No," I say. "No, I haven't."

He nods. Gives me something that resembles a smile.

"Will you be able to let go of this, Stella?"

I wish he wouldn't ask so many questions. I'm not in the mood for a cross-examination.

"I think so," I say.

"Maybe you want to talk to somebody. Maybe the woman you used to meet, Birgitta? Is she still working?"

"I don't know."

I stretch my hand over the table. I have to try, even if it's already too late.

Henrik takes my hand. He looks at me and seems to be thinking through what he should say. He's going to tell me about Jennie.

The doorbell rings. He lets go of my hand, gets up, and goes out to the hall. I hear him open the door, talk to someone. He comes back.

"Stella." His tone of voice makes it clear this is something serious. I stand and go around the table. I see a black woman and a short white man standing behind her in the hall.

"Stella Widstrand?" the woman says. She seems to be around my age. Tall and slender, not a single wrinkle on her face. We shake hands. Her fingers are a little cold. Her handshake is firm.

"Yes, that's me," I say.

"My name is Olivia Lundkvist. I'm a detective. This is my colleague, Mats Hedin."

He doesn't seem friendly. He's shorter than Olivia Lundkvist, with a thick neck and square body. Strong upper arms and a scarred face. His eyes are suspicious. He looks at me the way Per Gunnarsson did.

I don't say anything, just wait for them to explain why they're here.

"Can we sit down somewhere?" Mats Hedin says.

Henrik shows them to the living room. They settle down in a corner of the sofa. Detective Olivia Lundkvist looks around.

"Nice place you have," she says. "Very nice."

"Thank you," I say and remain standing.

"Do you know why we're here?"

Am I supposed to say something? And if so, what? I glance at Henrik; his brow is furrowed.

"Not a clue," I answer. "Does this have something to do with Alice? I mean, Isabelle? Did something happen?"

I can feel Henrik staring at me.

"Maybe you should sit down," Olivia Lundkvist says.

I try to swallow, but my throat is dry. Henrik pulls me down on the other end of the sofa and puts a hand on my leg. *Settle down.*

The rest of the conversation is like an out-of-body experience. I hear the questions. I answer them. But it's like I'm somewhere else. When Henrik puts his head in his hands, I realize that everything is in ruins.

Isabelle

There's a knock on the door to my room. Mom is up, but I'm still in bed. The door opens and a shock of purple hair comes into view. Johanna looks in and grimaces. *At herself, for yesterday, I suppose.*

"Your mother made breakfast, Bella," she says.

"Okay, I'm coming."

"I'm gonna do this first."

Johanna jumps down beside me in bed. She hugs me and kisses me on the cheek.

"Thank you," she says.

"For what?" I say and wipe my cheek off with my sleeve. Johanna laughs and says, "Isabelle Karlsson."

"Yes?"

"Do you know that you're completely out of it sometimes?"

At first I feel a bit hurt. But her huge smile tells me what she means.

"You're right," I say, laughing, too. Mom comes in and sits down on the side of the bed. She looks at Johanna; she looks at me. She puts her hand on Johanna's cheek and then on mine.

"Crazy kids," she says. "You are lovely. But off your rockers."

I know she doesn't think Johanna is a good influence on me. The nose ring, the purple hair, the tight clothes, and the boys and the parties, and everything, everything, everything. But then I think of what happened yesterday. I take my mother's hand and squeeze it. Our eyes meet.

Everything is good again.

That rarely happens. *If I'm being honest, basically never.* But right now I feel proud of my mom. She's usually so worried and strict, full of contempt for anyone who isn't. And when Johanna came home after the policemen left, I thought Mom might explode. Johanna's boyfriend, Axel, had dumped her, and afterward she got drunk. She drank a ton of shots, a bunch of beers, and a bottle of wine. As soon as she came through the door she threw up on the rug in the hall.

And Mom saw it all.

I felt so sorry for Johanna. But it was embarrassing as well. I closed my eyes, waiting for Mom to start chewing both of us out. I knew exactly what she was going to say. *This is what happens when you aren't careful, this is what comes from running around with boys* who only have one thing on their minds, *this is what happens when you break away from your parents, when you think you're more grown up than you are.*

Mom didn't say anything.

Not a word.

Instead, she picked up a bucket and helped me hold Johanna while she continued to vomit. Mom wiped off Johanna's face with paper towels (she was very careful with the nose ring) and whispered comforting words to her. Like she used to when I was little and hurt myself or felt ill.

Then Mom and I helped Johanna into the bathroom. She draped herself over the toilet and vomited again. And as she did, she started to cry. She lay on the floor and sobbed. Tears flowed, and she screamed that nobody loved her, she didn't want to live in this shitty fucking world anymore. Where everyone treats each other like pigs, especially all the fucking men who are worse than pigs.

Mom stroked her hair and said that everything would be fine now, that she didn't need to be sad. Mom had me grab a towel and clean clothes. I did as she said while Mom undressed Johanna, put her in the bathtub, and showered her. Then she dried her off, helped her get on some sweatpants and a long-sleeved T-shirt. We took her under each arm and dragged Johanna into her room. Mom tucked her in and sat by her until she was asleep. I stared at them from my seat on the floor. And that's when I felt it.

Mom was sitting there so calm and safe, stroking Johanna's hair and cheeks, humming quietly. I don't remember ever loving Mom more than I did in that moment. I don't think I've ever been so proud of her.

And then, when Johanna fell asleep, we drank coffee in the kitchen. I told her I felt angry when she got here, but I didn't feel that way anymore.

"How do you feel now?" Mom said.

"You're the world's best mom," I said, hugging her. Mom cried, I think. *She almost never does that.* Her cheeks felt moist. We held each other for a long time. I asked forgiveness because I'd been so mean, and Mom said everything was fine now. Now that I'd asked for forgiveness.

Then she talked about the things we used to do together when I was little. Some I had forgotten, some I remembered quite clearly. It was probably our sweetest moment together since Dad died. It's a pity we couldn't be like that more often. Maybe it's my fault. Mom hasn't had it easy.

"If you want, you can come home with me for a few days," she said. "I don't want to force you, Isabelle. But I miss you, you know that."

I promised to sleep on it. Then we didn't talk about it anymore. We didn't talk about the visit from the police, either. It felt like that could wait, as if it were out of place in this moment. But Mom said she was open to discussing anything.

"I know I've been tough on you," she said. "But I will try to change."

I've been unfair to her. She isn't at all as horrible as I imagine sometimes. Maybe we'll end up with a better relationship? I think so. I want that for us. And I know Mom does, too.

"Come on, girls," Mom says. "Breakfast is ready."

She goes back to the kitchen and leaves us alone for a while.

"Your mother is something else," Johanna says. "If that had been my mom, I would have caught hell. She would have chewed me out. And then I would have had to take care of myself. No one's ever taken care of me like your mom did."

"She does that," I answer. "Mom likes to take care of people."

"Maybe that's why she works in health care?"

"I guess so."

Johanna wants to give me a kiss, but I push her away.

"Your breath stinks."

I throw off the blanket and climb out of bed.

"And you smell like farts." Johanna laughs and slaps me on the butt.

We go to the kitchen, sit down at the table. Mom has prepared a lavish breakfast for us. Coffee for me and Mom, green tea for Johanna. Juice and milk, yogurt, freshly baked rolls, and cheese and meats and spreads she's brought with her.

"Dig in," Mom says and sits down.

After breakfast, Johanna wants a smoke. We go out on the balcony while Mom clears the table and does the dishes.

"Do you want a cig or not in front of Mommy?" Johanna says.

"You know I hate smoking. It's disgusting."

"It's cool."

"I didn't know you started again."

"I always smoke when I'm depressed. It makes me feel better."

Johanna takes a deep drag and blows the smoke in my face. She glances in at Mom, who's bustling around the kitchen.

"Did you get rid of your virginity yet? I heard Fredde was here."

I wave away the smoke.

"How do you know that?" I say.

"That you're a virgin?"

"Oh, Johanna, you are so annoying. No, that Fredrik was here, of course."

"Your mother thought you had somebody here. I knew it had to be Fredde. Calm down, I didn't say anything. Not because I don't think your mom can handle it. She's a lot nicer than you made her sound."

"Yes," I say. "I guess she is."

"Well?"

"What do you mean?"

"Stop." Johanna pulls her jacket tighter around her. She squints her eyes at me and holds her cigarette in the corner of her mouth. She looks cool, in a way I never will. "Your secrets are safe with me. You know that."

"About what?" I say and still don't understand what Johanna means. She blows out a blue cloud of smoke against the sky. Looks down at the crotch of my sweatpants.

"Your virginity?"

I'm still not as comfortable as Johanna talking about these things. I've mostly listened to her long commentaries on the various boys and men she's been with. But when I think of how Fredrik and I got dressed in a hurry, how he pushed me against the wall of the elevator, and how we made out all the way down, how I wrapped one leg around his body, I do really want to tell her. He mumbled that we should have done it as soon as he arrived. Then we would have had time. We giggled and kissed again. Before he left he stroked my hair and my cheek and asked me to call him. I had to get myself together for a moment after that, rearrange my hair, before meeting Mom. *I feel warm inside just thinking about it.*

I look in through the window. Mom is busy sorting the dishes on the shelves above the sink. She turns around and looks at me as if she knows I'm looking. She seems happy. I wave to her and she waves back.

I turn to Johanna, lean against her and whisper, "Almost. It was sooo close. He is so wonderful. But then Mom showed up."

"Is he big?"

"What?"

"Tell me, I want to know."

"What do you mean, *big*? Do you mean . . ."

Johanna nods. I don't understand how she can ask such a thing, and I have the urge to tell her to shut up. But then we look at each other and burst out laughing.

It's cold outside but we stay on the balcony for a little longer. Johanna talks about Axel, but meanwhile I think of Stella. And what Mom said about her.

And about the police officers who were here.

They asked me about my psychotherapist, and I told them I thought I saw her outside my apartment and near KTH. But I'm not scared of her. *Not at all.*

However, I am afraid this has gone too far. Mom exaggerates her worries. She also talked to the police officers, a man and a woman. Mom didn't really say anything that's not true, but it didn't sound good. Stella will surely catch hell for this. And I think what I said might have made it worse.

I asked the police why they were asking questions, what they were planning to do. Why were they here, I hadn't called them. They didn't answer that. They said thank you and good-bye, we'll look into this. Don't worry. *But they already made me really worried.* I was supposed to tell them immediately if I heard from her again. I was planning on meeting her every Wednesday for a long time to come. But it didn't feel like the right time to say that.

Mom followed them out and continued talking to them in the hall. I couldn't hear what they said. Don't even know if I want to know.

I'm trying to put the pieces together. They don't fit. There's something about it that bothers me, confuses me. But I don't want to think about it. Not right now. I just can't. It will have to wait.

Johanna puts her cig out in a flowerpot, and we go inside again. Much to my surprise, Mom asks if Johanna and I want to play Scrabble. Johanna says she'd love to. And gives Mom a big hug.

My phone dings. I pick it up and check. A text from Fredrik.

Everything okay? Can't you come over soon?! Miss you! XO

I go into the bathroom and answer.

All is well here, just been really busy. Miss you, too! Longing for you. Call you tonight. XO

He answers immediately.

Longing for you, too. Come here!

As soon as Mom goes home, I'll take the subway straight to him and forget everything about dead children and police interrogations.

Stella

I've been accused of threats and harassment. Maybe unlawful pursuit and stalking as well.

Henrik's eyes. I can't stand to meet them. He looks at me as if I'm some madwoman he stumbled across on the street. He looks at me with disgust. A poisonous cloud of disappointment lies between us.

Detective Olivia Lundkvist asks the questions. Mats Hedin studies me with a fixed expression. I've been tied to the pillory, and there is no escape.

Yes, I know Lina Niemi.

Yes, she's been in therapy with me.

Yes, it was alleged that she tried to commit suicide, but that's not the whole truth.

No, I saw no sign that she was suicidal.

Yes, I know her parents think I crossed the line and was overly personal. That's not true.

Yes, I am aware that they reported me.

To the Health and Social Care Inspectorate. You know that, too. It's no secret.

Yes, I know Ulf Rickardsson.

Yes, he's in therapy with me.

Am I usually so personal with my patients? Everyone who works in this kind of profession is, to some extent. But not in the way you make it sound.

Not at all. That's not true at all. I never touched him.

No, that's not right, either.

I didn't scream at him. Maybe I raised my voice. He felt threatened? Physically?

My colleagues? When?

No, I took today off.

No, I forgot to inform anyone about it.

That's right. Isabelle Karlsson is my patient.

She participates in group therapy at my clinic.

I haven't cut off contact with her. Not yet. No, I *know* she's my daughter. Listen, I . . . Can't you at least listen to me?

I try to catch Henrik's eyes. He gets up and stands looking out the window toward the garden. I close my eyes.

Inhale. Exhale.

Yes, I have been to Vällingby.

Outside the building where she lives, yes.

I don't understand. What do you mean?

I have been to Borlänge, too.

No, I did not go onto the property. The neighbors are lying. It's a lie. No, no, I sat outside in the car.

I know she is studying at the Royal Institute of Technology. Only once.

I've called Isabelle a few times. Yes, I left messages.

Don't remember what I said.

I did not act unprofessionally in our therapy sessions. No, I didn't.

Meet me outside of group therapy? It was just a suggestion. Completely within the bounds of therapy.

Henrik turns to Detective Lundkvist. He still hasn't looked at me once.

"Does this concern a *current* patient who is accusing my wife of harassment and God knows what else?" he says.

"Yes, it does," Olivia Lundkvist replies. "Along with Lina's parents. There's a fairly high risk that Stella will lose her license. She's already been reported to Health and Social Care. And now there's a police complaint on top of that. It really does not look good for her."

Olivia Lundkvist looks urgently at me, with a kind of seriousness that says the guilty need to be reminded just how bad their situation is.

I've been judged in advance.

"What happens now?" Henrik wonders.

Olivia Lundkvist talks about a formal interrogation, a preliminary investigation; the decision of whether or not to prosecute will be made by the prosecutors.

It's quiet at home. Henrik left a while ago, not long after the police.

He asked me questions, too.

Why in the hell did I continue to keep things from him? How can I lie straight to his face time and time again? What makes me do it? What is driving me?

I told him that it was all a big misunderstanding. I said I would never intentionally subject someone to this. Least of all him.

Henrik wondered how it could be a misunderstanding. I admitted I've been following Isabelle, calling her and continuing to meet her. Contrary to what I told him. And apparently I still think she's Alice? I wasn't at work today, contrary to what I said. What did I do all day?

I was at Alice's headstone.

And Borlänge? What made me go there? Is there more he doesn't know? I tell him that I wasn't home that weekend he and Milo were in Nyköping. I was at Strandgården.

More lies.

Henrik pulled on his coat and slammed the door. I heard him start the Range Rover and drive off.

I'm lying on the sofa. I sit up and look out. Someone is in the garden. Somebody in a shapeless coat with their hood obscuring their face. I can't move. Can hardly breathe.

We stare at each other.

I close my eyes.

When I look again nobody's there.

A broken tarp has blown in and been caught by the tree. I stand up slowly and go to the window. I look out into the garden, inspecting every corner of it.

Have I started seeing things? Things that aren't there, which only exist in my own disturbed consciousness? What more did I imagine?

Alice?

The thought is unbearable.

I go out to the kitchen.

I open a bottle of wine. I drink straight out of it.

Stella

I wake up on the sofa with a headache. The wine bottle is gone. Henrik must have cleaned up after me. Probably so Milo wouldn't see how bad it was. My phone shows it's a quarter past nine. I see that Henrik texted me shortly after eight.

Text me when you wake up.

A moment later:

Stay home, promise me. I have to take care of something at work. I'll come home as soon as I can, we'll talk then.

No *I love you* or *xo* or *hugs*. No *it'll work out*.

Most of all, I want him to tell me everything will be fine. If he thinks that, maybe I can, too.

In my mind, I go over yesterday and the last few weeks. There's a lot I could have done differently. All of it, really.

That I continued to be Isabelle's therapist was a terrible lapse in judgment. It was wrong. My colleagues, my patients, they've all lost faith in me. I lack the ability to maintain professional distance.

I am no longer a psychotherapist.

I should be under the care of one.

I should be a patient.

Isabelle has canceled our last few meetings, and I understand why.

I followed her; I stalked my patient.

Daniel doesn't want anything to do with me ever again.

And my husband. The way he looked at me yesterday, as if I were a stranger. But I don't blame him. I've become a stranger, even to myself.

Henrik keeps his distance, he's cold and unreachable. And it is entirely my own fault. He thinks I've gone mad. That I'm mentally ill.

Why didn't I talk to him? Why couldn't I be honest?

Because I'm terrified.

This fear has been with me for more than twenty years, and it has ruined my life.

I'm afraid of myself, afraid I'm sick.

I'm afraid Henrik is better off without me, Milo, too. I'm terrified. And it is alienating. My fear is a self-fulfilling prophecy. I will never find out what happened to Alice. We will never see each other again, never have the chance to get to know each other.

Henrik calls around ten. I don't answer. Just stare apathetically at the phone. He hangs up.

Calls again. I don't answer. I realize I can't avoid him forever. I sit up. Feel queasy and rush to the bathroom. I heave and sob over the toilet, but nothing comes out. I go back to the sofa.

He calls a third time. I don't respond. Stare at the phone while it lights up and vibrates. His name, a picture of him smiling on the display. The phone slides across the table in my direction, as if it wants me to pick up. It stops glowing, stops vibrating.

I lean over it, see myself mirrored in the dark glass. That person is someone I don't want anything to do with.

That woman is insane. Disturbed. Sick. Psychotic.

Her blank and shiny eyes flash at me. Her mouth moves as if trying to say something. I strike her with my fist. Again and again until she shatters and falls to the floor.

Stella

The apartment building on the other side of the street. Near the mall. I'm here again.

I'm not sick, I'm not insane. I'm healthier than I've ever been in my life. What I'm doing is right. Beyond any choice, beyond any option. Beyond a doubt. The only thing left is the truth.

Alice. I'm here now.

I know you understand. My beloved daughter. We will be intertwined forever. Our bloodstream binds us together. You live. You live in me.

I feel your breath in every beat of my heart.

No one can stop me. No one can impede me. What brings me here is larger and stronger than anything else. Larger and stronger than me.

And now I see you. If only you'll listen to me. Listen for a few minutes. I know we have something special. I know I can reach you.

You're coming toward me. I see that you see me. You freeze. You stop. You don't look scared, but you are wary.

Why?

Trust me. Believe in me. Tell me you're mine.

I stretch a hand toward you, to show you I'm not dangerous. I know you understand. I know you feel it, too. You live in me, you always have.

You are here inside me.

In my blood.

Isabelle

I'm on my way home from the store. The sky is overcast, the clouds heavy with rain. I feel much better, no fever anymore. It felt good to get outside a bit.

Johanna is in school, but not me. I feel stressed because I've been absent a lot lately, but it's been cozy to be home with Mom, too. Still, I don't plan to follow her when she goes home today. I need some time by myself. Need to absorb everything that's happened. Maybe I'll go down next weekend instead. Or after my exams.

Stella. I think of her more than I'd like. I wonder what the police want with her. Will it be weird to go to group therapy next Wednesday? It feels like I haven't been honest with her. At the same time, it makes me uncomfortable that she followed me. *Given what Mom told me.* I don't want to think about it. I push away thoughts of Stella Widstrand and think of Fredrik instead.

I was looking forward to calling him from the store. Now I'm remembering how he sounded, the words he said, and I'm so tired of waiting. I'm counting the seconds until I'm in his arms again. *It may not have to be so long.* I smile to myself and wonder what I should wear. I cross the square and then the street.

I see her standing outside the building staring up at our window.

In the same way as last time.

She usually has on something nice, her makeup perfect, her thick, curly hair arranged just so. She usually looks so healthy. But not today.

Her hair is in a messy bun; she has dark rings under her eyes. Her dress is wrinkled; it looks like she slept in it.

I wonder what she wants. Why she came here. But then I realize the police probably talked to her. *She is angry with me, of course.*

"What are you doing here?" I say.

She almost stammers, as if she were unprepared to see me.

"I-I had to meet you."

"Why?"

She looks sad. Distressed.

She looks like she might break down.

"I just wanted to know what happened," she says. "I thought you liked our conversations? I felt we had something in common."

I look down at the ground. *Don't scrape your feet like that, Isabelle!* I stop. Straighten up. I force myself to meet Stella's gaze.

"I did," I say.

"But why didn't you come? Not on Monday or Wednesday? Why did you report me to the police?"

I don't understand. I don't know what she's talking about. Then I get a hunch. I glance up at the apartment, but don't see Mom behind the curtain, spying, keeping watch. *What has she done?*

I look at Stella again. She points to a nearby bench.

"Do you want to sit with me for a while?"

I don't want to, but still I follow her to the bench. I sit at a distance from her.

"Maybe you didn't know about that?" Stella says. She sounds understanding, but doesn't wait for answers. "It doesn't matter; I just want to clear up any misunderstandings."

"I didn't know," I say. "I'm sorry, but I didn't know."

"It's all right," she says and strokes my back. "I've thought about what you told me. About your upbringing, about your thoughts. The relationship between you and your mother."

"Okay?"

"I once had a daughter," Stella says. "A long time ago."

I recognize the look in her eyes. It was there when she told us about her grief. That tone was in her voice. As if she were desperate, as if she were driven by such powerful emotions that she lost control of them.

"She disappeared one day," Stella continues. "I never found out what happened. Everyone said she drowned. Everyone thought she was dead. Not me. I knew she was alive. Knew someone had taken her."

Stella looks into my eyes. I look down, can't endure her wild, intense stare.

"Have you ever wondered if Kerstin is your biological mother? Your real mother?"

I stand up from the bench. "I have to go now."

"Please, Isabelle, listen. Please let me finish before you go."

Stella roots around in her handbag and takes out a photograph. Her hand is shaking.

"Just look. This is Maria. I haven't told you about her. But you reminded me of her from the moment I met you. More than that, you're like copies of each other."

I look at the photo. It could be my sister.

"Maria is your aunt," Stella says and takes out another picture. "And here, this is a photo of you. Of my little girl, when she was ten months old. Look at her black hair? The ear? The dimple?"

She waits. Lets me look before going on. "Do you have any photos of yourself as a baby? I don't think so. I think you have a lot of questions about that time."

I've had enough. I don't want to see or hear more. Stella takes a toy out of her purse. A cloth spider.

"This spider was your favorite. You loved it," she says with tears in her eyes. "I believe you're my missing daughter." She stretches out a hand toward me.

"You're wrong," I say, taking a step back. "You are wrong. You are totally fucking crazy."

"I understand this comes as a shock."

"Stop!" I scream. "Stop following me. She was right; she said you would say this."

The buzzing in my head is getting louder and louder. I press my hands over my ears.

Stella stands and goes over to me. Hugs me.

"Who was right? Kerstin? You know, I want to meet her. I want to know what she has to say about all this."

"Why?" I hear I'm sobbing. "Why are you doing this? I thought you were good; I thought you cared about me. It felt like you were the only one I could talk to. But you've just been pretending. This whole time. You're sick in the head." I push her away. She falls back and sinks down onto the bench.

"Isabelle, if only you'd give me a chance," she pleads. "Think about it. You've wondered why you're so different, why she doesn't feel like a mother."

"I've already lost my dad. She's all I have left. And right now things are better between us than ever. What makes you think you can do this to me? Spread these lies?" I'm screaming again.

Stella reaches out her hand.

I slap it away.

"Go to hell! You're worse than Mom when she's crazy. She's not perfect but at least she's honest. You're a fake. You lie, you manipulate. Get lost and leave us alone."

Stella stares at me with pleading eyes and an imploring expression.

"I'm your mother," she says. "Your name is Alice. You are my daughter. I knew you would come back to me. I've been waiting for you ever since you disappeared."

I run as fast as I can. Reach the door, push in the code, tear open the door, and slam it behind me. I forgot the groceries. I look toward the bench. A shrunken woman sits there. Alone with her photos and a toy she says was mine.

Kerstin

I saw them. Couldn't hear a word, of course, but I didn't need to, I saw them. I'm so angry I'm shaking.

Is it strange a mother would want to defend her child at any cost? Is it wrong? Is it unnatural for a mother to react with rage when her child is threatened?

No. It's not wrong. It's natural. That's the way it should be.

Isabelle opens the door and enters the hall. I continue folding the laundry. She enters the room. I look up at her. She's crying. Standing there on the threshold not daring to go in or out. And she looks just like she did when she was little. She's my little girl again.

I drop the sheets I'm holding. I go to Isabelle and take her in my arms. She's sobbing. Her tears stream down her face, she sniffs and sniffs, she sobs and tries to catch her breath.

There, there, my little darling. Mommy is here now, and nothing can hurt you. That's what I should say.

That's what I usually say.

I usually stroke her hair and whisper comforting words. Show her I understand, that I'm here to help and support her, to talk.

Not this time.

I hold my little girl, I do. But I'm silent, don't say a single word.

I want Isabelle to know how dangerous that woman is, how sick and crazy she is. I offer no words of comfort, let fear work on her for a while. Now finally she has the chance to really understand. To toughen up and find the strength within. She's still weak. She needs me. Her mother. And I'm here. I will always be here for my baby.

Still, Isabelle doesn't understand much about life. But she will.

Stella

I lie on the floor in the hall. Lie on my back with my coat on, staring up at the ceiling. Defeated. Crushed. I cried through the whole of my drive home. At one point I even had to turn off the road so I could calm down enough to make it the rest of the way.

I can't stop going over my meeting with Alice. What I said.

What she said.

How I said it.

How she reacted.

I scared her; I made her despise me. I made her feel angry and disgusted. All I wanted was to talk to my child, to my own daughter.

My humiliation is total.

My instinct, was it wrong? My intuition, my emotions?

I'm aware I'm not doing well, that I'm far from stable. I understand that I'm entering a manic state. But so long as I have the ability to reflect on what I feel and think, I'm not completely out of my mind. If I were, I wouldn't be able to lie here thinking through my situation. And right now I'm prepared to see the truth as it is, I'm ready to bow to reality.

So what's real? What is true? The answer is Alice.

Alice is real.

And the fact that she is my daughter is true.

Everything begins and ends with her. My problems began when I started my investigation. When I started asking Isabelle questions about her background. That's when the threatening letter arrived, that's when the man in the raincoat first stood outside on the street. It's not my imagination, these aren't fantasies. This is real.

Or am I wrong? Is it just another way for me to hold on to a delusion?

No, everyone else is wrong. I am right.

I just can't prove it.

The phone rings; I wasn't even sure it worked anymore. It must be Henrik. I can't bring myself to check. Stay at work. If you came home and found me like this, you'd commit me. And I don't want to go there again.

It rings again and again. In the end, I grab the fucking phone. Look at the cracked screen. Unknown number.

I answer.

"Is this Stella Widstrand?" The voice sounds distant.

"Yes."

"I'm calling about your son. Milo Widstrand."

I sit up.

"Yes?"

"He was on a class trip today. They couldn't find him when they were supposed to head back. Now he's absent from school. He's gone."

"Gone? What do you mean, gone? Who are you?"

"Unfortunately, I don't know any more than that. I was just supposed to call you."

The voice sounds even more distant now; it's scratchy. My phone must have been damaged by the blows; I can barely hear anything.

"Who is this? Were you on this excursion? What happened? What have you done to my son?" The call cuts off.

I'm running down the hallway toward the school office. I beat on the door. A woman I don't recognize opens it. I scream at her.

"My son has been abducted. Who's responsible? Have you called the police?"

"Abducted? I don't know anything about that. What's your son's name?"

"Milo Widstrand, 7B. They were on a class trip. Don't you have any fucking idea of what's going on?"

The woman fetches a binder. She fumbles with some schedules. It takes way too long.

"Where are they? Where is his class?"

"In their classroom," she answers and looks at me with fear in her eyes.

I storm down another hallway. Pass a kid who is absorbed in his phone. I push him away. He flies into the wall, falls onto the floor, and drops his phone. He screams after me, "Fucking bitch." I keep running.

I throw open the door to the classroom. Everything stops, everyone's eyes turn toward me. I stride over to the teacher. He's younger than me, has a hipster beard and glasses. I push him up against the whiteboard. Pound on his chest.

I don't scream. I howl, "Where is my son? Who took him? Where is Milo?"

"Mom?"

I swing around. Milo is standing by his desk looking at me. His face has lost all color. His eyes are wide with shock and shame.

The whole class is frozen. It's dead quiet.

I sob and rush over to Milo. I drag him into my arms, squeeze him, tell him I love him and I never want to let him go again.

The principal, Jens Lilja, enters the classroom followed by the woman from the office.

"What's going on here?" he says. "Peter?"

The teacher nods and readjusts his glasses.

"Everything's fine," he says.

"Stella." Jens lays his hand gently on my shoulder. "What is this about?" I turn to the principal. Still holding Milo tight, pressing him against me.

"I got a call," I say. "You were on a class trip. My son was abducted." I point accusingly at the principal, at the teacher, at the woman from the teachers' room. "You owe me an explanation."

Jens Lilja turns to Peter; they speak quietly to each other. After a while, the principal nods to Peter and says, "Stella, no one from this school called you."

"I got a call," I say. "Somebody called me. Someone from here."

"We didn't take a class trip today," Peter says. "That was in September."

"And as you can see, Milo is here," Jens Lilja continues. He takes a firm grip on my arm. I cling to Milo.

"Somebody called," I say. "Somebody from this school called me and told me he was gone."

"Is that your mom, Milo?" someone whispers.

"Great mom," someone else says.

"What a psycho."

A wave of giggles and scornful laughter passes through the classroom. Milo twists out of my arms. He runs out and slams the door behind him.

"Come on, Stella," Jens Lilja says in a quiet and friendly voice. I allow him to lead me out of the classroom. Their eyes burn into my back.

I want to die.

Stella

Henrik and I are sitting in his car in the parking lot outside Milo's school. He took my car keys, made sure someone would drive it home. Who, I don't know.

He's calm. But more cold and distant than ever. He asks me over and over again. I try to reproduce the phone call verbatim. Do a worse job of it every time he asks.

"Who called?"

"I don't know. It was a woman, I think, but she didn't say . . ."

"What time did she call?"

"Just before I drove here."

"Did she say that Milo was abducted?"

I push my fingers to my eyes and think.

"No, but . . . No. He, let's see now . . . he disappeared on his way back from a class trip, but I think . . ."

"A class trip that didn't exist." Henrik is dogged.

"I didn't know that then."

"Are you sure that's what you heard?"

He leans back in his car seat, looks out over the parking lot. "Did anyone even call?"

"What do you mean?"

"Or could you have been mistaken?"

"Mistaken?"

I take out my phone. Hand it to Henrik. "Look at the call history. Check and you'll see I'm not hallucinating."

He takes the phone and sees that the screen is cracked. "What happened?"

"I dropped it on the floor this morning."

I can tell he doesn't believe me. He puts in my code, my birth year. "And when did you get the call?"

"I already said that. Just before I drove here."

"That's strange. Your phone is dead." He holds it up and shows me. It can't be unlocked.

"In other words, you don't believe me?" I say.

"I've heard this from you before. Supposedly, I asked Erica to call you and tell you not to pick up Milo. Which I didn't do. Which Erica herself says she hasn't done." He looks at me. "Are you really sure someone called?"

I know exactly what he's worried about. I know. He doesn't say it, but all his thoughts and feelings are clear on his face. And I can see what he's most afraid of. And I realize he's right.

"Damn it, Stella. Don't you see what's happening?"

"You think I'm imagining things. That I've lost my mind?" I say.

He points to the school building. "What do you think?"

I don't respond.

"You need help," he says, starts the engine, and drives out of the parking lot. "You need to be in a hospital."

We're at St. Görans Hospital's center for affective disorders. Dr. Janet Savic is a small and energetic woman. She's direct, tells it like it is. Compassionate and sharp, you can't bullshit her. She's been my doctor since I was a teenager. We've met when I've been feeling good, and when I've been depressed and anxious. She knows more about my life than anyone.

I wonder when Henrik called her. Before he got to his car, I suppose. After calming Milo, after calming Peter and the school administrators, Henrik Widstrand takes care of his wife. She has a psychosis and suffers from total mental confusion.

Dr. Savic examines me. Listening to my heart and lungs, shining lights in my eyes, checking my blood pressure. A routine checkup. Completely unnecessary, but I let her carry on. Resisting would not be helpful in this situation.

We talk over the last few weeks. I'm honest, tell her everything. I hide nothing.

I tell her about Isabelle. About Alice. I tell her about what happened at the clinic. My outbursts. The panic attacks. How I followed Isabelle. How I went to Borlänge.

Dr. Savic listens with her head leaning on her hand. She's crossed one leg over the other, her foot bobs.

"Everything I've done is because of Alice," I say. "Because she's alive, she's come back. That's the only reason."

My voice sounds weak. Pleading for understanding. Pleading not to be committed.

"I'm sure you understand why I would like to keep you here for a couple of days," Dr. Savic says.

I look at her without answering. She observes me; the wrinkle between her eyes means she is still uncertain.

"I don't want that," I say. "If you would allow me to go home, I'd be grateful."

"Are you sure you can handle that? That it wouldn't just make things worse?"

"Yes."

Dr. Savic studies me. I stare down at the floor, overcome with shame, powerlessness, and regret. Knowing that she can see my every weakness, every justification I've used to protect myself, it's too much. I don't want to be committed. Won't.

She rises; she opens the door and calls for Henrik. He comes in and sits down next to me. She turns to him now. I already know what he will say.

"Is Stella eating like she should?" she asks.

He throws me a quick glance. "No, I can't say that she is. She eats very little."

"Is she sleeping properly?"

"She gets up at night. Sleeps fitfully. Drinks too much."

Dr. Savic lowers her glasses and looks first at Henrik, then at me. She tells us to listen. She's made a decision.

Her assessment is that I have been under tremendous stress. It was good that Henrik brought me here. I've lost weight. My blood pressure is way too high. I have gastritis. My hands tremble sometimes. I've had several panic attacks.

"We'll beat this before you become manic," she says. "You're on sick leave from now on. I'm prescribing you sleeping pills and some antianxiety meds as well. And from this point on you need to stop drinking. Completely. The chemical cocktail in your brain reacts poorly to alcohol. I'm not going to commit you. Even though that might be for the best. But you have to stay home from now on, Stella. You are to do nothing but rest. Okay?"

"Yes," I say. "I'm just going to rest."

"And it would be good if you started therapy again. Birgitta Alving has retired, but I'm referring you to another therapist I know."

Henrik nods. "That's a very good idea," he says.

Dr. Savic types away at a furious pace. She sends my prescriptions to the pharmacy, prints out my certificate of illness.

"In two weeks, I expect to see you again, Stella," she says. Henrik takes the paper with my next appointment time and the certificate. I'm no longer trusted to handle such important documents.

"Home and rest. Let your husband take care of you. And promise me you'll take it easy now."

Henrik stands, shakes Dr. Savic's hand.

"Thank you," he says.

I say nothing, just leave.

Maybe I should be happy. He didn't take me straight to the emergency room. I'm not committed.

Not yet.

The rain starts to fall as I walk toward Henrik's Range Rover. He catches up with me. We walk side by side but keep our distance. Henrik unlocks the car and opens the passenger-side door to me. His arm stops me before I step in.

"Do you have something to say?" he asks.

"What should I say?" I focus on a point in the distance.

"That you're pissed off at me?" he says.

"Pissed off?"

"Yes."

"Why would I be?"

"For this?" He points toward the entrance to the hospital.

"I'm not."

"No?"

"I can't blame you."

"Do you understand why I'm doing this?"

I don't answer. He apparently believes I'm completely out of it.

"If it were you?" he says. "If I'd been acting like this. What would you have done? If I'd been reported to the police, not by one, but *two* of my clients. If people contacted you about me, asked how I was. If I freaked out at home, stood screaming at Milo's school. Acted completely irrationally? What do you think *you* would have done? Please tell me. I really want to know."

He's controlled, but desperate, fury and impotence still leaking out.

I look at him. "I told you I don't blame you."

Henrik drops his arm, walks around to the other side of the car, and opens his door. He climbs in and closes the door. I sit in the seat next to his. He waits until I close the door and put on my seatbelt, and then he starts driving.

He puts on his sunglasses and drives in silence. He stops outside the pharmacy. Asks me to give him my driver's license. I give it to him. I'm just a child who doesn't know what's good for her. I refuse to look at him.

He comes back. Puts a bag on my lap. Medicines I don't want. I hate them. Hate their blunt effect.

"Mom and Dad picked up Milo from school," he says. "He's going to the country with them this weekend. Please, Stella, think about what you're up to. This isn't working. Not for Milo and not for me."

We drive on through afternoon traffic. Henrik in his sunglasses. Me in my cloud of misery.

"You don't trust me," I say quietly.

"What did you say?" Henrik sounds formal. His tone is excessively polite. Which he knows I hate.

"I'm afraid of losing Milo," I say, blinking and swallowing.

I don't want to cry. Don't want to have an outburst. Can't have another one.

"I have already lost one child. Does that make me mentally ill? It's easy for you to judge."

"You're exaggerating," Henrik says. "I don't want to hear any more of that."

I throw the folder that was lying between us onto the floor. All the papers spill out.

"Is it really so fucking weird that I'm afraid?" I scream.

Henrik jerks the steering wheel to the side. Turns into a parking lot and slams on the brakes. He throws off his sunglasses.

"I've always been here for you," he shouts. "I've always trusted you. I've let you be protective of Milo for all these years. I understood why."

"And that means I'm sick?" I scream back.

"Milo. Is. Not. Alice."

"I know, I know, I know. Stop making me feel like an idiot."

"Take a look at yourself. At how you've acted lately. How you sound. I don't even fucking recognize you anymore."

The sunglasses go on again. He starts the car and turns back onto the road. I stare out the passenger-side window. We sit in silence all the way home.

Henrik enters our driveway and parks next to my car. His phone rings. He picks it up and looks at the display. He listens, laughs. I hear in his voice that he's talking to a woman. They're talking about a party.

"I'll see you later," he says. He laughs again, pretending I'm not there. "Are you still in the office? No, no, everything is fine with Milo, thank you for asking. Good, see you soon."

Again, he looks at the screen, does something, writes something he doesn't want me to see.

I'm crushed.

"I have to go," he says. "I'll ask your mother to come here and keep you company."

"I don't need any fucking company," I manage to get out. Henrik takes off his sunglasses and looks at me. My own husband doesn't recognize me anymore.

I don't recognize him.

We are total strangers now.

"Whatever you want," he says. "You decide, Stella. But take this opportunity. If this doesn't help"—he makes a gesture to the bag in my lap—"I won't hesitate for a second to have you committed."

He looks at his phone again, waiting for me to climb out. I leave the car and slam the door as hard as I can. Henrik speeds off. I stand there looking after him as he drives away.

Everyone has decided that I'm nuts. And they're right. I'm totally fucking crazy.

Isabelle

It's evening. I'm sitting in an old garden chair looking up at the stars. Here in Barkargärdet, they are so clear. In Stockholm you rarely see them. It's cold tonight. The air feels fresher and cleaner. But the best thing about being home is the silence. Listening to the wind whisper through the trees. It feels easier to think here. In Stockholm there's always some noise coming from somewhere.

I don't regret going home. And it made Mom so happy. It feels good that we're getting along so well. Mom has actually changed. She's not as difficult as before. But I can't stop thinking about Stella and our meeting this morning. It can't be normal to seek out your therapy clients in your free time. *Mom says therapists aren't allowed to do that.* All those questions about my childhood, about Mom. It feels so wrong.

Still, I can't help thinking about what she said.

Could I be her missing daughter?

Am I Alice?

No.

Not a chance.

Stella just wishes it was so. She's ill. It's terrifying to think how a person could end up like that. I feel sorry for her, I do. And I still like her. I wish it hadn't turned out like this. But maybe there's a good explanation.

My phone dings. Another Snapchat from Fredrik. Every time I get that same feeling. It's a selfie with a filter that gives him silly little dog ears and a pink nose. He looks intentionally depressed and has written this on the picture: *Do you have to be gone all weekend?!*

I laugh. He makes me feel something I've never felt before. As if I'm just like everybody else, not some stiff, odd person with the world's weirdest life. I hold up the phone and take a picture of myself. I mimic his sadness and choose a filter with a flower wreath around my head. I ponder what to write. *Two whole days!*

Five seconds later I get a text message.

Too bad. I was hoping you'd come over tomorrow.
Sleep over.

Why did I go home? It was impulsive. Being here doesn't change anything. If I'd stayed in Stockholm, I'd be at Fredrik's. Sleeping over tonight. Now I'm going to drive myself crazy with longing.

I think about how to answer. Choose to call instead. He answers right away. His voice makes me miss him even more. And I tell him that.

I ask him if he remembers that time I thought somebody was watching me at KTH. Tell him my therapist turned out to be kind of weird. That she tracked me down again, and that's why I went home for the weekend.

He's understanding, considerate, wonders how I feel. I'm on the verge of tears. *I hope he doesn't notice.* I say I'm fine, it's nice to be home, but I'm already looking forward to going back. And I miss him.

He misses me, too. He says he longs to kiss me again. To eat more ice cream and hold each other in bed. And he says a few more things that make me warm, words that make my body tingle. I know he's as frustrated as me. I can hear it in his voice. And I'll think of him when I lie down. Imagine what we would do if we were together.

If I went home tomorrow.

We end the call after forty-eight minutes.

As soon as we hang up I get another Snapchat. A happy Fredrik with a thumb up.

He has on a black tank top; his hair hangs down over one eye. He's reclining on a sofa, and he's so hot. Despite the cold I take off my jacket, unbutton the top buttons on my blouse. I lean back and see my hair spread around me like sunbeams. I send a Snapchat back, where I'm smiling happily with my head to the side.

My chin is pointed; my dimples are deep. My skin is pale, my hair thick and black. My eyes are big and green. I look pretty good, I think.

And feel immediately embarrassed by that thought. *Pride goes before the fall, as Mom always says.* Even though I get a text where I'm told I'm so fucking sexy.

I would have liked to keep texting back and forth like that, but it's getting icy cold outside. I go in.

The house is a mess. Every room looks wretched—the only exception is my room. It looks the same as the last time I was home.

A pipe in the bathroom upstairs is leaking, and it drips from the kitchen ceiling. Mom has only put a bucket underneath it. She says she can't keep up with everything since Dad died.

I feel guilty. I've felt that way constantly since I got home. I should have come here earlier, like she asked. I can't go back tomorrow. She would be so disappointed. After everything she did, both for me and for Johanna. I should be more grateful.

Stella

I'm sitting on the floor in the corner of the living room staring straight ahead.

I stink of sweat; my hair is stringy.

I don't have the energy to do anything about it. Can't move. Can't drag myself all the way up to the bathroom.

I'm close to being committed.

I've been forced onto sick leave.

I've been reported to the Health and Social Care Inspectorate.

And to the police.

Henrik is gone.

Milo is gone.

Alice is gone.

Everything is over.

I've lost my life.

Psychologically unstable. Ready to be locked away. Poisoned by suspicion. Who have I become? My thoughts race. Can't sleep. Isabelle. Alice. Where are you? What are you thinking? Milo. How are you doing? Do you hate me now? Henrik. I know what you think of me. What I don't know is if you're meeting Jennie this evening. I have to know. Have to, but I don't want to.

I get up from the floor. Fetch the iPad and open the app.

Henrik is logged in to Facebook. It's been a long time since he updated his status. He's shared a few links from his company's website, a friend wrote a greeting in August. A bunch of congratulations on his birthday in May. Otherwise nothing. No new friends added. No tagged photos. I close the app.

Notice he's installed Instagram. Since when? Milo doesn't use it. Does Henrik? I push on the icon. The username is the name of his company. I remember how he snorted at it. "How many new clients are we gonna get on Instagram?"

I scroll through the pictures. They are well composed, trendy, and professional. No weird angles or trashcans in the background. Images from construction sites. Close-ups of drawings. The open-plan office, the lounge. A happy team, everyone loves their job. Young and hip. Stylish, smiling, and successful.

Pictures of Henrik.

Smiling, he holds up the coffee mug Milo gave him on Father's Day, the one with Superman on it. Engaged in conversation with a colleague, checking something on his iPad. Giving presentations on various occasions, a big screen in the background. He looks good. Well dressed. Relaxed. Professional. His shirtsleeves rolled up as they often are in the afternoon. A successful man who loves his job and knows he's damned good at it.

I scroll up again. Click on a picture. What's he doing here? Dancing in the lounge? He's captured mid–dance move, with his arms above his head. He's laughing. Self-confident and charming. White T-shirt and jeans. Those light, worn-out jeans that make his butt look good.

#thebossrocks #funattheoffice #tgif

One hundred and eight likes. I click on them. See a long list of likers. "Likers," so obnoxiously corny. I look through the list. What silly usernames people choose. I'm about to shut it off when I see that jennie_89 liked the picture.

Jennie, you're amazing!

I feel sick.

Click on the username. Pull up a grid of her photos. I recognize her from one of the group pictures of Henrik's employees. She must be new.

All those long days, late evenings at the office.

Henrik is there on the top row of her Instagram.

I look through the other pictures. A lot of selfies, of course. She's good-looking. She's skinny. She's blond. She has pouty lips and saucy, pert breasts that she displays prominently in her tight T-shirts and blouses.

Henrik is featured in another picture farther down as well. Smiling at the photographer. His eyebrows raised in order to say, *Stop messing around.* Easygoing. Playful.

Happy.

The blood buzzes in my ears. My hands shake, and I open and close them several times to make it stop.

I click on the latest picture of him. Posted just two hours ago.

There they are. Henrik and Jennie.

There are other people around them, but I only see Henrik and Jennie. His hair is messy, his eyes shiny. He has a beer bottle in one hand; he smiles straight at me. He's smiling his sexiest smile. He is leaning toward Jennie. Her hand rests lightly against his chest. Her head back is thrown back in laughter.

Office party with the best boss, she's written. Fourteen different emojis.

#bestnightever

Fifty-six likes.

One of the comments: "Sexy boss!" Four emojis.

Another comment: "You look good together!" Five hearts.

I have never been unsure of him. Not once. I know he's not a cheater. But this is different. All the phone calls, his accidental text. And now these pictures on Instagram.

I've driven him away from me. To jennie_89.

I lie awake in bed waiting. It's three-thirty in the morning when I hear him open the front door. He stumbles up the stairs. He hits his toe on the bureau and swears loudly. He's wasted. Stinks of beer and cigarettes. Smells of her.

Henrik and Jennie.

I can see him in front of me taking a swig of his beer. Sharing a cigarette with Jennie. Whispering in her ear. She presses her hot, fit body against him. Crawling all over him. Henrik laughs. She laughs. They laugh together.

They're laughing at me.

He takes a drag and gives Jennie his sexy smile. She caresses his neck, whispers that she wants him. They kiss each other. *You are the best I've ever had,* he tells her as they fuck.

I, his police-reported, soon-to-be forty-year-old wife, am waiting at home. A stinky, psycho wreck of a human being. I want to ask how long it's been going on. Pull every little detail out of him. But the words don't come. He looks at me, takes his blanket, and staggers out the door.

He doesn't even want to sleep next to me.

I lie there. Inhale. Exhale.

I can't stay here.

I go down the stairs and see him on the sofa. I have the urge to push away the hair hanging over his eyes. I sit down next to him, hear him snoring lightly.

I remember when I saw Henrik Widstrand the first time. When his light blue eyes looked into mine. I remember how he admired me, his sexy smiles. All those nights we sat up laughing and talking about everything. He went with me to Alice's grave, held my hand. He never judged me.

He became my best friend, my lover, my husband. I remember our first kiss, our first night together. How we moved into a place on Industrigatan and worked hard, he built his company, I studied. His happiness when I told him about Milo, the best thing we've ever done, and now here we are.

I stand up, hurry into the hall. I take my car keys and struggle out the front door, rushing into the cold. I can't stay in this house anymore. Can't be where he is. He carries her with him. Her scent, her deceitful smile.

He has betrayed me.

My husband has left me for a younger woman.

Out in the cold, out in the rain. It's freezing. I'm barefoot, wearing sweatpants and a tank top. I jump into my Audi and drive away.

I've lied, I've kept secrets from Henrik. I've tried to hide what I'm up to. I have been dishonest.

But most of all I've lied to myself.

I should have seen this. The signs were there. I've been blind. All I could see was Alice.

Henrik, drunk and happy. Newly in love, newly fucked. He has someone else now. He has Jennie. Young and beautiful and sexy and blond. With a perfect body that's never given birth to children, no rolls or stretch marks.

He's made his choice. I hate him. But I understand him, too, which makes me hate myself even more. Who wants a psycho, middle-aged woman drowning in self-pity? His patience is gone. He's had enough.

I'm an unstable, aggressive woman who's lost her grip on reality. Who pushes away everyone who comes near her. Who refuses to listen to the people closest to her when all they want is the best for her. Who refuses to see the truth.

I'm sick.

And Alice is a part of my disease.

I need help.

I stop the car, get out. I walk, then run. Ice-cold rain, ice-cold wind. Walk and run. I stumble. Tumble and collapse.

I end up on the street, crying.

Isabelle

It's Sunday and I would have liked to be in Stockholm now.

But Mom got a migraine just as I was about to buy my ticket. It's been a long time since she was this ill. She got really sick, and I just couldn't leave her alone. Luckily, I don't have to miss any school. Other than studying for our exams with my group.

Being home this weekend reminded me of how isolated my childhood was. Now that Dad has passed away, it's even clearer how lonely Mom is. She doesn't hang out with anyone. Ever. It's strange that you could live in such a small place and yet still avoid any contact with other people.

I miss Fredrik. And Johanna. I miss my independent life in Stockholm. We've been texting a lot, Fredrik and I. He writes things to me that make me feel like I'm floating in the clouds. *That make me long for him and fantasize about him all the time.*

But it's been good to be home, too. I've helped Mom with the worst of the mess. I took care of the dishes and vacuumed in the kitchen and the living room.

Right now we're cooking a late lunch together. The radio is on, and Mom is setting the table with her finest dishes. She feels better, humming and even taking small dancing steps, making me laugh. We eat and look at the collage sitting on the kitchen table. Remember every picture, where they were taken and what we were doing. It's cozy.

"Mom."

"Yes, my darling."

"Who is my real dad?"

She tenses up immediately. She doesn't want to talk about this.

"We were better off without him, believe me," Mom says harshly. "He was a horrible person. A bad man."

Maybe she's right. I mean, he hasn't exactly tried very hard to contact me. Still, her reply makes me sad. Mom is turning off, putting up a wall. Like she always does when I ask about my childhood. She hasn't thought it was important for twenty-two years. Still, I thought over the last few days we had started building something different. My questions might be uncomfortable ones, but it is my life we're talking about.

"You've made a lovely collage of us," I say.

"Yes, isn't it?"

"Why aren't there any photos of me as a baby? I don't think I've ever seen one of me under the age of one."

"You know you were born in Denmark."

"Yes."

I wait for an explanation. *But one never arrives.*

"Is that why, is that what you mean?" I say.

Mom sighs. She gets up and puts on a kettle. Takes down two cups and tea bags.

"We moved back to Sweden. It happened in a hurry. We weren't able to bring the photos with us. Do you want to make me feel guilty for that, too, now? What else have I done wrong?"

"What was it that made you move home? Were you fighting with him?"

Mom doesn't answer. She turns her back to me, showing me she doesn't want to talk.

"Was he around at all? Why has he never contacted me?"

"All you need to know is that he was a very dangerous man."

"Was he mean? Did he hit you? Was he a criminal?"

"Isabelle." I jump when she slams her fist into the kitchen counter. She turns around. "All these questions. You know how they exhaust me. You know I can't take your snooping. I'm getting a migraine again."

She sees that she's scared me and takes my hand. It's not as easy between us as it was when we were in Vällingby. One minute everything's great, the next it's like this. I don't know why. Maybe it's because we're here, in this house. Too many years of ingrained behaviors. Or maybe it's me. My questions, my talk about how I miss my friends, my tendency to disappoint her.

It was a mistake to follow her home.

"You haven't been this inquisitive since you were five years old," she says, forcing a smile. "Do you remember how you drove me crazy? When, how, where, why?" Mom squeezes my hand and pulls me up. "Come."

I follow her to the library, behind the kitchen. She tells me to sit down. I do as she says. She hands me my cup. I warm my hands on it and sip the tea. It's sweet. Mom has poured in a lot of honey. She tells me to close my eyes. I obey.

I hear her unlock the cabinet under the desk with the key she keeps hidden in the bookshelf. I know its hiding place, but she doesn't know that.

"Now you can look," she says, sitting next to me with a binder.

"Here are the papers from Hvidovre Hospital in Copenhagen," she says. "That's where you were born. On August 29, 1993." It's been ages since I've heard her voice sound so soft and loving. "I'd wanted you for so long."

"And that was the best day of your life," I fill in.

"Who told you that?" she teases.

I'm surprised. It's not often she makes a joke.

"Yes, of course it was," she says. "But also it was the worst thing I've ever experienced. I was a hairsbreadth from death. You almost cost me my life, little lady."

I lean against her arm. "Tell me again. I'm Rh-positive and you're Rh-negative and our blood got mixed? Is that right?"

"That's exactly right. I ended up with acute blood poisoning. Hovered between life and death for several days. I didn't even see you until you were three days old." She runs her fingers through my hair.

"But isn't it the baby who gets sick if the blood becomes mixed?" I say. "That's how I understand it. And usually, it's the next child who is in the most danger. Immunization, they call it."

I've read up on it since we talked about it in group therapy.

"But I said I got blood poisoning, didn't I?" Mom says.

"But you said it was because of . . ."

"Please, sweetie." Mom puts a hand on her forehead. *A migraine again.* "You know I hate when you twist my words like that. Doesn't the tea taste good? You sat outside in the cold for so long. You mustn't get sick again."

I drink up the rest of the tea. Might as well do as Mom says. She continues flipping through the papers.

"You were pretty small, see here? Six pounds, four ounces; nineteen inches. And you had a very thick, curly, blond lock of hair. Right in the middle of your head. You were my doll."

"Curly? And blond?" I wrinkle my forehead. Look down at the hair hanging over my shoulder.

Mom slams the binder shut with a bang and stands up.

"Yes, it's not uncommon."

Now she's gotten sad. Sad because of my questions. I've ruined our moment.

"This accursed headache. Now I have to go to bed," she says. "That psycho bitch. She's twisted your mind completely. You should have listened to me. Instead, you think you need to question everything. Destroy things between us. I hope you're satisfied."

Mom stands up, locks away the folder, and puts the key in the bookshelf. She forgets to tell me to close my eyes. She leaves the library and goes out to the hall.

"I'm sorry," I cry after her.

She waves it off and continues up the stairs with heavy steps and a self-conscious huff. *How many times has this scene played out?*

I wish I hadn't destroyed our moment. But there's so much I don't understand. So many answers I want. But Mom keeps everything to herself.

Maybe I've been more affected by Stella than I realized. Mom has had it hard, I know that. It's wrong of me to push her this way. I put my cup in the kitchen. Go up to my room.

As usual, I have a big lump in my throat. As usual, I lie in bed, weeping into my pillow. I wish Fredrik was here to take care of me.

Isabelle

The house should be quiet, but it's not. It creaks and scrapes in the stairs and the walls. The wind makes the roof howl and the gutters shake, and in the cellar the boiler rumbles to life.

I've never liked the atmosphere here, but now it feels like a direct threat: the house is alive; it sees me. It's waiting for me to stumble and then it will strike, slice me open with a knife or make me seriously ill. *There is some invisible essence here, an evil shadow that wishes me ill.*

I tell myself I'm being childish, ridiculous. But the feeling won't pass. I open the door to my room. Stand there listening. I tiptoe out into the hall, stop outside Mom's bedroom, put my ear close to the door. Not a sound comes from inside.

I hurry down the stairs, head outside, grab my bike, and head in the direction of Ornäs. Traffic noise roars above me as I bike through the viaduct under the highway.

I keep biking. After a while I see the Ornäs kiosk and pizzeria. I wonder how many times I convinced Grandma to take me there for a pizza instead of eating real food. *Like Mom wanted.* I bike on past the railroad crossing. Fortunately, there's no train, or I'd end up waiting here for several minutes. I cycle over the train tracks and turn left, roll down the hill toward the village where Grandma lives.

The river is flowing at full force next to the brick mill. The sun breaks through the clouds, and fields spread out on either side of me. In the distance, Lake Ösjön glitters, and to my right the Ornäs House sits on the cape. Every time I pass by, I wonder if it's true that King Gustav Vasa fled from the Danes through the latrine, or if it's just a legend. It's a good story anyway. And every year the tourists come here to drink super-expensive coffee and take selfies in front of the ramshackle old outhouse.

The ride uphill is long and I have to stand on the pedals and push hard when I pass the tennis court at Haganäs. There's a beach down there, but I've never been. Only employees at the steelworks have access to it, which is quite strange considering Sweden's freedom to roam law. What would happen if you went swimming there anyway? Do guards check to make sure you're entitled to be there?

The big red house on the right side is an old village school. It's been closed and abandoned for what seems like forever. After that it's not far left to the village sign. *Kyna.* When I was young I thought it sounded so exotic. As if Grandma lived in China.

I know every twist and turn of the road between Ornäs and Kyna, the curves between the fields, how the landscape changes with the seasons. This is my home, more than Barkargärdet ever was. When I'm homesick for Dalarna, this is what I'm longing for.

If I kept riding straight a few hundred feet, I'd end up at the maypole. They leave it standing there most of the year, until just before midsummer, when it's taken and covered with new leaves. I've celebrated midsummer here many times, picked buttercups, wild chervil, and clover out on the meadows and in the dikes. I've run around while Grandma worked with the others to get the pole ready, wrapping the flowers we picked around the rings and heart of the pole. She taught me how to make flower wreaths and put seven different wildflowers under my pillow at night. I've listened to the fiddlers fiddling in their folk costumes, bought raffle tickets and hoped I'd win. When the celebrations were over, our tradition was to walk home hand in hand and get a good night's sleep, just Grandma and me.

Just past the maypole, there's a path down to the spot where I've gone swimming every summer of my life. Except this year.

I consider going down there, just touching the water, but slow as I near Grandma's place. I look over my shoulder and turn left onto the gravel road. I speed up on the downhill and see Grandma's house on the other side of the railroad tracks. The smell at that railroad crossing is special. When the sun has been on it all summer, it smells like tarred crossties. I roll through the gate, throw the bike on the gravel path, and bounce up the stairs.

Grandma doesn't usually hear when I knock. The door is unlocked, so I go in. I find her in her armchair in front of the TV. She jumps when I shout hello, happy to see me. She gets up without help, waddles over to me, and gives me a warm hug.

She brews some coffee and pours milk for me. She puts out some cinnamon buns and several kinds of cookies. I wonder how many times I've sat like this: huddled on a stool at the kitchen table, with a glass of milk and a pile of cookies in front of me.

Grandma says it's so cozy to finally have me home again. I ask how she is; she tells about her ailments and the volunteer work she's doing with newly arrived refugee children. She wonders how I like Stockholm, and I tell her all I miss is her. We talk until it's starting to get dark outside.

"So how is Mom doing these days?" I say.

"Why? Did something happen?"

"Have you seen her house lately? She's been acting strange. More than usual."

Grandma hesitates. "We haven't talked much lately," she says, wiping crumbs off the kitchen counter.

"She's very demanding, needs a lot of love all the time," I say. "If she doesn't get exactly what she expected, she has fits of rage. But when she's happy, she's very sweet and easy. I've never understood what makes her moods change. It just happens."

Grandma sits down at the table. She hesitates again, seems to be thinking how to formulate something.

"We probably should have got her some help. We wondered if she had some kind of diagnosis. But when she met Hans, she seemed more stable; we thought she was better. And you were her world. You were often sick, and Kerstin was so good at taking care of you."

"No one told me this. It feels like I don't know anything about my own mother."

Grandma looks at me. "Don't judge her too harshly, Isabelle. She came to us as a foster child when she was twelve, you know. Then she moved away from home far too young. She didn't want anything to do with us for several years. Then one day she came home again. With you. You're the best thing that ever happened to her."

I try to smile. "What about her parents? I don't know anything about them, either."

"Kerstin's mother had very serious problems. She drank while she was pregnant, drank and took drugs when Kerstin was with her. She was brutally mean. I think she might have been a prostitute, but I'm not sure. We never knew the whole of it."

"What about her father? My grandfather?"

"He wasn't in the picture at all. Kerstin looked him up one time, I think. I don't know what came of that meeting. She never wanted to talk about it."

"And my father, then? Do you know anything about him?"

"All I know is that Kerstin was afraid of him."

"Why?"

Grandma looks at me. She seems sad.

"I don't know, Isabelle. I don't know anything about your biological father. Your mother refused to talk about him."

She asks if I want more cookies and holds out a jar. I feel nauseous and put a hand over my mouth.

"Sweetie, how are you? You look so pale."

"Maybe I ate too many," I say.

"Do you want to lay down for a while?"

"I have to go home and pack. I'm headed back to Stockholm early tomorrow."

Grandma smiles. "I'll drive you. I won't have you wheeling around on those roads at night."

When we stop outside the gate, she pats my arm. "I'm glad you've found your place in life. Have you met someone?" She winks at me.

"Yes, actually," I say, pushing a hand against my queasy stomach. "Fredrik is his name. He's so cute. I have pictures, but I couldn't find my phone before I left."

"Could you send me a picture later?" Grandma says. "I'll see if I can get it open on my phone."

"You're the best, Grandma," I say, laughing.

"My little sweetheart," she says, stroking my cheek.

Stella

Voices. I recognize them. A woman and a man arguing in the hall.

"Where is she? Surely she's still here?"

"Lower your voice."

"Why did she come here? Why didn't you let me in yesterday?"

"You were hungover. You were angry. That was the last thing Stella needed."

"Where is she?"

"Calm down. Or you'll have to leave."

"I am calm. But I was worried when she just disappeared. She was asleep when I got home."

"When did you get home? Early Saturday morning? And where were you? Who were you with?"

"Who? I haven't been anywhere with anyone."

"You're just like Hampus's dad. I can see you're lying. It's obvious."

"We had an office party, if you must know."

"Ah, an office party."

"Pernilla, I . . ."

"What happened when you got home?"

"Nothing. Stella was sleeping."

"Then why did she come here? There *must* have been something."

"Nothing happened, Pernilla."

"I found her on the street, frozen and confused. I heard someone screaming, looked out, and there she was. She'd fallen on the ground, and she was lying there sobbing. It was terrible. I dragged her up here and tucked her in on the sofa. She rambled on about Alice and Milo. And about you and Jennie."

"Jennie?"

"Who is she, Henrik? And what the hell did you do?"

He doesn't answer.

"How could you leave Stella alone and go out to *party*? With Jennie? You're a fucking idiot. What the hell have you done?"

"Nothing, Pernilla. I haven't done anything at all. It was just an office party, for the staff. Can I talk to my wife now, please?"

"Not until you've calmed down."

"I am calm. I'm super fucking calm."

"You'd never know."

"I'm worried about my wife, Pernilla."

Silence.

"Okay, but not for long. Then you have to leave."

Henrik sits down next to me. He holds my hand and says he wants to help me. He just doesn't know how. I look at him. He's transparent. I see straight through him. He's all thinned out, disappearing. I tell him so. He says he doesn't know what to do. He kisses my forehead. Rises.

He tells Pernilla that they should take me to the psychiatric emergency room. She tells him that she's taking care of me. He's no help in this situation. It's better if he goes home. Yes, she'll make sure I take my medicines.

He bends over me. Is he crying? Or is that me? I watch as he walks out of the room.

He's no longer there.

He's gone.

Stella

Sandy eyes, dry throat.

My head feels full of clay.

Pernilla is lying on a mattress beside the sofa. I pick up her phone and look at the screen. Morning, Tuesday, October 20. I've been lying here for three days.

I sit up in the sofa. See that I'm wearing a pair of leggings that aren't mine and a sleeveless gray T-shirt. I rush to the bathroom. Pee, wipe. My reflection in the mirror above the sink scares me. I have dark rings under my eyes, and I'm deathly pale. My hair is a tangled mess; I put it up in a knot in the middle of my head. I rinse off my face and drink water from the faucet.

I search for the cigarette pack Pernilla hides in a cookie jar in the kitchen. I take a glass of juice out onto the balcony and sit down on the small wooden bench. I light a cigarette and take a deep drag. The air is cold on my bare arms, but the sun warms my face.

Even though my life has gone to hell, the world outside is still out there. Karlberg Palace still stands on the other side of the water. Joggers and parents with strollers walk by on the street below. I watch the smoke float away and scatter. I have no idea how I got here.

Pernilla comes out.

"It's not exactly warm," she says.

"Well, at least it's sunny," I say.

"How are you?"

"I'm alive," I answer and pull on the cardigan she's offering me, take the cup of coffee. She sits down next to me, pulls a blanket over our knees, and takes the cigarette. She has a drag and hands it back.

"I won't nag you about taking your medicines."

"Good."

Pernilla puts a phone on the table.

"Henrik wants to know when you wake up."

I look down. It's my phone case, but the screen is whole.

"Did he bring me a new phone?"

At the moment, I feel so broken that even the smallest kindness makes me cry. Though I don't want to, Henrik's thoughtfulness makes my tears flow.

"You scared us, Stella," Pernilla says. "He came here on Saturday, crazy with worry. Hungover and angry. I drove him away, said you needed some peace and quiet. He came back on Sunday and sat with you. Do you remember?"

"A bit."

"Do you remember how you got here?"

"Not really."

"Shall I tell you?"

"Please don't."

"Okay, we don't have to."

"Thank you."

"Henrik left you the phone and a bag of clean clothes."

I put out the cigarette. Pernilla puts an arm around my shoulders. We sit like that a long time.

"What happened last Saturday?" she asks. "You told me about Alice. Said she was gone forever. Dead. Milo is gone forever. Henrik, too. And you were gonna kill someone named Jennie."

"Did I say that?"

"Yes."

"That I was going to kill her?"

"You hate her, you said. You were going to murder her."

"Did I say that?"

"Yep. Bash her head in."

I laugh. "Sure, sure."

"Who is she?"

I light a new cigarette. Then I explain what made me so suspicious and jealous. Admit that I was snooping around online. I tell her about jennie_89.

Pernilla takes up her phone and searches for the images on Instagram. Looks closely at them.

"Damn you, Henrik," she says. "What a pig."

I laugh out loud. It sounds hoarse. Miserable.

"Do you really think he's cheating?" Pernilla asks. "With her?"

"What do you think?"

"You've barely had sex since last summer, you say. Then here comes this hot, blond thing." Pernilla looks at the picture again. "She is a cutie. And obviously she's into him. It can be hard to resist. He is a man, after all."

"Thanks, now I feel better."

"Middle-aged wife in crisis, a hot blonde who's fifteen years her junior."

I look out over the water. "Not a hard choice," I say.

"Or maybe there's an explanation," Pernilla says. "He's only ever had eyes for you. Do you really think he's sleeping with her?"

I light a third cigarette, feel Pernilla's gaze. I hold up the cigarette, stare at it.

"Smoking clearly offers some relief from anxiety," I say. "Do you know how common it is to start smoking at the psych ward? We had a smoking room. In ward five. Or we'd go out onto a balcony with a high fence. It was like being in a chicken coop. There to protect us from the temptation to jump down four floors. I don't know which Helena thought was worse. Seeing me drugged and anxious, or smoking a cig to calm my nerves."

"She cares about you, Stella."

"I haven't made it easy for any of you lately."

"No, you haven't."

"Henrik told you everything?"

"*You* should have told me a long time ago."

I take one last drag, stub it out.

"Sorry."

"And Alice. When you came here, you said she was dead. Do you still think that?"

On a whim, I pick up my phone. Look through the pictures and find the screenshot I took. Pernilla takes the phone and looks.

"What is this? Is this her?" Her expression changes. She zooms in and gasps. "She is a copy of Maria." Pernilla looks at me. "What are you gonna do?" she asks. "What do you want to do? Do you know?"

"Yes," I answer. "I know what I want."

"Tell me."

"I want to take a long, hot bath."

I go into the bathroom, fill the tub with hot water. Put my hand in; it's scalding hot. I take off my clothes. I open the window, let in autumn air that makes my naked skin turn to gooseflesh. I take out all the medicines Henrik picked up for me. I throw them in the trash under the sink.

I climb into the steamy water. The heat stings my skin; I hold my breath. I put my hands on either edge of the bathtub, close my eyes, and sink down. I breathe in short, panting breaths.

I lean back, stare up at the ceiling, and inhale the cold streaming in through the open window. All my thoughts scatter into that steam. All my questions. All my guilt and shame. My foolish choices, my desperate attempts. All my failures and all my lies.

Everything fades and drains away.

The water is ice cold by the time I get out of the bathtub. I look in the mirror. The woman I see there looks at me curiously.

I know her, know her well. I know her better than anyone else. I know everything about that woman. She has no secrets, can't hide anything from me.

And I'm tired of her.

Tired of her delusions. Tired of all the problems she creates for herself, her limitations, the consequences of what she does, I'm tired of all of it. She knows that. And I look at her, and she understands.

I hold my hands in front of me. Steady, strong. They're not shaking anymore. I close the window, wrap a towel around my chest. I brush my hair out with long, powerful strokes. Open the medicine cabinet, find the scissors. I pull my index finger along the edge and manage to cut myself. A drop of blood drips out of the wound.

The scissors are sharp. They're perfect.

Kerstin

I've taken care of her for days. And now she's gotten sick. Good thing she wasn't sitting on a train to Stockholm when it hit her. She'll have to stay home until she's well again.

I've been cleaning. Dusting, vacuuming, polishing, putting everything in its place. I even watered the flowers. Isabelle helped a bit.

The house is coming back to life again. There's no other way to describe it. *I've* come back to life. Despite all my misfortunes and my grief after Hans. Despite the fact that I've lain sleepless with worry lately.

It's me and Isabelle. It always has been. And it's good for her to slow down for a while. She's been encouraged to search for "the truth." If only she knew who her real father was, why he wasn't in her life, then that would solve things. How can she believe that? She doesn't know what she's talking about. But I do. Isabelle has no idea how vicious the truth is. If she were ever told, she'd regret asking. She wouldn't want to meet the man she calls her real father. And it's just as well that it will never happen.

How could it help her to dissect my life, my choices, my decisions? The truth is never as liberating as you think. On the contrary. The truth hurts. The truth demolishes and destroys. The truth wounds.

Anyone can bring a child into this world. Raising them, giving them character and strength, loving them, that's something else.

Hans was not Isabelle's biological father. But he was more father to her than her real father could ever be. I made a mistake with him. A mistake I had to correct. Rummaging around in the past makes no sense. It won't fix anything.

Isabelle and Hans were very close. I am grateful for that. He was a good father to her. She should be content with that. I just wish she appreciated me a little more. That she showed more love, like when she was little. We love each other. She loves me, I know that. But I'd like to see her show it. I'd like to feel it. We are flesh and blood after all.

Those eyes. The jibes. The questions. The suspicions.

She didn't used to be like this. And those days together in Stockholm were different. Now her questions wash over me in torrents. Suddenly there's an awful lot she just has to know. I answer them as best I can, but still she's not satisfied. She's changed. She's been poisoned. The lies that were planted inside her, those lies have set this in motion.

I could spend my time fretting over the choices I've made. I choose not to. It is what it is. Should Isabelle have known earlier that Hans adopted her? I'm far from sure.

I try to be patient. It's difficult. Life is no bed of roses. Kids these days are spoiled, they've got it so good. But their opinions are inflexible, obvious, and not based on experience. They pretend to be tolerant and open-minded, but as soon as somebody disagrees with them, then you're the hater. They feel insulted, embattled. Kids these days blame everything on their parents, and they want to judge and sentence them.

Grow up, I say. Stop whining. You don't know anything about real suffering.

My own mother was worthless. An evil person, a drunk. I've done pretty well anyway. I would never have gone to a therapist crying about how mean she was. I would never openly question her choices. You don't do that. It's wrong. Allowing some stranger to root around inside you. Letting a stranger give you all the answers. Of course that's wrong. It's unnatural.

But I swallow my vexation. That's what you do when you're a mother.

I know Isabelle thinks I'm being silly when I comment on her clothing. But it's shocking to see how different she is from the girl who left home.

If it were just a question of fashion, I might have understood. Maybe. But she's been angry, critical, unpleasant, totally unlike herself. Like she *wants* to act in another way. As if she wants to be *someone else.*

I'm just waiting for a tattoo or piercing to show up next. But even there I try to hold my tongue. Instead of arguing, I serve her tea and tuck her in. She'll be well soon. She'll be herself again.

She'll come back to me. Everything will work out in the end. Of course she misses Stockholm, but I live in the present. I'm trying to teach her to do the same.

Rest.

Drink your tea.

Keep your feet warm.

The rest will take care of itself.

Everything will be good again. I'll make sure of that.

It will be just like it was before.

Stella

A long curly lock of hair falls to the floor.

One by one they fall.

When I'm done, I contemplate the results in the mirror.

Then I put on the clothes Henrik brought for me. Black stretch jeans, a white tank top, and a gray hoodie.

The kitchen smells delicious. Pasta, garlic, shrimp, fresh cheese, tomatoes, spices. My stomach grumbles, I'm hungry.

Pernilla sees me. She stops in her tracks with her mouth wide open.

"Stella, what have you done?"

"Made a change," I say, popping a shrimp into my mouth.

Pernilla touches my hair.

"You haven't had it this short for years. Not since junior high," she says. "Do you remember your school pictures?"

"All too well."

She laughs. "Daring or foolish, I don't know which. But this time it looks good. You look different."

"I feel different."

After we've eaten, I grab my bag. Take out my MacBook Air and my calendar, a reminder that I once had a job. I browse through it. It's been forever since I used it every day. Made appointments, notes, had a life. A paper lies folded inside it. I take it out and unfold it. My death notice. I have no idea who the man in the raincoat is or why he wants me dead, but I refuse to be afraid anymore.

"Don't forget to call Henrik," Pernilla says. "If you don't call him, I'll have to. I promised we'd call."

I put the laptop, my calendar, and the death threat into the bag. Then I call the clinic and talk to Renate. She tells me Henrik has already been in contact with them, and they know I'm on sick leave. The conversation is short.

I call Henrik, who picks up on the second ring.

"Hello," I say.

"Hello," he says.

It's loud wherever he's at. Soon the sound is muted, he's gone into his office.

"How are you?" I ask.

"Well, you know," he replies. "How are you?"

"I'm good. And Milo?"

"He's been asking for you."

"What have you told him?"

"That you've been under a lot of stress lately. That you're at Pernilla's resting up."

"I miss him."

"What happens now?"

"I'm coming home."

A long silence.

"I know what you're thinking," I say. "But I feel much better now. And I want to talk to Milo about Alice."

"Why?"

"What do you mean?"

"I'm just thinking about what's best for him."

"He's my son, too, Henrik," I say. "And Alice is his sister. Milo is entitled to an explanation."

"What are you going to say?"

"That I believe she's alive."

"Do you have to? It'll be one more burden to bear for him."

"Whether I'm right or not, it's the reason that all this happened."

Henrik clears his throat. Says that we shouldn't discuss this over the phone. Milo is going to Jonathan's tonight. He'll pick me up around five-thirty so we can talk before Milo gets home.

I say no to the ride. "I'll go directly home instead."

"After Milo has left."

"Yes," I say. "After Milo has left."

We finish the call. It gives me time. Time to take control.

Time to get answers.

Stella

I turn onto Paternostervägen in the suburb of Hammarbyhöjden. I park on the other side of the street, opposite the apartment building. I grab my bag, climb out of the car, and look up toward the apartment where Lina Niemi lives.

The building is a dull gray. Three floors, small balconies with white rails except for the farthest ones to each side, which for some reason are painted green. Small satellite dishes, forgotten flower boxes, lowered blinds. I'm taking a big risk just by coming here.

I look around before crossing the road. A man is exiting through the door I want to enter. I run the last bit, grab the door before it closes. Go up to the second floor.

Börje Niemi opens the door.

His eyes narrow when he sees who it is.

He yells, "Get away from here" and tries to close the door. His wife, Agneta, comes out in the hall.

"Who is it?" she wonders.

I put my foot in and push the door open. I pass by Börje and go into the hall. Both of them look terrified.

"Is Lina home?" I ask. "We need to talk."

Neither answers. They stare at each other, stare at me. A door opens and Lina comes out. She leans against the doorframe, chomping on gum, trying to look cocky. She looks more like a lost and sulky child.

"Hello, Lina," I say. I go inside and sit down at the kitchen table. I gesture to her parents to sit down, too. They do so, albeit reluctantly.

"I apologize for this," I say. "But there are some things I need to figure out."

Agneta avoids my eyes. Lina chomps on gum disinterestedly. Börje crosses his arms over his chest.

I take the calendar out of my bag, pull out the death notice, and put it in front of Lina.

"Is this from you?" I ask.

She reads it. She looks up at me with fear in her eyes. Not so confident anymore.

"What is it?" Börje asks and grabs the paper.

"My death notice," I answer. "It was put into my mailbox a few weeks ago. I thought Lina might have been at my house again."

She starts. Her eyes dart back and forth between her parents.

"We saw you outside our house this spring," I continue. "On a few occasions."

"What the hell . . ." Börje starts. I raise a hand to stop him.

"It should not come as a surprise," I say. "I've already told you as much. But you didn't want to listen."

"It wasn't me this time," Lina says.

"I'm not angry," I say. "I just want the truth." I pause, looking at Lina again. She looks down at the table. I lean forward, look her in the eye.

"I know about the blog," I continue, "and I know your parents reported me. And they also talked to a woman and told her your story. That woman reported me to the police for unlawful threats and harassment. These are serious things you started, Lina."

"I didn't write that," she says, nodding to the paper.

"No?"

"I never wanted you dead. Never. I just wanted to be part of your family."

"So you went to my husband's job?" I ask. "You followed us when we were out?"

"Yes," she says quietly.

Börje swears, Agneta gasps.

"Why did you want to be a part of our family?"

"Because you seemed so happy. Because you were always so understanding. And kind. And your husband also seemed kind."

"Do you still think I behaved inappropriately? That I made you dependent on me?"

Lina looks through the window. She shakes her head slowly.

"I got angry," she says. "And scared. I didn't want another therapist."

"There's been someone standing outside my house again. The last time was two weeks ago. Was it you, Börje?" I say and look at him.

He face turns red. He glares at me but says nothing.

"Did you write the death notice? You've made no secret of what you think of me."

"No," he answers. "I would never."

I don't even ask Agneta. She's too timid to do something like that. I look at them, one at a time. Then I apologize for disturbing them. I stand and walk toward the door. Lina catches up with me in the hall.

"Stella, wait." She pulls down on her T-shirt, stares at the floor. "Forgive me."

"I already have, Lina," I say.

"I'll cancel the complaint. It was wrong. I never should have done it. I felt really shitty about it."

"I hope everything works out for you," I say as friendly I can, and I mean it.

I exit the apartment building and stand on the sidewalk outside the front door for a while. Lina didn't write the death notice, neither did her parents. Her dad wasn't standing outside in a raincoat, and I'm sure they're not lying. The man hiding his face under that hood could be anyone.

The sun and heat of the morning have been replaced by lead-gray clouds. It's dark, and thunder hangs heavy in the air. The rain pours down as I drive across Traneberg Bridge.

I pull into our driveway and park behind Henrik's Range Rover. I throw open the car door and run into the house. When I get inside, I see Henrik standing in the kitchen. He has his back to me.

"Hello," I say. "Has Milo left?"

Henrik looks at his wristwatch.

"Yes, he took off maybe thirty-five, forty minutes ago."

"Took off?"

"He's walking to Jonathan's. He usually does."

"I didn't mean it like that. I was just thinking about the weather; it's raining cats and dogs."

"I told him to wear a raincoat and take an umbrella."

Henrik is loading the dishwasher, then he turns around. He stares at me. "What did you do to your hair?"

"What do you think?"

"It's unexpected."

He's cautious. I understand that. After my breakdown he has every right to be careful. I put the phone on the bureau in the hall, take off my coat.

"You feel better?" he says.

"I do."

My phone rings. I pick it up again, look at the display.

"Unknown number," I say and answer.

Once again a call from an unknown person. Once again it's about Milo.

Isabelle

It's been a long time since I've felt this sick. I booked a ticket and was finally about to head home again. Home to Stockholm. How long have I been here? What's wrong with me?

I hover between sleep and wakefulness. I think I might have been unconscious for a while. Mom fusses around me. She gives me tea to drink. Speaks encouragingly to me.

I don't want any more tea. *I don't even want to be here.* Mom doesn't listen. She tucks me in and tells me to rest. *Don't fight it. You won't get better faster by fighting it.*

A few days ago, I felt more alert. Then I got worse. Today I feel better again, but my body is weak. I can sit up on the side of my bed for a minute or two, but no longer. *It's absurd.*

I feel so alone. But I have friends waiting for me in Stockholm. People in my life who care about me. It makes me happy. I wonder what Mom has told Johanna. I asked her to call and tell her I'm here, that I'm sick. And Fredrik must be wondering why he hasn't heard from me. My phone is gone, don't know where I put it. I'm not strong enough to search for it, and Mom can't find it anywhere. She's turned the house upside down looking for it, and she says I'm careless. I'm sure I didn't lose it. It's too important. But I'm too tired to argue with her.

The flowery sofa next to my corner window. Dad bought it for me secondhand, even though Mom freaked out and thought it was ugly. I've sat there so many times, looking out and dreaming.

I crawl over the floor, drag myself onto the couch, panting from exertion. I want to enjoy the daylight before it disappears.

I see Gunilla on the other side of the hedge. I try to lift my hand and wave. Can't. I look down toward the front side of the property. Remember how I used to play there when I was little. The mailbox. Just looking at it upsets me. I don't know why, but memories and emotions from my childhood are coming back to me. Images float to the surface and then disappear again.

Is it because of therapy? Because of Stella? Maybe it's these days in this horrible house. Or is it fever dreams?

Something has happened that makes me remember. But I'm not sure if I want to.

Stella

Milo has been in a hit-and-run accident.

He lost consciousness and has been taken by ambulance to Astrid Lindgren Children's Hospital.

I tell Henrik and put my coat on again. I grab my purse and run out to my car. Henrik is right behind me. When we get to the emergency room, Milo has not yet woken up. The doctor there tells us Milo has an injury to his temple, probably the part of him that hit the sidewalk as he fell. He has scratches on his face and arms and legs. His left leg is broken in several places. That's all they tell us. We sit in the waiting room. Henrik is pale, clenching his jaw. I've called my mom and his parents. I told them what's happened and that we're at the hospital, waiting for more information. Damage to the skull and brain swelling have to be ruled out.

I browse through the brochures. Stare out the window. Browse through brochures again. Walk down the corridor. Sit down. Flip through a newspaper. Have no idea what I read. Stand up, read the signs on the wall one at a time. The hospital needs more blood donors.

GIVE BLOOD.
LIFE: 1 DEATH: 0

An unpleasant slogan. I don't want to think about death.

I do the same procedure, same round, same brochures, same newspaper, same window.

Henrik stays on the sofa, immobile. I sit down next to him and lean my head against his shoulder. I tell him everything will be fine, Milo will beat this. Henrik doesn't answer, but takes my hand.

· · ·

We have been here forever. Maybe longer. When we see the doctor walking down the corridor toward us, Henrik squeezes my hand so hard it hurts.

Milo has a concussion, but no life-threatening injuries. He's awake, and we can see him now.

Milo is lying in a hospital bed in the middle of the room. He looks so small. Whatever skin isn't black and blue on his face is pale and colorless. He has a bandage wrapped around his head, and his arms are covered with bruises. I can see that his left leg is swollen under the yellow hospital blanket.

"Mom," he says in a weak voice. I stroke his cheek and kiss his forehead.

Henrik whispers that he loves him.

"Does it hurt?" I ask.

"Everywhere."

I call for the nurse. She comes in and smiles widely, introduces herself as Ellen. She chats with Milo, explains what she's doing, and gives him something for the pain.

His leg has to be operated on, but not tonight; Ellen tells us that Milo needs to sleep. It would be good if we got some rest, too. She leaves the room.

"How could a person hit a child and then just leave?" Henrik whispers. "It's unthinkable. Milo could have died."

I don't have any answers.

Evening turns to night. Milo sleeps deeply. Henrik is leaning back in his armchair, his eyes closed.

"Are you asleep?" I wonder.

"No," he says, stretching and looking at me. "Impossible to sleep."

"Do you want to come with me for a bit? Maybe we can find some coffee somewhere."

We run across a nurse in the hallway who shows us to a kitchen. I take two mugs, put one in under the coffee machine, and press the button. When it's done gurgling, I hand it to Henrik, who's sitting on a sofa against the wall. I grab the other mug and sit down next to him.

"I understand if you're angry with me," he says after a while.

"Why would I be angry?"

"Because I let Milo walk there by himself," he answers. "Because he was hit by a car and injured. Because he was alone."

"A few weeks ago, I would have let him walk there alone. He's been doing that lately."

"The last time I saw you, you felt like shit. What happened?" he asks.

I tuck my legs under me on the sofa, take a drink of my coffee, and consider how to answer.

"I don't want to be afraid anymore," I say.

"So now we just go on like usual? We just forget everything?"

"That's not what I mean."

"Good. Because you think I'm sleeping with Jennie."

I look up at him, see the challenge in his eyes.

"I know you're not," I say. "I was wrong."

"I thought you trusted me."

"I do." I take his hand. "I was doing so badly. I was terrified. I panicked."

"Why do you always have to be so damn dramatic?"

"When you left me that afternoon, I hit bottom. I had an episode. Realized I would never know what happened to Alice. I'd acted terribly to Milo, and I was so scared that I'd pushed both of you away."

Henrik rubs his eyes. "Why Jennie?"

"Because she texts you and calls you so often."

"She works for me. As you may remember?"

"I didn't know that. Maybe because she's young and super hot? Because she's into you."

"Stop."

"Maybe because you sent me a text that was meant for her?"

Henrik wrinkles his forehead, as if he has no memory of that. "Did I?"

"Maybe because I saw a picture of the two of you on Instagram that night?"

"What kind of picture?"

"You didn't even want to sleep next to me."

"I didn't want to wake you up!"

We fall silent as two assistant nurses pass by and look in at us. After they pass, I shrug my shoulders.

"Doesn't matter. I'm tired of being afraid. Everything has ended up so distorted."

I put my mug on the table and scoot up next to him. He puts his arm around me, draws me closer.

"I've missed you," he says. "What happens now?"

"With Isabelle, you mean?"

"Yes."

"Nothing."

"Nothing?"

"There's nothing more I can do."

I draw back so I can look at him, his arm still around my shoulders.

"She never wants to see me again."

Milo is asleep when we return. His breathing is deep and regular. We stand in the darkness looking at him.

Stella

Milo's voice wakes me up. I've been lying curled up on a cot in an uncomfortable position, and my lower back aches. I sit up and see Henrik sleeping in the armchair next to the hospital bed.

"Mom?" Milo's voice is weak. "It hurts."

I sit on the bedside next to him.

"I'm here."

"I missed you, Mom."

"I missed you, too, sweetie."

I bend over him, kiss his forehead and breathe in his scent. "I'm so sorry for what I did. Can you forgive me?"

Milo hugs me, sniffles.

"Your hair is shorter," he says, observing me.

"Maybe time you cut that mop, too?" I touch a strand of hair that is sticking out from beneath the bandage.

Henrik stretches and sits up. His chin and cheeks are covered with stubble, his eyes tired. I stroke his cheek, and he leans his head against my hand.

Soon a new nurse comes in and tells us Milo is going to have his operation this morning.

"Unfortunately, you won't be able to eat any breakfast," she says.

"It doesn't matter," Milo says. "I'm not hungry anyway."

Henrik reminds Milo of the Super Hero game we used to play when he was little. What power would we choose if we were superheroes? What power is best when you have an operation? Not feeling any pain maybe. Super healing powers? The power to make time go by quickly?

"I'd wanna go back in time and skip all this," Milo says. "Never get run over in the first place."

Milo says it was raining so hard he barely saw anything. And it was dark. He heard a car behind him, and he turned around. It slowed down, then suddenly it accelerated. Drove straight into him.

"The driver should have seen me. I had your red umbrella, the one with reflective stripes on it."

He keeps talking, but I don't hear anything after that.

Milo had my umbrella. My red umbrella. He was brutally run over. In the rain and darkness.

Somebody thought it was me.

Stella Widstrand has suddenly and unexpectedly left us. She will not be missed. No one mourns her.

Whoever left that death threat was serious.

Who is he?

Stella

I sit with Milo while they put him under in the operating room. Then I go out to Henrik.

And we wait.

I think about my son. Milo, alone on the road, my umbrella in his hand. Someone slows, then floors it, and plows straight into him. Then drives off. Leaving him unconscious and bloody in the rain.

Milo in a hospital bed, in a light yellow room with cheap paintings and floral curtains. Pale and bruised. Afraid and brave.

My son, the victim of attempted murder. It should have been me.

Whoever did this doesn't hesitate to kill.

Among all the male patients I've treated over the years I can't think of a single suspect. My life has never been threatened before.

"It should have been me."

Henrik looks at me.

"What do you mean?"

"He had my umbrella. My red umbrella, which can be seen from miles away."

"What are you talking about?"

Henrik's body language shows he doesn't want to hear more.

I open my bag and pull out the death notice. "Do you remember this?"

Henrik looks at the paper with the text and cross and says nothing.

"That threat and my red umbrella are the reason Milo is lying on an operating table right now. Someone also called and lied to me about Milo. A man in a raincoat with the hood obscuring his face has been watching me."

Henrik hands back the death notice and sits down next to me. He studies me carefully.

"You said yourself that you had an episode. You may be imagining things. Again."

I meet his eyes. "I haven't been imagining voices that aren't real. Or events that haven't occurred. Someone called me about Milo. Twice. A man *stood* outside our house. Also twice."

Henrik looks down at the floor. "I don't know, Stella. I still feel unsure about you."

"Isn't this real?" I hold up the death threat.

"Lina could have written it. Or her parents. Maybe one of them called you about Milo."

"It wasn't them. I talked to her. I talked to her parents, too. They didn't do this."

"When? When did you talk to them?"

"Yesterday. I had to know."

"You're under investigation. You're not allowed to have any contact with Lina or her family."

"They're withdrawing the complaint."

"Are they? Well, that's good." Henrik looks surprised. "Then who is this? Who hates you so much that he's prepared to go this far?" He points toward the operating room.

"I don't know. But I got this right after I first met Alice," I say. "It *must* be someone who knows the truth about her disappearance. Who doesn't want it to come out. They want to make me seem unbalanced."

Henrik laughs. A short, joyless laugh. He doesn't follow my reasoning.

"It's clear no one will believe me if it seems like I'm imagining things," I continue. "For example, not picking up Milo, or believing he's disappeared from school."

"That's pretty far-fetched, Stella."

"If I'm reported to the police, then I can't meet Alice again. What exactly am I accused of? Really?"

Henrik leans back and shoves his hands into his jeans pockets.

"I haven't done anything to Isabelle," I say. "I've never behaved in a threatening or violent way. I haven't hurt her. It's strange."

"It's not that strange that Isabelle's mother would be worried when you thought her daughter was yours."

"Isabelle was never afraid of me. Not until that last time. And then it was as if she knew what I was going to say. As if someone had already told her what I wanted. That I was going to say she was my daughter. How could she know that? Who got to her with their version first?"

"What do you mean?"

"It wasn't a man standing outside our house."

"No?"

"It can only be one person," I answer.

"Who?"

"You know who. You've met her."

Isabelle

Mom hurls open the door. She enters the room and sees me on the sofa. I must have fallen asleep here. Must have been sleeping for a long time. It's light out again, morning I think.

Mom asks me what I'm doing up. Her voice is cold and hard. Her eyes mean. She draws the curtains.

I say I wanted some sunlight.

Mom answers that I'm sick. I don't need any sunlight, she says, I need to rest. Light is bad for you. It's better to sleep in the dark.

Then she tilts her head to the side and smiles. *Now she's her kind self.* It's best I eat some chicken soup. She's going to take care of me. Soon I'll be on my feet again. But first I have to rest. Lie down in bed and rest.

I let her stroke my cheek, I eat some soup. It smells bad, tastes bad. I don't want any more. Mom forces the rest down me. How can I get better if I don't eat?

She looks happy. Says we might go on holiday when I feel better. She tucks me into bed. I hear that I'm whimpering, complaining my stomach hurts.

Mom shushes me, strokes my hair, and bathes my forehead with a damp cloth. She says everything will be okay. Everything will be just like before. Mom will make sure of it.

I feel sick again. I'm sweating.

The glass bowl on the shelf, I see it more clearly than ever before, I see it more clearly than if I was standing right next to it. Every variation of the rounded glass, every reflection of the light, all the irregularities and small air bubbles. The overhead lamp spins around and a crack appears, dazzling light streams out. The orange ceramic bird on the desk hovers in the air, turns toward me, looks at me with the unseeing eyes of the dead. The ceiling bends down and then up, like elastic skin, and the walls slide away, slide in again, the floor is water, waves ripple through my room.

Dad talked to me. Said he was down in the garden. He was waiting for me. Asked me if I wanted to help him wash the car.

And then the wind came through the trees and sang.

From inside my torpor, they arrive.

From inside my dream, before I rise to the surface again.

The memories.

The mailbox at the gate. I thought it was magic when I was little.

No one else had a mailbox that looked like a house. It was bright yellow with gingerbread trim, towers, and a porch, porcelain flowers climbing up toward the roof. I used to stand and stare at it, pretend I lived there instead. *Inside that house, you could never be anything but happy.*

One day I accidentally rode into it with my bike. I hadn't really learned how to use the brakes; I was going too fast and smashed right into it. The mailbox fell over and broke.

I cried. My side hurt; my knees were scraped. I was ashamed that I'd ruined something that belonged to Mom.

Dad hugged me and said it was just a thing. He picked up the mailbox, promised Mom he'd fix it when he got home after work. After he left, she dragged me in by my arm, sat me down on a chair facing the wall. I sat there forever. Crying and begging for forgiveness. She walked back and forth behind me, screaming how I'd hurt her, how I was worthless. She'd done everything for me, but I showed no appreciation. I said it wasn't on purpose. She slapped me. Then she left. After warning me not to move.

After my legs and my butt had fallen asleep, she came back. I don't know where she went or for how long. She pulled me up, said she was my mother. You have to love and respect your mother. If you do, everything will be fine. Respect is love. Love is respect. They are the same thing.

Then she fussed over my wounds. She poured rubbing alcohol into them. It burned, and I cried even more. But now she comforted me. She hushed me and said it was necessary. She wiped my tears and hugged me hard, *too hard,* and then we baked a cake for Dad, and when he came home everything was like usual. Everything was good again.

We used to plant things in the garden together. Mom taught me about planting zones and hardiness. Our garden was tidy and beautiful. It was my favorite thing to do, to help Mom, to see her happy. One day I wanted to give her a bouquet of flowers. I took the tulips from the flower bed. Cut them off so only the stalks were left. After that, I was never allowed to help again.

When I was hurt or ill, she was at her best. She read to me, fixed my hair, comforted and bandaged me. But then her other side would shine through. One word, one look, one question put the wrong way was enough. I have never felt safe with her. I learned to be always on my guard. I had to choose my words carefully if I wanted to keep Mom in a good mood.

The cellar staircase. The dark, steep cellar staircase. The stairs rising up at me, swirling and hitting me, hard edges beating against my head, my arms and my legs. I land on my back on the basement floor. I look up and see a dark outline in the doorway. First, I don't know who it is. I ask: *Who are you? Why did you push me?*

The light in the ceiling turns on. The dark figure is gone, and now Mom is standing there looking surprised. She puts her hands in front of her mouth and screams. She rushes down the stairs, takes me in her arms.

She comforts, comforts, comforts. Says I must have stumbled in the dark. *You have to learn to be careful, Isabelle. Oh, my little girl, what have you done?*

Did Dad know how she treated me? I don't know. I don't think so. Not entirely. Perhaps he didn't want to see. He hated conflict. But those times when she went off the rails in front of him, he protected me. So she chose her occasions. *When we were alone.* And I never told anyone. It was my own fault that she got angry and I didn't want to turn Dad against me, too.

Now I understand my hate for her. I understand why I've wished she would die. I don't know how many times she's died in my imagination. How many times I've spit on her grave. But underneath the hate and rage there has always been fear. And that fear has kept me from remembering. I have been terrified of my own memories.

Mom has always been good at making everything better again. And when things were good, they were really good. I didn't want to ruin the good moments. And I still do that. Wish so much that those kind periods were for real. But I know her true self. Even though I haven't acknowledged it to myself, I know who she is. It scares me more than anything else.

She tells me she loves me. But it is a demanding kind of love, entirely on her terms. She wants me to love her back just as much. But I've never known how. Because it's never enough.

She was jealous of my relationship with Dad, I know that. Though she needed him, too. He was more important than I understood.

Since he died, that look of hers is back. I've seen it before; I know it and I'm used to it.

But it's stronger now.

It never disappears completely.

I wonder what she sees within herself.

I wonder what she sees when she looks at me.

And I realize that it's not my memories I'm afraid of. It's her.

Stella

Henrik crosses his arms and waits for me to continue. I stand up slowly and go over to the window. Turn around and walk back.

"It's the same person who told you I thought Isabelle was Alice," I say. "Already, she was sowing doubts about my mental state. She wanted to make me seem mentally ill. Deranged, in need of care."

Henrik wrinkles his forehead and looks at me doubtfully.

I myself wonder how it's possible. How did she know? Has she been watching me all these years?

It was her the whole time. She was the one who saw me when I was near her house in Barkargärdet the first time—not the neighbors, like I thought.

And now she knows I know.

She's afraid the truth will come out, afraid enough to try to stop me. To kill me.

Henrik says, "The woman I met was kind and pleasant. A worried mother. She was definitely not the psychopath you want to make her into."

I put the death notice back in my bag. It's not a good idea to talk about it now. Nothing has changed since yesterday. And we have to focus on Milo.

"I'm going to buy a cup of coffee," I say. "Want one?"

Henrik doesn't answer, just shakes his head.

I take the elevator down to the entrance hall. The sign hangs down here, too. *Become a blood donor.* I buy coffee in the café and ride back up again. Step out and stand at the panorama window in the corridor near the elevators.

The sky looks like a slate. The cemetery opposite the hospital is covered with fallen leaves. The E4 highway runs next to it, a traffic jam of cars headed out of the city. All of those people on their way somewhere on this ordinary Wednesday. Living their lives as if nothing has happened.

Group therapy will begin in the lounge soon. Will Alice be there today? Wonder who's taken over. It doesn't matter. None of it does anymore.

The surgery went well, and Milo is in the recovery ward. The left leg has a cast up to the knee. The bandage around his head has been removed, but not the one on his temple. He's still pale. And he's asleep.

When he wakes up, they roll him back into the light yellow room. We talk and play cards. Milo shows me a game on his phone. The bruises on his face have darkened slightly. It will look even worse in a couple of days, the doctor doing rounds tells us.

"It'll look cool," Henrik says, and Milo smiles.

Later, his grandparents come for a visit. Margareta gives me a big hug. I hug her back, hold her for a long time.

"You seem to be feeling better," she says. "I like your new haircut."

"We should eat," Henrik says. "You must be starving, Milo?"

"I want a Big Mac, supersized. With an extra cheeseburger."

Henrik laughs.

"I'll see what I can do." He turns to me.

"I'm not hungry," I say. "Coffee is enough for me."

"You have to eat sometime," Henrik says. "Soon you'll have more coffee than blood in those veins."

I stare at him. "What did you say?"

"What?"

"What did you say?" I say.

Henrik grimaces. "You should eat, you haven't had anything for—"

"No, no, the other thing. About the coffee."

"More coffee than—"

"Than blood in my veins."

A silly comment. But one that makes me realize something obvious. I should have thought of it a long time ago.

GIVE BLOOD.
LIFE: 1 DEATH: 0

Isabelle

Shrill and piercing. The sound penetrates this fog. *It never ends.* After a while it falls silent. Then it starts again. And again. It never ends, and it doesn't help to cover my ears. Our old landline sounds frightful. I wonder why Mom doesn't answer.

I get up and sit on the side of my bed. Vomit rises in my throat, but I swallow it again. I manage to get up on my feet, lean against the wall, and shuffle out of my room.

That terrible ringing is coming from the phone on the table in the upper hall. I want to get there faster, but my body has a will of its own and won't obey me.

By the time I get there, the phone has fallen silent. I sink down on the floor, lean against the wall. Don't have it in me to go back.

It rings again. I stretch out my hand and grab the receiver, bring it to my ear. It's so heavy, I can barely hold it up.

A woman on the other end says my name. She repeats it several times. I think I recognize the voice, I'm not sure.

All I'm able to get out is "Hello?"

She becomes eager, she asks me to listen. The woman asks what my blood type is.

"Why?" I wonder.

The woman says I'm a blood donor. Explains in detail about blood types. I don't understand.

Everything she says flows out of the receiver and into my ear, then it flows from my ear and down into me, into my chest, into my stomach. The words swirl inside me, around and around.

I feel sick again.

"Slower," I say. "You have to. Talk slowly."

The woman speaks more slowly. She explains it again. And now I know who she is.

"Stella," I say.

I crawl over the floor to the stairs. I turn around so I go feetfirst. I lie on my stomach and slide down. Just like when I was little. I wasn't supposed to, because it drove Mom crazy. She's not here now. *But she could come at any moment.*

One step at a time. Rest, lay my head down. Breathe, wipe the sweat out of my eyes. Next step. And next.

I'm down now. The wall leans over me. I close my eyes, look again. The wall has stopped leaning. I'm sweating. Feel sick again. Legs won't comply. My arms, hands, nothing will do what I want.

I crawl, then I sit up. I lean against the walls, go to the hall. My wallet is in my jacket. And inside that is a paper. I wrote it down, like I always do. In the blood bus outside KTH. Blood pressure and blood values. And blood type. Scrawled on a piece of paper, placed into my wallet.

It's too difficult. Too heavy. Too tough. Too complicated.

But I promised Stella. Have to try.

I go over to the hat rack, grab hold of my jacket. Find the inner pocket. Grab the wallet. My hands shake; I drop it. Down on my knees, down on the floor. Grab the wallet, look for the paper.

The numbers and letters dance in front of my eyes. I squint, hold my breath, force my eyes to focus.

BP: 110/60. Hgb: 129. BT: A neg.

Drag my body across the floor, crawling through the hall. Faster, I have to move faster. Mom cannot see me down here. The library inside the kitchen. The room I hate most of all the rooms in this house. The brown walls, the worn fishbone floor, the gray curtains in front of the small windows. A room filled with quiet secrets.

The key is in the bookshelf. I grab it, I hold it in my hand and look at it. I have never snooped in her stuff. Never. I know what she'll do if she finds out.

My hands are sweaty; I drop the key. It lands on the floor and slides under the desk. Down on my knees. Down on my stomach. Stick my hand under the desk and feel with my fingers, groping. Breathing in dust, the rug smells bad. Find the key, feel it with my index finger. Grope for it, it's under my palm now, I grab it. I hold on to it. Close my fingers around it hard.

I move as if deep underwater. Everything feels sluggish and plodding. I will never make it. Mom will be home soon. She'll kill me.

I sit up. Sweat pours off me, and I need to go to the bathroom. I hold the key with both hands. Breathe, breathe. Hands still, still. The key scrapes, scratches the cabinet under the desk. I open my eyes wide, peering, open them up. Close one and aim. The key scratches, slips away.

If Mom comes home. If she enters the room. If she sees me.

I wipe the sweat out of my eyes with my shirt. Swallow a sour belch. The key in both hands. I aim, get the key into the lock, and turn it. I open the cupboard. The binder is lying there. I pull it out, lay it on the floor. I breathe, breathe. I did it, I made it. I'll read through, find what Stella wanted to know, and then I'll put it back. And then I'll get up to my bed again. Before Mom comes home.

The birth certificate lies on top.

Girl. Born 08-29-1993 at 18.52.

Six pounds, four ounces. Nineteen point two inches.

I read, read, read. And then I see it. She's right. Stella is right.

Mother's blood type O RhD-, child's blood type B RhD+.

No Rh immunization. Blood poisoning.

The child is B positive.

On my note from the blood center it says A negative.

Mom's acute condition was not due to blood mixture. She's lying.

There is something in a plastic pocket at the back.

Photographs. *Kerstin and Isabelle, Copenhagen, February 1994* is written on the back of the top one. She said there are no pictures left of me when I was little. She's lying about that, too. Why?

I turn over the picture. A younger version of Kerstin. She looks up at me and smiles. She's holding a baby. A girl, a few months old. She has blond curls all over her head.

Another photo from the same occasion. Close-up of a happy Kerstin. And a blond baby.

I study the girl carefully. She smiles, but has no dimples. Her right ear does not look like mine. Who is she? Is this the real Isabelle? And if so, who am I?

I slam the binder shut. Try to put it back, but something is in the way. I lay the binder on the floor and the photos fall out. I see what's lying on the shelf inside. My phone. My phone has been locked in Mom's cabinet under the desk. Another lie.

I have to get well. I have to get out of here. The front door opens. A voice calls my name.

The sound of steps. They stop. I hear a long sigh, and my heart starts to hammer.

I twist my head and look up.

Mom is standing in the doorway. She looks at me. She looks at the desk. She looks at the binder and the photos scattered across the floor.

She comes over, leans down toward me.

I pinch my eyes shut, raise my arms to protect myself.

Stella

She never called back.

I've been waiting for her call for hours.

Something has happened.

Henrik and Milo are sleeping. But my bunk is hard, and I've been awake the whole time. I turn and look at the phone: 2:16. Alice won't call this late.

She was just going to check some papers, she said. She sounded drowsy, as if she were drugged. I'm not sure I was able to make her understand she had to leave there at once. But she promised to call back.

Kerstin has proven what she's capable of.

What will she do if she finds out Alice spoke to me?

I should take the car and go directly to Borlänge, but I wait. Milo needs me here. And Alice went there voluntarily. Of her own free will, she said. I believe her. As long as Kerstin doesn't know she knows the truth, she's in no danger. That's what I tell myself. At least for now.

I look at my phone again: 2:48. Nothing. I turn over and close my eyes.

Henrik wakes me up by shaking my shoulder. He's already dressed and squatting down next to me.

"We have to talk," he says. "Come with me to the kitchen."

He does not wait for me. I pull on my pants and a shirt, throw on Henrik's cardigan, and follow after him. He has a cup of coffee waiting for me.

"The police are on their way here. They want Milo to give them the details of what happened. Do you have any objections?"

"As long as he feels up to it," I say.

"The doctor has approved it," Henrik says.

"Okay. Might as well get it over with."

Henrik looks at me over the edge of his mug. "Are you going to say anything?"

"About what?"

"Will you accuse someone of attempted murder?"

"Wasn't it attempted murder?" I say. "He was run over. Left to die on the side of the road. And no one is responsible?"

"You know what I mean."

"I called her yesterday."

Henrik looks at me. "What are you talking about now?"

"You said that I have more coffee in my veins than blood," I say. "I realized that Isabelle's blood type has to be wrong. I had to call her."

I see that Henrik is becoming annoyed but I continue. "And you know where she is? In Borlänge. At Kerstin's."

"You know what, I couldn't care less."

I put down my mug. "You can't be serious. Kerstin tried to kill our son. Don't you realize she's capable of doing anything to hide what she's done? That she stole my daughter."

Henrik slams his mug on the table with a bang.

"You're the one who doesn't understand. Your daughter has been dead for more than twenty years, Stella. Your son is alive. Milo is here. Now. And he needs you."

"I'm here for him," I say. "I'm here, Henrik."

"What needs to happen to make you stop? How far will you go? Are you prepared to sacrifice everything? Milo? *Us?*"

"Is that an ultimatum? My daughter or my son? Is that what you're saying?"

He doesn't respond, just shakes his head and looks down at the floor.

I leave him and walk out into the corridor. Go into a bathroom. I ball my hands into fists and slam them against the wall as hard as I can. I sit on the toilet lid, lean my head into my hands, and let my rage drain away.

Men are strange creatures. It's impossible to understand them once their stupidity sets in. And the stubborn kind of stupid Henrik is displaying right now drives me crazy.

I pick up my phone and only now do I see that someone sent a text message. I unlock it and see a red number one on the green message icon. I press it. Don't recognize the number. I read the message but I don't understand what it means. Then I read it again and realize it's from Kerstin.

Kerstin

My poor little girl. You're sick, so sick. Mom is taking care of you. You'll get better soon. Stop vomiting, stop feeling so nauseous, soon it will be over. When the poison is out of you. When the evil leaves you. It may take time, but I'll help you. I'll never desert you.

The phone rings. It rings over and over, and it worries Isabelle so. Even though she's barely awake, she flings herself around. I pick up the phone, say my name, and ask who's calling.

A gruff male voice: "This is Mats Hedin. With the Stockholm Police Department."

I almost hang up. I'm definitely not interested in what he has to say. But I swallow my vexation. As I always do. Kerstin Karlsson does what she should. Kerstin Karlsson always does her best.

"Oh, really?" I say. "And how can I help you?"

"I have a few questions about your daughter, Isabelle Karlsson," Mats Hedin says.

I hear what he says. What I don't understand is what he wants from me.

"Hello?" he says. "Are you still there?"

"Questions? About what?" I say.

"Have you seen her recently?"

What's he getting at? What's he after? I have already said all I have to say about Stella Widstrand.

"Have I seen Isabelle?" I say. "Why do you ask? Of course I've seen her. I just came home from Stockholm."

"Your daughter was reported missing," Mats Hedin says. "Her friend Johanna saw her last Friday morning. Before Isabelle went to Dalarna with you. According to her, Isabelle was supposed to be back on Sunday, four days ago. But she never arrived. She hasn't been in contact, and she can't be reached. Johanna says she tried to reach you but couldn't."

"Reported missing?" I burst out.

"Because of your previous police report, that she's been threatened and harassed, we're taking this very seriously. But we have to rule out if she's with you."

"No, no," I say. "There's been a misunderstanding. She's not here. She just took me to the train in Stockholm, that's all. I don't know where Johanna got that idea."

"Really? So when was the last time you heard from her?"

"When she waved good-bye to me at the central station. She accompanied me there, like I said. You surely don't think something has happened to her?"

Mats Hedin is quiet for a moment. "We don't know yet."

"That woman. Stella Widstrand. I know it's her. If something has happened to Isabelle, if my daughter . . ."

"There, there, nobody is saying that something happened."

"She showed up in Vällingby. Just before I left. Showed up on the street. Where my daughter lives. I saw everything myself from the window. She was crazy. Threw herself at my daughter, scared the life out of her. Fortunately, Isabelle broke free and ran away from her. She was inconsolable when she got up to the apartment. Cried until she shook."

"Why didn't you report that?"

"How many times do I have to report a person before you act? I already told you she's dangerous. She thinks Isabelle is her child. She's trying to take my daughter away from me."

"You haven't heard from Isabelle since last Friday, either?"

"No, I haven't."

"And you haven't tried to call her? Not once?" Mats Hedin sounds judgmental. Insolent.

"I try not to call Isabelle all the time. She doesn't like it when I do. She has her own life down there in Stockholm, and I respect that. I thought she might be with her boyfriend. Didn't want to disturb her."

I'm crying now, I'm so worried. Sniffling into the phone.

"Even though she's been harassed again, by the same woman you reported to the police?"

"I don't understand why you're being so accusatory toward me. What did I do wrong? No matter what I do, it's wrong."

"Nobody is accusing you, Mrs. Karlsson," Mats Hedin says. "The boyfriend, what's his name?"

"Fredrik. Fredrik Larsson. They're in the same class, I think."

He's silent for a moment. Then he tells me to be in touch if I find out anything. They'll interview Stella Widstrand immediately. I wonder why they haven't already done so. I wonder why she hasn't been arrested.

"This is a priority for us; we're taking this seriously," Mats Hedin assures me again. "But we can't lock someone up without any proof."

I don't say anything. There's no point.

I don't give a shit about proof. I've never gotten any help when I needed it. They never took me seriously. I had to take justice into my own hands. Like always.

Mats Hedin says they'll talk to her boyfriend, too, and be in touch later.

I cry, express my thanks, and say once again how terribly worried I am. Then I hang up. I don't have any more time for this. I have other things to take care of.

The boyfriend. That Fredrik will never become Isabelle's boyfriend. I've read the messages he sent to her phone. Every single one. I've read what she answered. I know everything. All the filthy things he wants to do to her. How she *longs* to do filthy things to him. It's so disgusting it makes me want to vomit.

I've seen the pictures she sent. Indecent pictures. She offers herself like a whore. Trying to make him horny. And sure enough, he gets horny. He doesn't say it like that, of course. He tells her she's beautiful, that he misses her, that he's longing for her. Longing for what is no secret. I saw her messy bed. Who knows what they're up to.

She doesn't understand the forces she's playing with. Despite what I've told her, despite all my warnings, she hasn't learned anything.

Men are only after one thing. It starts with pretty words; it starts with promises and sweet smiles. Then he takes what he wants, and he prefers to do it with violence.

He takes a woman again and again, he takes her violently.

Then he leaves her.

Leaves her lying unconscious in her own blood.

Her body was all he saw, all that he wanted.

What she had between her legs.

He wanted to violate and soil her.

Squeeze the life out of her.

Then throw her away once he's used her up.

He wants to fuck her.

Rape her.

He forces himself on you even though you don't want him.

He hits you in the face, spits on you.

He calls you slut; he calls you bitch.

He calls you whore.

And it hurts, it hurts so damn bad that you scream.

Until you can't scream anymore.

You're injured.

You bleed and bleed.

You pay for your suffering in blood.

How something so ugly, so shameful and vicious could create a baby I will never understand. A doll for you to hold, who's all yours.

The finest, most beautiful thing in the world.

Dear sweet Isabelle.

If you only knew what you were playing with.

But you're lost and confused.

You are poisoned.

You are weak.

You think it's love, think it's something beautiful.

You should be glad I saved you, that I protected you.

You should be grateful I'm your mother.

Stella

I'm running down the corridor. I go into the kitchen and hold the phone up in front of Henrik. He takes it away from me and reads. I see the shock spread over his face.

> Pity he survived. Pity you didn't get to see him dead. Then you'd have no children left.

> It's your fault your son is hurt. It should have been you. You're a worthless mother. You put him in danger. Like you always do to your children.

> She's mine now.

Ellen, the nurse, comes in.

"Sorry to interrupt. The police are here."

"We're coming," I say.

Henrik takes my hand and looks into my eyes.

"Milo has to give his statement," he says. "Then we'll report that this was no accident. It was attempted murder."

Henrik and I are sitting beside Milo. Detectives Olivia Lundkvist and Mats Hedin knock on the door and enter the room. I don't understand why they're here.

Shouldn't it just be some regular uniformed police officers?

Henrik and I look at each other before he stands up and stretches out his hand. Mats Hedin takes it, nods to me. Olivia Lundkvist does the same. I stay seated next to Milo.

"Hi, Milo, my name is Mats. My colleague here is Olivia. Quite the bump you got there."

Mats Hedin plops down across from us, lays his powerful arms across the table. Milo looks at him seriously. Henrik sits down again. Olivia Lundkvist leans against the wall. And though I avoid looking at her, I can feel her observing me.

"We heard you were in an accident," Mats Hedin says to Milo. "Can you tell me what happened?"

Detective Mats Hedin behaves quite differently when he's talking to our son. He radiates warmth and calm.

"I left home around five-thirty," Milo says. "On Tuesday. In the afternoon. I was gonna go to Jonathan's house, he lives pretty close. Not more than a mile away. It was dark outside, pouring rain. I walked on the sidewalk, and there are streetlights everywhere. Plus I had my mom's red umbrella with reflective stripes. I should have been pretty visible."

"You didn't do anything wrong," Mats Hedin says. "There's good lighting at that spot. And I've seen the umbrella, you were definitely visible. Right, Olivia?" She nods and smiles at Milo, who smiles back.

Milo tells them how he heard a car behind him. When he noticed that the car was slowing down, he turned around. He didn't know what kind of car or the license plate number, just that it was a dark hatchback or SUV, maybe black or dark blue. Then the driver stepped on the gas and drove straight for him. He doesn't remember any more after that. Maybe he tried to jump out of the way, he isn't sure.

"Thanks, Milo," Mats Hedin says. "We need to borrow your parents for a minute. Is it okay if you go with Ellen to the kitchen? Maybe get some breakfast?"

Ellen opens the door as if she heard what Mats Hedin just said. She smiles at all of us and goes over to Milo and helps him out of the chair. I stroke his arm as he passes by and whisper that I love him.

Detective Olivia Lundkvist sits down on a chair. She crosses her legs and clasps her small hands together on the table. She turns to Henrik.

"We have a witness who confirms what Milo just told us," she says. "A person saw the car slow and then speed up and drive straight at your son. Milo jumped away. Which probably saved his life. The driver didn't seem to be under the influence. Both Milo and the witness described the actions as controlled. The witness also had the impression that the driver hit Milo on purpose."

I clench my hands hard on my knees. I want to explain to them that I know who did it, who was driving the car. I want to tell them that they should arrest Kerstin Karlsson. The woman who stole my daughter. The woman who almost murdered my son.

"It's impossible to get a description of the driver," Mats Hedin continues. "He probably had a hood or ski mask over his head."

I look at Henrik. He returns my look, and I know that he understands I was right the whole time. He holds out his hand and I take it.

"Unfortunately, the witness also couldn't tell what type of car it was, but both say it's a dark model, SUV or hatchback, no license plate number noted." Mats Hedin looks serious. "We hope that the driver will come forward and take responsibility for the accident."

"It was no accident," Henrik says.

"No? What do you mean?"

"Milo had Stella's umbrella. The driver thought he was my wife."

"And what makes you believe that?" Olivia Lundkvist says.

I take out the death notice. Lay the paper on the table. I show them the text I received during the night.

"I know who they're from," I say. "And I know who ran over Milo."

"You mean it's the same man?" Olivia Lundkvist says.

"Same woman."

"Same woman?"

"She's been watching our house. Wearing that same raincoat with her face obscured by a hood. That same woman drove into our son."

Detective Olivia Lundkvist pulls the paper with the death threat close to her.

"Have you reported this?" she asks.

"No," I answer and feel Henrik's arm around my back. Feel his support. "But maybe I should have."

"Maybe," Mats Hedin says. "Is this common?"

"What?"

Mats Hedin takes a deep breath and slowly exhales. "For a therapist to get death threats?"

"It happens now and then that a patient threatens their therapist, but it's not exactly common," I answer. "Somebody who's wrestling with an affective disorder, or who lacks impulse control, maybe someone whose problems include aggressive behavior as one of the symptoms."

"And why would somebody want to kill you?" Olivia Lundkvist asks.

"As it says in the text message, she has my lost daughter . . ."

"So you also have a daughter?"

"I told you that the last time we met," I say. "She disappeared twenty-one years ago. It's the same person. The woman who kidnapped my child drove into Milo believing he was me. She wants to stop me, make me stop."

The detectives exchange glances. Olivia Lundkvist picks up the phone again and reads.

"But that's not exactly what it says here, is it?" she says, looking at me. "It doesn't say anywhere here that she kidnapped your daughter twenty-one years ago?"

"No, not in so many words," I say. Impatient now. "Read it. It says she wants to see me dead. It says that I should let them be, because *she's mine now.* She writes that I put all my children in danger, then she must know something about my daughter, too, right?"

"I'd like to ask you about that. In what way have you put your son in danger? Can you tell me about that?"

I clench my jaw. Feel like I might just fly into a fit of rage.

Henrik squeezes my arm. "What is the purpose of these questions?" he says. "We are reporting that our son has been run over. That my wife has been threatened. In addition, we have confirmation that she was the target. You read the text. Shouldn't you focus on that? Or do you not take that seriously?"

"Of course we take it very seriously," Mats Hedin says with a smile I don't like. "But unfortunately, Stella, we have to ask where you were last Friday."

Both of them look at me. Henrik, too.

"Last Friday?" I say. "I have no idea what I did last Friday."

"I'll help you remember," Olivia Lundkvist says. "You tracked down Isabelle Karlsson. Do you remember now? Or do you need more detail? You were outside her home, even though you'd been instructed to stay away. You were so upset you threw yourself onto her on the street outside her door."

That was *that* Friday. My last desperate attempt.

"I was there, but I didn't throw myself on her."

"According to our information, you behaved in both an aggressive and confused way."

"I was not aggressive. Absolutely not."

"But you were confused?"

"I might have been out of balance."

Olivia Lundkvist puckers her lips. "And what time did this happen?"

"Around eleven, twelve, I think."

"And what did you do the rest of the day?"

"First, I went home for a while. Then to Milo's school, maybe around three. Went out with Henrik for a bit in the afternoon."

Olivia Lundkvist looks at Henrik.

"Sound right?"

"Yes," he replies.

"And later that night? Between, say, six and ten?"

"Then I was at home."

"Can you confirm that?" Olivia Lundkvist looks at Henrik again.

I know he can't, and I start to get a sinking feeling in my stomach.

"What is this about?" he wonders. "Do we need to contact our lawyer?"

"You are free to do as you please," Olivia Lundkvist replies. "But it will make things easier if you cooperate."

"I wasn't home," says Henrik. "I dropped off Stella around four-thirty, five, I think. Went directly to an event at work. There are at least twenty-five, thirty people who can confirm where I was."

"No need," Olivia Lundkvist says. "Did you party?"

Henrik looks at her steadily. "Why? Is that illegal now?"

"When did you get home?" she asks.

"Late. I may have a taxi receipt somewhere."

"Half past three," I say. "I drove to a friend's. Shortly after Henrik came home. You can ask her when I got there. Pernilla Dahl."

"Why did you go there?" Olivia Lundkvist asks.

"We had a fight."

"What was the fight about?"

"Nothing."

"Nothing? In my experience fights are almost always about something. But maybe that's not the case for the two of you?"

"There was a misunderstanding," I say, looking at Henrik. He smiles. I look at the police. "Just a silly misunderstanding."

"Doesn't sound like nothing," Mats Hedin says. "What kind of misunderstanding are we talking about here?"

"I thought my wife had met someone else. I was jealous," Henrik says. "That wasn't the case. I was wrong. Satisfied?"

Mats Hedin squirms, and Olivia Lundkvist looks scornfully at Henrik.

"So between half past four in the afternoon and maybe four the next morning nobody can confirm where you were?" Mats Hedin says to me.

"No. Why do you want to know this?"

"Isabelle Karlsson has been reported missing," Olivia Lundkvist says.

"Missing? But I know where—"

"Wait." Detective Olivia Lundkvist holds up her hand. "Isabelle has been missing from school. Which has apparently never happened before. She hasn't updated her status on Facebook. There has been no social media activity since last Saturday. She hasn't answered her cellphone for several days. Her boyfriend and roommate are convinced something has happened to her."

Olivia Lundkvist leans forward and studies me.

"According to Isabelle's boyfriend, she was worried someone was stalking her. You've had a report filed against you for just that reason. Besides her mother, you are the last one to see Isabelle. Which you have just confirmed. You might as well tell us. Or do we have to take you down to the station?"

"We're done here," Henrik says. "This conversation is over. If you have any further questions, please take them up with our lawyer." He is about to stand up, but I put a hand on his arm.

"I know where she is," I say.

"Oh, really?" Detective Olivia Lundkvist leans back. "Then I think you better tell me."

"I called Kerstin Karlsson yesterday and—"

"Why?" Olivia Lundkvist interrupts. "You were supposed to keep your distance and not contact them. Not under any circumstances."

"But can't you hear what I'm saying? Isabelle is in Borlänge. With Kerstin Karlsson. She's the one you need to talk to."

"We have already spoken to Isabelle's mother," Mats Hedin says. "And Isabelle is not there."

"Kerstin is lying. She *is* there," I say. "I spoke to her. She sounded drugged. Call your colleagues in Dalarna. Send them immediately before Kerstin disappears with my daughter. Again."

"Isabelle is Kerstin's daughter, as far as we know. But we know you have another opinion."

"Is this how you do your police work? You have a missing person, and I know where she is. Isabelle is in Borlänge, on Faluvägen. Look it up."

"You need to calm down," Mats Hedin says. "You're the one who has a complaint against them. Nobody else. And if I were you I'd try to remember that. You're also a hairsbreadth from being under suspicion for the disappearance of Isabelle Karlsson. There is nobody else who has such a strong motive. Who's already shown such excessive interest in her."

I stand up and raise my voice. "My daughter was kidnapped. My son has been run over. Do something. Before it's too late."

"Now I need you to calm down," Olivia says, pointing to the chair. "Sit down."

I continue to stand. The two officers look at me as if they're ready to arrest me.

"You're the ones who need to settle down," Henrik says. "Our son was almost killed. My wife has been under enormous pressure. Your attitude just makes everything worse."

"We have a job to do," Mats Hedin says. "Please sit, Mrs. Widstrand."

"We're finished with this," I say and stay standing. "You can go now."

"We want you to stay here in town. Make yourselves available."

I don't respond.

"Did you understand what my colleague said?" Olivia Lundkvist raises her eyebrows.

"I'd like to go be with my son now. If there's nothing else?"

"We'll be in touch," Mats Hedin says. He rises and leaves the room. Olivia Lundkvist follows, but stops in the doorway.

"People like you are always hard to deal with," she says.

"Like me?"

"People who think they know better than everyone else."

I go over to her. "I don't give a shit if you like me or not. All that matters now are my children."

Detective Olivia Lundkvist's face isn't far from mine. For a moment, I think she'll reply with another sharp comment, or maybe just drag me down to the station. But then I see a smile at one corner of her mouth.

"Okay," she says, turns around, and leaves.

Stella

Henrik takes me in his arms. We stand in the middle of the room for a long time, holding each other. I lean against his chest, feel his breath in my hair. So much has happened lately we'd need to talk about it for days, weeks. But at this moment we don't need words.

Milo returns to the room and lies down in bed. I sit next to him and tell him about his big sister. I tell him she's alive.

"I thought she was dead," he says.

"I did, too. But not really. It sounds strange, but I can't explain it better than that."

"But she has a grave. And a stone with a white dove on it."

"They never found her. Nobody is lying there."

"But why do you think she's alive?"

"I've met her."

"Alice?"

"Yes."

"When?"

"A few weeks ago. I wasn't sure at first. It's been so long. That's why I've been so weird."

Milo fidgets with his blanket.

"You've been super annoying."

"I know I should have told you a lot sooner," I say and stroke his cheek. "Told both you and Dad. I'm sorry about that."

Milo looks at Henrik. "What do you think, Dad? Is it Alice?"

"I'm absolutely sure it's her," Henrik says. "Your big sister."

I show them the picture I have of her on my phone. Milo and Henrik study it carefully.

"She has dimples just like us, Mom," Milo says.

"She does," I say.

"You've always said she favors Maria," Henrik says. "But I think she looks like you."

"But what happened?" Milo asks. "Where has she been?"

"It's a long story. I'll tell you everything later. But first, I'm going to go get her." I give him a long hug and a kiss on his forehead. Then Henrik follows me into the hallway.

We kiss each other. He hugs me hard, and I look into his eyes. He nods slowly. Even if he doesn't want me to go, he knows I have to.

Stella

The driveway in front of the house is empty. I drive past and continue onto Faluvägen. I go by a few houses and approach an abandoned factory on the other side of the road. I pull off and stop, then turn the car around and go back toward the house again.

Once again I pass by and drive onto a narrow dirt road to the right. I park and turn the engine off, see a glimpse of the house between the trees. Perhaps I should call the police after all. But after this morning's meeting, I know it's useless. I'm the suspect. And I am strictly forbidden to be here. I get out of the car, walk in between the trees, and continue toward the house.

I stop behind a thick spruce and peer out between the branches. The house seems empty. The curtains are drawn, and the blinds are down.

I walk over the lawn, up the stairs to the front door, and push the bell. It doesn't work. I knock, put my ear to the door and listen. I push down the handle and try the door. It's locked. I go back down the stairs and look at the kitchen window, where the blinds are only half down. I climb up onto an old dishwasher standing under the window, lean against the glass, and look in. Table and chairs, a striped plastic rug on the floor.

I walk around to the back of the house and come to a patio. A few crows fly off, their loud calls stop me in my tracks. Next to the back door sits a black bag of garbage. Egg cartons, empty cans, and leftovers are scattered about it. I walk up to the glass door, look through the gap between the long curtains. I see the kitchen and a room with brown walls adjacent to it. A desk has been overturned.

She has papers. In the desk. I am going to look.

I pick up the phone and dial the number. I can hear it ringing inside the house, but nobody answers.

I look for something heavy to throw through the glass door and find a brick. I look around, then I throw it close to the handle. The sound of glass breaking shatters the silence. I hold my breath, but no neighbors pop up before I'm able to put my arm in, twist the latch, and open it.

I enter the kitchen, stand still, and listen. Water is dripping somewhere. I look around. A yellow plastic bucket stands in the corner. Water oozes from the ceiling.

On the kitchen counter are several medicine boxes. I turn them over and read: Zoloft, omeprazole, zopiklon, Nozinan.

I continue into the room behind the kitchen and turn on the ceiling light. Someone went berserk in here. A bookcase has been turned over, the others are empty, the books are scattered across the floor. An ornamental table sits upside down against the wall. A lamp with a broken glass shade is at the far end of the desk. It lies on its side next to a cupboard door that is ajar. I hunch down and open it. Empty. I stand again, looking around the room. On the floor where the bookcase stood lie strings of dust, long and gray like molted snake skins. I lift the lamp and see an iPhone lying half hidden under a book. I pick it up and start it. The background image becomes visible.

Alice.

She has her eyes closed, laughing. A blond guy is kissing her neck. I try to unlock it, but need the code. The battery is low, and the phone is dying. I put it in the bookshelf. Some photographs are scattered across the floor. I pick up one of them. *Kerstin and Isabelle, Copenhagen, February 1994* is written on the back. Before I can look at it, I hear a voice behind me. I put the photo in my coat pocket and turn around. A woman with copper-colored hair stands in the doorway. She sweeps her eyes over the mess and then looks at me urgently.

"Who, may I ask, are you?"

I take a few steps toward her and stick out my hand. She doesn't take it.

"Stella Widstrand," I say and lower my hand. "I'm looking for Kerstin Karlsson. I went around back and saw there'd been a break-in."

The woman looks me over from head to toe. Does she see through my lie? Maybe she heard me break the glass?

"Have you seen anyone else here?" I say.

The woman bends down and picks a porcelain figure up from the floor.

A deer missing its legs. She puts it in the bookshelf and looks at me. A pendulum clock ticks on the wall. I'm waiting for her to tell me she's calling the police.

"My name is Gunilla, Kerstin's neighbor," the woman says. She puts out her hand, and we shake. "I'm not sure if there's been a break-in. Last night we heard horrible sounds coming from in here. Shouting and screaming. I wanted to call the police, but my husband didn't think we should interfere."

"Last night?" I say. It must have been after I called Alice.

"All morning I saw her running between the house and the car in that awful raincoat she always wears. Throwing in bags and suitcases."

"Where was she headed?"

"I never asked. Kerstin doesn't like to chat. She thinks you're snooping."

"Too bad," I say. "I really wanted to talk to her."

"I don't think she's feeling so good," Gunilla says. "You can see it on her. She mumbles to herself. Stays inside with the curtains drawn. And she's been neglecting work. It's been going on since Hans died last spring. That was her husband."

"How unfortunate," I say. "Where does she work these days?"

"Worked," Gunilla says and snorts. "The last thing I heard was that she'd been fired from the nursing home—Hällsjö Home. I know people there, you see."

"Where is that?"

"Close to here." She points. "You just go down Faluvägen a bit, then take a right on Hemgatan. There's a sign, you can't miss it."

"Thank you," I say, passing by her and going out onto the patio. As I walk down the path, she comes out and calls after me.

"Hello? Are you leaving already?"

I hurry back to my car. Gunilla shouts that she wants me to stay. I climb into the Audi, start it, and back out onto Faluvägen. Then I call Henrik, who answers on the first ring. He asks what's happening. I tell him I missed them and the house has been turned upside down. I've found medicines, and I'm afraid of what Kerstin has done to Alice.

Henrik thinks I should call the police immediately. He's contacted a lawyer and forbids me to take any more risks.

"I just have to check one thing first," I say and hang up.

Isabelle

I'm lying in the backseat of the car. Mom is driving. She's muttering to herself and shaking her head. I only catch a fraction of it.

I stare out, but don't recognize anything. Where are we heading? How long have we been driving? I close my eyes and memories appear as if through a blurry and distorted lens. The sound has been cut; the movement is out of focus.

Mom comes home. I'm leaning against the desk. She sees the binder I'm looking at. She sees the photos. She screams, howls, drags me away. Throws my head against the wall, rips everything out of the bookshelves, turns one of them over, and throws books at me. I curl up in the fetal position on the floor with my arms covering my face. I try to crawl away. Mom screams that I don't know what's good for me; she asks me over and over again why I hate her, despite everything she's done for me. When I don't answer she throws the desk onto my legs. Then she leaves me there and goes to the living room. She turns on the TV; I hear her swearing over the sound of the news. She walks around and around the room talking to herself.

When she comes back, she tells me I make her sad. I beg for forgiveness, trying to placate her and make everything okay again. Mom says she'll give me another chance. Even though I don't deserve it. She moves the desk, consoles me. Promises everything will be fine. She helps me to the sofa. She makes tea, tells me to drink all of it. *I obey.* She strokes my hair and hums. The TV is loud, some British series about upper-class people living in a castle. I pass out.

The landline is ringing.

I look up and wonder if it's Stella. Mom answers, her voice sounds artificial. She lies and says I'm not here, that I never went home with her. She talks about Stella, says she's dangerous.

I have seen Mom angry before. I've seen her be manipulative. But for the first time, I realize she's sick and she will never be well. That *she* is the one who is dangerous.

And she's no longer trying to hide it.

Mom forces me to drink more tea. I suspect there's something in it, that it's poisoned. I spit it out when she's not looking. Put my fingers down my throat and vomit when I'm in the bathroom.

She leads me out of the house and into the car.

The sun shines in my eyes, the light is blinding. My left thigh aches where the desk hit it. Gunilla and Nils are almost always outside. But now they're nowhere to be found. Not a human in sight.

Where are you? Why aren't you doing anything? Why are you letting her do this to me?

All those times I went to the school nurse. Scratches and bruises, stomachaches and headaches. Real and imagined pains. Why didn't she react? Not once did she ask how things were at home.

The car rolls out onto the road. I turn around and look at the house. I know this will be the last time I ever see it.

Mom stops at a gas station. I pretend I'm still sleeping and watch her. She leaves the car, walks in, and talks to the guy at the checkout. He follows her outside. She's a different person now, happy and easygoing. How does she do it?

She's always been fake. She lies and pretends in front of other people. She has the ability to make people trust her, confide in her even. No one has understood her true nature, not even me, and I grew up with her.

The guy looks so friendly. I want to make him understand, wish with all my heart he could see who she really is. That he'd understand how insane she is. But he just smiles and laughs.

Kerstin

The guy at the counter smiles at me. I smile back. I feel so stupid, I say, but I think one of my blinkers is broken. Is there any chance he could help me change the bulb? I don't want to annoy the traffic police, don't want to get pulled over.

Of course he can help me, that's a quickie. Right now he doesn't have much else to do. We chat for a bit in the meantime. I tell him I just picked up the car from the garage, but they apparently weren't very thorough. He's friendly and accommodating. We laugh and he thinks I'm pleasant. I can be if I want to. I know how to do it.

He wonders how my daughter's doing. She seems to be sleeping pretty deeply, he says.

That's good, I answer. She needs it. I tell him she's sick.

He hopes she'll get better soon.

Thank you, I'm sure she will.

I don't like the look he gives her, but choose to be indulgent. He's been helpful. And my blinker is working again. I walk around to the trunk and take out my water can, then I follow him back into the gas station again. I put some canned food into a shopping basket, pay, and thank him for the help.

Hans always took care of these kinds of things. Now that he's gone, I have to manage on my own. And I do. The problem with Hans was that he made me weak. But I can't afford to be weak, I have to be strong. For my child's sake. For my own sake. And I am. Stronger than anyone can imagine.

Hans wanted to come between my daughter and me. He wanted love that was meant for me. He should never have tricked Isabelle into moving to Stockholm. He never should have encouraged her to stay there over the summer.

I was forced to get rid of him.

And with his last breath, my weakness disappeared. I could see it in his eyes. He finally understood. It was his last gift to me.

A large SUV with raised ride height has parked in front of the exit. The music is thumping. So-called music. It sounds more like one unending primal scream. Several young people are leaning against the car, a few sturdy guys and some scantily clad girls. They stare at me as I come out, make faces at me and laugh.

A young guy with his cap on backward walks toward me. He bumps into my shoulder as he passes.

"Be careful," I say.

He glares at me like it was my fault. Then he gives me the finger and calls me an ugly word.

As I always seem to be doing, I swallow my vexation and walk on. Rude little snot.

I go around the corner and fill the can with water. It's heavy and thumps against my leg as I carry it back. I stop and change my grip.

Finally, I arrive at the car. It's empty.

Isabelle

I see Mom and the attendant go back into the gas station. I manage to open the car door and get out. My heart is pounding, blood rushing in my ears like a waterfall. My body feels heavy, and I'm unsteady on my feet.

There are other cars in the parking lot, but nobody is sitting in them. There is a bus not far away and a truck next to it. I stumble toward the road and wave my arms at a car that swings in my direction. The driver sees me. An older man in a brown cap wearing glasses with thick frames. He waves back, passes by, and disappears.

More cars go by on the main road. No one sees me, no one notices my frail attempts to wave my arms. I scream for help, but my voice is too weak. I wipe away the sweat running down my face with my sleeve. I look down and see that I have no shoes on. The grass where I stand is wet, my purple socks are soaked.

I look to the right, then to the left. We could be anywhere in Sweden. Red and white flags with the name of the gas station chain. A playground to the right, the highway to the left, and on the other side of that are fields and meadows. A few houses and a barn just past them, and then forest. I turn around and see a sign with bright green letters across a red extension. I peer, trying to see. *Ringarum Restaurant,* it says.

I have to find someone who can help me. Before Mom comes out and sees me. I go back to the bus. A fat man in a driver's uniform is lighting a cigarette. I ask if he can help me. He looks at me and wrinkles his forehead. He calls me a junkie and tells me to get lost.

"I need help," I say and go closer. "Please, can I hide on the bus?"

The man shoves me and leaves. I sink down onto the asphalt. My thigh spasms with pain. My head is pounding from when Mom threw me against the wall. I try to get up but my body is completely exhausted.

"Hi there," says a voice. A young man with long hair and a beard squats down next to me. "Are you okay? Did he hurt you?" He puts his hand on my shoulder.

"Help me."

"Are you alone?" He stands, looks around, and glances at the gas station.

I grab his hand and pull him down toward me. I whisper: "Have to get out of here."

He helps me up. "My car is over there," he says, pointing toward a silver Volvo.

I link my arm with his as fast as I can; he puts his other arm around my shoulders as support. It's way too far to the car. Mom can't see me.

He opens the door and I climb into the backseat. A girl with a buzz cut and Asian features is sitting in the front seat; she turns around and looks at me.

"What happened to you? You look like you got beat up."

"She needs to go to a hospital," the man says. "She's been beaten."

"Do you want us to take you to the hospital?" the woman says.

I shake my head. They start to discuss it with each other. I beg them to start driving.

"We're going to Västervik," he says. "Do you want to come with us?"

I nod.

Finally, he starts the car and drives toward the exit.

I close my eyes and lean my head against the window.

Stella

Hällsjö Home is a large brick building with a green roof and three rounded annexes in the same color. I go through two sets of doors to enter. Once inside there's a glass case with some crafts displayed, probably made during art therapy. Pot holders, wooden butter knives, a wall hanging with text embroidered on it.

One long corridor extends down the entire length of the first floor. Gaby's Hair Salon is located to the right, next to a place where you can get pedicures. A café and a pharmacy are located on the left. Straight ahead I see the elevators and beyond that a meeting room with tables and chairs in light wood. Outside the large windows there's a valley and a subdivision of small houses.

According to the bulletin board next to the elevator, the nursing home wards are on floors two, three, and four. I step in and ride up to the fourth floor. As I leave the elevator, a woman in white pants and blue scrubs comes running toward me. She hurries past and doesn't seem to notice me.

I take the corridor to the right and wonder why I'm even here. Kerstin surely wouldn't have brought Alice here.

"Can I help you?" A sturdy woman with a Finnish accent steps out of a storage room.

"I'm looking for an acquaintance of mine who works here," I say.

"Who's that?"

"Kerstin Karlsson."

The woman's expression darkens.

"Kerstin?" she says. "She doesn't work here anymore."

The nametag on her scrubs says *Ritva*. She shuffles back into the storage room. I follow and stand in the doorway.

Ritva is unpacking disinfectant from a box and says, "She missed several shifts and didn't even notify us. And even when she was here she was getting complaints."

"Complaints?"

"She's always been a bit off, but lately she's been mean to the old people. Rough and angry. And medicines have gone missing." Ritva straightens up and looks at me. "Are you a friend of Kerstin's?"

"Isabelle's."

"Kerstin's daughter?" Ritva says. "She used to come here sometimes when she was little. Very cute and sweet girl."

"I haven't been able to reach her for several days," I say. "Thought I'd ask if Kerstin knows where she is."

Ritva closes the storage room door and walks down the corridor. "It's been a long time since I saw Isabelle. She lives in Stockholm now. She was always a good kid." She stops outside the staff room. "Hope you get ahold of her."

"I hope so, too," I say, staring at a framed picture on the wall. A tree with photographs stuck at the end of each of its branches.

"That's the staff here," Ritva says, pointing. "Here's me. And here's Kerstin."

She taps her finger on a photo at the top right. The pictures are bleached and faded; Ritva and Kerstin have been working here a long time.

"Sad to see a person change like that." Ritva leaves me and goes into the staff room.

I study the photo again. Her face is round, eyes small. Her hair is thin and appears dyed. Underneath the photo is taped a handwritten label. *Kerstin Karlsson.*

I've met her before.

But she was using another name.

Isabelle

We're getting closer to Västervik. I feel free. With every mile we put behind us, my worries feel lighter.

I stare out the passenger window through half-closed eyes. Behind the tops of trees, the white-gray clouds look like they're just about to break open and release the sun. A haze hangs over the fields. We pass by farm after farm. Horses and cows grazing. Forests that go on for miles.

Hanne and Ola are discussing which grocery store to go to. They seem to bicker quite a bit. But they also laugh often and touch each other. I miss Fredrik so damn much.

"Could I borrow a phone?" I ask.

Hanne turns around and hands me her phone. After a few rings, he answers.

"Fredrik, it's me."

"Isabelle? Where are you? I called you like a million times. Do you know you've been reported missing?"

"Mom went insane," I say.

"Oh my God," he says. "How are you? Are you hurt?"

"I'm okay," I say. "I got help. I'm on my way to Västervik now. But I don't know how to get home."

"I'll help you," he says without hesitation. "I'll borrow my mom's car and pick you up. Can I reach you at this number?"

"For a while," I answer.

"I'll call back in ten minutes."

"Okay."

We hang up. I dry my tears and hand the phone back to Hanne.

"Who were you talking to?" she says.

"A friend. He's driving down from Stockholm to pick me up. Can I stay with you until he comes?"

"Of course," Ola replies. "Right, Hanne?"

"Absolutely," she says. "We won't let you go until we know you're safe."

She smiles at me and I smile, too. I realize how lucky I am to have run into Hanne and Ola. Without them I never would have been able to escape. I have no idea what Mom had planned for me. But I have a feeling that trip would have ended badly.

After a while, Hanne says she needs to pee. Ola asks why she didn't do it at Ringarum.

"Because I didn't have to back then," she says.

"We can't stop here," he says.

"Yes, we can."

"No, we can't."

"Yeeeees."

"Nooooo."

"Stop at the Hjorten Inn."

"I hate that place. Mom and Dad always stopped there for coffee when I was a kid."

"Stop being silly, Ola."

"You can't just go in and pee. You have to buy something."

"Buy an ice cream at the kiosk."

"It's not summer now, Hanne."

"A coffee then." She turns to me. "Do you want coffee, Isabelle?"

"Yes, please," I answer.

"There, you hear that?" she says, giving Ola a teasing pat on the back of his head.

"Ooowoo," he bursts out and pretends it hurts. Both laugh loudly, and I laugh, too.

We drive with a lake on our right and pass by a sign: *Hjorten Inn.* After five hundred feet Ola turns off, and I see a low red building that overlooks the water. He doesn't even have time to park properly before Hanne opens the door, jumps out, and runs toward the restaurant.

Ola rolls his eyes at me in the rearview mirror. He adjusts the wheel and looks over his shoulder, about to start backing up. Suddenly there's a violent bang, and the car is pushed aside. The seatbelt snaps into my chest, and I see Ola's hair fly back and forward again in slow motion as his head is thrown against the wheel.

Then silence.

Quick steps over the asphalt. A shadow outside the window. At first I can't see who it is. And by the time I understand it's already too late.

I fumble with my belt while the door is opened. Mom grabs hold of my hair and pulls. I scream and stumble out of the car.

Ola throws himself out of the front seat and stands in her way. He's holding his head and grimacing in pain.

"What the hell are you doing?" he screams at her.

Mom shoves him aside and pulls me toward her car. I summon every ounce of strength I have to struggle against her.

"Stop it, goddamn it!" Ola roars and grabs Mom's arm. She turns around with her arm in a wide bow and strikes him.

A fountain of blood sprays out of his throat. Ola stares at her in surprise and sinks down next to the car door. His shirt is quickly soaked in blood. I feel it splash on my face, see my own shirt becoming stained. Only now do I see Mom is holding a screwdriver. She throws it away from her and drags me to the car.

A long shriek pierces the air, and I wonder if it's coming from me, until I see Hanne running toward us.

She throws herself down on her knees next to Ola, presses her hands to his throat, trying to stop the bleeding.

My eyes burn, and I can feel tears flow down my cheeks.

Mom pulls my hair and hisses that I should know better.

Mom's hands are hard and indifferent, they pull and push and shove and hit. "Get in the car."

I ask her why she's doing this, what does she want from me.

Mom looks at me coldly. She tells me she's my mother. I'm her child. She'd do anything to protect me. She'd kill for me, if that's what it takes.

She's holding a black flashlight. She lifts it over her head, and I raise my arms to stop the blow.

Kerstin

A silver Volvo SUV pulled over near the exit. A long-haired, bearded man behind the wheel next to a girl or boy, impossible to tell which, with a buzz cut.

But you, Isabelle, were sitting in the backseat.

I waved and shouted at the driver not to go. I screamed at him to stop: *My daughter is in his car.* He didn't hear, didn't see. He was pretending, of course. There was no way he couldn't see me.

He took my child. Stole her from me.

Why?

Stupid question. I already know.

And the idea of what he planned to do to her makes me ice cold with rage.

He doesn't know who I am. What I'm capable of. He doesn't know I will follow him to the ends of the earth to get my daughter back.

Why, Isabelle? Why? You deliberately deceived me, pretended to be asleep and then ran away and tried to escape. I should have known; I should have been more vigilant.

But don't be afraid. I'm here.

It hurts now. But there's a reason for this, too.

Pain makes you strong. It won't be long, this will be over soon. Afterward I'll comfort you, take care of you, just like I always do. I'll wash the blood from your forehead, I'll wipe away your tears. We can do some baking, if you like? How about some chocolate muffins?

You're sleeping now. That's good.

You'll soon be well again. When I make you well.

And then we'll start over again. We always do. Because this isn't like you. This isn't you. It's the weakness in you. I will always be here to guide you onto the right path. I hope you know that. I think you know how important you are to me.

I wanted you for so long before you came, you should know that. You are life's gift to me.

Why can't you just love me? All I want is for us to love each other. For you to let me take care of you. When you've hurt yourself, I've comforted you. When you've injured yourself, I've bandaged your wounds. When you've been sick, I've tended to you.

I've received a lot of praise for my care. Everyone has seen what a self-sacrificing mother I am. There's nothing better than when I'm taking care of you. When you let me hold you, comfort you. Please, don't look so scared. My funny little kid, it's for your own good.

It's a beautiful day, the sun is shining for us. Soon we'll be there. Soon we'll be back.

Soon we'll be home.

Stella

I stare at the photo of the smiling woman.

I've met her, we talked to each other. We drank coffee together at Coffeehouse by George.

The photo I'm looking at is of Eva.

She was warm and sympathetic and she made me open up about everything. I told her about Alice, how I'd found her. That I was sure Isabelle was my daughter, my missing child. Eva encouraged me to keep searching for the truth, even though everyone thought I was crazy. I told her I went to Vällingby and to KTH hoping to see Alice. I told her about Henrik, and that I hadn't told him anything. I revealed that he once took me to the psychiatric emergency room, and that I wasn't sure he would believe me.

I shared my life with her, I completely opened up. I told her about my fears of becoming a mother again. About my sorrow at not having more children. And I told her about Milo. My fear that something would happen to him, that he, too, would be taken from me.

Eva listened. Eva understood. Eva comforted me and gave me good advice. Eva liked my red umbrella.

I'm just about to leave the nursing home when I remember the photograph in my pocket. I stop and take it out. A younger Kerstin with a baby in her arms. *Kerstin and Isabelle, Copenhagen, February 1994*. The baby has curly blond hair. She's laughing but she has no dimples. It's not Alice. It's another child.

And if it's not her, who is it?

I go to the parking lot outside the entrance. I sit down in my car, lean back in my seat, and begin again from the beginning.

That rainy September day when Isabelle first entered my clinic. She shook her long black hair and smiled at me. I knew at that moment she was Alice.

My diary. All those memories.

Daniel and our story.

The mistake I made in not being honest with Henrik from the beginning. The fear of not being believed, the fear of being wrong. The fear of being committed again.

Eva fooled me into telling her everything. Kerstin fooled me.

Kerstin tracked down Henrik and used what I'd confided in her against me. Her calls about Milo made me go to his school and make a scene. Which made Henrik take me to Dr. Savic.

Eva's duplicity, Kerstin's lies.

She ran over Milo believing he was me.

My visit to Sven Nilsson. The tip he talked about. *He was going to tell us everything. He died suddenly. Before he could say more.*

Strandgården closed shortly after we stayed there. Elle-Marja talked about a daughter who didn't want to run things after Lundin died.

He died suddenly.

Kerstin must have been at Strandgården in August 1994, but I have no recollection of seeing her. What was she doing there? She wasn't staying in any of the cottages, of that I'm sure. We talked to the other guests, we pushed the stroller around, or walked on the beach.

Roger Lundin died unexpectedly.

He was going to tell everything.

Did *he* know something? And if so what?

He had a daughter. *She moved here for a bit that year and then she disappeared again. She had a baby . . . this place was too much to take care of on her own.*

The photograph I found. *Kerstin and Isabelle, Copenhagen, February 1994.*

And I hear Alice's voice: *I was born in Denmark.*

I take out my phone, google for Elle-Marja's number. I make the call.

"Hello?"

I recognize the voice, nasal and thin.

"Hi, Elle-Marja, my name is Stella Widstrand. We met at Strandgården a few weeks ago."

I wait. Hear a dog barking in the background.

"Yes, hello?" Elle-Marja says.

I try again, say my name and remind her that we've met before.

"Yes, yes, I remember you," Elle-Marja says. "I remember you very well. Quiet, Buster, I'm on the phone."

"I need your help," I say. "I need to know something about Roger Lundin of Strandgården, about his daughter."

"Yes?"

"You told me he died in 1994."

"He died at home on his sofa, God bless his soul," Elle-Marja says. "His daughter was the one who found him. She called an ambulance, but he was dead by the time they arrived."

"What did he die of?"

Elle-Marja has a coughing fit, then apologizes. "He had diabetes. That last summer he got a little deep into his cups, if you know what I mean. It was the kiss of death, if I may say so."

"You said his daughter had moved home?" I say. "And she'd brought a child with her?"

"I met her a couple of times with the baby. It was in the spring, March or April, I think. Quite adorable. Like a little angel."

Several months before we arrived. What happened to that baby? What happened to the real Isabelle?

"Then at the beginning of the summer she shut herself in," Elle-Marja continues. "Just stayed indoors, didn't meet a soul. There were rumors."

"What kind of rumors?"

"People said she had a problem."

"Alcohol? Like her father?"

"More like mental problems. Nobody really knew. But that's what people said. And when Lundin died, she and the child moved away."

"What was her name, Lundin's daughter?"

"She wasn't here long. And now the whole place is a ruin. It's really too bad. Can you imagine if she'd just taken care of it instead?" Another attack of coughing.

I'm getting impatient. "Elle-Marja, listen to me," I say. "Do you remember her name?"

"Unfortunately, no. Can't remember."

"Kerstin? Was her name Kerstin Lundin?"

Elle-Marja hesitates. "No, I don't think so. Wait a second. I'm just going to look . . ."

There's a scrape and a crackle; I hear the old woman muttering in the background. I wait. Listen to her talk to herself and putter around.

"Found it," she says at last. "I have a book on local history, you know. It was at the very back of my bookshelf."

Elle-Marja explains that the book contains a list of the buildings in Storvik and its surroundings. Who's owned them over the last hundred years. Historical events, anecdotes, and pictures of places back in the day and now. I could surely get a copy if I want, it's available for purchase from the woman who wrote the book. Berit Larsson is her name. Elle-Marja knows her. It's not at all expensive and quite nice to flip through if you want to know more about Storvik and Strandgården.

I wonder where she's headed with this. Probably nowhere. Another old person who just wants to talk for a while, but has got it all wrong. Who's confused and ends up sidetracked. And for a moment, I think maybe she's also suffering from Alzheimer's.

"Aww, here it is, a wonderful picture of Strandgården at its height," says Elle-Marja. "Flowers everywhere. Taken June 1994. The caption reads: 'Roger Lundin, proud owner and entrepreneur who has been operating Strandgården since 1969. Also pictured, his daughter, Kerstin, and his grandchild, Isabelle.'"

Kerstin

The first time I came here, flowers covered the verandah. Hanging flowerpots, balcony boxes, pots. The flower beds were in bloom, well cared for and beautiful.

I loved helping Dad with that part of the work. Apparently, I inherited his green thumb. We spent a lot of time together when I first moved here. I felt so comfortable, so safe. Slowly but surely I started to come back to life.

Why couldn't I have grown up here at Strandgården with him? It would have changed everything. Instead, I moved from foster home to foster home. Nothing to hold on to, never at home anywhere. Not even with Aina, where I landed when I was twelve. She meant well. She was kind, but I moved out as fast as I could. Moved around again until I ended up in Copenhagen.

After I got rid of Isabelle's biological father, I looked up my own father. And when we got back from Denmark I knew it was here we were going to live, my girl and me. Here she could have a nice and harmonious upbringing. I'd give her everything I never had.

It didn't turn out like that.

Nothing ever does.

I park, get out of the car, and stretch. The trip was more strenuous than I expected. And getting Isabelle into the house is a struggle. She fights me, fussing and being willful. I explain that she needs to come in and sleep for a while.

To rest, after everything she's been through. Just one little sleeping pill this time, enough to make her feel calm.

She cries, she whines. No, I don't want to, she moans. You did this when I was little, stop, I don't want to. You killed Ola. She doesn't know what she's saying, she's still in shock of course.

I explain that I saved her. That man got what he deserved. It was self-defense. And now you need to rest. Don't you understand that?

Sleep, rest.

Like all good children do.

They rest, they sleep. They're silent. Children need to take naps. Mothers need some peace and quiet sometimes, nothing strange about that. All mothers need a little time to themselves now and then.

She was too active. She was too wild. Whine whine whine.

Scream scream scream.

Cry cry cry.

We couldn't go on like that.

You have to be calm and quiet, you have to be peaceful.

You have to be still.

And then, finally, you are.

I stay with her for a long time. I stroke her hair.

Everything happens for a reason, I'm sure of it.

There's still wood and kindling stacked next to the wood-burning stove. I find some matches on the shelf above, open the hatch, arrange the wood, and light the kindling and some newspaper. I wait for it to catch, and then add a few more chunks of wood. The house soon feels warm and cozy.

I go outside, down the stairs, and turn to the right. Below me I see Strandgården. The long main building with its patio, the cabins beyond, the miniature golf course, and the shower and bathroom facility that stands next to the campsite.

It's a long way from its former glory. But this is my place on earth. My place in life.

I turn around and head to the lookout point near the cliff. I caress the deer where it faithfully stands watch over my and Isabelle's history.

That girl, she is my everything. My miracle. Who could imagine the pain I endured would give me Isabelle?

She needs to sleep now. It takes a while, she has a stomachache and she's crying. She cries and cries and cries.

I spank her a little. Carefully, carefully. Spank her just a bit harder. She protests, screams even louder. I hold her with one hand, spank her with the other. Pushing her head against the pillow. I'm careful, but determined. Children need boundaries. I hold her down and spank her. Spank and hold her. She tries to fight me, of course, she's such a lively, spunky little thing. You have to be firm, show her who's in charge. A mother can't back down. Routines are important—without them everything turns to chaos. The girl needs her sleep. I hold her head down and keep spanking. Singing to her, humming.

Now she's sleeping in her cradle, and I fall asleep next to her.

Then I wake up. But Isabelle is still sleeping.

She sleeps and sleeps and sleeps.

I hold her in my arms. Speak sweetly and kindly to her. But she's completely still; her little body is limp. Then it's cold. She mustn't get cold. I shake her a little bit, just a little bit. She doesn't wake up. I shake her just a little, but it doesn't help. I shake and call her name. I shake her, even slap her a few times. She still keeps sleeping.

Silly kid.

Silly, silly, disobedient little kid.

Dad thinks it's my fault.

He doesn't ask me what happened, but I can see it in his eyes.

I see he's scared of me. He thinks I did it. How could he think I'd hurt my own daughter? She's my everything.

I didn't do anything wrong. I'm a good mother, I always do my best.

I *am* a good mother.

The days go by. She is always with me. I read her stories, she sleeps in my bed. I wash her, I brush her hair. We have breakfast together. We go for a walk. She lies wrapped in a blanket on the floor, and I sing to her. Everything is easy, she's stopped crying. She's with me all the time. I tell her that it's okay if she cries. It doesn't matter, Isabelle, I promise.

But she's only silent.

You sleep and sleep and sleep.

One night, Dad enters my room. Isabelle is beside me, wrapped in her pink blanket. She's so small and defenseless. I want her next to me forever. Why can't he understand that? That I have to protect her from all evil?

He ignores my tears, and I plead and beg. He pushes me aside and picks her up. He puts her in a trash bag, puts in some stones, and ties a nylon rope around it.

I scream: I hit and kick. It has no effect on him. It doesn't matter what I do, how much I cry, how hard I beg. I stand at this cliff and watch him row the boat out. He lifts up the little bundle, throws it over the side. My child sinks down into the deep dark water.

Every evening, I sit out here by her. Stay long after the sun has gone down. I want to be close to my girl. Show her I haven't abandoned her. I bring the stone deer up here. It's watched over her ever since.

Then one day *they* arrived.

They were beautiful; they were happy. They came to Strandgården and acted like they owned it.

I can see them now. A perfect little family. Watch them walking along the beach again. Watch them laughing and teasing each other. And they touch each other in a way you shouldn't in public. They're not even adults, just a couple of snotty teenagers. Spoiled brats from the big city. Who happen to have a baby. They play with her, laugh loudly. They don't have a care in the world. They think they know what happiness is. They think it will last forever.

Do they know what sorrow is? Have they felt fear and self-hate push down on them every day like a yoke around their necks?

Never.

They fuck. Enjoy themselves. They sound like animals. They have no clue what it's like to have a hand pressed over your mouth while another rips off your underwear and gropes you down there. What it's like when your legs are pushed apart. How the pain and shame take root in you forever. How rage and impotence burn through your body like poison. How your vagina becomes a wound that never stops bleeding.

They fuck. They enjoy it. They have a beautiful, healthy baby.

Have they known the agony of having a child and then losing it? Never.

They should not have a child. They're no more than children themselves.

I follow them. Follow and am disgusted by all I see and hear. Caresses, kisses, moans. Lustful, writhing bodies moving together. Even though a small child is asleep in the same room.

Someone should teach them, show them anything can happen. Anything. Someone should show them the other side. Show them what life is like when happiness is gone.

I go there again and again. Go there to watch and listen. It's as if I'm driven to seek them out. As if I have to do it. As if some invisible force is driving me.

And then I see it.

I see what no one else can see, no one else can understand.

As I expected. As I hoped, as I wished, she came back.

My little girl has come back.

My Isabelle.

There you are.

I was tested, and I overcame. I proved my strength, not weakness. Now it's that conceited bitch's turn to be tested. I lift up my love, carefully, carefully. I kiss her forehead and her soft little cheeks. She's with me, where she belongs.

I'm her real mother.

I want to show Dad the miracle that has happened. We are sitting in the rocking chair next to the fireplace when he comes home. I'm cradling Isabelle, and it doesn't matter that she's crying. She cries a lot. I comfort her. I sing and hum. Shush her quietly.

Dad doesn't understand. Even though I'm calm, even though I explain. He doesn't want to listen; he doesn't want to understand. Isabelle has come back to me. See, Dad? Can't you see this miracle?

He doesn't want to listen; he doesn't want to understand.

My father is weak. He always has been. A weak and timid man. Otherwise, he never would have left me with my whore of a mother.

He says I scare him. Says I'm sick. He says I make him afraid.

Why are you afraid? I don't understand. It's me, your daughter. Why would I scare you? How can you say I'm not like myself? That I am sick? How dare you say that Isabelle is not my child?

I lift her up and show him. It's *Isabelle,* your granddaughter. We're going to live here together. You and me, and my little love.

Dad refuses. He fetches a bottle and drinks until he's drunk. Until he's drunk as a skunk. Just like my mother. A disgusting pig. A wreck of a human being who's lost all his dignity. I'll never be like that.

Later I hear Dad calling the police. He slurs that he has information about the girl at Strandgården. The one who disappeared. He says he knows what happened. *Come here tomorrow morning. I'll tell you everything.*

My heart breaks. I tell him that I heard him. My own father, you have betrayed me, you are a traitor. I hate you. Dad says, *Everything will be okay, Kerstin, everything will be fine.* He has tears in his bloodshot eyes. And I know what he's going to do. He's going to take my child away from me again. Wrap her in a blanket and put her in a trash bag. As if she's a piece of garbage that needs to be thrown away. He'll sink her to the bottom of the sea.

He's drunk. Slurring and stumbling around the house. Babbling like a madman. He's crazy. *He* is the one who is sick.

In the end he passes out on the sofa.

Dad, have you taken your insulin? I'll help you. Here's your dose.

It's easier than I thought.

Just like when I took care of Isabelle's father. That one overdosed on heroin.

I feel joy, I feel relief.

I feel free.

Still, I weep as I inject the insulin. I have feelings for my dad, despite all the evil he has done to me. And I don't know it then, but I will feel the same thing with Hans. I'll cry every time I give him the blood thinners.

Life and death.

There is a way through everything. I know that from experience.

My beloved father is gone.

The policemen come the next morning, at the same time as the ambulance I called. I beg them to be quiet because my little girl finally fell asleep. She was anxious all night, crying. She's learned how to say "mama."

Mama, Mamamama, Maaaaamaaa.

She cried out like that all night. The happiness I feel is indescribable.

I open the door. "Good you came so fast. Dad is in here." The EMTs and one of the police officers come in.

"He was drunk yesterday," I say. "He drank all night long. And as usual it got to be too much. I found him this morning. He probably had hypoglycemia."

"Hypoglycemia?" the police officer asks.

"Low blood sugar," I say. "It's not the first time that's happened. He has—he *had* diabetes."

Sven Nilsson is kind. It's easy to deal with those kinds of people. They're easy to dupe. Regular, nice people who've never seen the other side of life. Never been forced to live in the shadows.

"As you know, a little girl disappeared from Strandgården," he says. "Your father said he knew something. I understand if you're upset, but I have to ask."

"I heard about that. So horrible. So sad. We talked about it yesterday, but he was drunk. He drinks a lot. Drank, I mean. I have a daughter myself, it must be so horrible what that mother is going through."

"What did he say? Do you remember?"

"About what?"

"About the girl. Alice. That's the name of the girl who disappeared."

"I'm sorry," I say. "I can't help you."

"He said he knew what happened," Sven Nilsson says. "He was going to tell us everything. Do you have any idea what he meant?"

"He said the stroller was near the water. The currents are very strong right there. He knew the waters around here like the back of his hand. But Dad always liked to talk a lot when he was drunk. I didn't hear half of it. The little one was having such a hard time sleeping, so I was mostly with her."

I dry my tears. I have so much to think about now. My dad is gone. I'm in shock. My poor dad is dead, and my grief is overwhelming. My beloved father. He was the best father anyone could wish for. We had a wonderful relationship.

Sven Nilsson is very understanding. He apologizes and hopes he hasn't been too much trouble. The police leave.

We got a second chance, Isabelle and I. We got a new life. And now we're back in the place where it all started.

Isabelle

A ringing in my ears, a light flashing.

The last thing I remember is my head exploding.

It still throbs in pain. I try to move, to get a sense of where I am, but my neck isn't strong enough to hold up my head. I run my hand over my scalp; something sticky has dried in my hair. I have an iron taste in my mouth, the smell of blood in my nostrils. I'm in a dark room with a blanket over me.

I'm lying on a lumpy mattress; the smell of mildew lingers. Cold moves across the floor and through the walls. The air is raw and moist. A faint light trickles in between the shutters on the window.

I don't want to think about what happened to Ola, but I see him in front of me. His eyes, the shock and the horror inside them. The blood spraying, pumping out of his throat no matter how hard Hanne tried to stop it. The front of my shirt is stiff from his dried blood.

And I think about Fredrik. What is he doing now? Has he talked to Hanne, and what did she say? Has he called the police? Are they looking for me?

I pull off the blanket and sit up. I stretch out my arms and legs. My joints are stiff and aching. My whole body aches, especially my hip. I'm barefoot, my socks are gone. I'm hungry. Despite a down jacket I'm shivering from the cold.

There's a rustling sound inside the walls. Is it a mouse? A rat? I pull my feet up from the floor and look around me in the dark. A table, a few chairs, an old chest of drawers, and a bookcase stand against one wall.

There is a tin bucket and a roll of toilet paper in the corner. I get up from the mattress, pull down my jeans, and squat over the bucket. When

I'm done peeing I go over to the door. I stand very still, breathe as quietly as I can and listen. Nothing. I push down on the handle.

Locked.

I go back to the mattress. Feel something under my foot. I bend down and pick it up.

A brochure.

Welcome to Strandgården
The Pearl of the Baltic Coast
Sun, Wind, and Water
for the Whole Family

Under the text on the front is a picture of a happy family romping around the water's edge on a sun-drenched beach. The brochure disintegrates as I try to peel apart its moisture-damaged pages.

After a while I hear steps. Yellow light streams under the door. A key rattles in the lock. The door opens.

Mom is holding a kerosene lamp. Her face is illuminated from below, and I barely recognize her. She's humming and smiling. Her eyes are as blank and glassy as marbles. I don't dare ask her what she's planning to do.

Without a word she takes me by my arm and leads me from the room. We walk through a hallway and enter a kitchen. There's more light in here than in the locked room; there are no shutters over the windows. I see, in the kerosene lamplight, that it's just as dirty. Nobody's been here for many years. But it's warm. The heat from the woodstove fills the room, and my feet tingle as they thaw.

I look around. The kitchen is large and open; there are windows facing a garden and the sea. There are benches along the walls, pale green cabinets. A wide-planked table stands in the middle of the room with six chairs around it.

Above the sea, the sky is ablaze in colors a child would delight in. Orange and pink and red. It will soon be night.

Mom hums continually. She cleans the blood from my forehead, says all will be well again soon. *Poor baby, such bad luck you had. But you were careless, you have no one to blame but yourself.*

I recognize how she's looking at me. That glimmer in her eyes. I saw it every time I hurt myself and she tended to me afterward. She loves to tend to, to care for, to lavish attention. Show everyone what a loving mother she is.

For the first time, I realize this is what she's always done.

The insight makes the pain in my head fade. The fear deep in my body recedes. It's as if I'm waking up from a stifling, lifelong dream. I'm not terrified anymore.

I'm angry.

"Every time I hurt myself, all those injuries. It was you. It was always you," I say.

Mom stops. She tilts her head and looks at me.

"My darling," she replies. "You needed to learn. I thought you understood that." She bathes the wound again with a soft cotton ball. It stings, and I jerk my head away, look at her.

"And when I wanted to go to Gröna Lund with my class? You slammed my arm in the car door. Many times. You didn't care that I screamed and begged you to stop. Why? What did you get from hurting me?"

"I couldn't let you run around down there. Not with her close by."

"*Who? Who* was close by?" I want to make her say it. I want to hear the truth.

"I've never hurt you, Isabelle. Never. I protected you. I raised you." She takes out a Band-Aid and puts it on my forehead. "I wanted to make you strong. That's what a mother does. She cares for you, protects you."

"Where are we?" I say.

"This is our very own hideout. It might not look like much to the world, but it's ours. We're going to have a lovely time here together."

"At Strandgården? Where is that?"

"In paradise."

She whirls around, takes a saucepan from under the kitchen counter, and opens a jar of pea soup. "We should start by eating, I think. You must be starving."

Mom smiles at me and caresses my cheek. Her touch sends a shiver down my spine.

"You're sick," I say. "You are completely insane."

She laughs. Laughs loudly like I've just said something very silly. I, too, press out a laugh, just to show her I'm not afraid of her anymore.

"I think it's time to go home," I say in a calmer voice. "We can start over at home. It'll be like before. It'll be even better. Now that we've gone through this together. We are even stronger now. Stronger than ever."

I'll say anything to convince her. Maybe it will work, if I just say what she wants to hear. If I pretend that what she did doesn't matter. If I pretend everything is normal.

"And I really have to call Johanna," I say. "I've missed some mandatory seminars. She's probably starting to wonder."

Mom sighs. "She wasn't good for you, Isabelle."

"If you want, I'll move home. We can be together all the time."

She stares out through the window while slowly stirring the ladle in the saucepan. The reflection of her face in the window reveals a hollow-eyed and twisted creature. Is she even listening?

Mom stops stirring. "It hasn't been long since you were going to leave me," she says. "You were planning to meet *her*." She says the word with disgust.

"I quit therapy. I will never see her again."

"It was your fault that her boy was run over. I had no other choice. And that awful umbrella misled me. I thought it was her. And she should be busy with *him* now. Instead of trying to get ahold of *you*. Making you snoop around. But she doesn't care about her other child, either. That's who she is. Always thinking about herself."

A wave of nausea washes over me. What has she done? How many more has she killed?

"What are you talking about?" I whisper.

Mom looks at me. She smiles again, puts out a loaf of bread and a knife. "Sorry, my darling. We can't go home. She won't give up. She never will. She found us there. She'll find us here, too."

"And why does she want to find us? Tell me."

"It's her fault that we have to flee. Everything is her fault. Think about it, Isabelle. How have you felt since you met her? You haven't been yourself. What do you think it's like for me to see my daughter feeling so terrible, changing so much, and still be unable to do anything about it? You won't listen to me, either."

She starts cutting the bread, but holds up the knife and looks at it. It's not a bread knife. It's sharp and pointed, a deboning knife for meat.

Her facial expression shifts.

Rage. Sorrow. Bitterness.

"She had everything, but she didn't deserve it. She never cared about you. Believe me, I did you a favor. Haven't we had it good, you and me?"

"I'm not your daughter," I say. "I have the wrong blood type. You're not my mother."

"None of that matters. You are my child now. And I'm your mother."

"Who was the baby in those hidden photos?"

Mom spins around. She raises her arm and throws the knife at me before I can respond. It passes by my arm, and I hear it strike the wall behind me, then land on the floor.

The silence afterward is deafening. Mom pinches her eyes closed, stands with her hands pressed against her head. She shakes, rocks. I look at the front door and wonder if it's locked. But even if it was wide open, I wouldn't get far.

"My sweet girl. Now look what you did." Mom's face is friendly again. Her voice is mild.

She walks over to me and touches my hair. Stroking it over and over again.

"You've always been mine. I knew immediately that you'd come back to me. Don't worry, Isabelle. We will always be together. Hans tried to destroy the connection between us. But I stopped him."

I don't want to hear any more. But Mom goes on.

"I had no choice, you have to understand. I had to let him go. But don't be sad, my love. He didn't feel it. It didn't hurt."

She lifts my chin and tries to catch my eyes. I look aside.

"You don't understand yet, Isabelle. But a mother has to be ready to do anything to protect her child."

Stella

It's evening by the time I turn onto the road that leads to Strandgården. I park the car, step out, and close the door. The only thing I hear is the wind in the trees, the waves beating against the shore.

The sunset has turned the sky pink, orange, and yellow. It all feels surreal. The knowledge that Alice is here, at Strandgården. The knowledge that I've been heading toward this moment since the day she disappeared.

Over the years I've imagined so many different scenarios. How I'd get her back, how we'd reunite. I've had daydreams and nightmares. My longing for her and the fear that it would consume me.

I walk to the main building. There are no signs that someone has been here. The shutters are still locked. The cottages are empty and deserted. I turn and walk toward the Path of Problems. The house up on the hill must have been Lundin's home. I walk past the Ring of Troubles, but after a few feet I stop and turn back. I pick up a rock, weigh it in my hand. I put it in my pocket and keep going.

I climb up onto the plateau and see the house. A yellow light shines in the windows, and a car is parked outside. A dark Nissan.

The car was dark, maybe black. Or dark blue. A hatchback or SUV. When it slowed down I turned around and looked. Then the driver stepped on the gas. Headed straight for me.

I pick up the phone and call Henrik. He doesn't answer. I send a text message and tell him where I am. Then I walk on toward the house. It's adorable with gingerbread-like trim on the windows. I'm almost to the doorstep when the door opens and a woman in a baggy sweater steps out. She's holding a kerosene lamp in her hand.

"I knew you'd come," she says. "Would you like a cup of coffee?" Kerstin looks at me and smiles. She's been waiting for me.

She goes back into the house.

I follow her.

The hall is spacious with high ceilings; the kitchen is located directly to the left.

More kerosene lamps have been placed around in here. It's dirty and the windows need cleaning. The electricity seems to have been shut off—and no wonder, the house has been uninhabited for more than two decades. The heat in the kitchen comes from an old wood-burning stove.

A toaster and a marble mortar and a few cans of food stand on the kitchen benches along with a full water can. A stack of newspapers lies on the table; the top one is dated 1994. All covered with dust.

"What a nice house," I say.

Kerstin tilts her head. Stares out through the window. "Yes, it was. But now it may as well burn down." She lights another kerosene lamp and smiles once more.

Eva.

Kerstin.

My new friend.

"That would be a shame," I say, looking at the knife on the floor beneath the kitchen table. Kerstin has her back to me; I take a few steps toward the table. I can see myself bending down, grabbing it, holding it up to Kerstin, and forcing her to tell me where Alice is.

"And we've met before," I say. "In the Kronobergs Park." One more step. I move slowly: one more step, then another.

Kerstin swings around, hurries over to the table. She bends down and grabs the knife. She points it at me and slowly shakes her head.

"You should have listened to me then," she says. "I warned you. Didn't I tell you to let it be? Didn't I tell you to leave things as they were?"

"You ran over my son," I say. "You almost killed him."

"You left me no choice. I had to stop you."

"Still, you were the one who told me to find the truth."

"Because I understand you," she says. "Losing your daughter like that.

What a tragedy, especially when it was your own fault. I feel for you, I really do. But you have to understand that Isabelle is *my* daughter. *That's* the truth."

She believes what she says. She's convinced she's right.

"You've been outside my house," I say. "I've seen you on the street, in a raincoat with your face hidden under a hood. You left a death threat in my mailbox. You've called me, told me lies about my son. Why?"

Kerstin laughs. Then she turns serious. "You've always been so self-righteous. Thought you were superior to other people. Despite the fact you were always walking on the edge. It wasn't hard to push you over." She pours water from a plastic can into a coffeepot, puts it on the stove, and measures out some powdered coffee. We're like two old acquaintances about to make small talk over some coffee. I sit down at the kitchen table.

"You made it easy for me," she says. "Told me everything I wanted to know. *My husband, he'll never believe me. He'll think I'm crazy.* You felt so sorry for yourself, of course. It must not have been easy for someone as remarkable as you to end up in the funny farm."

Her voice is compassionate and understanding.

"You don't know me," I say. "You have no idea who I am."

"Don't be so sure about that. I know more than you think."

"Tell me, I'm curious. Have you been keeping an eye on me all these years?"

Her eyes narrow; her face stiffens with rage. At first I think she's going to attack me with the knife. But in the next second she's calm again.

"You're not so important as that," she says. "But of course I found out who you were, what you were up to. You met that upper-class fellow. You married rich and came up in the world," she says. "He's very pleasant, your husband, I'll give you that. When I met him, told him about you, he behaved in the right way. And he's handsome—you wouldn't be happy with anything less. But I know how men are. Deep down. Like pigs. Like wild animals. There aren't many who show you respect, not like Hans did. He left me alone, never touched me."

Kerstin sits down opposite me.

"And of course you had a kid. You apparently thought you were meant to be a mother again. And you bought a nice house in a good neighborhood. You had everything you could wish for. You didn't deserve it, not after what you did. But I was happy for you, you should know that. Cried a tear or two."

"It must have been terrible for you," I say. "Isabelle came to me. Of all the therapists, she was referred to me. Do you believe in fate, Kerstin? In karma? Do you think our bad deeds are punished? That truth wins in the end?"

Kerstin rises and wipes off the kitchen table. Then she sets out a tray of buns. Still holding the knife in her hand.

"That sort of thing is for cowards," she says after a while. "For the weak ones. Like you."

"But you're strong? You have the right strength?"

"You'll never understand," Kerstin says. "You haven't been tested by life like me. At the slightest misfortune you fell apart completely."

"I know Isabelle is my daughter," I say. "She's Alice."

Kerstin looks at me. "You never deserved her. You said it yourself, that you may not have it in you. You're a bad mother, we both know that. You let your daughter disappear, let your son get run over. You're really a worthless mother. This was for the best. Don't you think so, too?"

"*You* ran over my son. *You* took my daughter. What kind of person does something like that?"

Kerstin's voice is scornful. "The kind of person who does what needs to be done. The kind of person who takes control. Don't you think I've suffered?" she says. "Don't you think I know what it means to be excluded from what everyone else takes for granted? Do you know what it feels like to be broken? To have your life destroyed? I don't think so. And why should you escape? Why should you get everything for free, without paying dearly for it, as I have?" Kerstin pours the boiling water over the powder.

I put my hand in my pocket and squeeze the stone. I could do it now. Beat her in her head with it. Beat her unconscious.

But I wait. First, I have to find out where she hid Alice.

"Where is she?" I say.

At the same moment my phone rings. I put a hand in my other pocket, fumble for it, turn off the sound. I take up the phone under the table and check the display.

Henrik.

Kerstin gently puts the coffeepot on the table. She looks at me and stretches out her hand. If I answer, I'll never see Alice again. I hand over the phone. Kerstin takes it, watches it ring. Then she opens the door to the stove, throws the phone into the fire, and closes it.

"You don't need that anymore."

"I'll ask you again," I say. "Where is she?"

Kerstin doesn't respond. She takes a kerosene lamp, goes out to the hall, and gestures with the knife for me to follow her. We pass a living room with furniture covered in white sheets. I jump at the dull bang of the phone battery exploding in the stove.

The sun has gone down, only a few glowing red stripes linger in the sky. The long windows offer a striking view of the sea.

We stop in front of a door at the far end of the corridor. I dread what I'm about to see. My hand squeezes the stone in my pocket. Kerstin puts a key in the lock and turns it. She opens the door.

Furniture is stacked in one corner. In the other corner there is a bucket and a roll of toilet paper. It stinks strongly of urine. There's a mattress on the floor, a dirty blanket.

And there she lies.

She doesn't move. Am I too late?

"What have you done?" I say. "What did you do to her?"

I take a step forward, but Kerstin grabs my arm.

I try to pull free and take out the stone. She digs her nails into me and holds on. Kerstin is strong, her nails are sharp as claws. She raises the knife toward me. The tip is an inch from my neck.

"She belongs to me now. She is mine."

Isabelle

The room is darker than before. I can hardly see anything anymore. And despite the coat and blanket, I'm shaking from cold. The heat from the woodstove doesn't reach here. But I'd rather be here than in the same room as her.

She wept at Dad's funeral. How could she, when she was the one who'd killed him? I don't know who she is. What she is. And I don't know what she's planning to do with me.

If I had strength left, I'd resist. Struggle. Try to escape again. But I have nothing left.

If I say I'm her daughter, will things be okay again? If I pretend I belong to her and no one else?

In the dark, it's easy to hear things. I thought I heard a choir of voices. Hundreds of people whispering and singing. It took a while before I realized it must be waves.

Then I imagined a car was approaching. And I heard a dog barking. I thought about Stella, about how she never gives up. I thought maybe she was coming to get me. My real mother. I crept over to the wall, pushed my ear against the wallpaper, and listened. All I heard was my own breath and my heart pounding.

I felt angry with myself. Disappointed. So like me to fantasize, to escape into dreams, to make things up so I'll feel a little better. Stella has no idea where I am. And she won't show up to save me. No one will. Not Fredrik, either. He won't find me here.

I'm alone.

When I think about Fredrik, I can see in my mind's eye how the rest of my life would have been. A life filled with lovely people. I would have become a civil engineer, got an exciting, well-paid job. Married the love of my life and been happy. We'd travel, see the world together. We'd have children someday. A boy and a girl, maybe.

None of it will ever happen.

I'm alone and nobody knows where I am.

My friends are worried; the police are looking for me. But time is running out. And I've vanished without a trace. Maybe I'll be in the news for a while. On TV, in the newspapers, on the Internet. But nobody will ever find me.

Lost forever.

A dim light creeps in under the door. I've been sleeping again.

I hear her voice.

Distant and faint, but I hear it. *Stella is here.* She came for me. She didn't give up, she kept searching.

But I hear Mom's voice as well. Cold and scornful. I hear the rage just below the surface.

The door opens. I don't dare look up. I wait.

Stella asks Mom what she's done to me. Mom answers triumphantly that I belong to her.

I push my hair away and look up. Kerstin is holding tightly to Stella's arm. I loathe when she does that. When her nails dig in.

And she's holding a knife. The same knife she threw at me earlier. She lets go of Stella, walks over to me, and pulls me up on my feet.

"Are you hurt?" Stella says, sounding dismayed.

"It's not my blood, it's—"

"Are you awake now, my darling?" Kerstin interrupts. "Come, there's coffee and buns."

Stella clenches her hands, as if she'd like to rush forward and throw herself over Mom.

But no—Kerstin is not my mother. She never has been. I will never call her that again.

I want to warn Stella not to do anything hasty, warn her that Kerstin is unpredictable and more dangerous than she could ever imagine.

Don't you see that glimmer in her eyes?

I try to make Stella understand by staring at her as intensely as I can. And she does, she understands. She gives me a quick nod, which means she knows what I want to say.

I lean against Kerstin as we walk down the hall. I glance at the knife in her hand, but Kerstin is holding me in a viselike grip. A warning.

We go back to the kitchen. There are kerosene lamps here and there, but the light they offer is dim. Outside, a full moon hangs like an unpolished silver coin above the ocean. Stella sits opposite me at the table. Kerstin puts a coffee cup in front of each of us. She sits down and watches every move Stella makes.

I don't drink the coffee. It took far too long for me to realize she was drugging me. Every time I ate, every time I drank. Stella mustn't drink it, either. If she does, neither of us will get out of here.

I hold the cup in my hands. When Kerstin stands up to fetch the sugar bowl, I tap it a few times and make a face. Stella looks at her own cup and pushes it away. She shapes her mouth to a noiseless question: *Are you okay?*

I nod, but can't stop the tears. I wipe my cheeks with a clumsy movement. Stella stretches out her hand toward mine.

"Stop it!" Kerstin screams. The marble mortar crashes onto the table, close to Stella's hand.

"Drink," Kerstin says. "Drink your coffee." She puts some candles on the table and sits down. She holds the knife in front of her. "I want to give you a chance to make everything right, Stella."

"What should I do?" she says.

"Ask her for forgiveness." Kerstin nods toward me.

"Forgiveness?"

"Ask her to forgive you for being such a worthless mother. Take this opportunity. While you can."

Stella says nothing. Instead she rises slowly, takes a candle, and walks over to the wall. Kerstin keeps her eyes on her the whole time. Stella holds the light in front of a framed newspaper clip. A picture occupies the upper half of the spread, a smiling man standing in front of a building. Flowers fill the porch behind him.

"Your father, right?" Stella turns around. She puts down the candle again. "Roger Lundin. He knew what you did, and he was about to tell the police. But he died. Before he could."

"He was a traitor," Kerstin says. "A drunk, just like my mother. He never should have taken my girl from me. She didn't need burying. And thank God she came back to me again."

What is she talking about? Who is the girl, and why was she buried? And what do I have to do with it?

Stella roots around in her jeans pocket. She takes something out and puts it on the table in front of Kerstin.

"Is this your girl? Is this Isabelle?"

I see the photograph I found in the cabinet under the desk at home. I don't understand how Stella got hold of it.

Kerstin looks at the photo.

"The real Isabelle." Stella speaks softly. "Your daughter."

"My baby," Kerstin says. "My beloved little girl."

"*Your* girl, Kerstin. Not *mine*. Not Alice. This is the real Isabelle, right?"

Kerstin looks up at Stella with a questioning look.

"The real Isabelle," she says, pointing the knife toward me. "She's sitting right there."

"My name is not Isabelle," I say. "And I should have grown up with Stella. You stole me from my mother. You stole my life."

Kerstin turns to me. "That's not true. You're speaking lies now," she whispers.

"You're the one who's lying. You always do. None of what you say is true. *None of it.* My whole life is one big lie. I've grown up with a psychopath. A murderer."

Kerstin pleads, "I love you, Isabelle. But you've never loved me. Oh, how I've tried, how I've struggled to do my best for you."

Stella pulls a stone out of her pocket. She rushes toward Kerstin and aims a blow to her head. Kerstin bends away and drives the knife into her arm. Stella screams and drops the stone. She holds her arm and stares at Kerstin with a furious look.

Kerstin stands behind me. She's holding the knife to my neck.

Its sharp edge slides across my skin.

Stella

Alice is paralyzed. She's deathly pale and stares at me with terror in her eyes. Her face is bruised and she has a Band-Aid on her forehead. A childish, colorful Band-Aid, too small for the cut. Kerstin stands behind her with a knife pressed against her neck. I have to find a way to divert her.

"I just want to know one thing," I say, holding up my arm and pressing my left hand against the wound.

"What's that?"

"Is Isabelle buried up by the stone deer?"

Kerstin pulls Alice by her arm, holds her close to her as they walk toward the door.

"Grab a lamp. I'll show you." She keeps the knife at Alice's throat as she exits. I grab a lamp and follow them.

The sky is an enormous dome of black crystal. The stars shine like shards of crushed ice. A cold wind sweeps in from the ocean and our breath turns to smoke. We walk in silence, side by side, through the darkness. Kerstin keeps Alice between us, with a tight grip on her arm. The moonlight glitters on the blade. Not for a moment does she lower the knife, just keeps it pointed straight at my daughter's throat. I can't do anything. It's too risky. I wonder how far Kerstin is prepared to go.

I can barely use my right hand. I have difficulty moving my fingers, and the pain will soon take over. It feels like the wound is on fire, and it radiates up toward my elbow and along the whole inside of my arm. Kerstin throws me suspicious looks, but I pretend not to notice them. Don't know if it's working, but I want her to think I've stopped fighting.

Doubtless Kerstin was hoping I'd know where she took Alice, and that

I'd follow them to the Strandgården. But what's going to happen now is impossible to know.

We arrive at the stone deer that sits next to the cliff. A full moon shines on the sea and the wind tears at the branches of the trees, at my hair and my clothes.

"This is a wonderful place," Kerstin says. She sounds happy, as if we were out on a brisk evening walk and had found a beautiful view.

The stone deer stares out over the water. Kerstin pulls Alice down toward the ground, squats and strokes the animal's back before getting up again. She points the knife toward the sea.

"She rests down there. My little girl."

I put the lamp on the ground. Try to stretch my arm. The pain is worse now, and I can't move my fingers anymore.

"How did she die?" I ask.

"She slept and slept and slept. She never woke up. Dad didn't understand. He rowed her out there and sank her into the water. But I took back what was mine." Kerstin looks at Alice, then at me. "She became mine. She became my Isabelle, who came back."

"Alice has never been yours," I say. "You took her from her stroller when she was sleeping."

Kerstin grabs hold of Alice's hair and pulls her up to her feet. Alice whimpers and clutches her head.

"And you've never been her mother," Kerstin hisses. "She doesn't want anything to do with you. She wants you to disappear and leave us alone."

I move closer.

"We love each other," Kerstin says, backing up with her arm around Alice, pushing the knife to her throat. "She's my child. I'm her mother."

"Then take the knife away. You're hurting her."

"You're still just as full of yourself. You didn't deserve her then, and you don't deserve her now."

They're close to the edge now. Alice stares at me and the look in her eyes says it all. This is the end.

Isabelle

The knife scrapes my neck. I hold my breath as the razor-sharp blade presses against my larynx. I don't want to die.

"There's a reason for everything," Kerstin whispers into my ear. "You and I have always been on our way here, Isabelle. We never left this place." I try to pull free, but don't have the strength.

Stella comes closer. She stretches out her unhurt hand and points to the knife.

"You've proven your strength to me. It's enough now."

Kerstin sounds disappointed. "You haven't understood anything," she replies. "Why aren't you listening? Isabelle's father made the same mistake. My own dad, too. And Hans. None of them listened."

"Give me the knife." Stella still holds her arm outstretched.

"If you want it, you'll have to take it from me."

I can see on Stella that she knows: it's over now. I try to tell her I'm sorry for all this, but can't get out a word. Kerstin's grip tightens. She takes another step back. I glance to the side and see how far down it is to the water. One more step, and we'll both be crushed on those rocks.

"We were happy!" she screams. "You should have let us be."

Stella throws herself at us. She grabs hold of Kerstin's hair and jerks her to the side. Kerstin loses her balance and lets go of me. I stumble away from the edge and collapse on the ground.

They hold on to each other, a still embrace. Kerstin has an arm around Stella's back, Stella has both arms around Kerstin. A slow dance under the full moon.

Then Stella turns her face to me, her eyes widen, and she gasps.

Kerstin has buried the knife in Stella's stomach. She pulls it up to land one more vicious stab, pulls back her arm again, but Stella breaks free. Kerstin loses her balance. She grasps at the air for something to hold on to.

Stella pushes her and she totters on the edge.

Kerstin holds out a hand toward her, but Stella does nothing. Just watches as she falls.

Kerstin's scream stops when she lands on the rocks below. I crawl forward and look over the edge. She's stretched out with her body in an unnatural position. The blood flows from her head, her eyes are wide open, and the water washes over her legs.

Stella sinks down next to me.

"How are you?" she asks. Her voice is no more than a whisper.

I lean against her without answering. Stella twitches and whimpers from pain.

I straighten up and look at her.

She tries to smile.

Stella

We stay there, looking out over the sea. The waves break against the rocks below where Kerstin lies.

I pushed her. I killed her. Let her fall without taking her outstretched hand.

Alice says she's happy Kerstin is gone. She asks if that makes her a horrible person. I tell her it doesn't.

My body has started to shake. I breathe in short, intense bursts, and my heart is racing. I'm terribly thirsty, wish there was something to drink.

Alice asks how badly I'm hurt. I open my coat to see. A black flower of blood has spread over my stomach and down onto my legs. She puts her hands to her mouth, and I see the shock in her face. We both know it's bad. Then she pulls off her jacket and presses it to my stomach. She feels my brow, says I'm ice cold and have lost all color.

I hear the sirens approaching. See the blue lights shining in the dark. Alice asks me to hold on, says help is on its way.

I fall to the side. I lie on the ground looking out over the water as it glitters in the moonlight. Alice leans over me, and I want to tell her that this is the second time we've looked at the full moon together here. But I can't move my mouth anymore. All that I want to say to my daughter. But no words will come.

Alice holds my face between her hands and looks into my eyes. She says something, but I can't hear.

She puts her head against my shoulder, and I feel her sob. I wish I could comfort her.

Isabelle

The sun-dappled meadow is dotted with poppies and yellow buttercups. Cornflowers and flax and pink clover. Oxeye daisies and wild chervil. Everything is in bloom.

I walk through it slowly, running my fingertips along the high grass. The sun is on my back, a lazy wind in my face. The smell of newly cut hay. In the distance, I see the horizon lying like a blue ribbon.

I want to stay here forever.

"Alice."

I turn around.

You're sitting on a horse. The sun streams from behind your face and blinds me. I shade my eyes with my hand.

The sun is shining brighter and brighter. I squint but it doesn't help. The sun is coming closer; it changes and spreads an icy cold instead of heat. That corrosive light obliterates everything.

I call after you. Shout your name as loud as I can, but you're already gone. The sun is growing, burning into me.

I scream.

"Isabelle?" Another voice.

I can't move my body. I try to close my eyes and turn my head away.

"Calm down, Isabelle," a man says. "Can you see me? Do you know where you are?"

The man holds a flashlight in one hand, and he's lifting my eyelids with the other. He's wearing glasses and a white coat.

"My name is Björn Söderberg, and I'm a doctor here at Oskarshamns Hospital. This is Lotta, your nurse. How are you feeling?"

"Where is Stella?" I want to sit up, but something is hurting my hand.

A needle sits there, connected by a tube to a clear bag of liquid. There's another needle in the crook of my arm.

"Where is Stella?" I ask again. "How is she?"

"Who can we contact to tell that you're here?" the doctor asks.

"How is she?"

"Let's just focus on you for now, make sure you recover." The doctor looks down at a few papers. "Maybe you have some . . ."

"Why won't you answer me? I've asked several times since I got here, but nobody will tell me anything. What's going on?"

"She was operated on during the night," Lotta says.

"Is she gonna make it?"

"It's too early to say anything," the doctor says. "She hasn't woken up yet."

There's something about his voice, how he avoids looking at me. It scares me.

"Will she make it?" I look at the nurse. She hesitates.

"She's in critical condition," she says. "She's lost a lot of blood and her heart stopped several times."

The doctor gives her a stern look, and she takes out a blood pressure cuff.

"We just have to check a few of your vitals . . ."

I swat away her hand and start to sit up. "Where is she? I want to be with her."

Lotta tries to hold me back, but I struggle against her.

The tubes get caught on something, and my hand stings. She grabs my arm.

"Please, Isabelle, calm down."

"Where is she?"

"There's nothing you can do right now," Lotta says.

She can't be gone. She just can't.

The doctor takes me by the shoulders and tells me to breathe deeply. The two of them help me back into the bed.

"I'm sorry," he says.

"No," I sob. "Please."

"You need to rest for a while now." The doctor nods to Lotta, who injects something into one of the tubes.

A feeling of ice on my skin, the cold spreads through my veins. Then I sink back into bed. And continue sinking. I disappear into warm, gentle water. Above the surface a man and woman look down at me. I see in their faces that they know. They know, but don't want to tell me.

It's too late. Everything is too late. Stella is gone.

She's dead.

Isabelle

It's raining outside. The wind tosses itself at the window, and there's the patter of raindrops on the glass.

The emptiness inside aches, inside my head, behind my eyes.

A man is sitting on a chair next to the bed. He didn't notice that I woke up. He looks tired, and as if he's been crying. I have a suspicion of who he might be.

I change position, and the man looks up.

"Hello," he says. "I was supposed to let them know when you woke up."

"There's no need."

"Do you want something? Are you thirsty?" He opens a water bottle standing on the table next to the bed and pours some into a transparent plastic cup. He hands it to me. I take it and drink it all.

"Are you my father?" I regret the question when I see how surprised he is. I feel ashamed and stare down at the yellow hospital blanket. The man takes my hand in his. It's warm.

"No, I'm not your father," he answers. "My name is Henrik."

"Are you Stella's husband?"

He nods.

"Do I have a dad, do you know?"

"His name is Daniel."

I pull my hand away and shift position again. I feel the tube attached to my hand. There has been blood flowing beneath the tape next to the needle. It's unpleasant, and I wish I could get it off. I wish I didn't have to be here at all.

Henrik studies me. His eyes are red. "Stella never stopped thinking about you. Never stopped hoping."

I don't want to talk about Stella. I take the water bottle, screw off the top, and drink directly from it. Then I put on the lid again and place the bottle back on the table. I can feel Henrik's eyes on me, but refuse to look up and meet them.

"It's all my fault," I say.

Henrik leans toward me. "That's not true. You shouldn't feel like that. If anyone is to blame it's me. If only I'd believed her, none of this would have happened."

"I never even got to know her."

Henrik looks at me with a look I can't interpret. "What do you mean?" he says.

I don't have time to answer. The door opens, and the doctor comes in.

"How are you, Isabelle?" he says.

"So-so," I answer.

"That makes sense."

The doctor explains that I was suffering from hypothermia when the police brought me to the emergency room. I have some minor injuries, and I'll probably be in pain for a while. The kinds of events I've been through have a traumatic impact on the whole body.

"We have a social worker here who you can talk to. Just so you know."

I don't answer, just want them to leave me alone.

"I'm here, too, Isabelle," Henrik says. "And, sooner or later, Stella, too."

I stare at him.

"Stella?"

"It was a complicated operation," the doctor says.

"Her heart stopped," Henrik says, taking my hand again. "She was gone. No one thought she'd make it."

"She survived?"

"We're taking it one day at a time." He smiles. "But Stella is the most stubborn person I know."

"Do you mind if I borrow Henrik for a moment?" the doctor says. I shake my head. Henrik stands and tells me he'll be back soon. The doctor turns around in the doorway.

"A nurse will be here soon to take a few of your vitals. And the police want to talk to you. See you soon, Isabelle."

"I'm not Isabelle," I say.

The doctor looks at me questioningly.

"My name is Alice."

ACKNOWLEDGMENTS

I would like to thank everyone who contributed to the creation and publication of this book.

To my agents, Jenni and Lena at Grand Agency, for your dedication and amazing work. Lotta, Umberto, and Peter, too, of course.

To Jonas and Lovisa at Polaris, my Swedish publisher, always so cheerful, positive, and professional. And to everyone at G. P. Putnam's Sons, my American publisher.

Thank you to my whole family, to Mom and my sisters, who always believed in me.

And to my husband and my children, I like you. A lot.